HONOR RECLAIMED

What Reviewers Say About BOLD STROKES Authors

ی

KIM BALDWIN

"*A riveting novel of suspense* seems to be a very overworked phrase. However, it is extremely apt when discussing Kim Baldwin's [*Hunter's Pursuit*]. An exciting page turner [features] Katarzyna Demetrious, a bounty hunter…with a million dollar price on her head. Look for this excellent novel of suspense…" – **R. Lynne Watson**, *MegaScene*

ی

ROSE BEECHAM

"…her characters seem fully capable of walking away from the particulars of whodunit and engaging the reader in other aspects of their lives." – *Lambda Book Report*

ی

GUN BROOKE

"*Course of Action* is a romance…populated with a host of captivating and amiable characters. The glimpses into the lifestyles of the rich and beautiful people are rather like guilty pleasures.…[A] most satisfying and entertaining reading experience." – **Arlene Germain**, reviewer for the *Lambda Book Report* and the *Midwest Book Review*

ی

JANE FLETCHER

"*The Walls of Westernfort* is not only a highly engaging and fast-paced adventure novel, it provides the reader with an interesting framework for examining the same questions of loyalty, faith, family and love that [the characters] must face." – **M. J. Lowe**, *Midwest Book Review*

ی

RADCLYƒFE

"…well-honed storytelling skills…solid prose and sure-handedness of the narrative…" – **Elizabeth Flynn**, *Lambda Book Report*

"…well-plotted…lovely romance…I couldn't turn the pages fast enough!" – **Ann Bannon**, author of *The Beebo Brinker Chronicles*

HONOR
RECLAIMED

by

RADCLY*f*FE

2005

Credits
Editors: Ruth Sternglantz and Stacia Seaman
Production Design: Stacia Seaman
Cover Design By Sheri (GRAPHICARTIST2020@HOTMAIL.COM)

By the Author

<u>Romances</u>

Safe Harbor

Beyond the Breakwater

Innocent Hearts

Love's Melody Lost

Love's Tender Warriors

Tomorrow's Promise

Passion's Bright Fury

Love's Masquerade

shadowland

Fated Love

Distant Shores, Silent Thunder

<u>Honor Series</u>

Above All, Honor

Honor Bound

Love & Honor

Honor Guards

Honor Reclaimed

<u>Justice Series</u>

A Matter of Trust (prequel)

Shield of Justice

In Pursuit of Justice

Justice in the Shadows

Justice Served

Change Of Pace: *Erotic Interludes*
(A Short Story Collection)

Stolen Moments: *Erotic Interludes 2*
Stacia Seaman and Radclyffe, eds.

Acknowledgments

The Honor series began with the idea that it would be fun to write about a Secret Service agent who fell in love with her protectee. It was the perfect recipe for romance: political intrigue, an inherently dangerous personal situation, and a forbidden relationship all rolled into one. *Above All, Honor* was conceived as a stand-alone, but the ending of that book was clearly just the beginning. I have been asked if writing a series is easier than writing a stand-alone. The answer is that it is not easier, just a different kind of challenge. The individual characters change from book to book as we explore the ever-increasing depth of their personalities and relationships. The cast of characters expands and circles back, always drawing energy from the central pair. Without Blair Powell and Cameron Roberts there would be no series, but this has become much more than their story. It has become the saga of friends, lovers, and a country in the midst of change. I am honored to have so many readers share in this journey and ask for more.

Thank you to my editors, Ruth Sternglantz and Stacia Seaman; my readers and proofreaders: Athos, Connie, Denise, Diane, Eva, Jane, JB, Mary, Paula, and RB; my many Internet supporters on the Radlist, and Helen, who began the list and has kept it going all these years. A big, big thanks to Becky and Janette at Bella Distribution for getting the books out day after day.

Sheri surpasses my expectations each and every time with her ever-evolving vision. I am grateful to have her covers grace my books.

Lee stands always ready to encourage, cajole, and occasionally browbeat me into believing that I still have stories to tell. Her belief in me is my daily inspiration. *Amo te.*

Radclyffe 2005

Dedication

For Lee
For All The Days After Tomorrow

CHAPTER ONE

Thursday, September 13, 2001

Secret Service Agent Cameron Roberts opened her eyes in the one place she had never expected to awaken—on the second floor of the White House in a 200-year-old bed. A Thomas Sheraton original. And curled up naked beside her was the daughter of the president of the United States. Blair Powell's cheek was pillowed against Cam's breast, her breath soft and warm, caressing Cam's skin with the to-and-fro cadence of sleep. Cam cradled Blair with one arm curved around her shoulders, her fingertips gently smoothing the bare skin of Blair's upper arm in long slow strokes.

The room was dark, the heavy drapes pulled closed over the floor-to-ceiling leaded-glass windows on the far side of the spacious room. She judged it was probably not yet five and still dark outside. The house seemed utterly quiet, although she knew that at the far end of the hall the president slept and that one floor below, the halls would be teeming with Secret Service agents and members of the Metropolitan Police division who patrolled the White House grounds. While the first family was in the private quarters on the second and third floors, the Secret Service did not physically guard them. But as soon as they left that sanctuary and stepped into the public areas, sensors located in every hallway and room tracked their movements and the Secret Service agents assigned to each family member resumed their surveillance.

She was one of those Secret Service agents, and the family member she was charged to protect was lying in her arms. A year ago she would have denied even the possibility of such an occurrence, but that was before she had been reassigned from the investigative arm of the Secret Service to the protective division, and had reluctantly accepted the responsibility of safeguarding Blair Powell. Now, Blair was central to her life, and although protecting her remained her solemn duty, it was also the critical focus of her days. The urgency and importance of that charge had always been clear to her, but never more so than in the last forty-eight hours when terror had struck the nation in the form of multiple hijacked commercial airliners that had been turned into enormous airborne missiles. A simultaneous, near-successful assault on Blair within the confines of her own heavily fortified Manhattan home merely underscored the first daughter's terrible vulnerability with devastating precision. Unconsciously, Cam tightened her grip on her sleeping lover.

"It's all right," Blair murmured, stroking her palm up the center of Cam's abdomen to her chest. "I'm right here."

Cam rested her cheek against the top of Blair's head and covered Blair's hand with her own, pressing the warm fingers to her breast. "How can you know what I'm thinking when you're asleep?"

Blair laughed softly. "I can sense you when you switch into protective mode. Your whole body feels like you're ready to throw yourself in front of me, even when we're lying in bed."

"Sorry."

"You don't need to be. In a crazy kind of way, I like it." Blair pressed a kiss to the side of Cam's breast. "At least, I like closing my eyes and feeling totally safe. I don't like the idea of you protecting me with your body for real."

"I know."

No other words were needed. Because Cam had put herself between Blair and danger more than once, and the first time had nearly cost her life. Blair's guilt over that event had almost kept them apart, and they still lived with an uneasy truce regarding Cam's role as Blair's personal security chief—a position that at any moment could force Cam to sacrifice her own life for Blair's. And now, in the aftermath of tragedy, that possibility had escalated a thousandfold.

"I can't believe it really happened," Blair whispered. "God. All those innocent people."

"No," Cam replied, her voice thick with fatigue and sorrow. "Neither can I." She sighed. "I guess it's more fair to say I don't *want* to believe it. But I *am* lying here with you in the official presidential residence, and only something as catastrophic as a direct assault on you—Christ, on the heart of the nation—could have brought that about."

"It's sad, isn't it, that it took something like that to bring us together under my father's roof." Blair rubbed her cheek against Cam's breast, seeking comfort. "Love wasn't enough, but the death of thousands was. Now the fact that you and I are lovers is of no interest to anyone."

"It doesn't matter to anyone *today*," Cam said with a trace of bitterness, "but in a week or a month, it will. When the media frenzy over this has wound down some, then your personal life will be headline news again."

Blair raised up on an elbow and struggled to see Cam's face in the dim light. She was unused to hearing frustration and anger in her lover's voice and knew even without being able to make out Cam's chiseled features that her dark gray eyes would be nearly black with pain. It was rare for Cam to be unable to hide her anguish. She always dealt with reality, no matter how difficult, with a cool head and a steady hand. But then, they, like every other citizen of the United States, had been deeply shocked by the events of September 11. Their mad flight to safety from New York City and the subsequent evacuation to DC had left them little time to deal with the aftermath.

Cam had lost one agent in the assault on Blair's apartment, her second in command—Mac Phillips—had been critically wounded, and another agent under her command had actually been part of the assassination attempt. Blair had often seen Cam assume responsibility for things over which she had no control. It was one of the things that Blair loved best about her as well as one of the things that frustrated her to no end. She ached knowing that Cam was blaming herself now, and suffering.

"What happened in New York wasn't your fault."

"Blair," Cam said gently. Wordlessly, she kissed her. She wanted to point out that one of *her* team members had come within a heartbeat of shooting Blair, but she didn't want to resurrect that terrifying memory in Blair's consciousness when it was still so fresh. She knew that the horror of that moment was not over for either of them, but for now, they had to deal with more immediate concerns. If there had been one traitor on her team, there might be others. And it was far from clear that the nation itself was safe, that another attack wasn't imminent. She and every member of the law enforcement community had to be concerned with one thing, and one thing only—ensuring that the nation and those critical to its survival were safe. Her official part in that was to protect Blair. Her private obligation was to track down those responsible for the attempt on her lover's life. "You're going to need to stay here for a while."

It was Blair's turn to stiffen. "I don't live here. My home is in New York City. My place is with you."

"Your safety is what matters, and this is the safest place in the world for you right now."

"And where will you be, Cam? Where will *you* be while I'm sequestered here, with someone watching my movements twenty-four hours a day? When will we have time to be together? Where will we have the privacy to touch?" Blair hadn't raised her voice, but her tone was rough with fury. "Is that what you want? For us to be separated?"

Cam slid her fingers beneath the thick blond hair at the nape of Blair's neck and massaged the taut muscles on either side of her spine. Her voice was quiet, calm, because she knew that Blair's anger was born of pain. "You know I don't want that. I love you. I want to lie down with you every night and open my eyes with you beside me every morning. I want that more than anything in my life."

"Oh Cam," Blair sighed, resting her forehead against her lover's. "I'm sorry. It's just the last thing I want right now is for you to... disappear."

"Jesus, I wouldn't." In a swift lift of her hips, Cam rolled them both over until Blair was beneath her, their legs entwined. She levered her body above Blair's on her bent arms and lowered her head to kiss her. She had meant only to reassure her, but the first touch of Blair's lips to hers sent a shock of need coursing through her. A kaleidoscope of images skittered across her mind—Foster with his automatic pointed at Blair's heart, a fusillade of bullets streaming around her and Blair in the alley behind Blair's building, Parker and Mac lying in crimson pools of their own blood. *They came so close to killing you. Jesus, I almost lost you.*

Cam moaned, an agony of loss in the quiet sound, and pressed her body hard against Blair's, her tongue thrusting deep inside Blair's mouth. She needed her, needed to feel Blair's heart beating in her every cell.

Blair felt the call of Cam's passion, and her blood fired hot in an instant. She was always ready for Cam—ready to hold her, take her, give herself *to* her—ready to answer whatever need arose between them. It had always been that way, since the first moment they'd touched. For the last two days they had run for their lives, uncertain of when or from where the next assault might come. She had seen agents—not just her guards, but her friends—shot and killed. She'd seen her lover struck yet again by a bullet that had been meant for her. The sudden reality of all she might have lost swept over her, and she drove her hands into Cam's hair, clenching her fists in the thick dark locks as she arched into Cam's body, desperate to obliterate any barrier between them. A moan that might have been a cry caught in her throat and ended on a gasp as Cam drove a hand between their bodies, between her legs, and inside her. She wrenched her head away from the kiss.

"Oh God." She clamped her fingers hard around Cam's wrist to still her motion. "Stop. You'll make me come."

"Yes." Cam's voice was rough, hard, but her hand was gentle as she pushed deeper, then stroked. "Yes. Yes."

Had Blair wanted to wait, she couldn't have, because the unexpected force of her lover's desire had already broken her control, and her body surged toward the first peak. But she had no desire to hold anything back. Cam's need was her need; Cam's passion, her own. They gave and took, called and answered, with nothing between them but the whisper of skin on skin. They were as close as they had ever been, as joined as they ever could be.

When she came, Blair pressed her face to Cam's neck, her open lips against the heartbeat in Cam's throat. Her cry of release was one of wonder and surrender, and for long moments after, she felt Cam still deep within her. "I love you," she finally murmured.

"I love you. Jesus," Cam groaned, "I love you."

"Cam?"

"Hmm?" Cam lay full-length along Blair's body, fingers still gently enclosed by the warm, faintly pulsing muscles inside her. She never wanted to move. When they were like this, so intimately connected, she forgot everything that haunted her. There was no danger, no threat of loss, no loneliness. All she knew was the rightness of being with this one woman. She sighed and rested her cheek against Blair's shoulder.

"We just made love in the White House."

"Mmm-hmm." Cam stiffened. "Jesus." She raised her head and squinted in the gray light that stole around the edges of the window drapes. She could just make out the laughter in Blair's blue eyes. "I think we may have committed a state offense."

"Several."

Cam shifted her hips and pressed her pelvis lightly against the hand she still cupped between Blair thighs. "Wanna do it again?"

Blair's lids fluttered at the sudden pressure deep inside. Her laughter fled on a soft moan. "Oh yes."

"Let's try it a little slower this time." Cam eased away enough to bring her mouth to Blair's breast, where she lightly circled one small, tight nipple with her tongue.

"Why?" Blair curled her fingers on the back of Cam's neck and forced her lover's mouth harder against her breast. "I've never minded fast."

Cam bit slowly as she began the soft slide of her fingers through Blair's slick heat. "I know, but I want—"

The bedside phone rang, and they both froze. A second later when Cam started to withdraw, Blair murmured, "Wait," and stretched an arm out toward the phone.

"Blair," Cam said urgently, "it might be your father. You can't talk to him with us...like this."

Blair found the receiver and pressed it to her chest to muffle her words. "Why not?"

Carefully, Cam pulled away. In a tight whisper, she said, "Because. It's against protocol."

"Oh, Commander. I do love you." Blair brought the phone to her mouth. "Yes?" She glanced at Cam and raised an eyebrow. "Hi, Dad... Uh-huh, she's right here."

Cam groaned.

"Yes. All right...What time?...We'll be there."

Blair returned the phone to the bedside table and rolled back against Cam's body. She pressed close, wrapping both arms around Cam's neck. "You have twenty minutes to finish what you just started."

"And then what?"

"We have a meeting with the president."

"Christ. Talk about performance anxiety."

"Then don't talk."

CHAPTER TWO

"Paula, sweetie," Renée Savard whispered, gently tracing her fingertips over the smooth skin of the woman sleeping beside her. The sky had lightened just enough to paint the surprisingly youthful face of her lover with the soft, pale colors of dawn. At just after five, there was no sound in the hallway outside their hotel room, and they could have been anywhere in the world, just the two of them, alone with all that mattered within the circle of their embrace. For one wild moment, she wished she never had to leave that room. That she didn't have to return to the site of a horror so unimaginable that the mind rebelled and the heart was torn asunder. For the first time in her life, she wished that she weren't an FBI agent, that she hadn't sworn to stand for what was good and right and just. What she wanted was to close her eyes and lose herself in the sweet solace of this new love. She leaned down and kissed the corner of Paula Stark's mouth. "It's time."

Without opening her eyes, Stark replied, "Did you sleep?"

No. Because I knew what I would dream about. Renée pressed close against Stark's back, hoping that the warmth would penetrate the cold that had overtaken her days before and which she feared might never thaw. She rubbed her cheek against Stark's shoulder and then kissed the angle of her jaw. "I have to go."

"I know."

Renée caught her breath at the sight of a single tear escaping from beneath Stark's long dark lashes. "Oh no, sweetie. Honey. Don't."

"I'm sorry. It's just…I keep remembering how I felt when I heard that the South Tower collapsed. I knew you were there. I thought that you had been killed." Stark turned onto her back and opened her eyes.

Their normally vibrant brown was dull with fatigue and the remnants of a fear that she could not banish. Her voice cracked with the effort of holding back more tears. "It was as if this huge pit opened up in me and swallowed…everything. My heart and my soul just…died. After that, I was still walking around…doing my job, but there was nothing inside."

Renée caught her lower lip between her teeth to stop the trembling. Her ocean blue eyes swam with tears she feared to shed lest they never stop. "I know. I *do* know. I felt the same horrible emptiness when I heard there'd been an assault on the Aerie and that there were agents down." She closed her eyes and tried to take a deep breath. She couldn't. The memory was a physical pain. "I know you're never far from Blair. All I could think was that I'd lost you." She opened her eyes, met Paula's, and managed a weak smile. "The last thing in the world I want right now is to let you out of my sight."

"Maybe we can just stay here. Order room service. Unplug the phone. Hold each other for a year or so." Stark searched Renée's face, her eyes clouded with a mixture of hope and sadness.

Solemnly, Renée nodded. "It sounds perfect to me. Except you have a duty to Blair, and I have one to the thousands who were murdered on Tuesday."

"I know we can't just turn our backs on all of that, but sometimes it just…it feels like we're always saying goodbye."

Stark turned away, but not before Renée caught the glimmer of despair that eclipsed her normally exuberant expression. She slid down in bed until they were face-to-face and their bodies touched. With an arm around Stark, she circled her palm down the center of Stark's back as she kissed her. She kissed her until the memory of terror and the heartbreak of unimaginable loss faded to a faint scream in the recesses of her consciousness. Then she drew away. "We'll never say goodbye, okay? We'll just say 'until soon.' Because no matter where I am or what I'm doing, you're always in my heart, in my mind. Always, Paula. I love you."

"I'm not usually like this," Stark murmured, struggling to keep her voice even. "I'm tougher than this."

"Oh, I know." Renée's voice was gentle. "It was that tough Secret Service agent I fell in love with the very first day we met." She kissed

Paula again, her lips moving with tender insistence over Stark's full, generous mouth. "The one who made it very clear I was on *her* territory and not altogether welcome."

"Well," Stark said, grasping Renée's shoulder and pushing her flat on her back. The bullet wound in her upper arm throbbed, but she didn't care. She needed Renée. Just Renée. She followed her over and caught both of Renée's wrists in her hands, pinning her to the bed. "You're on my territory now too. And *very* welcome."

"And just how do you intend to stake your claim?" Renée's blue eyes were suddenly filled with questions.

Stark stopped halfway to the next kiss and searched her lover's face. The last two days had changed everything. A month ago they had talked about a three-week trial of living together. Just to see how it worked out, as if they had all the time in the world. And maybe they still did. And maybe Renée would walk out the door in thirty minutes and never come back. "Maybe we should start with you moving the rest of your stuff into my apartment."

"Maybe." There was a note of uncharacteristic uncertainty in Renée's voice. "I don't know what's going to happen when I get back to Manhattan. There was no real organization up there after…after the Towers. Every available agent was activated, but most of us weren't even working with our regular squads. We were just thrown into it. I got pulled off the Tower investigation almost immediately and sent up to the Aerie because of the attack on Blair. Then, eight hours later, I was reassigned to one of the counterterrorism units and back at Ground Zero. I might not even *be* in New York City after today."

"You have to live somewhere." Stark placed a quick kiss on Renée's mouth. She smiled, but her dark eyes were serious. "It doesn't matter where you're stationed, you still need a place to call home."

"I need…a little time." Renée brushed her fingers over Stark's cheek, then kissed her to soften her words. "It's not about loving you. It's just…these last few days. Sometimes I feel…numb. And then, suddenly, it's like every nerve is screaming." She laughed shakily. "I'm a bit of a mess."

"You were right there, honey. You were *in* the South Tower. I can't even imagine how bad that must have been." Stark eased back onto her side and drew Renée into her arms. "And then you worked for two days straight in the middle of all that horror. It's no wonder things feel off."

"I just don't want to start our life together when I'm not sure I can be totally there."

Stark's stomach went queasy, but she managed to keep her expression calm. The very thought of Renée going away, leaving her somehow, not loving her, was terrifying. She made the monumental effort to concentrate on what was happening for Renée and to set aside her own fear. Still, she barely managed to hide her hurt. "I love you. We don't have to decide anything right away."

Renée pressed her face to the curve of Stark's neck. She couldn't see the clock, but she could hear it ticking in her mind. Their time was almost up. She wanted to be close, she wanted to make love, and yet inside, she felt so cold. "Would you mind very much just holding me? Is that all right?"

"It's more than all right." Stark kissed her forehead and held her tightly. "It's everything."

❖

The chairman of the Joint Chiefs of Staff and the president's national security adviser exited the president's private dining room just as Blair and Cam walked down the hall. Both men nodded to Blair and ignored Cam as they passed. Secret Service agents were no more than background noise in the normal day-to-day life of the first family and were rarely acknowledged as individuals.

Blair knocked and, at the sound of a deep male voice calling *Come in*, pushed the heavy walnut door open and entered. Her father sat alone at a white-linen-covered table in the center of the room with a cup of coffee by his right hand and a half-finished omelet on a china plate pushed to one side. A stack of documents rested in front of him.

"Hi, Dad."

Andrew Powell, a trim and vigorous fifty-year-old with thick blond hair a shade darker than Blair's, was already dressed for the day in a white shirt and dark trousers. When he removed his reading glasses and smiled at Blair, his cobalt blue eyes were only faintly shadowed with fatigue. He showed no other outward signs of stress. "Hi, honey. Cam."

"Sir," Cam replied. She was always just a bit startled to see the strong resemblance between her lover and the president of the United States. Automatically, she stopped a few feet inside the door, in the position she would ordinarily take when guarding Blair in a social situation. Far enough away to afford privacy, but close enough to intercept an assailant or interpose her own body between Blair's and any source of danger.

Blair stopped and turned back with a soft smile. She extended her hand. "Cameron. Let's sit down with my father."

Cam glanced at the president.

"There's plenty of coffee," Andrew Powell said, gesturing to the silver carafe. "You two could probably use some." He glanced at his watch. "I have thirty minutes before I'm due in the operations room, and we have some things to talk about."

Cam and Blair took seats on the opposite side of the table and helped themselves to coffee. Then they waited.

"Blair," he said, "everything all right?"

Blair lifted a shoulder. What could she say? *I've been assaulted and nearly killed. My lover's been shot. Some lunatics have massacred thousands of people blocks from where I live. The world has gone crazy and I just want to be left alone.* "I'm okay, Dad."

The president studied her a moment longer, then nodded slightly and looked at Cam. "I've been briefed by the directors of both the Secret Service and the FBI about what happened at Blair's on Tuesday morning. I'd like your report."

"I apologize, sir. I haven't had a chance to prepare that yet."

Powell shook his head. "I'm not interested in paperwork. I want your opinion. I want to know what you think happened—and I want to know how and why it's possible that someone nearly assassinated my daughter in her own apartment."

"Dad," Blair said quietly. "Cam isn't respons—"

Both Cam and the president spoke at once.

"I am—"

"She is—"

The president held up a hand. "There's a difference between being responsible and being at fault." He smiled at Blair. "I have no doubt that Cam guarded you better than anyone else could have. What I need to know now is whether it's going to happen again." He swung his gaze back to Cam. "And how to prevent it."

Cam nodded gravely. "I agree. I don't have enough information yet to give you a complete report, Mr. President, but I can tell you that four heavily armed men with a knowledge of both the layout of Blair's apartment building and the placement of our agents carried out a well-timed and well-conceived assault." Her eyes never wavered from his. "I can also tell you that at least one of the Secret Service agents on Blair's personal security team was involved."

"Just one?"

"I don't know that, sir. But I intend to find out."

"Gut feeling?"

"He acted alone. The probability of two rogue agents assigned simultaneously to Blair's team is not impossible, but extremely unlikely. My feeling is that Foster is the key, and that's where our investigation needs to start."

"*Our* investigation?" The president's tone was mild but his gaze was intensely focused on Cam's face.

"I'm not leaving this to anyone else, sir. I spent twelve years in the investigative division of the Secret Service. I know how to uncover and infiltrate clandestine organizations."

Blair turned in her seat and stared at Cam. "And just when did you decide this?"

Cam shifted her attention to her lover. "It wasn't something that needed to be decided. The minute they came through that door, it was done."

For a millisecond, Blair closed her eyes, then snapped them open; her blue eyes were on fire. "You're not doing this. We have the entire FBI, the CIA, the National Security Agency, and I don't know what all else to do this kind of thing. It's not going to be *you.*"

"Sir. You tell her."

"What?" Blair snapped. She looked at her father, her body rigid. "*What?*"

"Honey," Powell said gently. "As your father, you are my number one priority. But the number one priority of the country right now, and therefore *my* number one priority as president, is to find out what happened in Manhattan on September 11, to bring those responsible to justice, and to ensure that it never happens again. Yes, a team will be appointed to investigate the assault on you. Good people. Dedicated people." He sighed. "But there's going to be pressure from all fronts to deal with the terrorist threat, and that's going to overshadow every other agenda. I need someone leading the investigative team who won't be sidetracked by politics—or anything else."

"Not my lover." Blair's voice was as hard and cold as ice. Her hands trembled and she kept them out of sight beneath the table. "Because I know Cameron. She'll find out who's behind it, and she'll go after them, and this might be the time that she doesn't win." She turned to Cam. "I don't want you to do this."

Cam's eyes were tender, her voice gentle. "Blair. It's the only way to be sure you're safe."

"It's the right decision," Andrew Powell added.

"I don't care about what's right," Blair shouted. "I am sick to death of hearing about what's right, about duty, and responsibility, and fucking *justice*. I'm tired of giving up everything that matters to me because of someone else's—" Her voice broke and she looked away, covering her eyes with a trembling hand.

"Hey." Cam slid her chair closer to Blair and wrapped an arm around her shaking shoulders. She brought her mouth close to Blair's ear. "It's all right. The last two days have been hell. We all need a chance to get our bearings again." She kissed Blair's temple. "It's all right."

Blair pressed her face to Cam's neck, her arm going around Cam's waist underneath her blazer. "I'm sorry. When they were shooting at us, when you and Paula were in front of me and all the bullets—I kept seeing you that morning on the sidewalk in front of my apartment building. I kept seeing the blood and then…then you stopped breathing. Oh God, Cam. You stopped breathing."

"Sweetheart, it's all right. It's all right." Even as she held Blair protectively, her expression grew fierce at the memory of the sick terror she'd felt not knowing if the bullets that passed her by had found their target in her lover's body. She cut her gaze to the president's and said with her eyes what she did not want to say aloud. Not now. Not when Blair was still so raw and the terrifying events of September 11 still so painfully vivid. *No one is going to hurt her. I'm going to be sure of that.*

He nodded, knowing that she did not blame him for sparing no one, not even her, to secure Blair's well-being. Knowing instinctively, too, that she would not allow anyone else that sacred charge. She would die for his daughter, not out of duty, but out of love. "Blair, honey. Let's all take a little while to think about it."

Blair shifted her head on Cam's shoulder and met her father's gaze across the table. "It's already decided. The two of you—you didn't even need to have this discussion because somehow you both already knew what you were going to do. Sometimes I really hate how alike the two of you are." She sighed and straightened. "And I love both of you for it too. So…how exactly is this going to work? Because I'm part of this too."

Chapter Three

Cam crossed her arms and leaned against the door inside Blair's bedroom. She watched in silence as Blair methodically stripped off the T-shirt and jeans she had hastily donned for the meeting with the president.

"I'm going to take a shower," Blair said quietly.

"Want company?"

A beat passed before Blair nodded. "Yes."

Cam shed her clothes, tossed them on the foot of the bed, and followed into the bathroom. Blair was already in the shower, and the glass enclosure was misted with steam. Visible through the haze, the outline of Blair's nude form swayed hypnotically beneath the spray. Cam stood still, holding her breath, watching. There were moments like this when she was overcome with the wonder of having Blair in her life. When she felt the longing and desire so acutely, it was like a pain deep in her chest. If asked, she couldn't have explained what it was about this one woman that settled in the very heart of her like none other. Blair was beautiful, intelligent, strong and willful and tender, and so many other things that Cam admired. But it was more than that. This thing, *love,* that she couldn't define or explain, was what shaped so much of what truly mattered in her life.

Cam gave a start as the shower door slid open and Blair looked out.

"Darling? What are you doing?"

"Just thinking." Cam stepped into the shower and closed the door again. She doused her head in the warm spray and flicked the hair back out of her eyes with one hand. She turned to find Blair leaning against the back shower wall observing her. "Are you angry?"

"You first. What were you thinking about?"

"Come here." Cam pulled Blair close to her beneath the spray. "You'll get cold."

"Don't change the subject." Blair wrapped her arms around Cam's neck and slid her wet body against Cam's until they fit together seamlessly, two parts of a whole. "You had this look on your face…like something hurt."

"No," Cam said softly, "nothing like that."

Blair tightened her fingers in Cam's wet hair and tugged. "You know I won't quit."

"I know." Smiling, Cam kissed her.

Blair leaned into the kiss, rolling her hips slowly between Cam's thighs, matching the deep, leisurely strokes of her tongue to the easy rhythm of her body teasing Cam's. "Mmm. Tell."

"Christ," Cam gasped, lifting her head from the kiss. Her stomach was in knots and her thighs trembled. "You don't play fair."

The corner of Blair's mouth lifted in a satisfied grin. "Then why take me on?"

"Because," Cam growled, gripping Blair's upper arms and pushing her against the shower wall, then following with her body hard and fast, pinning her there, "you make me crazy when you get tough."

Before Blair could answer, Cam's mouth was on hers, hot and hungry, and her hands were everywhere, closing over Blair's breasts, squeezing her nipples, running up the inside of her thighs to cup her sex.

Blair's hips bucked as fingers glanced over her clitoris and were gone. She hooked one calf around Cam's hips and drove her center against Cam's thigh. She moaned and thrashed her head, and still Cam kept her pinned, plundering her mouth while Blair rode her thigh. Blair felt the orgasm on the verge of careening through her, and she twisted her torso as she pushed away from the wall. She reversed their positions before Cam could stop her. Ignoring the climax that shimmered just beneath her skin, she went down on her knees with the water pounding on her back and sucked Cam's clitoris between her lips. She heard Cam shout, felt her stiffen, and then they were both coming, shuddering and groaning until their trembling limbs could no longer support them and they slid to the floor.

"God."

"You were saying?" Blair murmured. She snuggled against Cam's body, her head resting between Cam's breasts.

Cam's mind was fuzzy and her barriers down. "I was thinking how much I love you and that nothing else in my life matters except that."

"Why did that look like it hurt?" Blair asked gently.

"It never hurts unless I think about being without you."

"Oh no, never." Blair inched closer and tightened her grip around Cam's waist. She pressed her lips to Cam's breast. "Never."

"Promise?"

"Promise."

"Water." With another groan, Cam tried assembling her extremities into some kind of working order. "Water. Cold soon."

Laughing, Blair got to her knees, then stood with one arm braced against the shower wall. She turned off the water and stared down at her lover. "Why, Commander, I do believe you've been done in."

"Not so fast." Cam grinned up at her. "That was only a skirmish. There's plenty of fight left in me."

Blair extended her hand and tugged when Cam took it, pulling her to her feet. "Let's hope so."

When they stepped out and wrapped themselves in towels, Blair leaned her hips against the vanity and regarded Cam seriously. "You know I don't like it. What you're planning to do."

Cam stopped in the midst of toweling her hair. "I know."

"Then why do you do it? Since the moment we've met, this job— this *duty* of yours—has been between us."

"I know." Cam lifted a thick white robe from the back of the bathroom door and shrugged into it, then passed the matching one to Blair. "There are a lot of reasons. I'm trained to do it. I'm good at it. I have more reason than anyone else in the world to do it right."

Blair nodded. "All good reasons. But not good enough to put the smallest wedge of anger or resentment between us. I don't like anyone protecting me at the risk of their own life." She held up a hand when she saw Cam about to protest. "I understand that it's necessary. I know what my security means for my father, for the country. I know that, and I've accepted it as best as I can." Her voice trembled, but her eyes were dry and hot and hard. "*All my life*, Cam. All my life I've accepted it. And now I have you, and I'm supposed to be happy about risking you?"

She laughed harshly. "I don't think so."

"There's one other reason." Cam kept her hands in the pockets of her robe, because she wanted so much to reach out to Blair. She wanted to touch her, stroke her, soothe the hurt she heard beneath the anger. But she didn't, because Blair did not need that now. What she needed was the truth. "I have to do it, because if I leave it to someone else and anything happens to you, it will break me. I would rather be dead than lose you."

"Oh, Cameron." The anger left Blair's eyes on a wave of tenderness. "I feel the same about you. Can't you understand that?"

Cam closed the distance between them and caught Blair's face gently between her palms. She kissed her lightly on the mouth. "I *do* understand. I do. There's a reason I'm your security chief, Blair. It's because I'm *good* at it. Trust me. Nothing is going to happen to me."

"And what about this...other? Are you going to be the best at that too?"

"With your safety on the line?" Cam's eyes hardened to obsidian. "Count on it."

"I'll be so happy when the day comes that the only thing we have to worry about is paying the mortgage."

"Me too," Cam whispered. She rested her cheek against the top of Blair's head and closed her eyes. In the distance, she could see a future where they would be together, living an ordinary life, with ordinary problems and ordinary joys. But between this day and that, there was a war to be won.

❖

Stark paced in a tight circle around the perimeter of the surprisingly spacious waiting area. When she caught the eye of the slightly amused administrative assistant observing her, she abruptly sank into the nearest chair. She clasped her hands between her knees, fingers entwined, knuckles white, and stared at the door on the far side of the room with the neat, unassuming brass nameplate that said *Assistant Director*. She'd never been to Assistant Director Carlisle's office before. She'd never been to *any* assistant director's office. She'd taken her entrance exams, she'd had her psych eval, she'd gone through qualifying physical fitness trials, and she'd endured the Academy, all without ever having seen anyone higher than a regional director. Cameron Roberts, as security chief for the first daughter, held more rank than anyone she'd ever worked with.

The door from the hall opened, and Stark looked over to see the woman in question enter. As usual, the commander wore a dark suit with a slightly paler monochromatic shirt, opened at the neck. The jacket was flawlessly tailored and there was no telltale sign of a weapon, although Stark knew that the commander was one of the few who still wore a shoulder harness. Her own weapon rested in a belt holster on her right hip. Stark bounded to her feet. Standing, she was a head shorter than her chief and compact whereas the other woman was lean.

"Good morning, Agent Stark," Cam said.

"Ma'am." Stark cast a sideways look at the attractive blond behind the desk, who did not seem to be paying them any attention. "I received a call at 0600 to report, Commander. I would have called you, but I wasn't certain of the protocol."

Cam shook her head. "If the assistant director calls you to come in, you come in. No problem."

Stark glanced at the closed door. "Do you know what—"

The intercom on the desk buzzed, and the blond picked up a phone. A minute later, she replaced it and smiled at Stark and Cam. "Director Carlisle will see you now."

"Thank you," Cam said.

Stark followed silently, having no idea what to prepare for. Once inside the functional, unadorned office, she relaxed to a small degree. The silver-haired man behind the desk was in his mid-50s, sharp-eyed and intense looking, but not particularly threatening. When he nodded to her and Cam and said, "Sit down, please," Stark felt almost normal. Except for the pounding in her chest and the queasiness in her stomach. That had been there since their flight from New York City, and she was starting to realize it was her new *normal* condition.

Stewart Carlisle picked up two file folders and set them next to each other on the blotter. Then he opened one and flipped through several pages. When he finished, he looked at Stark. "Six years on the job, correct, Agent?"

"Yes, sir." Stark was very pleased that her voice did not waver.

"And"— Carlisle glanced down again—"two years as one of the lead agents on Ms. Powell's security team."

"Yes, sir."

Carlisle straightened, his hands resting palm down, one on each folder. "I'd like your assessment of the events of Tuesday morning, Agent Stark."

Stark struggled not to look at Cam. Something was going on, and whatever it was, the path she was about to walk was narrow, twisting, and fraught with danger. "In what respect, sir?"

"What would be *your* opinion on that?" he countered.

"There are several factors to be considered, sir. The origin, identity, and intent of the assailants. The extent of the security"—she struggled for a word and in the end, could find only one—"breach. The response of the security team. The potential compromise of the evacuation—"

"All right, Agent," Carlisle interrupted. "All valid points. Let's focus on our particular area of responsibility. Do you want to tell me how an armed assailant managed to be standing outside Egret's door at nine a.m. on Tuesday morning?"

For the first time, Stark glanced at Cam, who sat beside her, one leg crossed over the other, her forearms resting on the arms of her chair, her hands relaxed. In profile, her face was smooth as granite, her expression remote. Stark wanted to be anywhere in the world but sitting in this room. She turned her attention back to the assistant director. "With what limited information I have at this moment, sir, I would speculate that the details of the building's security system, the placement of our agents, and the daily shift schedule had been provided to the assailants by Agent Foster." Her throat was dry, and voicing the incomprehensible was like swallowing chips of glass. She had spent hours every day with the man, worked out with him in the gym, stood guard with him, played cards with him during those interminable nights when Blair slept in a hotel room nearby. She couldn't believe that she had suspected nothing. Blamed herself for noticing nothing amiss.

"How is that possible?"

She held his eyes. "I don't know, sir."

"Well, we'd better damn well find out." He leaned back in his chair and expelled a long breath. In a conversational tone, he continued, "It's customary during the transfer of command for the outgoing commander to brief the incoming commander on sensitive matters not included in the Eyes Only report."

He picked up the second folder, stood, and extended it across the desk to Stark. "Once you've reviewed this material, Agent Stark, Agent Roberts will brief you on any additional information pertinent to your new command. As of 0800, you are Egret's acting security chief. That will be all."

CHAPTER FOUR

Stark and Cam left Carlisle's office in silence. In the reception area, Stark hesitated, glancing at the file in her hand and wishing with all her heart she could throw it into the nearest trash receptacle. It symbolized something she fervently did not want.

"Commander—"

"Let's take a walk, Agent." Cam gestured with her chin toward the folder. "You're going to need to get a briefcase." She handed hers over. "Here, use mine for now. There's nothing classified in it."

Stark stared at the offered item as if it were a ticking bomb. "No, I—"

"You can't walk around the streets of DC with that in your hand. Go ahead." As Stark reluctantly accepted the briefcase and deposited the folder, Cam added, "It's not personal, Stark."

"I'm sorry, Commander. It feels that way to me."

Cam moved toward the door to the hall, pushed it open, and waited for Stark to pass. As they started down the wide, marble-floored hallway, she said, "I recommended you for the position because I trust you to do it."

"Thank you." Stark blushed and kept her eyes forward. "But with all due respect, ma'am, I don't want the job."

"I said the same thing almost a year ago."

"It should be Mac."

Cam shook her head. "I spoke to Felicia earlier. Mac is stable, but he's in for a long recovery. And I wanted you."

They exited on Fifteenth Street and walked south toward Pershing Park. Cam led the way to a bench in a deserted corner and sat down, stretching her legs out in front of her and pushing both hands into her pants pockets. Stark sat ramrod straight beside her, the briefcase balanced on her knees, held firmly with both hands. Her knuckles were white where her fingers curled around the edges. "There's no reason to replace you at all."

"What happened Tuesday at the Aerie was not only unacceptable—it was inexcusable," Cam said quietly. She looked out over the small, neat park, automatically registering the presence of the few tourists strolling through, but in her mind she saw, in stark black and white as it had played on the security monitors in Command Central, the lobby door of Blair's apartment building burst open and four heavily armed commandos rush inside. She saw Secret Service Agent Cynthia Parker take down the first assailant before a burst of automatic fire, silent on the monitor and evident only from the muzzle flare flashing on the screen, blew Parker off her feet. Cam had lost an agent in a surprise attack that had been orchestrated by one of her own people. Cynthia Parker's blood was on her hands. "There's no way I could be allowed to maintain my command."

"You saved Egret's life." Stark too stared into the past, experiencing a different take on the endless loop of nightmare images playing from the same silent reel. Cynthia going down; the smell of sweat and adrenaline and, beneath it all, fear; the hail of bullets and smoke; Mac bleeding on the ground; the gut-wrenching pain of the gunshot ripping her flesh. "You probably saved some of the rest of us too."

"Consider this our transition briefing," Cam said, knowing that they'd all been lucky to survive. Whenever she thought of how close Blair had come to dying, a surge of pain so sharp she lost her breath struck at the heart of her. No rationalization would ever erase the knowledge that she'd nearly lost her, and that Blair's death would have been her fault. "The entire team has been placed on administrative leave until the investigation into the assault on Egret is completed."

Stark swiveled her head sharply to stare at Cam. "Everyone?"

"Everyone except you. We need some degree of continuity or the new team can't function effectively."

"I..." Stark took a long breath. The decision had been made, and there was nothing for her to do but step up. "Thank you, Commander. I appreciate your confidence in me."

"I think we can dispense with the *Commander*, now," Cam said with a small laugh.

"No, ma'am, I don't think so. There's no way anyone's going to be calling *me* that."

"You *are* the first daughter's security chief, Agent Stark."

"Fine, then they can call me *Chief*." Stark's tone left no room for argument.

"I imagine that will work," Cam observed mildly. "Blair doesn't know yet."

"Oh, man."

"Assistant Director Carlisle advised me of the director's decision just before the meeting this morning."

"Does the president know?" Stark asked.

"I imagine he does, although the way these things work, he was probably informed by the security director after the fact."

Stark perked up. "Then it's possible he could still reverse the decision."

Cam shook her head. "No, I don't think he will. This action is the right one, and he'll recognize that. Plus, considering everything else that's just happened, he's not going to oppose any recommendation made by his security advisors. Or the DOD."

"I know that the conclusion looks right from the outside," Stark said, meeting Cam's eyes, "but those of us on the inside know it's just wrong. There's no one better for this job than you. And we need the rest of the team."

"I agree with the last part. I'm going to do everything I can to see that our people are cleared and back on the job just as soon as possible." Cam stood. "Let's walk over to the residence. I'll talk to Blair while you review the Eyes Only docs."

Stark kept pace by Cam's side, wishing she could talk to Renée. Wishing that she could share her misgivings and uncertainties, because she understood that outwardly she must never allow them to show. She glimpsed Cam's face as they approached the security checkpoint at the White House and saw nothing but calm. She wondered as she had so many times before what feelings the commander kept hidden from everyone, and at what cost.

❖

Blair looked up and sketched a wave in the air as Cam walked into her suite, then smiled into the telephone. "I miss you too. Believe me,

I'd rather be home than here." Her expression grew somber. "How is it up there?"

Cam removed her jacket and weapon harness and placed them on a small table just inside the door. The sitting room adjoined Blair's bedroom and was furnished much as the other rooms in the White House, with original American period pieces. She walked to the minibar tucked unobtrusively into one corner of the room, pulled a Pellegrino from the small refrigerator, and carried it to the sofa. Blair was curled up on the opposite end talking, Cam surmised, to her best friend and art agent, Diane Bleeker. As Cam sipped the sparkling water, Blair drew her legs up onto the couch and settled her feet in Cam's lap.

"I'm coming up with my father in the morning," Blair said. "I'll call you as soon as I'm free and we'll get together."

Cam rubbed her thumb up and down Blair's instep as she listened to the conversation. Clearly, her lover had been busy in her absence. The president would need to visit the site of the tragedy to show the world that the United States did not bow to terrorism, but the last place Cam wanted Blair was in Manhattan so soon after the attack. There was no way, despite the hundreds of local and federal law enforcement agents scouring the region, that the area could be remotely secure. Guarding the president was going to be a nightmare. Adding Blair to the mix would only complicate matters further. Cam switched her attention to the opposite foot and closed her palm around the delicate bones and muscles beneath the nearly translucent skin, kneading gently. Blair traced the toes of her free foot back and forth along the inside of Cam's thigh.

"You heard from her *already*?" Blair's voice rose in surprise. "Really—she's still in Manhattan? The news reports said there are hundreds of people still stranded because of the canceled flights." She stretched and pushed her foot higher between Cam's legs. "Well, I guess if she can't get a hotel room, she could always stay in your guest room for a few days." She laughed. "*Very* convenient. I'll call you tomorrow. See you soon."

"Diane, I take it?" Cam asked as Blair switched off the phone and placed it on the floor beside the sofa.

"Mmm. Apparently *Valerie* called, and she's temporarily stranded in New York. Diane is very pleased about that."

"Huh." Cam wasn't altogether comfortable discussing a woman with whom she had been intimate, although under extremely unusual circumstances and in what now felt like a different lifetime. And even though Blair knew about her liaison with Valerie, Diane did not. "What's this about you going to Manhattan tomorrow?"

"I'll fill you in on the details later." Blair pushed the heel of her foot gently against Cam's crotch. "You know, there's nothing on the agenda for today."

Cam grasped the foot teasing between her legs and stilled the entirely too pleasant motion. "I expect to get called back to Justice for my debriefing this afternoon."

Blair craned her neck toward the Seth Thomas clock on the mantelpiece. "It's not noon yet." She rocked Cam's thigh with her other foot and her expression grew distant. When she spoke again, the bantering tone had disappeared and her voice was thick, as if with unshed tears. "You know, I keep thinking about Cynthia and Mac. When I do, all I want is your skin against mine. I need to hear you breathe. You feel like the only solid thing in my world right now."

"Oh, Christ," Cam whispered. She lifted Blair's legs and slid closer to her on the couch before slipping her arm behind Blair's waist and drawing her into an embrace. She kissed her mouth, then nuzzled her face in thick blond hair that smelled of sunshine and roses. "I love you. And God knows, I *want* you."

Blair pulled back, her eyes narrowing. "But?"

"But we need to talk about a few things."

"What happened with Carlisle this morning?" Blair withdrew from Cam's embrace and inched away, as if she wanted space in which to carry out the conversation. "What's wrong?"

Cam shook her head, wishing that Blair could not read her quite so well. "Nothing's wrong."

"There's something you're not telling me. You promised me you wouldn't do that."

"No. Stewart called me right before the briefing this morning, so there was no time *to* tell you."

"Tell me *what*, Cameron?" Blair's voice had grown cold and her eyes were a hard, icy blue.

Fast and hard seemed to be the only way to do it, because Blair was best at handling sharp, swift pain. "I've been replaced. Stark's your new security chief."

Blair grew utterly still. "You can't be serious."

"I am."

"Son of a bitch!" Blair jumped up and paced in a small, tight circle before storming back to stand within inches of Cam's legs. "They can't do this. Does my father know?"

"I don't know. I think he does, bu—" Cam caught Blair's wrist as she was about to pick up the phone. "Wait."

"For what? For you to tell me one more time that I have to accept everyone else's decisions when they affect *my* life?"

"This is all *about* your life, baby," Cam said gently. "It's about taking care of you the best way possible."

"*You* take care of me. I take care of you." Blair pulled her arm from Cam's grip. "That's what lovers do."

Cam stood, but she did not try to hold her. "This isn't about us as a couple. It's about you as the first daughter. I've been relieved of my command because I almost let someone assassinate you. The entire team has been suspended, with the exception of Stark."

Blair's head jerked back as if she'd been struck. "Everyone? This is crazy."

"A board of inquiry will investigate what happened, including the possibility that other members of your security team were involved. As soon as our people are cleared, I'll push Carlisle to get them back on duty."

"Why did they make an exception for Stark?"

"Because I insisted. Because she put herself between you and the assailants, and had she been involved with the assassination attempt, she never would've done that."

Because she took a bullet meant for you.

Blair sank down on the sofa and rested her head against the back, staring up at the ceiling. "I'm going home. I can't stay here like this."

"Your apartment isn't secure. Hell, *New York City* isn't secure." Cam settled next to her and clasped Blair's hand. "Just give it a few weeks, please. Just until we have a better idea of the scope of these attacks."

Blair turned her head and stared at Cam. "While I'm living here under twenty-four-hour guard, where are you going to be?"

"I'll stay in my DC apartment. Your father wanted me to investigate the assault at the Aerie, and I'm still going to do that, one way or the other."

"What about us?"

"I'm not letting you go anywhere without me. If you travel, I'm coming."

A faint smile flickered across Blair's mouth. "Kind of like a groupie?"

"Your number one fan."

"What about at night?"

"With the press corps downstairs?" Cam's gaze flickered around the room, and she sighed. "I can't stay here every night."

"Then I'm staying with you at your place."

Cam groaned. "Jesus, if you can just be patient a few—"

"No."

"Blair," Cam sighed and brushed her mouth over the top of Blair's hand. "All right, as long you promise to stay *here* if I'm out of town."

"Until I go home."

"Agreed."

Blair smiled. "There, see? That wasn't so difficult, was it?"

"Perfectly painless." Cam leaned forward and kissed her, sliding her fingers into Blair's hair. She let herself linger in the soft, warm comfort of Blair's mouth, savoring the press of Blair's body along the length of hers. The connection steadied her, centered her, and she would need that in the days ahead.

CHAPTER FIVE

So what about that suggestion?" Blair slipped her fingertips inside the waistband of Cam's trousers and brushed the back of her fingers over Cam's abdomen.

"You mean the one where we ignore the fact that I'm out of a job *and* that we're in the White House where someone might notice if we never leave the bedroom?" Cam curled both arms around Blair's waist as they swayed together, hearts and bodies attuned. "God, you smell so good."

Blair laughed softly and pulled Cam's shirt free. Her laugh became a soft purr when her hand met skin, and Cam stiffened, emitting a throaty growl. "I was thinking more along the lines where we have a quickie, short but intense. Maybe right here on the sofa. I seem to remember you liking it quite a bit when I knelt between your le—"

The phone rang, and they both cursed simultaneously. With a sigh, Cam stepped away, automatically tucking in her shirt.

"Don't be so quick to give up on that idea," Blair muttered as she snatched up the phone. "Blair Powell...Hi...Yes, she's here... When?...Okay, fine." She clicked off the phone and tossed it onto the sofa, then faced Cam with a frustrated expression. "I feel as if I'm in that groundhog movie. The same goddamn scene keeps replaying."

"Your father?" Cam was already on her way to retrieve her jacket and weapon.

"Just about. Lucy Washburn."

Cam turned as she shrugged into her shoulder harness. Lucinda Washburn was the White House chief of staff and the second most powerful person in the nation. Others might assume that the chairman of the Joint Chiefs or the head of the State Department might hold that position, but Lucy Washburn was the president's confidante and his oldest adviser. She was also an accomplished politician in her own right and somehow always managed to juggle the simmering Capitol Hill rivalries, shifting loyalties, and internecine power struggles to the president's advantage. "She wants to see me?"

"Both of us."

Their eyes met in silent acknowledgment that a command appearance in Washburn's office was never good news.

❖

When they arrived in the West Wing, they were shown directly into the chief of staff's office. Lucinda Washburn, an imposing auburn-haired woman in a double-breasted, charcoal pinstriped suit, stood at the windows overlooking a lush garden, her back to the room. She turned at the sound of their entrance, the lingering remnants of sadness softening the strong lines of her jaw and deepening the shadows beneath her hazel eyes. She squared her shoulders and strode to greet them, indicating the seating area in front of her desk with a sweep of one arm. A thin gold filigree bracelet that matched her earrings encircled her right wrist. "Blair, Cameron. How are you?"

It was the first time the three of them had been together since Blair's evacuation from her makeshift sanctuary in Maine upon Marine One the day before. Blair still found it hard to believe that it had only been two days since the world had exploded. So much had happened in those forty-eight hours to alter the landscape of an entire nation's existence that time itself seemed to have been altered, each moment somehow stretching toward a point in a future that was clouded with questions and uncertainty. Blair reached for Cam's hand, instantly comforted by the warm, solid strength of the fingers that closed around hers. She glanced quickly at her lover, whose eyes said that the connection mattered to her too. Blair felt a wash of appreciation, because Cameron made it so easy to love her. She never let her unshakable strength diminish her tenderness, or her need. Blair smiled her thanks and turned to the woman whom she'd known since childhood.

"We're alive, Luce, and that's what counts." Blair sat on the floral brocade love seat in front of a wide, glass-topped coffee table, her hand still clasping Cam's. "But everything else has gone to hell. Cam's been taken off my security detail."

"Yes, I know," Lucinda said, settling into a chair across from them.

"So I guess my father does too?"

Lucinda nodded. "There really wasn't anything to be done. Considering everything that's happened, all we've been trying to do is follow protocol in an effort to reestablish some kind of order."

"That's ridiculous," Blair snapped. "My personal security detail has nothing whatsoever to do with national security. It has nothing to do with what happened—"

"It does, Blair," Cam interrupted gently. "The assault on the Aerie was timed to coincide with the airliners hitting the Towers. Those hijackings and the gunmen at your building were two arms of a single assault."

"Yes," Lucinda said, regarding Cam intently. "That seems to be the only conclusion." She looked at Blair. "Which means that *you* played a key role in a terrorist plan to destabilize the nation. Obviously, your ongoing security is now of the utmost importance."

Blair's fingers tightened around Cam's. "So we're going to high priority coverage."

Lucinda nodded.

"An agent physically in the room with me twenty-four hours a day. Doubling the number of agents on every detail. Limitations on social appearances and foreign travel." Blair shivered nearly imperceptibly, then held Lucinda's gaze. "For a few days, maybe. But for weeks? Maybe months? I can't take it, Luce. I just can't."

"We don't know *what* kind of time frame we're looking at." Lucinda's tone was kind but unyielding. "We don't know anything yet, Blair. We don't know if this was an isolated terrorist cell acting alone on orders from outside this country or if this represents just one faction of a highly organized national network that may be planning another attack right now on Chicago or Los Angeles or Dallas." She leaned forward, her expression intent, but her eyes gentle. "All we know is that you were singled out for elimination. We must assume that you are still a target."

"What makes this any different than any other day? The entire focus of my security team is to protect me from the potential of attack. And they do it very well." Blair looked at Cam. "Just like they did on Tuesday."

"From the limited intelligence we have available thus far," Lucinda said, "the attack on the Aerie was nearly flawless. You were all lucky to survive it."

"I agree with Lucinda, Blair," Cam said. "There might have been only one strike team capable of that kind of assault, and if that's the case, they've been eliminated. But we don't *know* that. We don't know that there isn't a second team already trained with a contingency plan for another strike. We just don't know."

"If that's the case, Luce," Blair argued, "then why take my most experienced agents away from me? Cam and the others are the best people to protect me."

"Ordinarily, I'd agree, and I have, in the past. This isn't the first attempt on your life, and we've kept your security team in place." Lucinda gave Cam a look that was as close to an apology as she ever offered. "But this time, there was inside help. A United States Secret Service agent was involved in an assassination attempt on the first daughter. Clearly, we have a profound breach in security. No one is above suspicion."

Blair stiffened. When she spoke, her tone was flat and deadly. "You're talking about my lover."

"I'm giving you the opinion of the highest-ranking members of our security services."

"I don't give a flying fu—"

"An opinion, by the way," Lucinda went on, "that I don't happen to share. And neither does your father. Which is why you're both sitting here right now." Lucinda smiled wryly. "And if you would simply let me brief you, I could probably save us all a lot of time."

Blair opened her mouth, then sighed deeply and settled back against the sofa. "I'm sorry. Go ahead."

"Justice and the NSA want to keep the investigation into the incident at the Aerie under their jurisdiction as part of the larger inquiry surrounding the terrorist attacks."

Cam spoke quietly, her tone mild and uncritical. Her eyes, however, shone hot with emotion. "It will take that kind of multijurisdictional commission two years to investigate something of this magnitude."

Lucinda laughed. "You're being generous, Commander. I would have ventured closer to three."

"Ma'am," Cam acknowledged with a tip of her head. "Your estimate is probably more accurate than mine. Either way, it's too long not to know the scope of the threat to Ms. Powell."

"Yes, well," Lucinda said, serious once more, "however long it takes, I believe we all can appreciate that regardless of intentions, the greater emphasis of any investigation must be on the *national* threat."

Blair saw a muscle along the edge of Cam's jaw flutter, and she sensed the utter stillness in Cam's body that she had come to know preceded the lightning strike of her lover's rare but powerful fury. "Are you baiting her, Luce? Because it's not a very good idea."

Lucinda kept her eyes on Cam's face. "No, I wanted to see for myself exactly why the president has such faith in her."

"Maybe it's because I love her," Blair said sharply.

"No," Lucinda said softly, "it's because she loves you." She settled back in her chair and crossed her legs, one smooth silky glide of tight flesh along tight flesh. "So let me explain, Commander, your new assignment. The president intended to be here, but he was called away for an emergency meeting. You may assume the orders come from him."

Cam nodded. "Yes, ma'am."

"You will head a special investigative team appointed by the president whose sole purpose is to determine the origination of the assault on Ms. Powell's apartment building, ascertain how deep the intelligence breach goes within our security ranks, and establish how this operation was associated with the attacks on New York City and Washington, DC."

"I'll need free access to various intelligence files, including those of the FBI, ATF, CIA, and Justice," Cam replied immediately.

"You'll be granted clearance and provided contacts, but your inquiries will need to be very circumspect."

Meaning that this is a secret commission. Cam did not voice the question, knowing that she would not receive an answer. "I want to choose my own team members."

"Granted."

"I want the original members of Blair's security team reinstated as soon as the Justice inquiry clears them."

"That will take some time, but I'll see to it." Lucinda lifted a shoulder. "Nothing makes their wheel turn quickly."

"When we find the people responsible, I want to coordinate the takedown."

"Cam—" Blair protested.

Lucinda broke in, "You'll coordinate any strike team efforts with a military liaison."

"Agreed," Cam responded.

"The president will name the liaison."

Cam considered arguing for her own choice of military personnel, but one did not question the president's authority during negotiations like these. "I want to attend the daily briefings of Blair's security detail."

"The new commander may take offense."

"Possibly," Cam said. "I would. Nevertheless, these are my terms."

Lucinda tilted her head and appraised Cam with interest. "What makes you think you have any bargaining power here, Commander?"

"Because you know that I'm going to investigate with or without your sanction, and you'd prefer to know what I'm doing. And what I find out."

"If you were to undertake an unauthorized investigation, you'd be placing yourself in violation of any number of security regulations. Theoretically, you could lose your clearance, possibly face prosecution."

"Lucinda, what the hell?" Blair started to rise, and only Cam's hand in hers held her back.

"It's okay," Cam said quietly.

Blair rounded on her, her blue eyes flashing. "If you think I'm going to sit here and listen to her threaten you, you're crazy."

"I'm not threatening her, Blair," Lucinda said. "I'm only laying out the facts. And the reason that you're here listening to this, against my advice, by the way, is because your father doesn't want to keep this a secret from you."

"And why did *you* want to keep me in the dark?" Blair sat forward on the edge of the sofa, her free hand fisted on her thigh.

"Because I knew you wouldn't like Agent Roberts heading this investigation, and your reluctance could interfere with her—"

"Bullshit, Luce. Nothing interferes with Cam's effectiveness, and you know it."

"Not her effectiveness," Lucinda said gently. "Her safety."

Blair jerked. "What? Do you think I would compromise her in some way? Risk her *life*?"

"No, I think your resistance would distract her, and distraction can lead to mistakes."

"I have *never* wanted her to do this job, and she knows it." Blair's words sliced the air as her body quivered. "Do you think she was distracted the day she stepped in front of me outside my apartment building and intercepted the bullet that was meant for me? Do you think she was distracted on Tuesday when she stood in front of me *again*—"

"Blair," Cam murmured. "It's—"

"But she's still doing the job." Blair's voice cracked but she continued, "because she has to, and I know that. Because not doing it would hurt her more than anything that might happen to her, even…" She finally lost her battle to block out the images that, under ordinary circumstances, she so successfully kept at bay. Now she couldn't *stop* reliving the nightmare of her lover dying. She turned her face away from Lucinda and Cam, closing her mind to the memories.

Cam stood, ignoring the surprise on Lucinda Washburn's face. "Let's go, baby. It's been a tough couple of days, and I need a break."

"I need a decision, Agent Roberts," Lucinda said.

Cam circled Blair's waist with one arm. "I'll let you know tomorrow. There are some people I need to speak to first."

"That's a bit irregular."

"These aren't normal times."

"I'll expect your answer in the morning."

Cam nodded as she and Blair turned to leave. "You'll have it."

Once they were beyond the hearing of Lucinda's deputy chief of staff, Blair asked, "What are you waiting for?"

"You and I need to talk, and I need to go to New York tonight."

CHAPTER SIX

B lair and Cam walked in silence through the warren of offices that was the nerve center of the nation. The West Wing at almost any hour of any day was alive with activity, but now the very air was charged with a sense of urgency. Aides, deputy chiefs, military advisers, and security personnel hurried through the halls, all looking as if they were on a mission of vital importance and already behind schedule.

They nodded to the Secret Service agents stationed at the elevator to the residential floors, and once inside, Blair asked, "Why New York and why tonight?"

Can looked as though she was about to answer, but when the elevator doors slid open and they stepped out, she nodded in the direction of Blair's suite. "Your security chief is here."

Paula Stark stood just outside Blair's door, her gaze fixed on some point on the opposite wall that appeared to hold great interest. She wore a dark suit, and her face was nearly the same shade as her white shirt. Blair's new chief did not look toward them as they approached.

"Paula?" Blair queried as she stopped in front of the Secret Service agent.

"Ma'am," Stark responded stiffly. "In case the commander hasn't yet informed you, I've been assigned as your new security chief."

"Yes, I know."

"I'd like to review your plans for the next few days."

"I don't know that I have any." Blair's voice held just the slightest edge of irritation. "And now isn't a very good time."

"I understand. I'll be happy to wait."

Blair stopped with her hand on the doorknob. "For how long?"

"Until it's convenient for you to meet with me."

"This is a new tactic," Blair said with the barest hint of appreciation in her tone. She glanced at Cam, whose eyes held a glint of humor. "If I don't decide to come out for forty-eight hours, you'll get awfully hungry out here, Paula."

"Yes, ma'am."

"And you already look done in."

Stark shifted and met Blair's gaze. "I'm fine, Ms. Powell. And I appreciate that you weren't given any notice of these changes, so I don't wish to disrupt your schedule."

"Your *presence* is a disruption. But you've always known that."

"Yes, ma'am. I should have said any *more* of a disruption than necessary."

"Fair enough." Blair smiled with a mixture of humor and bitterness. "So, can I expect you to talk like you have a stick up your ass from now on, then?"

"I'm not sure," Stark replied seriously. "I really haven't had time to work on a command voice."

Blair sighed and pushed the door open. "Come on in. Your approach is unique, and there's no way you could match Cam's command voice anyhow. But for God's sake, relax."

Just inside the door, Stark stopped and looked toward Cam, who had walked to the far side of the room, and gave her a brief shrug of apology. Then she returned her attention to Blair. "I'd like to say right now that I have no intention of replacing the commander. However, I've been given a job to do. A job which I consider vital, and I intend to do it in the best way possible. My way."

"Well. *That* sounds a lot like the previous security chiefs I've dealt with." Blair flopped down on one of the sofas and indicated a nearby chair. "Sit." She trained her head in Cam's direction. "Are you going to join us?"

"I've got some calls to make. And I think this ought to be between the two of you." She smiled at Blair and nodded to Stark as she headed for the adjoining room. "I'm glad to see you're on the job, Agent."

"Thank you, Commander."

"Let's get this over with, Stark," Blair said testily. "You'll find that the daily briefings are not one of my favorite exercises."

Stark took a breath and launched into her prepared speech. "The first team, at least temporarily, will consist of myself and two to three other agents, depending upon the circumstances. Right now, I don't have the duty assignments because I've just been given the names of your new team members."

Blair's eyes narrowed. "I'm not happy about working with strangers, especially if we're at Priority One."

"That's why I'll be on the first team. Outside the perimeter of the White House, I'll be your primary agent."

"It'll be tough, doing double duty as both the crew chief and my primary."

Stark's expression didn't change. "In my opinion, that's the appropriate action."

"All right. Thank you, that will make it easier for me."

"As to the commander—"

"There's nothing about Cam's presence in my life that's open for discussion." The faint warmth that had seeped its way into Blair's voice since they had begun talking quickly disappeared. "You and I are friends, Paula." In fact, for a few brief hours in what now felt like the distant past, they'd been more than that. "I hope you're not going to suddenly pretend that you don't know what she means to me."

"I was going to suggest that the commander attend daily briefings, since I'm sure you would both prefer that."

Blair tilted her head and studied Stark appraisingly. "And you don't mind that? My lover and your former boss observing your new command?"

Stark released a long, pent-up breath and leaned forward, her hands clasped loosely between her knees, her eyes holding Blair's unflinchingly. "It doesn't matter whether I mind or not. What matters is that your security team functions effectively, and I believe it will run more smoothly if the commander is aware of the daily plan." She separated her hands and curled her fingers over her knees, her voice softening for an instant. "But just so you know, I won't forget anything."

"They should have assigned more agents like you in the past, Paula," Blair said quietly. "I might not have found it necessary to disappear quite so often."

"I'd like it if you could promise not to do that in the future, Ms. Powell," Stark said, all business again. "Because the danger is far more than theoretical now."

"I can't." There was no aggression in Blair's voice, only an undercurrent of regret. "But I'll do the best I can."

Stark nodded. "Then we have a plan." She leaned back and unbuttoned her jacket, the first break in her formal posture. "We need to talk about the next few days."

"I'm flying with my father to Manhattan tomorrow to view…the scene."

"I'll discuss the itinerary with Agent Turner," Stark said, referring to the president's security chief. "And you'll be staying here tonight?"

"You're blushing."

"I've been working on that," Stark acknowledged conversationally. She grinned for a fleeting second. "No luck so far."

"I don't know where I'll be tonight."

"Ms. Powell—"

Blair interrupted. "It depends on Cam's plans. If she doesn't stay here, then I'll stay with her in her apartment."

Stark winced. "Security would be far easier to accomplish here."

"That's not my concern." Blair rose abruptly. "I have your number. I'll call you about my plans."

"Yes, ma'am." Stark stood. "Thank you."

Stark had nearly reached the door when Blair stopped her with a question.

"Have you heard from Renée?"

"Yes. She's…uninjured." Somehow *all right* didn't feel quite like the truth. Stark looked over her shoulder. "It sounds…bad…up there."

"I can't even imagine," Blair murmured. Her expression softened. "Get some sleep, Paula. I won't be going anywhere for a while. And I promise, I'll call."

"Will do," Stark lied, knowing that before she could sleep, she needed to review the dossiers on the seven new agents she'd been assigned and try to choose three whom Blair would be able to tolerate having in close proximity during her waking hours for the foreseeable future. "I appreciate the time, Ms. Powell."

"Lose the stick, Paula," Blair said with a laugh.

Stark smiled. "Working on that too."

❖

Cam, sitting on the edge of the bed, hung up the phone as Blair walked into the bedroom. She'd removed her jacket and weapon harness and had rolled up both sleeves to mid-forearm. "How did it go?"

"She's still standing."

"That good, huh?" Cam grinned.

"I'm glad you got them to appoint her as security chief," Blair said as she settled next to Cam. She threaded an arm around Cam's waist and leaned her cheek against Cam's upper arm. "It's so much easier with a woman, and one who knows about you and me. Because I can't go back to the way things were. I can't pretend that I'm not who I am and that we're not lovers."

"I wouldn't want you to." Cam kissed her temple. "In fact, I don't think I could take it either." She eased back onto the pillows and drew Blair back with her until they reclined, Blair curled against her side. "I can't pretend that I don't need you with me all the time."

Blair shifted until she lay full-length atop Cam. "Why the sudden change?"

Cam ran her fingers through Blair's hair, holding the thick blond strands away from Blair's neck so that she could raise her head and kiss her there in the sweet triangle just below her ear. "I'm sorry if you ever thought it was easy for me not to be with you. It's always been hell, but these last two days…" She caught Blair's earlobe between her lips and sucked it softly. When Blair stiffened, she released the small, fleshy morsel. "I don't want to let you out of my sight."

"Same here." Then Blair felt it coming, the powerful surge of tenderness and want and need that coalesced in her heart and body to become love and something far greater than she could define with words or contain with mere flesh. But still she tried to articulate with insufficient phrases and her woefully inadequate touch the places that Cam filled in her life. "I love you."

As Blair began to unbutton Cam's shirt, Cam tugged Blair's blouse from her jeans.

"No," Blair murmured. "Lie still."

"Blair," Cam protested.

"Shh."

Blair knelt astride Cam's hips, slowly loosing each button until the shirt lay open with a column of flesh exposed down the center of Cam's body. She edged her fingertips beneath the crisp fabric, crested the rise of Cam's breasts until she reached the tight peaks, and brushed lightly over the puckered nipples. She smiled when Cam's hips twisted against her thighs, and she carefully squeezed and molded Cam's breasts beneath her palms, drawing the swollen cores of the nipples between her fingers until she elicited a soft moan from her lover's throat.

"Oh God." Cam's pupils dilated until black eclipsed the gray and desire swam in the dark eddies left behind.

"I never get the chance to go slow with you," Blair said in a quiet conversational tone as she rocked back on her heels and ever so slowly slid the length of Cam's leather belt through the silver buckle at her waist. Ignoring the flutter of muscles beneath the smooth skin of Cam's abdomen, she deftly popped the clasp at Cam's waistband with one hand and drew the zipper down with the other in a single fluid motion. Then, as she turned her hand and slid her fingers into the soft curls she'd just laid bare, she leaned forward and caught a nipple between her teeth. As she closed her eyes and sucked, she circled her fingers over the base of Cam's belly, not touching the focus of her need, but knowing that the motion would tease the blood into the sensitive flesh only inches away. "Mmm. I love how hot you feel in my mouth."

Cam gripped the back of Blair's head and pushed herself hard against Blair's mouth, causing teeth to scrape across her hypersensitive flesh. Pleasure shot straight to her core and struck between her thighs, bringing her hips off the bed. In a voice so hoarse her words were barely recognizable, she rasped, "Bite it."

"Oh no," Blair whispered, pulling back to lick ever so lightly at the swollen nipple. "I don't trust you not to come."

Cam could only groan.

"And," Blair said, her breath rushing in and out as if she'd been running for hours, "there's no hurry." Then she pushed herself lower until her breasts were nestled between Cam's thighs and her cheek was against Cam's abdomen. As she sucked and nibbled on the pliant crescent of skin edging Cam's navel, she smoothed one hand up the inside of Cam's leg, briefly cupped the vee between her parted thighs, and then slipped inside her fly again. This time, she pushed lower until her fingertips found the hard rise of Cam's clitoris. She wanted it between her fingertips, wanted to tug and stroke and twist until she felt the rapid lengthening and swift swelling that always signaled Cam's rush toward orgasm. She loved that power, that unbelievable intimacy, that singular knowledge that she and she alone could do this to the woman she so craved. Shivering, she forced herself to grow still.

"Touch me."

"Soon, darling, soon." Blair pressed down once, hard, against Cam's clitoris, making her whole body twitch, and then quickly withdrew her hand. Getting swiftly to her knees, she grasped the waistband of Cam's trousers. "Lift your hips."

In seconds, Blair had her naked. Groaning at the magnificent sight of Cam, neck arched and hands lying open, palms up at her sides, Blair tore off her blouse and threw it aside. She ran both hands up her own abdomen and over her breasts, tugging her nipples in passing and moaning at the pleasure. Then, her control slipping, she threw herself down between her lover's legs. She stretched one arm up to close a hand over Cam's breast as she simultaneously took her into her mouth.

Cam arched off the bed, both hands tangling in Blair's hair. "Going to come."

"Wait," Blair mouthed against the swollen, pulsating flesh, too needy to stop her assault. She licked and sucked and drank of her lover's passion, tugging Cam's nipple to the cadence of her lips working the stiff shaft in her mouth.

"I gotta come." Quiet, desperate.

"Nooo," Blair breathed, lifting up just enough to slide her fingers into Cam's silky depths. She pushed.

"Gotta come." Wondrous, pleading.

Blair bit down gently.

Cam twisted and jerked. "That's it. Oh…that's it."

Blair never let up, never stopped the thrust and pull that kept Cam clenching around her fingers, even when she felt herself explode inside her tight jeans. Whimpering, she rode Cam's climax until they both lay limp and panting in a tangle of sheets and sweat-slicked limbs.

"You want to tell me," Cam gasped, "where that came from?"

Still stroking Cam lightly, Blair slid up beside her and kissed her. "Wanna tell me what's in New York?"

CHAPTER SEVEN

Cam hiked herself up onto an elbow and studied Blair through narrowed eyes. "Did you by any chance just screw my brains out so you could extract information from me while I'm in a weakened condition?"

"But of course," Blair said, sliding her lips over Cam's nipple. "It's a tried-and-true interrogation technique. Of course, we reserve it for the hard-core cases."

"Very effective." Cam caught Blair's chin in her palm and eased that talented mouth away from her breast before the pleasure eclipsed what remained of her control. She kissed Blair swiftly on the lips and then guided her lover's head down to her shoulder, curving an arm around Blair's waist to keep her close. "There are things I need to do up there that I should have done yesterday."

"Yesterday morning we didn't know if there was anyplace in the world we were really safe," Blair reminded her.

"I know. And the only thing that mattered was getting you back here. But once Marine One picked you up, I probably should've gone back to Manhattan right away."

Blair struggled to contain her protests. This was about what Cam needed, not her. "Did you stay here because I needed you to?"

"No." Cam hugged her. "I stayed because *I* needed to. Since the day I walked into that loft and saw you in that blue silk robe, I've been doing what I've needed to do instead of what I should have done."

"Sorry?" Blair made aimless patterns on Cam's stomach with her nails, listening hard for what lay beneath the surface of her lover's quiet musings. With Cameron, she had learned that the truth of what really lay in her heart was in all the things she did not say.

"Never," Cam said immediately. "But now you're safe, and there are things I need to do."

"You said that." Blair raked her nails harder across Cam's lower abdomen, eliciting a quiet groan. "Now explain."

"*That* distraction procedure is working too," Cam gasped.

"I know. I'm waiting."

Cam grabbed Blair's wrist and pressed her hand firmly against her stomach to stop the torture. "Your apartment building is a crime scene. I need to get a look at it firsthand before there's nothing left of the evidence."

"God, Cam," Blair said in surprise. "The FBI must have been all over that place already. There's not going to be anything left that they haven't already analyzed."

"I don't let other agents do my investigating for me. Besides, they're FBI."

Blair laughed. "Don't let Renée Savard hear you say that."

"She's the exception."

"What else are you planning?"

"To talk to whichever of our people are still around." Cam's voice held an edge. "I'd like to hear their reports before the special inquiry begins."

"You think they'll be under a gag order not to discuss anything about what happened?"

"Ordinarily, not from me, but now that my status is in question, I don't want to put them at risk for disciplinary action if anyone finds out they briefed me."

"I doubt they would pass that information along to the Justice people."

"A week ago I would have been certain of that."

"You still trust them, don't you?"

"I trusted Foster too." The bitter acid of self-recrimination burned her throat as she said his name.

Blair heard the frustration and regret in Cam's voice. "Hey. You're not the bad guy here." She circled her fingers soothingly in the hollow between Cam's breasts. "Remember, you saved my life."

That was my job, my duty, and I almost blew it. God. Cam brushed her lips over Blair's hair. "I know. You're right."

"Once those interviews are done, you'll be finished up there?"

"I also want to talk to Diane."

Blair sat up quickly, the sheet falling away and leaving her breasts bare. "Diane? Why?"

Cam ran her fingers up and down Blair's arm, aware of the steel bands of tension beneath the velvet skin. "Because she's your best friend. Because there isn't a better source of information about you on the planet. Because someone might have approached her without her even realizing it, and if they did, I want to know."

"She would never hurt me."

"I know that. But sometimes we say things innocently, without realizing the implications."

Blair shook her head vehemently. "No, not Diane. She's known me my whole life, and she's always understood the security issues. Christ, she used to fine-tune my alibi in boarding school when I escaped from my security details to meet my girlfriends. She would never let anything slip."

"I'm sure you're right, but I have to check."

"Of course you do. And of course you have to do it all yourself." Blair tried to keep her voice light, because she didn't want Cam to know how very much she didn't want to be apart from her right then. She knew she was safe in the White House and probably anywhere else she might go with the heightened security she was sure to have, although she never really felt as safe with any of the other agents as she did with Cam. But that wasn't why she didn't want Cam to be gone long. The attack on the Aerie—no, the attack on *her*—was more frightening than she wanted to admit. Mere blocks away, thousands of unsuspecting, innocent people had died for a reason no rational person could fathom. She had always known the danger was there, lurking in the background like an ominous shadow, but this had brought her true vulnerability home with undeniable clarity. Life felt so very tenuous, and being with Cam was the only thing that made it right. "How long are you going to be gone?"

"I had thought a couple of days. But if you're coming up with your father tomorrow, I want to be there. I may come back with you, it depends."

"Cam, I'll have a full security detail. Why don't you just—"

"No." A public appearance this soon after the attack was ill advised, but Cam didn't want to say that, knowing that Blair was not about to change her mind. Frightening her would accomplish nothing.

"It will be a new detail with a new chief. I want to be by your side. I'll get the schedule when you're en route and meet your vehicle when you arrive downtown."

"Stark can handle it."

"I have no doubt. But she's going to have a new team. And I won't know them."

"If being with me tomorrow means you going back to the city again in a few days, then I'd rather you just do what you need to do and get it done. I'll be fine."

"It's not going to get done quickly, baby," Cam said gently. "That assault team was too well organized and too professional not to have known the risks of discovery if they failed. We're going to have to dig, and dig hard, to find out who they were. And even that may not tell us who sent them."

"How long, do you think?" Blair shivered, but the cold was deep inside. Despite her best efforts, not knowing who had wanted her dead gnawed at the edges of her awareness, threatening her comfort and peace of mind. But if the question was to go unanswered for weeks and months, leaving the threat of another attack hanging over her, her life would never be her own again. Nor might her lover. Blair feared that Cam might become so immersed in the hunt that she would lose her to it. "How long?"

"Weeks, probably months. You're shivering." Cam tucked the sheet around Blair's shoulders. "Or we could get a break and have an answer in days." When Blair shivered again, Cam pulled her back down beside her. "Hopefully, closer to the latter than the former. You okay?"

Wordlessly, Blair nodded. The course of their days, it appeared, had already been charted. As had so often been the case throughout her life, she had no choice but to commit to the journey. And this time, with her lover by her side, she hoped that she would not lose herself along the way. "When are you leaving?"

"As soon as I shower."

A half hour later, Blair walked Cam to the private entryway that the first family used to come and go without the scrutiny of the ever-present press.

"You'll call me?"

"Of course." Cam looked past Blair back into the White House. A guard stood ten feet away, staring in their direction but appearing to register nothing about their actions or conversation. She glanced over her shoulder to the expansive gardens, noting the distant sound of traffic. Her shoulders tightened.

"What's wrong?" Blair asked.

Cam shrugged and grinned ruefully. "We haven't been apart for a long time. It makes me uneasy."

Blair smiled. "Sometimes, Commander, you say the most wonderful things."

"I love you." Cam leaned forward in full view of the uniformed officer and kissed Blair softly. "See you soon."

Blair put both arms around Cam's neck and pressed against her. "Be careful."

Cam kissed her again. "You too."

❖

The ground shook as a bomb detonated, and then she heard the thunder of incoming fire. The roar filled her head, so thick she couldn't breathe. She ran for cover, the smell and sound of destruction engulfing her. The air was a thick black blanket, nearly impenetrable. She ran blind, one arm stretched out in front of her, praying she wouldn't stumble down a dead-end alley or under the wheels of a vehicle. The whine of high-velocity projectiles assaulted her eardrums, and she knew with absolute certainty that she was going to die.

Renée Savard lurched to her feet, her weapon in her hand, and pivoted in an unsteady circle, searching for the enemy. She banged her shin on the edge of the coffee table, and the deep, sharp pain brought her fully awake. Still, the rattle of gunfire persisted until she snatched up her cell phone, its digital readout marking its place on the floor by the sofa.

"Savard," she croaked. The room was dark. The night outside the windows was black. She fumbled on the side table and finally found the lamp switch. The light hurt her eyes.

"Are you busy?"

"What?" Her blazer lay in a crumpled ball just inside the entrance to the apartment she shared with Stark. *What the hell?*

"Renée?"

"What? Who? Paula?"

"Hey, did I wake you?"

"No. I just…I just walked in." When had she left the search zone and come back to the apartment? When had she fallen asleep? "Sorry."

"Is everything all right?" Stark's voice was quietly cautious.

"Yes. Sure." Savard stared at her left hand. Her fingers were clenched around her service weapon. Jesus. Quickly, she holstered her weapon and sank down onto the sofa. "What time is it there?"

"It's seven thirty. The same time as it is where you are. Renée? What's going on?"

Savard scrubbed an unsteady hand over her face and took a long breath. She forced a lightness she did not feel into her voice. "Nothing. Just lost my watch. I'm always a little disoriented when I don't have it."

"You're done for the night now, right?"

Done for the night. When had been the last time she'd been off duty? She'd left DC before sunup, reported in at the local field office in Manhattan, and gone straight back to Ground Zero. Search teams were still scouring the massive area of destruction, still hoping for survivors even while gathering evidence of the unimaginable damage. She and her fellow agents were still at the stage of gathering physical evidence, and everyone was working frantically while trying to deny the devastating knowledge that they had failed. She hadn't slept in three days.

"Right. I'm off shift."

"Look, you sound really beat. Why don't you call me back after you've had a chance to unwind."

"No, hey. I want to talk to you." Savard struggled to call up the image of the woman who had touched her just hours before and made her feel alive, of the tender lover who had held her in the night and helped her forget the fear. Love and gratitude for that woman hammered against the wall of despair that had somehow appeared around her in the last seventy-two hours. She knew the emotions were there even though she couldn't feel them all the way inside. But she clung to the memories nevertheless. "How are you?"

"You're sure you're okay?"

"Yeah, yeah. I'm fine. Come on, sweetheart, tell me about your day." *Just talk to me. Just let me hear your voice.*

"Well, I've got some news."

"What?"

"The commander and the entire team are under investigation for what happened at the Aerie. They've all been suspended."

Savard straightened, her weary mind suddenly clear. "You've got to be kidding. That's ridiculous. Oh, sweetie, I'm so sorry."

"Not me, honey. I'm the only one they didn't suspend."

"Why not? I mean, I'm glad, but why not you too?"

Even through the phone line, Stark's voice conveyed her lingering astonishment. "I'm Egret's new security chief."

"Oh my God. God, Paula. Congratulations."

"I guess."

"That's incredible. I'm so proud of you." Savard felt it then, the swell of love and pride and tenderness, and close behind it, a rush of relief. Somewhere inside, she was still alive. "I love you."

"Oh man, I love you too. So much. I miss you."

"Same here, sweetie. I—wait a second, I've got another call." Savard looked at the number on the screen. "I'm going to have take this. It's a scramble."

"Okay. Look, call me when you can, okay?"

"I will. I love you." Savard switched to the second line. "Savard."

"This is Cameron Roberts."

"Commander. How are you?"

"Fine. I'd like to see you."

"Of course. When?"

"How about now?"

Savard pushed her fatigue and the pain of the last few days into the recesses of her consciousness where she kept all the other horrors she'd witnessed over the years. "Certainly."

Chapter Eight

Cam slowly circled the rental car around Gramercy Park. Blair's building was dark, as she had expected.

"What's the security situation?" she inquired of Savard, who had been silent for the short trip across town from Stark's apartment.

"What? Oh." Savard straightened and cleared her throat. "There isn't any."

"No one is detailed to watch the building?" Cam pulled to the curb around the corner from the entrance. "Didn't anyone consider that whoever ordered the assault might be just as interested as we are in what was left behind? Or that a second team might be waiting for Blair to return?"

"I don't know, Commander. I was pulled off the investigation the first day."

"Right." Cam fought back her anger at still further corroboration that this investigation would inevitably take a backseat to the greater threat of another terrorist attack. Added to that was the complete disruption of business as usual at the highest levels and the inevitable preoccupation of those in charge with what was sure to be a long siege of finger-pointing as to exactly which agency was responsible for the nation being taken by surprise. Still, seeing the clear lapse in protocol was a cold reminder that she couldn't count on anyone else to ensure Blair's safety. "Let's not assume that just because *we* aren't watching the building, no one else is. Is the rear door functional?"

"The door's there, but I'm not sure about the stairs. They blew the fire door from the lobby to the stairwell."

Cam remembered the thud of plastic explosives and the grating scream of twisting metal as she'd shepherded Blair out of the building toward the waiting vehicles. The men behind them had been so close, and Blair had been so vulnerable. A trickle of sweat snaked between her shoulder blades despite the cool night air. "Let's have a look. We'll walk south a couple of blocks, track back on Second Avenue, and approach the rear from the east."

"Yes, ma'am."

"Wait for me to come around." Cam stepped out of the car and walked to the passenger side, then leaned down and opened Savard's door. She'd worn jeans and a leather jacket to travel in and hoped that to anyone watching they would look like a couple headed out for an evening date. She extended her hand. "Just pretend we're together."

With Savard's hand in hers, Cam turned her back to Blair's building and walked south on Irving Place. Savard's fingers were like ice in hers, and she saw Savard shiver. Although the September night was chilly, she did not think it was the cold that bothered her companion. "The Bureau must be pushing hard on the evidence-gathering at the site."

"Every available agent is there."

"Working around the clock, I guess," Cam said mildly as she turned east several blocks later.

"Pretty much."

Savard spoke in a monotone, her usually animated expression flat. Cam resisted the sudden urge to put her arm around Savard's shoulders. Something told her the action might be welcome, but possibly more contact than Savard was ready to handle. She knew from experience that there were times when the only way to get beyond pain was to walk through it, unshielded and alone. "I'm going to need you to take me through the scene tonight. You were one of the first responders, and you saw it fresh. I'm going to need to see what you saw, smell what you smelled, feel what you felt—every detail. Can you do it?"

"Yes." Savard met Cam's questioning gaze. Even with her face illuminated only by the streetlights, the feverish intensity in her eyes was clear. "Yes. Yes, I can do it."

Cam nodded once as they turned north again. A few minutes later, they walked down the narrow access alley that ran the length of the block behind Blair's building. The turnaround where Mac and Felicia had parked the Suburbans was littered with the detritus of a hasty medical evacuation that marked the spot where Mac had lain shot and bleeding. Where Cam had left him to fend for himself while she took Blair to safety. She pulled a small, powerful Mag-Lite from the inside pocket of her leather jacket and shone it on the ground. While Savard watched, she walked the perimeter of the scene and then crisscrossed the area in a methodical grid, examining every square foot of concrete as she moved.

"The team from Quantico has been over this, Commander," Savard observed quietly.

"Uh-huh."

At one point, she squatted down and brushed her hand over the surface of the concrete. The stain from Mac's blood yielded no answers. She stood, clicked off her light, and pocketed it. "Let's go inside."

The steel security door was dented and the brick surrounding it for fifteen feet was pockmarked from the storm of bullets Cam, Stark, Felicia, and Mac had fired at the assailants. Cam's gaze swept over the bullet marks, her face registering nothing, as she fit her key card into the lock. The door opened and they stepped inside. Cam switched on her light and played it over the stairwell. Bits of plaster, shards of metal, and other debris from the explosion one floor up covered the stairs, but they were passable.

"You go ahead," Cam instructed, playing the light ahead of them as they climbed. Their footsteps in the cavernous space were a distant echo of the automatic weapons fire that had followed her down the same stairs only days before. Once in the lobby, she walked directly to the spot where Cynthia Parker had fallen. Traces of her blood remained on the scuffed tiles. Turning toward the entrance, Cam assessed the distance and knew that the assailants' plan had included eliminating the Secret Service agent on duty Tuesday morning. The security desk where Parker had been stationed was too far from the front entrance for any other scenario to have been possible. Parker had been lucky to get off a shot at all, and it was a testament to her skill that she had actually taken down one member of the assault team. They had come into the building planning to kill her, and they had known exactly where she would be positioned. Fury settled in Cam's stomach like a stone. Someone had set her people up to die, and it had taken more than a rogue Secret Service agent to do it.

"Okay—tell me what you saw when you arrived. The position of the bodies, what type of weapons, the amount of ammo the attackers carried, communication devices—all of it."

As Savard recounted her observations in a steady unwavering tone, Cam played her light over the area as if highlighting action on a stage. Once or twice she asked Savard to repeat a detail.

"Who has the tapes from the security camera up there?" Cam asked as she illuminated the corner opposite the front entrance.

"All the tapes are at the regional office."

Cam nodded. "I want them."

"Commander—"

Cam angled the light between them so that their faces flickered in shadow as their eyes met. "I'm going to run this investigation, and in order to do that, I plan on getting all the information there is, no matter who has it. I want you on the team."

Savard's lips parted in surprise. "But the World Trade Center—"

"Is critically important, I know that. And I know that you want to be part of it. But the attack on Blair Powell was a threat to national security too, and"—Cam shone her light on the dark brown stain where Cynthia Parker had lain dying—"this is personal. Parker deserves justice too." She studied Savard's face and saw her pale even in the gloom. She didn't have to say that this could easily have been Paula Stark's blood flaking like so much rust-colored paint on the floor. "They came after us where we live, Savard. We can't let that happen again."

"No, ma'am," Savard said softly. "We can't."

They moved through the lower floors quickly. The apartments were all corporate rentals and infrequently occupied by business executives in the city for short stays.

"We'll need a list of anyone who stayed here in the last year, and another search on all property owners. The FBI databases should be good for that," Cam noted.

"Got it," Savard replied.

In the command center, Cam halted in surprise when she saw all the computers still present and humming quietly on standby. "Who the *hell* was in charge of this field operation? Didn't they realize that our computers might have been hacked for some of the information the perpetrators needed to carry out their operation? They might have left a trail."

Savard shook her head. "It's been crazy, Commander. We haven't been able to put together a cohesive team since Tuesday. Agents keep getting pulled to different shifts, the SACs are being shuffled around and no one knows why, and everyone is paranoid that they were the ones that missed some key bit of information that would have tipped us to Tuesday. Especially those of us who were in the counterterrorism squad."

"The CTS was established to analyze and coordinate data, not gather intelligence. There's a huge difference, and we all know that," Cam said. "You guys weren't to blame."

"But that's not going to make any difference now," Savard said solemnly.

"No, probably not." Cam dialed a number on her cell phone from memory. "Are you still in the city? I've got a job for you...tonight. I need you to strip out the hard drives from the computers in command central and anything else that might help us find out what happened here." Cam listened, then laughed softly. "Low-profile...yeah, you might say that. It could get dicey. You sure?...I don't know. For now, why don't you take it all home with you."

Cam pocketed her phone and grinned at Savard, a grin completely devoid of humor. "We have another team member."

"Should I ask?"

"Soon enough." Cam took one last look around, knowing that they might never be returning to the command center again. The entire security system had been compromised. In all likelihood, Blair would need to find a new home. "I want to go up to the Aerie. I need to see what kind of shape it's in before she does."

"Her paintings...I made sure no one touched them."

For the first time since they'd walked together like lovers, Cam touched Savard's shoulder. "Thank you. If you don't mind waiting down here..." She handed over her Mag-Lite. "Here, take this."

"No, there's plenty of light from the window. You'll need it upstairs. I'll be fine, Commander."

"You will be," Cam said gently. "I'll be right back."

Five minutes later she stood in the doorway of Blair's apartment, Foster's blood a Rorschach print of anger and regret beneath her feet. She looked into the loft and remembered the first time she'd stepped across the threshold and confronted the first daughter. Blair had been angry, aggressive, and alluringly seductive. Cam had tried for months to pretend that she hadn't felt the sharp spike of attraction the instant she'd seen her. But the more she'd tried to deny it, the stronger the attraction had become, and the more time she'd spent with Blair, the faster her attraction turned to something far deeper. Now, she thought of the woman she loved and the conspiracy that had been hatched by nameless individuals to destroy her, and she felt the mantle of resolve settle on her shoulders. Beneath it seethed the desire for retribution, and at the heart of her, a clearer, cleaner paean for justice. But what drove her, and what *would* drive her until the danger had been annihilated, was the pure and simple fury that someone would try to take from her what mattered most.

She switched off her light and whispered into the darkness. "You made a mistake when you chose her. Get ready, because I'm coming for you."

❖

Diane Bleeker opened the door to her apartment clothed in the deep burgundy silk dressing gown that Cam remembered with graphic clarity. The subtly curvaceous blond with a mouth made for kissing smiled a slow, sultry smile as she leaned with one hip cocked and an elegant arm stretched out to the door. Her breasts slid under the silk like shadows beneath the surface of a still pond on a hot summer's day, and after one involuntary glance, Cam kept her eyes firmly fixed on Diane's laughing blue ones.

"Why, Commander, to what do I owe the pleasure of this late-night visit?"

"I'm sorry I didn't call ahead," Cam began, then stopped suddenly as another figure moved into her range of vision. Another blond, this one cool where Diane was hot, remote where Diane was tantalizingly available, and one, Cam knew, capable of rendering a woman helpless with lust and need. "Hello, Valerie."

"Hello, Cameron."

Valerie, or Claire, as Cam had known her when they'd shared a clandestine relationship, also wore a dressing gown. Hers was black satin and gave her willowy form the glint of obsidian honed to a razor's edge. Cam felt the pull of a familiar ache deep in her groin, a visceral memory of talented hands and a torturous mouth, and she shrugged the unwanted response away with an impatient jerk of her shoulders.

Valerie smiled, but while Diane's smile was always playfully seductive whenever she detected the slightest reaction from Cam,

Valerie's was sad. "I guess we're all a little surprised."

Cam looked questioningly from Diane to Valerie just as Diane cast an inquisitive glance at first Valerie, then Cam.

"Valerie is marooned here for a few days until the cross-country flight situation gets straightened out," Diane said. "She's, ah, using the guest room."

"Yes," Valerie added, her cultured voice completely composed. "Diane has been very gracious with her hospitality."

"I was wondering if I could have a few minutes of your time," Cam said to Diane. "Alone, if you don't mind."

"My, that sounds very officious." Diane's smile suddenly disappeared and she took a step forward, curling her fingers tightly around Cam's forearm. "Blair's all right, isn't she? I spoke with her on the phone earlier—"

"She's fine," Cam said gently. "She's still at the residence."

"Oh, but I bet that she hates that."

Cam grinned. "You could say that." Out of the corner of her eye, she saw Valerie studying her intently. She wondered what it was Valerie hoped to see, because it was no secret that she and Blair were lovers. What else was she looking for? "I'm really sorry to barge in on your evening."

"Believe it or not, we were on our way to bed even though it's only eleven." Diane sighed. "The last few days have just been... unbelievable. I'm drained."

"I'm sorry. I can come back in the morning and we can talk then."

"Where are you staying?"

"I was planning on checking into one of the hotels."

"What about your apartment?" Diane asked curiously.

"No room service," Cam said, seeing no reason to point out that if someone *was* watching Blair's apartment, they would be watching hers as well. For the time being, she preferred to avoid anyone's scrutiny, friend or foe. She'd taken special precautions driving to Diane's after dropping off Savard to ensure that she hadn't been followed. No one knew she was in the city, and she preferred to keep it that way.

"Then stay here, because there's nothing available in the city in the way of hotel space. Too many stranded travelers. The couch is comfortable enough, and I can promise you good coffee in the morning."

Cam shook her head. "I've already disrupted your evening."

"Don't be silly." Diane leaned up and kissed Cam chastely on the cheek. "Stay. And give Blair my love when you talk to her."

"Thanks. I'll just grab my overnight bag from the car."

Diane handed her a spare key that she retrieved from a glass bowl on a nearby secretary. "I'll see you in the morning."

"Good enough," Cam said. When she met Valerie's eyes and saw the question in them, she returned her gaze evenly. "Good night, Valerie."

"Sleep well, Cameron," Valerie murmured before turning away.

When Cam returned to the apartment, she changed into a T-shirt and boxers and stretched out on the sofa. Then she speed-dialed a DC number.

"This is Blair Powell."

"Hey, baby," Cam said softly as she closed her eyes and imagined Blair's face. "I miss you."

"You know, Commander, sometimes you say the most wonderful things."

CHAPTER NINE

Friday, September 14

Cam stood on the small balcony outside Diane's living room, watching the occasional headlights cut curving swaths through the trees of Central Park five hundred yards away. It was two a.m., and she couldn't sleep. When she'd said good night to Blair, she'd closed her eyes, hoping that the sound of Blair's voice would carry her into the night. Sometimes, just imagining Blair by her side was enough to settle her mind and dispel the lingering worries and concerns so that she could rest. That hadn't been the case tonight, despite the fact that the oversized sofa was comfortable, just as Diane had said, and that Diane had covered the broad surface with a fine-weave cotton sheet and left a down pillow for her. Behind closed eyes, Cam lay awake running the probabilities as to when and where the next strike might come.

She had been trained to expect the unexpected and to respond to the unanticipated with a combination of skill and instinct, and her instincts had always been accurate. It had been her *instinct* that had saved Blair three days before, and her instincts now told her that the danger was still much closer than anyone suspected. What bothered her was that she could no longer clearly envision the enemy or predict their weapons. She wasn't certain whether she should expect another armed assault, or another kidnapping attempt, or a car bomb. Not knowing what shape or form the threat might take, she felt the urgent need to prepare for everything. Sleep was a luxury she could not afford, so she finally got up, pulled on her jeans, and walked barefoot outside in her T-shirt. The cool night air felt good on her face and neck.

A few minutes later, the glass doors behind her slid quietly open, but she did not turn. When the distinctive scent of Monyette Paris drifted to her on the tail end of a breeze, she recognized who approached. Even so, the whiskey-warm voice sent a tremor down her spine. Her stomach tightened, and she closed both hands around the railing, the muscles in her forearms bunching with tension.

"Couldn't sleep?" Valerie asked as she moved close to where Cam stood leaning against the heavy wrought-iron balustrade.

"No." Glancing sideways, Cam took her in. Valerie would be naked beneath the black dressing gown, she knew, and Cam didn't need the moonlight to envision the swell of her breasts and the long sensuous curve of belly as it gave way to the smooth arc of hip. She'd run her hands over that body countless times and felt the sweet slide of passion-slicked skin on her own. The tangle of limbs, the swift rush of pleasure, and the cries of release—hers and Valerie's rising as one—were only a brief memory away. "You?"

Valerie shook her head. "I fall asleep, and then I dream." She shrugged. "And then I'm awake." She moved as if to touch Cam's shoulder, and then stopped. "Do you mind the company?"

Cam breathed in slowly, tasting the unbearably tantalizing mixture of perfume and desire. The last time she had stood on this balcony in the night, the woman beside her had been Blair, and she remembered the soul-deep longing and near-crippling hunger she'd had for Blair then. She looked at this woman—could feel the heat of Valerie's mouth on her body—and knew that she'd never wanted Valerie the way she wanted Blair. Wanted her then, wanted her now—*would* want her, always. The fist of arousal that had gripped her when Valerie first appeared released its stranglehold on her, and she was free. "No, I don't mind at all."

"Diane doesn't know about us."

"I know."

"Is it going to be a problem if she finds out?"

Cam shifted until she could watch Valerie's face. "A problem for whom?"

Valerie smiled. "You always were so careful, Cameron. For you, for Blair."

"Blair has known for a long time."

"Oh, I know. I was looking into her face the exact moment she understood." A small smile skittered across Valerie's mouth, transforming the perfect symmetry of her face for an instant, making her seem less flawlessly beautiful and more vulnerable. "I could see her struggle with her anger, knowing that I had touched you. I watched her win that battle. She's quite a remarkable woman."

"Yes."

"And you love her." Valerie was watching Cam just as intently as Cam watched her.

"With everything in me."

"You would, of course." Valerie settled her fingertips lightly on the top of Cam's hand. "She knew…Blair…that I was in love with you, but she also knew on some instinctive level, even that first night, that you did not love me."

"Valerie—"

"No," Valerie said quickly, curving her fingers over the edge of Cam's hand now, "you don't need to explain anything, Cameron. I always knew what you felt and what you didn't. You were always very honest about that."

"I'm sorry," Cam said, "for using you, nevertheless."

"Using me?" Valerie laughed, a deep genuine laugh. "Oh, hardly. You have no reason to apologize for the pleasure that we shared. That was our agreement, and anything beyond that was my responsibility." She took her hand away and turned to face the park, her shoulder resting lightly against Cam's. "I really shouldn't be here."

"Why are you?"

"I don't know," Valerie said pensively, reaching up to tame a stray lock of blond hair that the wind had whipped into her face. She pushed it impatiently behind her ear, the movement inadvertently exposing the pale, slender column of her neck, as if beckoning a kiss. "I could have found somewhere else to stay, or hired a car and driven into the country for a week or so. But when everything happened—when the entire world suddenly tilted, the first thing I thought of was Diane. So I called her, even knowing that I shouldn't."

"Why shouldn't you, Valerie?" Cam asked quietly. They'd had a liaison for almost a year, and for part of that time, Cam had been Blair's security chief. And during that time, there had been two attempts on Blair's life. Cam knew with absolute certainty that she had never divulged one single piece of information involving Blair or her security, but everyone in her life, everyone in *Blair's* life, was a suspect now as far she was concerned. And Valerie—Claire—remained a mystery on many levels.

"Oh, so many reasons." Valerie shrugged and laughed again, this time a small, self-deprecating sound. "I could strike some platitude such as *she deserves better*, which is absolutely totally true, or I could mention that her friendship with Blair might be damaged—"

"Blair will handle it."

"Yes, I imagine she will. But I wonder if *Diane* will when she learns that Blair knew about my *relationship* with you and didn't tell her."

"You can't ever know how anyone is going to react. You just have to go with what you feel."

Valerie turned, leaning a hip against the railing, and regarded Cam seriously again. "Philosophy, Cameron?"

"No, just lots of mistakes."

"Diane and I aren't sleeping together."

"Yet?"

Valerie moved her head from side to side. "I don't know about that."

"But you're here."

"Yes." Valerie sighed. "And now so are you. I heard you get up and come outside. I lay there thinking about the last time we were together. You wanted to make love to me that night, and I didn't let you. I regret that."

"Things have changed." Cam's voice was gentle, and she didn't move away when Valerie leaned toward her. There had been too much between them to turn her back.

"Yes, but...sometimes it just takes one last time to put the past to rest." As she spoke, Valerie slid her hand under the bottom of Cam's T-shirt and pressed her palm to Cam's abdomen. She made a small sound of pleasure when Cam's muscles twitched at her touch, and she slowly smoothed her fingers lower, turning her hand to edge her fingertips under the waistband of Cam's jeans.

Cam clamped her hand over Valerie's wrist through the T-shirt and stopped the caress. She'd gotten wet at the first touch. "There won't be another time."

Valerie, her mouth close enough to Cam's to kiss, stared into Cam's eyes for a very long moment. "God, you always did have exquisite control."

Cam grinned and withdrew Valerie's hand from beneath her shirt. She released her wrist, then let out a pent-up breath. "Sometimes looks can be deceiving."

"Perhaps." Valerie edged away, putting space between them. "But your message is quite clear. I won't make another pass."

"Thank you. Because you're a beautiful woman, and very desirable, and I happen to be completely in love with someone else."

"I knew that well before you did, Cameron," Valerie said with a soft smile. "I just wasn't certain how you'd handle it, and never really had the chance to find out. Now I know."

"What about Diane?"

Valerie closed her eyes for a moment. "I wish I knew. It's been so long since I've had an uncomplicated feeling for a woman, I don't know if I can recognize one any longer."

"I know what you mean."

"I believe you do." Valerie traced her fingers along the edge of Cam's jaw and then turned toward the apartment. "Remember tonight, Cameron. Remember that in this moment, there was nothing between us but the truth."

Cam watched Valerie open and close the glass doors and disappear into the darkness beyond. There was more to be said. Or perhaps confessed. Of that she was certain. As she turned back to the night, she wondered when she would find out what other secrets lay between them.

❖

Valerie stepped carefully across the dark living room by the aid of memory and the slivers of moonlight that hinted at the shapes in her path.

"We should talk," Diane said quietly, rising from her seat in the corner opposite the balcony. "I hadn't meant to spy, but I heard you get up. I was worried that you'd had a nightmare."

"A nightmare?"

"You do, you know. You cry out in your sleep. The first night," Diane said as she joined Valerie in the archway that led to the hallway and the bedrooms beyond, "I got up and opened your bedroom door. You were moaning and thrashing under the covers. I didn't know if I should wake you or not."

"I'm sorry. I didn't know."

Diane shook her head. "You don't need to apologize."

"But you didn't wake me."

"No. I walked to the side of your bed, and then I realized that you were naked and I just looked at you. I looked at you and I wanted to touch you, and then I knew I needed to leave."

"Diane," Valerie murmured, grazing her fingers down Diane's arm without thinking.

"I saw you outside with Cam. I couldn't hear what you were saying, but I didn't need to." Diane gently withdrew her arm from Valerie's grasp. "Blair Powell is my best friend."

"Blair knows," Valerie said quietly.

"I need to, too."

"Yes." Valerie sighed. "Let's go to your room."

Valerie followed Diane down the hallway and into the master bedroom suite. She waited while Diane opened the drapes enough to provide illumination for them to see one another. Diane did not turn on a light, and Valerie was grateful—their pain would not be exposed in the harsh clarity of lamplight, but muted by the forgiving luminosity of the moon. She sank down on one end of the small love seat that faced the floor-to-ceiling windows in the sitting area and waited to speak until Diane joined her.

"Cameron and I were...involved...for close to a year," Valerie said immediately, seeing no reason to pretend that the discussion was about anything else. "It's over now."

"It didn't look like it was over." Diane's voice held no hint of censure, only an undertone of sadness. "Of course, you don't owe me any explanation."

"I do." They were inches apart, and Valerie wanted to touch her, as if her flesh could somehow instill in the other woman a belief in the truth of her words. "I'm here, in your home, and I *do* owe you an explanation."

"I wondered why you hadn't responded to my"—Diane laughed—"not-so-subtle hints that I was interested in you. I hadn't thought to ask if there was someone else. Foolish of me."

"That wasn't the reason that I didn't respond," Valerie said quietly. "And I wanted to."

"Is it because of...Cam?"

Diane stumbled over the words, and Valerie knew that it hurt her to say them. What surprised her was that it hurt *her* to hear Diane's pain. "I'm sorry. No. It was because I wanted…" She stopped, considered carefully what she was about to say. "I wanted to be sure you never regretted anything that happened between us. And I knew that could never happen until I told you about Cameron."

"Were you going to?"

Valerie hesitated. "I don't know. It's not just me involved."

"You said that Blair knows. So I assume she knew the night of the gallery showing?"

"Yes."

"And you're still alive? Amazing."

"Blair knows her lover."

"*Any* woman can be tempted," Diane said bitterly. "Believe me, I know."

"Tempted, yes—but anything more than that is not going to happen with Cameron Roberts."

"But you want it to." Diane wrapped her arms around her body just below her breasts, as if to ward off a chill. The room was warm. "I could see from across the room how much you wanted her."

"I did, yes." Valerie drew one leg up onto the sofa so that she could turn and look directly into Diane's face. "I did want her, out there just now. When we ended things, there was a part of me that hadn't said goodbye. I wanted to say goodbye tonight." She extended her arm along the sofa back until her fingertips almost touched Diane's shoulder. "Now I have."

"Is it that easy?" Diane did not move away or lean into Valerie's touch.

"I've just accepted what I've known for a long time. So in a way, yes, it was easy."

"All right."

Valerie stroked Diane's shoulder and then pulled her hand back. "There's something else that you should know. About when Cameron and I were together."

"No, there isn't. Whatever it was or wasn't is none of my business." Diane caught Valerie's hand as she was about to move away. She clasped Valerie's fingers between her own and rubbed her thumb back and forth over Valerie's knuckles. "Why did you come here Tuesday night?"

"To be with you. I don't know why, but I wanted to be with you now. I…needed to be with you."

Diane nodded. "I'm glad."

"There are other things I haven't told you," Valerie said quietly.

"There always are."

Chapter Ten

This is Cameron Roberts. I'd like to speak to the chief of staff, please."

"It's 4:30 in the morning, ma'am," the polite male voice informed her. "I'll be happy to take a message."

"You might want to check your priority list before you do that." Cam heard a rustle of papers. When the duty officer spoke again, he sounded as if he were standing at attention.

"I'll put you right through, ma'am."

"Thank you. Scramble it, please."

"Yes, ma'am."

Within seconds, Lucinda Washburn answered, her voice brisk and sharp. Cam had no doubt she'd been awake.

"Problem, Commander?"

"Call it precaution, ma'am. I'm in Manhattan. I suggest you give Stark a few extra people for this afternoon." Despite the fact that their transmission was scrambled and therefore presumably secure, Cam left nothing to chance where Blair was concerned. She expected that Lucinda would get her meaning without further explanation.

"Any particular reason?"

"Just a feeling."

"That's good enough." Lucinda sighed. "And the Eagle?"

"I imagine Tom will already have that covered." Cam knew that Tom Turner, the president's security chief, would have pulled out all the stops for the president's first public appearance since the attacks. No doubt every FBI agent, Secret Service agent, and NYPD security officer available would be detailed for Andrew Powell's visit to Ground

Zero. "But Egret tends to fly far from the nest."

"God, that she does," Lucinda said with a fondness that was apparent even over the line. "You don't have anything specific?"

"I've only been here a few hours, but things are loose at the Aerie. I don't like it."

"Damn. Neither do I. You'll stay close this afternoon?"

Cam smiled, a cold, hard smile. "Count on it."

"I'll see that she leaves here with extra people."

"Thank you. Oh, and one other thing."

"I knew yesterday that you wanted something in particular," Lucinda said. "What is it?"

"Not *what*, who."

"Let's hear it."

"I want Felicia Davis detailed to me as of today."

"That's going to be difficult. The security clearance will take time, and there's only so much I can do to go around the Justice Department's special investigative committee."

"If we're going to find these people," Cam said with certainty, "it's going to be through some connection to Foster. I need a computer expert for that."

"I can get you someone…There is at least one Justice agent who is supposed to be the best they ever had. A bit of a renegade, apparently, but—"

"Won't work," Cam interrupted. "Felicia is one of mine already. She was vulnerable during the assault, just like Stark. She's lucky to be alive. There's no way she's involved."

"I'll see what I can do, but these things don't come free."

"Oh, I know that. If there's some price attached, I'll pay it. Now, as to the other team members—"

Lucinda laughed. "You've been busy since we talked yesterday."

"Things are bad up here," Cam said quietly.

"Yes. Whom do you need?"

Cam told her and waited.

"That shouldn't be a problem. Consider it done unless you hear from me by midday."

"I'll have them working by then."

"Yes," Lucinda said, "I imagine you will. Good hunting, Commander."

❖

Cam was thinking about the hunt as she poured her first cup of coffee at a little after seven a.m.

"I see you still remember where the essentials are," Diane said from behind her.

Turning toward the kitchen door, Cam smiled. "Hope you don't mind."

"Mmm, not at all. I like a resourceful woman, especially in the morning." Diane, dressed now in a pale green silk blouse, tan slacks, and low heels, glided across the burnished-steel-and-granite *Architectural Digest* kitchen to the counter. She reached past Cam for the coffeepot, and in an unusual move, was careful *not* to touch her.

Despite Diane's casual tone, Cam thought she detected signs of tears beneath her hostess's flawless makeup. "Rough night?"

Diane laughed and shook her head. "Don't you know that's something you should never say to a woman? It suggests either that my age is showing or that I simply look like hell."

"Neither is ever the case," Cam said seriously. "But it *has* been a hell of a week."

"Oh God, hasn't it?" Diane's hand trembled slightly as she raised the coffee cup to her lips. She sipped and leaned one hip against the counter edge, facing Cam. "Did you sleep at all?"

"Not much." Actually, not at all. After she and Valerie had talked, she'd tossed and turned on the sofa for several hours before retreating to the balcony again in defeat. She'd almost napped on the lounge chair, but the litany of things yet to do kept repeating in the back of her mind and prevented her from slipping completely into sleep. Finally, she'd given up and called Lucinda. Now, showered and dressed in black trousers and a dark polo shirt, she'd exchanged her fatigue for the exigency of the day to come. "Blair is coming up this afternoon with her father."

"I know, she told me." Diane narrowed her eyes, regarding Cam pensively. "You don't like that, do you?"

Cam grinned. "What was your first clue?"

Diane laughed. "How do you handle it? Your worry for her?"

At any other time, Diane might not have asked such a personal question, even given her long-standing curiosity. She respected her best friend's privacy, despite how envious she was at times of the obvious passion she witnessed between Blair and Cam. And she knew that Cam was, if anything, even more private than Blair. But in a world where annihilation could be delivered to one's doorstep on a bright sunny morning, there seemed little point to standing on convention. And for those who lived within the shadow of the tragedy, life had taken on an even greater sense of urgency, where caution and prudence had far less meaning.

"I'm paid to worry about her," Cam replied mildly. It was the simple answer, and the truth. Then, because she sensed the caring beneath Diane's question, and because Diane loved Blair, she told the rest of it. "I do my best not to let her know when I'm worried, because she needs to feel that she has a normal life. And when she's doing something like today that just about makes me crazy, I do everything I can to make sure she's safe."

"I imagine if she knew exactly how hard it was for you, she'd try to change."

"She might," Cam agreed. "And that would kill something in her." Cam rinsed her cup in the sink and turned it upside down on the grooves carved into the granite counter for drainage. "So I don't tell her."

"Of course not. And neither will I." Diane deposited her cup with Cam's. "You wanted to talk to me about something?"

"Do you mind sitting out on the balcony?" Cam asked as they started to leave the kitchen.

Diane stopped abruptly on her way into the living room, regarding Cam in surprise. "You don't trust Valerie?"

Cam remained silent as they walked toward the balcony. The living room was empty, and she couldn't hear any noise from the bedrooms down the hall. Diane said nothing until they were outside with the sliding glass door closed behind them.

"I can't think of any way to say this that won't be awkward," Diane said as she settled into one of the chaise lounge chairs. "I happened to be in the living room last evening when you and Valerie were out here, and afterward, we talked."

"And she told you about us." Cam leaned with her back to the railing, the sun behind her and her face in shadow. The interrogation technique was so automatic she didn't even think about it.

Diane shielded her eyes with one hand against the morning sun and nodded. "Some of it." She laughed. "No details, I'm afraid. I can't seem to find a woman who's willing to share you. Even in afterthought."

"Did she also tell you that Blair knows?"

"She did. I'd like to tell Blair that I know. Keeping secrets from friends is the fastest way I know to destroy a friendship."

Cam picked up on the pain in Diane's voice. "Blair didn't tell you because she was protecting me."

"And now you're protecting her." Diane smiled. "She has quite a champion in you."

"No." Cam took two steps and then sat on the end of the lounge chair facing Diane. She leaned forward, her elbows on her knees. "I just wanted you to know that she did it for me, and not because she didn't want you to know. In fact," she said with a sigh, "I think not being able to tell you has been tough on her."

"Are you sure you don't mind if I speak to her about it?"

"Not at all."

"You didn't answer my question. Don't you trust Valerie?"

"It's not a question of who I trust and who I don't," Cam said. "It's a question of protecting Blair's privacy and maintaining her security."

"You can't think Valerie is a threat," Diane said defensively.

"I don't discuss Blair in front of anyone." Again the truth, even if evasive.

"No. None of us who love her do. I understand." Diane appeared satisfied. "Tell me what you want to know."

"I want to know the name of every person who's asked you about Blair in the last year. I want to know about every *new* person who's come into your life in that same time period, business or personal. I want to know if there's anyone who stands out in your mind as being *off* somehow."

Diane laughed. "You're not serious?"

Cam merely nodded.

"My God, I run an art gallery. Sheila Blake is one of my clients, and everyone in the art world, at least, knows that Blake is Blair Powell. People ask me about her all the time with regard to her work."

"Anyone seem more interested than others? Persistent questions, repeat questions, returning to the gallery over and over for no good reason?"

"Not that I can think of, but I can go back through the gallery sales records and see if that jogs my memory."

"Good. Excellent. Ask your employees if they remember anyone inquiring about her schedule or personal information—address, phone, e-mail address." Cam leaned even closer, her dark eyes simmering. "Anything. It won't be obvious. These guys are pros. Tell them that."

"I will. I'll talk to them this morning." Diane frowned. "You said *personally*. You don't think someone I've been…intimate with…could possibly be involved?"

"I don't know. Have you met anyone under unusual circumstances, or anyone who seems almost too perfect in terms of the kind of woman who appeals to you?"

There was a moment of absolute silence as they stared at one another, the name hanging in the air between them. As if bidden, the doors behind them opened, and Valerie stepped out. Her ice blue blouse was an exact match for her eyes, which moved questioningly from Diane to Cam. Whatever she saw in their faces made her lift her hands in apology.

"I'm sorry. I'm interrupting, it seems." She brushed her hair back, holding it for a moment against the wind, her eyes on Diane. "I wanted to tell you that I'm leaving. I've called a cab."

"Right now?" Diane rose quickly. "Why?"

"It's a business thing. It came up just a few minutes ago—I just got a call from my employer." Valerie smiled and shrugged. "You know how these things are. When a client gets something into their head, you just can't put them off. I hate to run when you've been so kind."

Cam stood and headed inside to give them privacy. "I have some calls to make too." As she passed Valerie, she said, "Take care of yourself."

"I will. And you, Cameron." Valerie kept her eyes on Diane during the exchange. Once Cam was inside and the door closed once more, she said, "I'm so sorry about all of this."

"I thought we put that to rest last night," Diane said, moving to join Valerie. They stood facing one another, their expressions equally troubled and watchful. "We both have pasts. I won't apologize for mine, and I don't expect you to, either."

"You're very kind."

"To hell with kind," Diane said sharply. "You know damn well I'm attracted to you. *More* than attracted to you. Why are you leaving?"

"I told you...business."

Diane regarded her steadily. "I won't ask you *this* time what's really going on, because it's obvious you feel you can't tell me. But I will ask you this, and I want an honest answer. Am I going to see you again?"

Valerie hesitated, and then, instead of replying, slid her hand to the back of Diane's neck and guided her forward into a kiss. She kissed her softly at first—just a brush of lips—savoring her tantalizing taste, until suddenly she wanted more. More than just a whispered goodbye. She needed something to take away with her. Without breaking contact, she caressed Diane's mouth more firmly, a long slow slide with the tip of her tongue glancing between Diane's lips.

Diane caught her breath, first in surprise, then at the sudden tightening in the pit of her stomach. "Oh," she murmured, "don't do that and then leave me."

"I was hoping perhaps you would remember this," Valerie said against all good judgment, "until I return."

"Will you? Return?"

"If I can."

The regret in her voice was too genuine for Diane not to believe her. She settled her arms loosely around Valerie's waist, gratified when the other woman did not move away. "*When* you come back, will you tell me what it is you think I won't be able to handle?"

"If I can." Valerie couldn't help herself. She kissed her one last time, hoping desperately to satisfy the ache inside with something as simple as a kiss. Something she could explain away, if pressed, as a moment's indiscretion in the midst of a world gone mad. She knew she'd failed hopelessly when she found herself wanting nothing more than to keep on kissing her until there was nothing in her mind or her heart or her soul except Diane.

"Goodbye," Valerie murmured as she drew away. She reached behind her to open the door, her eyes still on Diane's.

Diane let her go. For reasons she did not understand, as she watched her leave, she whispered, "Be careful."

Chapter Eleven

"I appreciate you appearing with me at the press briefing this morning," Andrew Powell said as he passed Blair a plate of freshly baked muffins.

"You don't have to thank me, Dad." Absently, Blair broke off a corner of one of the White House chef's specialties. "I feel like there's so little I can do as it is. If it sends a message to whoever's out there that we won't be manipulated by terrorists, I'll go on television with you every single day."

"I have a feeling you'd get tired of that pretty fast, but I'll remember the offer."

"I'm glad there was no mention of what happened to me." She shivered and quickly forced a smile. "I already have my face on the front page of too many tabloids."

"It was a judgment call," Powell admitted. "The press will want to pillory me if it comes out that we held that kind of news back."

"Dad, you don't have to—"

"It was my call, honey. I'm happy with it."

"Why did you decide to keep it quiet?" Blair put down her muffin and watched her father intently.

"A number of reasons. Most importantly, your privacy. You've had the press fixated on your private life for months, and this kind of news would make you morning television news program material." Her father's voice held an edge of anger. "And I don't want whoever's out there—or here—focusing on you as a target."

"Thank you," Blair said softly.

"No need to." The president leaned back in his chair and regarded Blair with a small frown. "It's probably going to be pretty rough this afternoon."

"I know. I'll be okay."

"I never doubted it."

"I'm not coming back with you tonight." Blair pushed her half-eaten breakfast aside. "I want to go home. I can't hide here, and besides, it's already making me crazy."

"I'd like you to wait until my security advisers tell me they think it's safe," Powell suggested mildly.

"You know it's never going to be *safe*," Blair said with asperity. "If I have Stark and Cam looking out for me, I'll be fine."

"How about if I ask Cam's opinion as to the timing?"

Blair's eyes flashed with temper, and then she laughed. "Jeez, Dad, I can see you're going to need a crash course in the dynamics of lesbian couples. That's kind of like asking the husband if it's okay for the wife to do something."

"Ouch." Powell laughed, coloring slightly. "Okay, I've got that in focus now. So, is it all right if I ask your *new* security chief and your *ex*-chief about the situation, just so I feel better?"

"*Much* better. And you're going to anyhow, with or without my okay, aren't you?"

"You've been around this game too long, I can see." Powell suddenly looked serious. "Yes, I'll want to be briefed on the potential risk to you before you leave here."

"Will you tell me what they say?"

"Yes."

"Then I'll *try* to follow their recommendations."

"Thank you." He hesitated, then added, "I wouldn't say this to anyone else except Lucy, but we're playing catch-up here, Blair, all of us. The Department of Defense, the CIA, the FBI—all of us were caught flat-footed on Tuesday. It's going to be a scramble for months until we get a system in place to anticipate and counter another event of this kind. I'm worried about you."

Blair reached across the table and took her father's hand. "And I'm worried about you. I've *always* been worried about you. But that's the life we have, and we have to trust the people whose job it is to take care of us, right?"

"You sound as if things aren't quite as hard for you as they used to be. Is that true?"

She shrugged. "If you mean is it any easier for me to have Secret Service agents trailing around after me twenty-four hours a day, no." She laughed. "Even when one of them is my lover. But I'm happier because I have Cam. She makes everything easier for me."

"Then I'm happy for you." He squeezed her hand and let go. "In case I haven't mentioned it, I like her a lot. It's hard for a parent to imagine their child with an entire life that doesn't involve them. You and I have never had enough time together, and now you're building your own life. I'm glad it's with her."

"I don't think you've ever said anything like that to me before," Blair said thickly.

"I'm sorry that I haven't, because you've always been the most important person in my life."

Blair brushed impatiently at her tears. "Okay. Enough of this." She took a breath and smiled tremulously. "I'll talk to Cam later about me going home or *somewhere*. If she's totally opposed, then we'll figure something else out. But I'm not staying here much longer. This place is a museum. I don't how you stand it."

"I don't—" Powell stopped as the phone gave the distinctive ring that indicated an urgent call. He grimaced. "Sorry. I have to take that."

"No problem, Dad." Blair rose. "I'll see you later." She expected no answer and got none as her father turned his attention to the newest problem at hand. Still, for perhaps the first time in her life, she felt that her father truly understood what was important to her, and that was enough.

❖

Cam left Diane and Valerie on the balcony and returned to the kitchen, where she sat at the round, glass-topped table in front of the windows with her second cup of coffee. She dialed the residence and ran down her mental to-do list while answering the White House operator's usual questions. A minute later she was put through to her lover. Blair answered immediately.

"Hello?"

"Hey, good morning."

"Mmm, it is now."

"Yeah." Cam smiled. "How was your night?"

"Long. And lonely. How was yours?"

"Same." Cam leaned back in the chair and stretched her legs out in front of her. She was stiff and sore and tired, but listening to Blair's voice eased some of the tension that had knotted the muscles along her spine into a taut ladder of pain. "Have you been up long?"

"A few hours. I had breakfast with my father—well, part of one, at least, before he was called away."

"Everything okay?"

Blair sighed. "*Okay* is relative, isn't it? Apparently there was some kind of scare in a government complex in New Jersey. I'm not sure what it was all about, but I heard that he had to meet with someone from the NIH right away."

Cam frowned. She didn't like being outside the intelligence loop, even for a few hours. Ordinarily, something like this would have been brought to her attention immediately as Blair's security chief. She made another mental note to call Stark and inquire about significant developments that came up at the morning briefing. "How are *you*?"

"I want to see you. I want to be where you are." Blair made a small sound of disgust. "God, I sound pathetic. But I've made my obligatory media appearances with my father—we've shown the world we're not afraid, and they'll believe it when they see us in Manhattan this afternoon if they're not convinced yet. I've done my part, which hardly seems enough."

"You're doing everything you can, baby."

"Thanks for saying that." Blair hesitated. "Do you feel like I do when we're apart? Like nothing is quite right?"

"Every minute."

Blair laughed. "Even if you're lying, I don't care. I love you for saying it."

"I'm not lying," Cam said with utter seriousness.

"Did you sleep?"

"Some."

"I know you, Commander. That means probably not at all. You can't run yourself into the ground, Cam, or you won't be any good to your investigation or me."

"I know. I won't."

"Uh-huh. Right." Blair made a low murmuring sound in her throat. "But I know how to put you to sleep. We'll take care of that later."

Despite her fatigue, her worry, and her hyperadrenalized awareness, Cam felt herself respond. "Jesus, don't do that now. I have to work."

"What's the matter, did I just make you twitch?"

Absently, Cam brushed her palm over the inside of her thigh. "More than that."

"Oh, good."

Cam laughed and closed her eyes, allowing herself the simple pleasure of enjoying the company of the woman she loved for just a few minutes.

❖

Savard bolted awake, bathed in sweat. She rapidly scanned the space around her as if it were a battlefield, searching for danger, until she placed the room—*bedroom, Stark's...no, our place now.*

With a jerk, she threw the damp sheet aside and stumbled into the bathroom, then directly into the shower. She twisted both knobs on full and barely flinched when the first blast of icy water struck her in the chest. Her skin tingled, and it felt good. She was alive. She was alive.

Five minutes later, wrapped in a towel, her hair still dripping, she sat on the side of the bed and dialed Stark's cell phone.

"Stark."

"Hi, sweetie. Are you busy?"

Stark had to forcibly hold back a surge of wild laughter. Oh hell, no. Not busy. She suddenly was responsible for guarding the first daughter in the midst of a national crisis, with a team of newbies and a reluctant protectee. Hell no, she wasn't busy. "I've got a couple minutes. We just briefed."

"How was it?"

Stark lowered her voice. "My legs aren't shaking anymore."

"You're going to be fine. You were a good agent before the commander came on board, and now you've spent almost a year watching her work. You know what to do. Just do it your own way, and you'll be fine."

"Thanks, honey. What about you? How are you doing?"

"Fine," Savard said quickly. "Is it still a green light for today?"

"Yes. This afternoon."

"Any chance we'll be able to get together later?"

"I don't know. I want to. It's going to depend on...well, you know."

Yes, Savard thought. *From now on, my lover's life is going to be determined by Blair Powell's schedule. It's going to be even harder now for us to connect. Maybe it's just as well. Maybe I shouldn't see her until I don't feel so...crazy.*

Stark picked up on the silence. "I'm sorry. I want to see you so mu—"

"Hey. It's okay." Savard glanced at the clock by the bedside. "God, it's almost nine. I'm late. Listen, sweetie, I've got to run. Call me if you can."

"I will. I love you," Stark said hastily.

"Me too. Bye."

Savard pulled the towel off and wrapped it around her hair as she hurried to the closet. She was surprised someone hadn't already called her to find out why she hadn't shown up for her shift. As she pulled clothes from a hanger, her cell rang.

"Damn," she muttered as she grabbed it off the bedside table. "Savard."

"This is Roberts. Where are you?"

"Stark's."

"Good. I'll pick you up in fifteen minutes."

"Uh...what about my other assignment? Should I call—"

"Already taken care of."

"Yes, ma'am," Savard said briskly. "I'll be waiting downstairs."

"Very good. Goodbye."

"Yes, ma'am," Savard whispered. Fifteen minutes. Fifteen minutes to get herself together enough so that no one would notice she wasn't who she used to be.

❖

It was the smell that plummeted Cam back in time—that unmistakable mixture of antiseptic and death that permeated the air in the hallway leading to the intensive care unit. Six months before it had been her lying in one of the glassed-in cubicles, tubes and monitors attached to her body, swimming in an ocean of pain. She had only fragments of recollection of the first three days following the shooting—her mother's voice, Blair's touch, and always the fucking pain. Suppressing a shudder, she shoved her hands into her pockets and shook off the memories. Despite what she insisted to Blair—that the chance of her ever being shot again was infinitesimal—it was always a possibility. And that was something you didn't think about if you wanted to do the job.

"Davis told me they're supposed to move him out of here today," Cam said to Savard as they pushed through the double gray steel doors with the red letters proclaiming *Trauma Intensive Care Unit.*

"Good. That's good," Savard said quietly.

Two minutes later, after clearing their visit with the nurses, they approached Mac's bedside. To Cam's great relief, he no longer had a breathing tube and was able to croak a hello. Her former second in command, Mac Phillips, was ordinarily a vigorous thirty-three-year-old—tall, blond, and handsome. Now he looked pale and vulnerable, and Cam felt the fury rise again.

"How are you doing, Mac?"

He smiled weakly. "Not bad, Commander."

Cam nodded at the statuesque African American woman with the model-perfect face standing on the opposite side of the bed. "Agent Davis."

"Commander," Felicia replied in her smooth alto voice. "Hello, Renée."

"Hi." Savard leaned over and kissed Mac lightly on the cheek. "Hello, honey."

"My day…is looking…up," Mac said, grinning.

"We heard they're moving you to a regular room later today. That's terrific," Cam said as she stepped over and closed the door. They were all completely visible to anyone in the rest of the intensive care unit, but their conversation would not be overheard. Turning to face Mac and Felicia again, she said, "The whole team—with the exception of Stark—has been placed on administrative leave until Justice completes the investigation of Tuesday's events."

"God," Felicia said, "that could take *months.*"

"Probably will. But you've been detailed to a special team," Cam informed her. "As of now, you and Savard are with me, and our only job is to find out where those bastards who hit the Aerie came from."

"What about...me?" Mac said immediately.

Cam squeezed his shoulder. "Your assignment is to get better. Once you're out of this place, I'll pick your brain to make sure we're not missing anything, but no field work for you."

"The bullet...missed the good stuff," Mac said. "I'll be good...to go...in a week or so."

"That's not exactly what the doctor said, baby," Felicia interjected. "Six to eight weeks is what I heard."

"We'll keep you in the loop," Cam assured him, "but you're an armchair quarterback on this one."

"Yes, ma'am," he said weakly, his eyes flickering closed as he obviously tired.

"So, Davis," Cam said, "we need a new command center. I should have an address for you later today. You can transfer the equipment then."

"Yes, ma'am."

"The first order of business is an ID on the four men who hit the Aerie. You and Savard are on that."

"Yes, ma'am."

"Savard will coordinate when I'm not available."

Savard jerked slightly at the announcement, but Felicia appeared unfazed. "Understood."

Cam looked at her watch. "For now, get copies of everything the FBI has that relates to the attack—forensics, intelligence, background on paramilitary groups and terrorist cells, gossip, rumor, innuendo—I don't care. Everything."

Felicia glanced at Savard. "Can you get me into the computers?"

Savard nodded. "Yes."

"Then you'll have it within twenty-four hours, Commander."

"Good," Cam said briskly. "You've got eighteen. We brief tomorrow at 0700. Now I've got to meet Marine One."

Chapter Twelve

Cam made the thirty-mile trip from Manhattan to White Plains in just under an hour. She pulled into the parking lot of a small private airfield and walked toward a line of four gleaming black Suburbans that were idling on the far side of a chain-link fence. She hadn't gotten twenty feet from her rental car before the passenger doors of each vehicle opened and three men and a woman jumped out and hurried through the gate on an intercept path with hers. Anticipating this, Cam held out the badge case she carried in her right hand.

"Secret Service. Roberts."

"Stay where you are, please," the lead man, a stocky African American in a well-cut dark blue suit, called out.

Dutifully, Cam stopped. These field agents had probably been pulled for emergency duty from regional offices all over the country. It was doubtful that anyone in the service didn't know that *an* Agent Roberts was the first daughter's lover, but they didn't know *her,* not by sight.

"Hold the badge in two fingers and put your arms out at your sides, please," a tight-bodied blond woman ordered brusquely. Her eyes never moved from Cam's body as she plucked the badge from Cam's loose grip, handed it to the first agent, and flipped open Cam's jacket. "She's carrying. Service-issue weapon."

"You might contact Paula Stark. She'll verify that I'm expected." Cam kept her arms straight out while the female agent removed her automatic from the shoulder holster below her left breast. She didn't move a muscle as every inch of her body was patted down, quickly and efficiently.

"This is a restricted area," the male agent said, studying her credentials. "How did you get in here?"

"The same way you did," Cam replied mildly. "I showed my badge to the officers at the checkpoint you set up at the main entrance. They let me pass." She could tell by the expression on his face that he wasn't happy. Despite the fact that she had a Secret Service ID, someone should have called the ground team for clearance. It would take time before the various state and federal agencies were able to coordinate the new level of security required, which was one of the major reasons she didn't want to be too far away from Blair. No matter how good the first team might be, there were too many other links in the chain that might weaken and break, leaving Blair at risk.

"Christ," he muttered under his breath, then handed Cam her ID. "Stay here."

"You can lower your arms," the blond said, her expression impassive behind impenetrable sunglasses.

Cam did, slowly, and glanced up at the sky as she heard the distant sound of rotors. Ten seconds later, the lead agent jogged back through the gate.

"Give her back her weapon, Calhoun. Sorry, Commander."

"No problem," Cam said as she holstered her automatic and accepted her ID. "I would've been a lot more upset if you hadn't braced me."

"Let's go," he said, already heading back to the airstrip on the other side of the fence. "They'll be on the ground in a minute."

Cam fell in behind the ground team, her eyes on the sky as the VH-3D presidential helicopter descended. With the rotors still churning, a stairway unfolded from the side of the Sea King and four fully armed Marines from the elite HMX-1 squadron based at Quantico clambered down to flank the exit route from the chopper. The Secret Service ground team stationed themselves in a similar fashion, creating a continuous corridor that led to the waiting vehicles. Cam stayed by the side of the third Suburban in line. Andrew Powell and Blair stepped out together and descended the stairs briskly. Stark flanked Blair, and Turner had a similar position on the president's opposite side. There were two men and a woman behind Stark whom Cam recognized as senior Secret

Service agents. These would be the new members of Blair's first team. As the president and the first daughter approached the vehicles, the local Secret Service agents split into two groups and fell in behind the first teams. Blair walked directly up to Cam and kissed her.

"Hi," Blair said.

"Hi." Cam threaded her arm around Blair's waist and turned with her toward the Suburban, where Stark stood holding open the rear door. "Chief," she said with a nod toward Stark.

"Good to see you, Commander."

Cam and Blair slid into the spacious rear compartment with Stark and the female agent taking the seats across from them. One man joined the driver and the other took the keys to Cam's rental from her to drive it back to the city. While Stark murmured into her microphone, ensuring everyone was in position, Cam extended her arm on the seat and Blair settled naturally against her side.

"How are you doing?" Cam asked quietly.

Blair smiled. "Good now."

As they pulled out of the airport, Stark said, "Commander, this is Agent Patrice Hara. That's Greg Wozinski up front and Leonard Krebs in your car."

"Ma'am," the woman next to Stark said.

"Agent," Cam said, shaking the outstretched hand while making a rapid assessment. Five-four and compact, forty years old, jet black hair that fell straight to her shoulders, dark almond-shaped eyes testifying to her Japanese heritage, wedding ring on her left hand. Hara accepted the scrutiny with no sign of discomfort. Satisfied, Cam turned back to Blair. "Trip go okay?"

"Fine." Blair laughed. "Every time I see that thing settling down on the South Lawn, I think there's no way I'm getting into it. But it beats Beltway traffic all to hell."

Laughing, Cam dropped a light kiss on Blair's temple. Across from them, Stark and Hara stared out their respective windows. "Diane says hello."

"I know. I called her on the way up here."

"Oh?"

"I thought I'd stay there tonight." Blair leaned back far enough to look into Cam's face. "I take it I'm not going to be able to stay at my place yet?"

"No." Cam didn't think this was the time or place to tell her that in all likelihood she would never stay there again. When they caught the perpetrators, there would still be no way of knowing how much information had been disseminated about the physical layout of the command center and Aerie. Even with that variable aside, the security there had been fatally compromised. There was no going back. "I *thought* I saw a suitcase being loaded into the back."

Blair smiled. "Aren't you going to tell me all the reasons why I have to go back to the White House?"

Cam rubbed her thumb over Blair's chin, then lightly caressed her mouth. "No. Because you already know. Let's talk about where we're going to stay a little later, though." Suddenly, she realized that it wasn't going to be her decision any longer. Stark would have to approve. That was going to take some getting used to. "And of course, we'll have to discuss it with your security chief."

"Cameron," Blair said as she rested her head against Cam's shoulder and wrapped an arm around her waist. "I never asked *your* permission to do anything when you were my security chief. Why do you think it's going to be different now?"

Cam settled her cheek against the top of Blair's forehead, smiling to herself when she saw a muscle twitch at the corner of Stark's eye. "No idea."

❖

"Was it horrible?" Diane asked, passing Blair a crystal glass filled with ice and scotch. They were sitting side by side on the sofa in Diane's living room. Blair still had on the suit she had worn to tour Ground Zero. Her shoes and slacks were gray with the residue of ash that covered everything there. Cam and Stark were in the kitchen, their muted voices creating a comforting backdrop.

"Yes." Blair's hand trembled as her eyes met those of her best friend. "I've been doing nothing but watching the television news reports since Tuesday, and I've seen all the pictures. But..." She took a healthy swallow of the liquor, grateful for the sharp burn that brought some feeling back into her body. Her mind, however, still felt numb. "It's so huge...the destruction goes on forever, it seems. And everyone there—the cops and firefighters and EMTs, the investigators, ordinary people on the streets—everyone just looks so shell-shocked.

And underneath it all, you can feel the anger." She closed her eyes and leaned her head back against the sofa. "God."

"I saw some of the news footage of your visit today. Your father was fabulous. I felt better—safer—listening to him."

Blair smiled faintly. "Yes. He's really great. Sometimes I'm amazed that this man that the whole world considers one of the most powerful people on the planet is my father." She turned her head toward Diane and opened her eyes. "Sometimes I feel guilty wishing that he were *just* my father."

Diane slid closer and put her arm around Blair's shoulder. "I know. I don't blame you. Do you want to run away somewhere?"

"Can I take Cam?"

Diane smoothed her hand up and down Blair's arm. "Can I watch?"

"Watch what?" Cam asked as she walked in from the kitchen.

"Never mind," Blair replied.

Cam squatted down in front of Blair and put both hands on the outside of Blair's thighs, rubbing gently. "You doing okay, baby?"

Blair covered Cam's hands with hers. "I'm fine. I'm just tired."

"Do you still want to stay here tonight? I think we can cover that safely with the people Stark has."

"God, yes. I don't want to travel anymore. I just want to take a shower and curl up in bed and go to sleep."

"Honey," Diane said. "It's only eight o'clock."

"All right, then, I'll take a shower and curl up in bed with Cam and go to sleep a little bit later."

"Please don't put those pictures in my head," Diane said quickly. She brushed a kiss over Blair's cheek and rose. "Why don't you and Cam relax out here for a few minutes. I'm going to have some Thai delivered, and don't tell me you're not hungry because you will be when it gets here."

Cam took Diane's place on the sofa. "I'm hungry now."

"What about the spookies?"

"Hara has the night shift. I imagine she'd appreciate something to eat."

At that moment, Stark emerged from the kitchen, clipping her cell phone to her belt.

"How about you, Paula? Shall I put you down for some takeout?" Diane asked.

"Thanks, no. I'll be staying here tonight, but I need to go out for a couple of hours. I'll grab something while I'm gone."

Cam looked up, surprised. "Two on site overnight?"

"We're still at Priority One."

Stark spoke with quiet confidence, and Cam noticed. She settled back on the sofa and took Blair's hand in hers. "Your call, of course, Chief."

"Agents Krebs and Hara will be here for the evening," Stark said to Blair. "I'll be back before midnight. Please call me if you change your plans about staying in."

Blair shook her head wearily. "Believe me, Paula. I'm not moving from this apartment."

"Very good, then," Stark said. "Have a good evening."

"You too," Blair said. "Oh, and Paula?"

Stark turned. "Yes, ma'am?"

"Don't forget about the stick."

Stark grinned. "That's on my list, ma'am."

When Cam and Blair were alone, Cam said, "I spoke with Lucinda just now. She's working on a temporary apartment for you."

Blair raised an inquiring brow. "*Lucinda* is?"

"We need a safe house that's never been recorded by the Secret Service. Preferably one that no one knows about except the president, his security adviser, and Lucinda. We can't tell how far our internal security has been compromised."

"How long do you think it will be before I can move back home?"

"I don't know, baby." Cam cradled Blair's hand between both of hers. There was never going to be a good time for this. "It may never be secure enough for you to move back into the loft, Blair."

Blair jerked. "What? You mean I'm going to have to move?"

"Probably." Cam kissed Blair's palm. "I'm sorry."

"It's not your fault," Blair said dully. "God, I can't think about that right now." She closed her eyes. "I hate staying in safe houses. They feel so goddamned sterile."

"Just temporarily."

Blair stood abruptly, the frustration and fatigue finally winning. "How long is *temporarily*? A few days? A few weeks? I can't paint with people in my back pocket all the time. I need to be alone. I need my own space to work."

Cam stood as well, but she did not touch Blair. "I know. I know what you need to work. I'll make it happen as fast as I can. I promise." She watched Blair stalk away, her arms wrapped around herself, and wanted to comfort her. She stayed where she was.

"Can I at least go by the apartment for an hour tomorrow? I need to get my canvases, Cam."

"We can send someone for them."

Blair shook her head. "There are dozens, and it will be impossible for me to tell anyone else which ones I want. Besides, I need to look at them to decide." She whirled away, unwilling to allow Cam to see the tears that were as much impotent fury as sadness. "Send a goddamn armed guard with me. I don't care. I'm going to the loft in the morning. I'll pack up my work, and I'll go wherever you tell me to after that."

"Blair," Cam said gently. "I'm sorry."

"Stop saying that." With her back to the room, Blair stared out through the glass doors of the balcony into the gathering night. After a moment, in a quieter voice, she asked, "What if we went somewhere that no one knew about, not even Luce?"

"Have you got some place in mind?"

Blair swung back around. "What about Whitley Point? It's isolated, we were safe there earlier this week, and we can bring the entire team and anything else you think we need. I'm sure that Tanner can find us a house to rent. It's off season, and there won't be very many people around." She took a few steps forward. "And I can work there, Cam. I can work and"—she drew a shaky breath—"maybe start to feel normal again."

Cam considered it. She'd have to bring her entire investigative team, or let Blair go alone. The second choice was not an option. Fortunately, thanks to Davis's computer skills, her investigation could be run from anywhere in the world. "Okay, go ahead and check with Tanner. If she can find us a place we can secure, I think Stark will agree that it's a reasonable solution. I'd be happy for you to be out of the public eye for a while."

"I'll call her right now." Blair took two steps toward the bedroom where she'd left her overnight bag and cell phone and then stopped, suddenly uncertain. "And you'll come with me, right?"

"Of course." Cam did go to her then and took her into her arms. Holding her close, she murmured, "We're together now. Remember?"

Silently, Blair nodded and pressed her face to Cam's neck, breathing in her scent, centering herself in the feel of her body and the touch of her hands, beginning to allow herself to believe.

CHAPTER THIRTEEN

I've been thinking about this all day," Blair said with a sigh as she slid naked into bed beside Cam just after eleven p.m. She turned on her side and drew her leg up over Cam's thighs, fitting herself into the curve of her lover's body as she rested her head on Cam's shoulder and her hand between Cam's breasts. She gave a small groan. "You feel so good."

Cam curved an arm around her and kissed her forehead. "So do you."

"I'm so tired."

"Me too."

Blair kissed Cam's throat, then her mouth. "I want to make love."

"Mmm."

"I think I'm too tired."

"Uh-huh." Cam covered Blair's hand and moved it to her breast. "Me too."

"I'll catch you in the morning," Blair said drowsily, her fingers playing over Cam's nipple.

"Deal," Cam muttered, already drifting into sleep.

Blair felt Cam's body relax and smiled to herself. As much as she loved to excite her, to share with her the passion she gave to no other, she reveled in the knowledge that here in her arms, Cam could relinquish the vigilance that occupied her every waking moment. Satisfied in a way she had never imagined, Blair surrendered to her own weariness and slept.

❖

With trembling hands, Savard stroked Stark's face even as she shifted out from under her. "I'm sorry. I think I'm just too tired."

Heart pounding, her mind and body still absorbed with the urgent need to feel her lover's passion, Stark rolled away, panting. She captured Renée's hand as it stole between her thighs and drew it upward to her stomach, trapping it there. "No. I'm okay."

"Oh, sweetie, you're not. Let me touch you."

Stark shook her head, trying to gather the fragments of her reason. "No. Really." She pulled Renée into her arms and held her tightly. "I just missed you so much. I didn't mean to push."

"You weren't pushing, sweetie. I wanted you too." Savard's heart ached to hear the note of apology in her lover's voice. "God, it's just that I can't…" *Feel anything. Only so cold inside, so numb, so disconnected from everything.*

The awful void that had been flirting at the edges of her consciousness all week yawned before her, threatening to suck her into darkness, and a wave of dread rolled over her. She needed to feel something other than the horror, or she feared she would be lost. With a cry, Savard climbed on top of Stark and kissed her hard, thrusting her tongue deep inside her mouth. She dug her fingers into Stark's shoulders, desperate for connection, not even noticing when her lover flinched at the unexpected onslaught. Gasping, she drove her hips between Stark's legs. The pressure deep inside, born of panic rather than passion, was unbearable. Eyes closed, sweat beading her face, she forced herself upright on trembling arms and thrust wildly, but still her climax eluded her.

"Oh God, oh God," Savard moaned. "I can't, I can't…"

"Renée," Stark soothed, cupping her face with both hands. "Baby. Honey. Easy, it's okay."

Mind and body screaming for release, Savard focused on Stark's voice and let the sound of love pull her back from the edge of that terrifying abyss. Her arms finally gave out and she collapsed into Stark's embrace. "Hold me, oh please, Paula, just hold me."

"I've got you," Stark whispered, wrapping her arms and legs around her and rocking her. She kissed her forehead, her eyes, her damp cheeks. She had no idea what was happening, but Renée was shaking uncontrollably, and that scared her more than just about anything ever had. "I'm right here. I'm right here. I love you."

"I'm sorry, I'm sorry." Savard pushed her face into Stark's shoulder, her mouth open against the warm body—desperate for the taste of her skin, the comfort of her flesh.

"Don't say that." Stark stroked her face, her neck, her back. "Whatever you need, it's okay."

"Did I hurt you?"

Stark forced Savard's head up with a hand beneath her chin. "Renée," she said firmly. "Look at me." She waited until Renée opened her eyes and then kissed her, her own eyes open and holding her lover's gaze. "I love you. You didn't hurt me. You couldn't. But *you're* hurting. Tell me what's happening, honey."

Savard's eyes burned with tears. "I don't know what's wrong with me. I think…" She looked away, retreating from the pain, then laughed shakily. "Just a *really* lousy week."

"Yeah, I know." Stark searched her face, knowing there was more, and saw the fear shimmering in Savard's eyes. She forced herself to be patient. She guided Savard's head back to her shoulder and kissed her forehead. "Maybe you need a few days off."

"I can't. Not with this new assignment."

Stark chose her words carefully. "I think the Commander would probably understand—"

"No," Savard said sharply, pulling away from Stark's embrace. "This is too important. No one gets time off now. You know that, Paula."

"You're right," Stark said quietly, realizing that she would feel the same herself. Nothing could get her to take time off when the nation was at war. No matter what name was put to it, that was the situation. "I only thought—"

"I just need some sleep." Exhausted, Savard settled back down into Stark's arms.

"I can't stay tonight," Stark said miserably. "I want to."

"It's all right." Savard kissed her into silence, then turned on her side and pulled Stark's arm around her body. She clasped her lover's hand between her breasts. "Just hold me for a little while."

Stark brushed her lips over the back of Savard's neck, wishing there were some way to reach into her heart and ease her pain. She gave the comfort of her body, praying that for now it would be enough. When she carefully slipped away an hour later, her lover was asleep. She left a note on the coffee table next to Savard's badge and gun.

I love you. See you soon.

The words seemed so inadequate, but they were all she had to give.

❖

Blair drifted lazily upward through the mists of sleep, a gradual awareness of pleasure coalescing in her consciousness. She sighed and shifted restlessly, her body already nearing climax but her mind not yet registering what was happening. The muscles in her legs tightened as a shiver coursed through her spine, and she opened her eyes to the first whispers of orgasm. Unable to focus, she reached out blindly, finding first Cam's shoulder, then her face. She cupped Cam's cheek with trembling fingers and surged against her mouth, on the brink of exploding.

"I'm going to come," she said in wonder. And she closed her eyes again, drenched in pleasure. The ripples of release broke hard, one riding fast upon the next, each more intense than the last, and she cried out in surprise. Dimly, she felt Cam's fingers thread through hers, and she clutched the steady hand to anchor herself amidst the chaos.

When finally freed from the grip of her orgasm, she laughed weakly and tugged at Cam's hair. "You started without me."

"Mmm, guilty as charged." Cam worked her way up the bed and stretched out on top of Blair. She kissed her lightly, a tease of tongue over warm, soft lips. "Good morning."

"The best I've had in quite some time." Blair caught Cam's head in her hands as she pushed her thigh between Cam's legs, grinning when Cam jerked and caught her breath sharply. "I want to watch you come."

Cam groaned and rocked on Blair's leg, slicking her skin with the proof of her need. "Won't take…long."

"Keep your eyes open. Cam, *Cam.* Don't close your eyes." Blair was nearly breathless, desperate to absorb each glimmer of passion revealed in her lover's face. "So beautiful."

"Oh, God…"

The cell phone on the bedside table rang, and Cam groaned.

"Don't you dare," Blair warned.

The phone rang again, and with her last ounce of will, Cam pushed herself over onto her back and swept the phone up with a trembling hand.

"Roberts."

"Good morning, Agent Roberts," Lucinda Washburn said.

Cam stared at the ceiling, struggling to even out her breathing. "Ma'am."

Blair made a grab for the phone, and Cam curled onto her side, blocking her lover's arm. She felt Blair's teeth on the back of her shoulder and stifled a gasp.

"I've discussed the issue of temporary relocation with the security advisor, and we both agree it's a workable solution."

"Good. Thank you." Cam flinched away at a harder bite, grinning even as she started making mental plans for the move. "Is Stark aware? Because I'm sure Blair will want to leave today."

"She'll be briefed next."

"I want to take my team with me. There are two buildings on site—a smaller guesthouse that will work for my people."

"There's been a development in that regard," Lucinda said in a tone that put Cam instantly on guard.

Displacing Blair, she sat up in bed, totally focused. "Yes, ma'am."

"There'll be one more agent joining your team, as well," Lucinda said.

There it is. The price I have to pay for Savard and Davis.

"Coming from where?"

"Ah, that's classified, but I'm sure the agent will fill you in as needed."

Cam almost laughed. She'd be told what the NSA or the DOD or the CIA wanted her to know, and nothing else. Whether it would be the truth or not was always in question. She lifted her watch from the bedside table. 0545.

"I'm briefing with my team at 0700. Your agent can catch up—"

"Not *my* agent," Lucinda interrupted with a hint of uncharacteristic annoyance. "I don't appreciate having this forced on me any more than you do."

"Sorry, ma'am. I was out of line."

Lucinda sighed. "You're just not accustomed to up-close-and-personal politics, but I'm afraid that we're all going to get a lot more used to it in the future."

"I don't play politics where Blair is concerned."

"Things have changed. We *all* have to play the game now, Cam."

Blair felt Cam stiffen and heard the anger in her voice. She shifted closer, tucked her arm around Cam's waist, and then gently kissed the tip of her shoulder. "It's okay, sweetheart."

Cam caught back the next ill-advised comment and stroked Blair's hair. Then she took a deep breath and gathered her control. "Once I know today's schedule, I'll give you a contact time and place for the agent to join us."

"That won't be necessary. I expect she'll be arriving at your location in about forty-five minutes."

"Someone's in a hurry to find out what we're doing," Cam said dryly.

"There's a great deal of maneuvering going on down here between the various agencies. No one knows who's going to come out on top in the scramble to reorganize the security network, and everyone is afraid of being cut out."

"I can't be worried about egos and personalities. Everyone on my team has to be willing to take orders from me."

"You have my word on that."

"Thank you," Cam said, knowing that was the best assurance she could have. Still, she knew that this new agent would be reporting whatever intelligence they uncovered to her own superiors. Cam would have to keep a very close watch on the flow of information, because she had no idea whom she could trust.

"And, Cam," Lucinda said, "I wasn't given a choice about this. Be vigilant."

"Yes, ma'am. I always am." Cam disconnected and tossed the phone onto the bed. "Son of a bitch."

"What did she say?" Blair asked.

Cam made a conscious effort to rein in her temper. She stroked Blair's shoulder and back, waiting for her irritation to fade. "We're a go for Whitley Point."

"Oh, good. God, I'm glad. Can we go today?"

"Yes." Cam kissed Blair and drew her more closely into her embrace. "As soon as you collect your canvases and Stark gets the team together."

"What else did she say? What upset you?"

Cam shrugged. "Oh, just the usual bureaucratic bullshit. It's nothing."

Blair pushed herself up on her elbow, sweeping her hair out of her face with an irritated gesture as she fixed Cam with a hard stare. "Don't give me that crap. I heard your voice. You were furious. What did she say?"

"I'm getting another agent foisted on me from somewhere. FBI, NSA, who the hell knows. Probably someone being put in place to report on anything we turn up."

"You mean like…a snitch?"

Cam laughed. "Christ, that's a good word for it. I believe, though, they would be considered a counterintelligence agent. Someone whose job it is to gather intelligence about possible threats to national security. It's a very vaunted position."

"Well I'm sure it is, but we don't need them spying on *us*."

"I'm surprised Lucinda couldn't block it," Cam confessed. "Someone with a lot of power behind them wanted this to happen."

Blair relaxed against Cam's shoulder, aimlessly smoothing her hand up and down Cam's stomach. "I'm sure you can handle it."

"Your faith in me is inspiring," Cam said in a lighter tone. "I should get up. Our new team member is due here in half an hour."

"They were certainly eager to get him on board."

"Her."

"Oh really?" Blair's hand stopped moving. "You know, I seem to be surrounded by an inordinate number of female spies."

Cam laughed. "Baby, we're not spies."

"Oh, all right then, spooks." Blair began stroking again, her fingertips brushing back and forth through the curls at the base of Cam's belly. "Still, I wonder what that's about."

"Probably coincidence." *Or maybe someone thinks you'll be more open around women. They don't know you very well.* Cam covered Blair's hand and guided it lower. "I have to get up in two minutes."

Blair bit Cam's shoulder once more and slipped her fingers slowly inside her. "Make it five."

Cam lifted her hips to take her deeper and instantly felt her clitoris surge back to life. "Don't think so."

"Try," Blair murmured as she rose above her, angling her arm to claim her more fully. "And don't close your eyes."

"Christ," Cam muttered, her vision wavering, "you're tough."

Aware only of Blair inside her, somewhere beyond the boundaries of her flesh and blood, she climaxed to the beautiful sound of Blair's laughter.

Chapter Fourteen

Saturday, September 15

Blair found Diane entertaining Stark, Patrice Hara, and Greg Wozinski with stories of their youthful indiscretions over coffee and croissants in the living room. Fortunately, they seemed to be getting the G-rated version.

"Diane," Blair said mildly as she reached for the coffee carafe, "I prefer that you not educate them in *all* my techniques for eluding surveillance."

All three Secret Service agents laughed, although Hara and Wozinski cast obvious sidelong glances at each other. Blair caught the looks and surmised that they had heard of her tendency to ditch her assigned protectors with regularity. Laughing, she said to Stark, "I see you've briefed them thoroughly."

Stark answered with a deadpan expression. "Of course. That's standard operating procedure."

"Where's Cam?" Diane inquired.

"She'll be right out. She's…" Blair had been about to say *arranging a briefing with Savard* when it occurred to her that Cam might not want to disclose the nature of her special investigation to Stark or the other Secret Service agents. "She's on the phone."

"Here," Diane said, holding out a cup of coffee. "Why don't you take this to her in case she's going to be a while. She's probably ready for it by now."

"Thanks." Blair accepted the mug and turned toward the hallway, but at that moment, Cam walked in.

"Is that for me?"

Blair held it out. "Compliments of Diane."

"Thank you," Cam said before taking a sip. She looked at Stark and said, "Can I see you for two minutes, Chief?"

Stark quickly set her cup aside and bounded up. "Sure thing, Commander."

They walked to the other side of the room and stood facing the balcony. Cam kept her voice low when she spoke. "I'm expecting an agent to meet me here in the next few minutes, so you might alert your ground team. Then I'm going to head over to your apartment for a quick briefing with Savard and Davis. I imagine Blair will want to go to the loft as soon as possible."

"I've got the vehicles standing by, and I called in two extra people from the swing shift," Stark said. "We're covered."

"I'd prefer it if you could wait for me, but I know she's not going to want to. I'll have to meet you there." Cam looked once in Blair's direction and saw that she was deep in conversation with Patrice Hara. "Make sure you check the high ground, Stark, before you let her exit the vehicle."

"Yes, ma'am."

"And send in an advance team to secure the lobby before she enters the building."

"Yes, ma'am."

"And the elevators…Don't forget she gets off last and that you need—" Cam stopped abruptly. "Christ. Sorry."

Stark's eyes never left Cam's face. "I understand, Commander. It never hurts to run through procedures again."

Cam let out a long breath. "I know you know the job, Stark. I, uh…she's just…"

"Yes, ma'am. She is."

"Savard told you about our investigation?" Cam asked, changing the subject with relief.

"Uh…"

"Don't worry—there's no problem there. I advised her to. There's no way we can run an operation of this magnitude without Blair's security team being aware of it. Hell, we're all going to be working and probably *living* in close proximity for the next few weeks, if not months." She inclined her head toward Patrice and Greg. "They don't need to know the details, but the basics will be apparent. We have to assume that Justice looked at the new team members thoroughly, but I still don't want to take anyone into complete confidence on this except you."

"I'll handle that, Commander."

Cam gave Stark's shoulder a brief squeeze. "Thanks. It helps that you—"

Stark's radio sounded and she listened for a few seconds. "Double-check the ID." She glanced at Cam. "An agent, asking for you." She listened again and raised her eyebrows. "CIA."

"Perfect," Cam muttered. CIA agents were notorious for not being team players. No one in the other services really trusted them, and with good reason. They showed little allegiance to anyone except their own director, never shared intelligence—and what they did share was always suspect. "Do you have a name?"

"Lawrence."

Cam shook her head. The name rang no bells.

"What shall we do with her, Commander?"

"Send her up. We might as well get a look at her."

Stark relayed the message and signed off.

"Kind of strange, isn't it?" Stark asked. "CIA doesn't usually get involved in domestic issues."

"All bets are off, now. And besides," Cam said pointedly, "we have no idea what they might know about the situation that we don't. Let's hope we can work this street both ways and learn as much from them as they *think* they're going to learn from us."

"Now there's a plan I can get behind."

The buzzer sounded and Cam said, "I should be at the Aerie by 0830."

"Yes, ma'am. See you then."

Cam crossed the living room while the others continued to talk and opened the door. She felt a wave of dizziness, as if the room had suddenly spun three hundred and sixty degrees while she stood rooted in place. Then her natural instincts surfaced and she felt nothing but a cold calm. Valerie looked different than she had ever seen her before. She was just as beautiful—dressed just as elegantly as ever in a Prada business suit and low Ferragamo heels—and her eyes held the same glimmer of compassion that had always drawn Cam in. But this morning she wore a weapon on her right hip, although no one who wasn't very good at detecting such things would have noticed because of the excellent cut of her suit jacket. But the core of steel that Cam always knew Valerie possessed was very close to the surface now. It was evident in the way she stood and in the sheer power of her gaze. She radiated the supreme confidence that some agents had, but few deserved.

"Agent *Lawrence*," Cam said quietly. "Is it still Valerie?"

"It is, yes."

Cam glanced at her watch. "We have a briefing in twenty minutes, so if you don't mind, I'd like to leave the introductions until later. Although, of course, I'm sure you know everyone's names already."

Valerie's eyes skimmed past Cam to where Diane sat on the sofa, laughing at something that Blair had said. At that instant, Diane turned her head, a look of shock crossing her face when she registered Valerie's presence. Diane stood quickly and took two rapid steps forward, her expression of pleasure quickly turning to one of uncertainty.

"I just need one minute," Valerie said, her gaze still fixed on Diane's face.

Cam didn't need to turn to know who Valerie was looking at. "I'll say goodbye to Blair."

"Valerie?" Diane asked, her voice raised in surprise.

"I only have a few seconds right now," Valerie said quickly. "Everything I said to you was true. But there—"

"What are you doing here?"

"Just *listen*, Diane." Valerie touched her hand so fleetingly it might have been an accident. "I couldn't tell you everything before. I'm a federal agent. I—"

Diane's expression shut down, her face going as blank as if she'd suddenly donned a mask. "Never mind. I don't want to hear it." She turned abruptly and without a word walked past Cam, who was on her way back to the door.

"Ready?" Cam asked.

"Yes." Valerie watched Diane until she disappeared into the far hallway, then met Cam's gaze without a trace of emotion. "Let's go."

❖

They'd been in the car ten minutes before Cam broke the silence. "Why did they bring you in now?"

"Since Tuesday, priorities have changed," Valerie replied.

"You must have been under for a long time to establish Claire's identity. I can't imagine they neutralize your kind of operative's cover lightly."

Valerie put her back against the door to face Cam in the driver's seat. "They don't tell me all the reasons, Cameron. But we all know how important Blair's security is." She saw Cam's hands tighten on the wheel, but continued evenly. "I know the players. And believe it or not, there are people who think that I can be helpful in the situation."

Cam swiveled her head and fixed Valerie with a cold stare before averting her gaze back to the traffic. "Well you know *me,* don't you?"

"You fell into the net by accident, Cameron. You were never an intended target."

A muscle in Cam's jaw bunched. "And I don't suppose you can tell me who you *were* supposed to be spying on, can you? When you weren't fucking them, that is."

"As you no doubt realize, my job description is counterintelligence, and Washington, DC is an excellent place to find out what our *friends* are really up to."

"Yes, it's amazing what you will reveal when someone's just fu—"

"Cameron, please don't," Valerie said quietly. "It was never like that with you."

Cam stared straight ahead. "Are you going to tell me that you never filed a report on me?"

"I'm not going to lie about that—"

Cam laughed bitterly.

"But there was never anything compromising in the reports."

"I guess reporting to the CIA that the first daughter's security chief is frequenting whores on Capitol Hill doesn't strike you as being *compromising.* Christ." She had to make an effort not to grind her teeth. "I'm surprised they didn't bust me out a long time ago."

"Everyone has secrets, Cameron. Sometimes secrets can be powerful currency."

Abruptly, Cam swerved to the curb and jammed on the brakes. She swiveled to face Valerie. "Was *any* of it true?"

"Every touch," Valerie said quietly.

Cam searched her eyes and saw the pain. She searched her own heart for the true source of the rage that had followed fast upon the disbelief at finding Valerie at the door that morning. She'd never been in love with her, but she'd cared. Deeply. And she'd let Valerie see things that she revealed to very few people—she'd exposed herself in her weakest moments.

"*Christ.*"

"I'm sorry, Cameron. But I can't apologize for doing my job, only that I hurt you in the process."

"Right." Cam grimaced, thinking that she'd said the same thing more than once herself. "We're going to have to work together, and frankly, I don't trust you."

"Camer—"

"I don't trust *any* CIA agents. On principle." Cam grinned briefly when she saw a true smile flicker across Valerie's full lips. "But as far as I'm concerned, whatever happened between us is personal. That's not part of the job now."

"Thank you." Valerie put her hand on Cam's wrist. "You were never an assignment, never work, for me."

Cam turned her hand over and slid her palm into Valerie's. Their fingers linked and their eyes held, a silent acknowledgment of what they had once been to one another. Then they separated, settling back into their seats as Cam started the car.

❖

"Agents Savard, Davis, Lawrence," Cam said, making rapid introductions as everyone found seats in the small living room of Stark and Savard's apartment. Cam took the end seat on the sofa and reached for the coffee mug that Savard had placed in front of her on the low wooden table. Absently, she noted that the fish tank against the far wall seemed to have a new batch of baby somethings congregated just below the surface in a shimmering silver cloud. Then the apartment receded from her view, and all her focus turned to Savard. "What do we know?"

"It's more what we *don't* know," Savard said. "We concentrated on the IDs of the four dead commandos, and the short answer is, no one knows who they are. Fingerprints haven't turned up anything in our databases or NCIC."

"Don't tell me these guys aren't ex-military," Cam said sharply. "These guys were professionally trained."

"Interpol?" Valerie asked quietly.

Savard gave her a long look. She'd recognized her from a previous investigation when a few agents very close to Cam and Blair had learned of Cam's liaison with a woman identified as a Washington call girl. Apparently they had been mistaken. "They're still checking."

"DNA?" Cam asked of Felicia.

Felicia shook her head. "Not yet, but Quantico expects results within twenty-four hours."

Cam didn't ask how Felicia knew that, and she didn't care. All that mattered was that she had access to whatever intelligence was available without delay. Even though she *should* be able to get any information she needed to run her investigation, if she went through regular channels there would be resistance at every level, and it might take weeks to learn what Felicia could discover in a matter of hours by hacking into the various databases.

"*Someone* knows who these guys are. Let's get their faces out to every possible source here and abroad." Cam turned to Valerie, who sat slightly apart from the others in an overstuffed chair that had seen better days. "Any place in particular we should be looking?"

"Our best guess," Valerie replied carefully, "is the Middle East or Afghanistan. Second-best guess, Libya, although we don't believe they have the contacts required to orchestrate Tuesday's attack."

"All right," Felicia said. "That's a place to start."

"In the meantime," Cam said, "if we can't get anything on the commandos, then we'll have to concentrate on Foster. I want to know everything about him from the minute he was born. I want the names of the people he roomed with at the Academy, the women or men he dated, the names of the agents he worked with on previous assignments, his previous partners, his travel itinerary for the last ten years. I want to know everywhere he's been, everything he's done, every last thing about him."

"Since the assault team members were all Caucasian," Valerie said, "I'd suggest looking at all the paramilitary organizations nationwide. That fits their profile." She looked at Savard. "The FBI should have a considerable file internally, but there has been some counterintelligence activity by…other organizations, as well."

Felicia smiled. "I'll have a look around."

"Good. Let's start putting together organizational profiles on every known paramilitary group," Cam instructed. "Personnel, geographic location, financial resources, political affiliations, publications, propaganda...anything that might hint at armed retaliation."

"Do we have anything that ties these guys to the World Trade Center?" Savard asked, directing her attention pointedly toward Valerie.

"No," Valerie replied, her expression completely composed. "From what we know now, the hijackers appear to have been foreign terrorists. The men who attacked Ms. Powell were not." She sighed. "And neither event was anticipated. Certainly not in the present time frame."

"We need access to your people's intelligence files," Cam said, deciding it was time to find out whose side Valerie was really on. "Can you get us in?"

Valerie hesitated. "As far as I have access, yes."

"If you open the door," Felicia said, "I'll—"

Cam's cell phone emitted a series of sharp, staccato beeps and she yanked it off her belt as she jumped to her feet. "Roberts."

"Cameron," Lucinda Washburn said with an urgency that Cam had never heard in her voice before. "There's been an incident at the Aerie. They've called for a HAZMAT team and quarantined the building."

Cam didn't hear the rest of the message because she was already running for the door.

CHAPTER FIFTEEN

The NYPD had worked fast. Cam ran into the first barricade two blocks from Gramercy Park. Patrol cars angled across the intersection and a bevy of uniformed cops milled in the street. Three helicopters swooped low over the tops of nearby buildings. She slammed her car to a halt nose-in against the curb, yanked the keys from the ignition, and jumped out. She was vaguely aware of shouts aimed in her direction as she ran, her badge extended in her left hand. Dodging and weaving around the bodies that interposed themselves between her and her destination, she just kept screaming, "Secret Service. Secret Service," and shouldering aside anyone who didn't get out of her path quickly enough.

When she rounded the corner of the gated square diagonally across from Blair's building, the congestion in the streets was magnified a hundredfold. Squad cars, ambulances, bomb squad armored vehicles, and official personnel from the police, fire, and emergency rescue departments clogged the sidewalks and streets. She rapidly scanned the building's façade, half expecting to see the top floors gone. The only thing she could imagine was that a bomb had detonated or was about to.

Her stomach cramped, her legs screamed with acid build up, and her chest burned with air hunger, and none of it was from her race through the crowds. It was from a terror that had gripped her the moment Lucinda's words had registered. Someone had gotten to Blair. Despite everything she had done, everything she had anticipated, everything she *was*—someone had gotten to her lover. *Christ. God. Blair!*

"Secret Service, get out of the way. Get out of the way," she barked as she pushed and shoved her way toward the double glass doors to the lobby of Blair's apartment building. "Secret Serv—"

Several pairs of hands grabbed her jacket and dragged her away from the door as a wall of blue closed around her. Blindly, she reacted with an elbow strike that found a target, as evidenced by a grunt and a muffled curse. Then her back was slammed into the wall, followed by her head, and the world spun in a dizzying circle, trees and sky and sidewalk flashing by in an off-kilter parade before her eyes.

"Commander. *Commander!*" A woman's voice shouted somewhere very close to her ear. "Ease up!"

Cam struggled to find her balance, her head still reeling. She knew that voice. She blinked, tried to focus. Hara. Hara and Wozinski. Wozinski had her pinned up against the building with a beefy forearm across her chest. Hara, one hand restraining Cam's right wrist in a viselike grip, was waving off an angry trio of NYPD officers with her other arm.

"Secret Service. We've got this," Hara yelled. "Back off. We've got this."

"Let me go," Cam said in a flat, hard voice.

Wozinski looked at Hara for direction, but she just shook her head and angled her body so that her back was to the cops who still stood muttering nearby. With her face very close to Cam's, she said, "If we let you go and you make a move for the front door again, those cops are going to haul you away, and we won't be able to stop them this time. We could use your help here, Commander. It's your call."

"Is she alive?" Cam asked, her eyes boring into Hara's.

"As far as we know, yes."

"I want to talk to her."

"NYPD has diverted all calls to their own channels. They're jamming cell signals in this sector. We can't—"

Cam twisted her wrist in a move designed to break the strongest restraining grip, and got as far as dislodging Wozinski's arm from her chest before both agents drove their shoulders into her midsection again. Their combined weight forced the air from her lungs and her legs deserted her. Only the two bodies jammed against hers kept her upright.

Hara continued speaking in a calm, even tone as if nothing had happened. "The NYPD is not taking any chances after what happened Tuesday. Right now, their antiterrorism team is running the show, and they're jittery as hell. If we want some control back, you're going to have to get it for us. Commander? Commander, are you getting this?"

"Yes," Cam wheezed. "I'm okay. Let me go."

"Okay, Greg, ease up," Hara said after a long look at Cam's face.

Immediately, Cam felt the pressure on her chest lessen, and she was finally able to get a full breath. She coughed, and her bruised ribs protested. "Sorry." Ignoring the pain, she gulped in another breath and felt her head start to clear. "Fill me in. Fast."

"We don't have much." Hara lowered her voice. "The chief, Egret, and Tony Fazio went up to the penthouse. Greg and I were detailed to the lobby. Waters and O'Reilly are on the rear door."

Cam wanted to shout *Tell me about Blair, God damn it!* but her years of training kept her focused. She needed to know everything if she was going to take charge. And if Blair was in trouble, she wasn't going to let anyone else take care of her. "What happened up there?"

"We don't know. The chief radioed a code red with orders to contain the building. While we were doing that, she must've called in a red alert to the NYPD, because the next thing we knew, we were overrun with uniforms and nobody's telling us anything."

"Have you seen a command vehicle?"

Wozinski pointed toward the northeast corner of the park. "Opposite side of the street, about halfway up the block. We couldn't get close."

"I can." Cam rubbed her chest unconsciously, but the pain wouldn't abate. She welcomed it. It kept her head clear. "You two stay on the door. No one goes up to that penthouse unless I'm with them, got it?"

"The only ones who have gone up there so far are the HAZMAT team," Wozinski said.

"I don't care if the next one in is the president, I go too."

Both agents visibly relaxed. Simultaneously, they said, "Yes, ma'am."

Cam straight-armed her way down the street, waving her badge and repeating over and over, "Secret Service. I'm looking for Captain Stacy Landers." Landers was the head of the NYPD security division assigned to liaise with the Secret Service and to provide additional forces whenever the president or Blair made public appearances in the region. Landers' division was also part of the antiterrorism squad, and Cam knew she'd be heading up the operation. "Landers. Captain Landers. Where is she?"

Finally, she got close enough to pound a fist on the closed door of the black armored van that bristled with satellite antennae. A face appeared at the small rectangular bulletproof glass window for a second and then was gone. A voice over the intercom next to the door instructed, "Hold your ID badge up to the camera, please."

Cam faced the video camera lens mounted above the door and held her ID next to her right cheek so that her face and the image on her badge were visible. Ten seconds later, the door slid open two feet revealing a giant of a man in a SWAT uniform. He wasn't smiling. "Come on in, Agent Roberts."

Three men and a woman were crowded into the narrow central aisle, clustered around a bank of video monitors that showed both limited views of both the exterior and interior of Blair's building as well as an aerial shot of the roof relayed from one of the helicopters Cam had heard circling overhead. The woman, a redhead in a tan jacket and slacks, looked over her shoulder at Cam. Her green eyes flickered for an instant with compassion, then went hard.

"Commander."

"Captain," Cam said, leaning over to peer at the monitors receiving images from the surveillance cameras placed throughout Blair's building. There was no view of the interior of the loft because she herself had ordered the video cameras removed from Blair's living space to protect her privacy. The rest of the building seemed eerily deserted. She hadn't expected to see Blair, but still the disappointment was like a knife cutting through her. She wanted to tear the van apart. *Procedure. I have to follow procedure if I want to get to Blair.* "Status?"

"Egret's security chief radioed a red alert fifty minutes ago," the captain of the NYPD antiterrorism squad reported. "Apparently they ran into some kind of foreign substance up there. We're assuming it's a chemical agent."

"Casualties?" Cam gripped the edge of a metal bracket securing the monitors to the side wall of the vehicle so hard that the edge cut into the skin of her palm. Her mind rebelled at the possibilities. *Cyanide, ricin, sarin. Oh my God.*

"None reported. We've shut down the building's exhaust units and the Public Works people are isolating the outflow from this grid into special holding tanks." She stopped abruptly and pressed two fingers to the earpiece cradled in the shell of her right ear, tilting her head as if to improve the reception. After a moment, she muttered, "Roger that, sir. Yes, sir, I have that," into her throat mike. She looked up at Cam, her expression grim. "That was the president's security adviser. I've been ordered to hold our HAZMAT unit outside the apartment until a team from Fort Detrick gets here."

"USAMRIID?"

"Yeah. They're already in the air. ETA twenty-five minutes."

It only took another second for Cam to make the connection, and then her stomach twisted. The U.S. Army Medical Research and Materiel Command located at Fort Detrick, Maryland was the only facility in the Department of Defense with a BSL-4 laboratory. *What the hell do they think is up there?*

"Open a line to the loft. I want to talk to Blair. Now."

❖

Blair jumped when the portable phone on her breakfast bar rang, staring at it as if it were alive. The last time she'd tried it, for what must have been the fiftieth time, it had been without a signal. None of their cell phones or radios worked either. That couldn't be a coincidence, or an accident. They hadn't heard from anyone in almost thirty minutes, and being kept in the dark as to what was happening really *really* pissed her off.

She snatched up the phone and snapped, "Blair Powell. Who the hell is this?"

"It's Cam, baby. You okay?" Cam tried desperately to keep the tremor from her voice.

"Hey," Blair said gently, her temper instantly soothed. "I'd be great if somebody would tell me what the hell is going on."

"You're not hurt? You're not sick in any way?"

"No. We all seem to be all right." Blair moved to the other side of the loft from where Stark and Fazio paced in tight circles, their useless cell phones clutched in their hands. "Where are you?"

"Right out front with Stacy Landers. Can you tell me what happened?"

"We were moving my canvases," Blair explained, "and there was a plastic bag stuck between two of them. We didn't see it there, and when we pulled the frames apart, whatever was in the bag spilled out."

Cam was struck by a wave of dizziness and braced a hand against the ceiling of the van to steady herself. "Spilled out or blew into the air? Do you remember?"

"Uh...a little of both, really. What's going on, Cam?"

"We're not sure just yet. Who actually broke open the bag?" *Who had the most exposure to whatever was in it?*

"Fazio—he was unpacking some of the crates for me. Why?"

"Stark and Fazio are both all right too?"

"Yes. We were instructed to move as far away from the problem site as possible without leaving the apartment. That was over half an hour ago, and that's the last we heard from anybody. Why are we being kept up here?"

Cam hesitated and then realized that the truth was the only choice. Blair could handle anything from her except a lie. "We have to assume that substance—the powder, whatever it is—is potentially harmful. We can't move you until the potential contamination is contained. We're bringing in a team now to do that."

"There's a HAZMAT team here somewhere, I heard them talking to Stark on her radio before we lost contact with everyone. Why aren't they in here decontaminating us, if that's what we're waiting for?"

"Washington is sending up a special team," Cam said. Her shirt and jacket were soaked with sweat, despite the fifty degree temperature outside and the powerful air-conditioning unit in the van that ran at full power to cool the electronic equipment. The inactivity was making her crazy. She wanted a firsthand look at the situation. She wanted to see Blair. "They'll be here any minute."

"Yeah, yeah. Any minute. I'll bet." Impatiently, Blair strode to the windows and looked down to the street. "God, there's five times as many people down there now as there were twenty minutes ago. What aren't you telling me?"

"We're all pretty much waiting on this team to arrive, baby. As soon as they touch down, I'll come up with them."

"That's grea—" Blair stopped her restless route around the perimeter of the room, her eyes narrowing. "They're coming from

DC. So someone either knows what this is or thinks they do, because they don't want the local people handling it. Just who are these people, Cam?"

"USAMRIID."

Silence ensued while Blair searched her memory for an association to the familiar-sounding name. "Wait a minute, isn't that part of the bioterrorism response unit?"

"Yes."

"So," Blair said thoughtfully, reaching behind her to grip a chair back. She suddenly felt light-headed, and the feeling frightened her. "What are we talking here? Ebola? Some kind of plague?"

"I don't know, baby," Cam said in frustration, hating the note of fear she'd heard in Blair's voice for the first time. "I'm waiting to find out, the same as you."

"I don't want you coming up here," Blair said sharply. *I won't have anything happening to you. Not again.*

"I'll come up with the containment team. I'll be perfectly saf—"

"*No.*" Blair saw both Stark and Fazio glance at her in alarm and she waved them off, mouthing, *It's okay,* when they started toward her.

"Listen to me, Blair. I need to see you. I need to be sure you're all right. I'm coming up."

"Cameron, *think.* My security chief is stuck in here with me. I've got no one on the outside who knows anything about me except Lucinda, and she's not capable of running the ground show. I need you healthy so that you can handle my security while they sort out whatever this thing is. If you get sick, or they even think you are, you won't be any use to me. Think, sweetheart. I need you out there, not in here." *Don't come near me. I won't have you die because of me.*

"We don't even know there's anything dangerous up there. I'll be well protected."

"Cameron, if you don't do this for me, I'll have Stark tell Stacy Landers to keep you away from here altogether."

Cam swore vehemently. The four NYPD officers hanging on her every word pretended not to notice. "Blair, don't do that."

"Promise me you won't come up here." She waited, the silence ringing hollowly between them. "Cameron. Promise."

"All right," Cam finally said. "*Unless* I get clearance from the USAMRIID team."

"Fine, but I want to hear it from their team leader." Blair let out a sigh. "Stark is waving to me. She wants to talk to you. I've got to go. I love you."

"I love you." Cam's throat was so tight she could barely speak. "I'll see you soon."

Stark took the phone from Blair with a nod of thanks. "Commander. I felt given the circumstances I had no choice but to—"

"It was a good call, Chief," Cam said. "Blair—all of you, you're all right?"

"Yes, ma'am. Any word yet on what we're dealing with?"

"Negative. You'll just have to sit tight until the biohazard team from Fort Detrick has a look."

"Fort Detrick? Oh man." Stark turned away from Blair and Fazio and cupped her hands around the phone. "In today's briefing there was a report about that team investigating a bioterrorism attack in New Jersey. They suspected anthrax."

Cam closed her eyes, but she could still see the white powder blowing in the air.

CHAPTER SIXTEEN

The dial tone that severed Cam's tenuous connection to Blair sounded as ominous as incoming shell fire. And this was an enemy Cam could not fight—not with force or skill or even her formidable willpower. This time she would have to rely on others to do that, and the prospect left her feeling helpless and impotent. Her fingers clenched the phone as the stifling air in the van closed in around her. A rush of anger and frustration filled her head, momentarily clouding her reason and fracturing her control.

"God *damn* it," she said as her fist struck the inside wall of the van with enough force to send a tremor through the vehicle. She didn't feel the pain as the skin split over her knuckles and a small fissure cracked in a bone in her little finger. She tossed the cell phone onto the narrow counter in front of Stacy Landers and pivoted toward the double rear doors, intent on reaching Blair. Someone behind her must have signaled, because the officer in the SWAT uniform blocked her way with an agile sidestep that she would have thought impossible for him to make, considering his bulk. "Step aside."

Her voice was once again modulated and calm. But her face was cold as death. From somewhere in the van, Captain Landers said, "I'm sorry, Cam. But you'll have to wait it out down here with the rest of us. There's nothing you can do up there now."

Perhaps it was the use of her first name, or the fact that Cam already knew that Landers was right, but she checked the movement that would have driven her shoulder hard against the SWAT team officer's chest. "I need some air."

"Good idea," Landers said. "Let her by, Lieutenant Maxwell."

"Yes, ma'am," the man said and smoothly shifted out of Cam's path.

She shoved open the rear doors and jumped down to the sidewalk. Immediately, she was surrounded.

"What's happened?" Renée demanded, her fingers clamped around Cam's forearm. "Has someone been wounded up there? Why the fuck won't they let us up? What about our people? What about Blair, Paula?"

Although the questions were reasonable, the tone of Savard's voice sent a warning signal that dissipated the remaining haze of Cam's anger. The FBI agent sounded as if she was about to crack. Cam took a close look at her, and what she saw made her shake off Savard's arm and point to the far side of the vehicle. "Let's talk over there, Agent."

Felicia and Valerie, standing nearby, moved to follow, but Cam shook her head and indicated they should wait. Both women looked impatient and concerned, but they accepted her orders. On the far side of the van, out of range of prying eyes and intrusive cameras, Cam said, "Let me fill you in, Renée."

"Paula? What about Paula? Is she hurt?"

"Paula is fine. I just talked to her. There's been exposure to an unknown substance, and they went to red alert status. SOP. We're waiting on a special decontamination team right now."

"I want to talk to her." Savard's speech was taut with tension and fear.

Cam shook her head. "You can't. You know the procedure. The longer lines are open, the more likely that transmissions will be intercepted and the greater the chance we'll have a media leak. In situations like this where the use of a biowarfare agent is a possibility, we could have widespread panic. Mass evacuations, civilian casualties. We can't risk it. You'll have to wait."

Savard's eyes flicked to the apartment building across the street, but what she saw were the Towers coming down and, everywhere, the devastation. The defenselessness and horror was suffocating. Gasping, she whispered in a tortured voice, "I can't."

"Yes, you can," Cam said quietly, placing both hands on Savard's shoulders and lowering her head until their eyes met and held. Her tone was firm, yet gentle. "You and Felicia and I are going to do whatever needs to be done to take care of the situation. Paula is counting on you to handle this, and so am I. This isn't like Tuesday, Renée. We're going to have a chance to fight back."

"I can't take it." Savard's gaze wavered as she opened and clenched her hands spasmodically. "I can't lose her. I can't. I just can't."

"I know."

Suddenly, Savard jerked, and her tormented eyes widened. Her pupils, dark passageways to her own personal hell, flickered wildly. "Oh my God. Blair? Is she—"

"Pretty pissed off," Cam said with a tender laugh. "But otherwise, she sounded fine."

When Savard saw the pain shadow Cam's face and heard the tremor of desperate love in her voice, she understood that she was not alone in her agony. She drew her shoulders back and straightened. Her blue eyes cleared, and some of the color returned to her face. "What do you need me to do, Commander?"

Cam's expression hardened as she squeezed Savard's shoulders and then let go. "I need you to tap into your sources and get me as much information as you can about a similar occurrence yesterday at a government complex in New Jersey—the nature of the suspected toxic agent, number and type of casualties, whether any perpetrators took credit for the attack—anything. Get me that as quickly you can."

"Yes, ma'am. I'll be back as soon as I have something."

As Savard turned away, Felicia stepped up to Cam with Valerie just behind her. "The bomb team is still outside the building, so I assume we're not dealing with explosives this time."

"No," Cam said with a quick look around. Seeing no one close enough to overhear, she rendered a rapid recounting of what Blair and Stark had told her. As she spoke, she watched Valerie's face, looking for some sign that the news of a biological weapon did not come as a surprise to the CIA. "Do you have anything to add, Agent Lawrence?"

"When is the team from Detrick expected?" Valerie asked.

Cam checked her watch. "ETA eighteen minutes."

"Let's take a little walk," Valerie said, edging through the crowd that was clustered around the command vehicle.

The three women cut briskly through the milling bodies until they reached the gated entrance to the east side of the park. Cam removed her keys and opened the gate, letting it swing closed and lock behind them. While outside the block-square oasis of trees and flowers and wending walkways the streets and sidewalks seethed with activity, inside the quietude was seductively soothing. Cam strode twenty feet down a narrow stone path and then turned abruptly to face Valerie. "What else don't we know that we should have been told? If you people put her at risk, I swear I'll make someone pay for it."

Valerie shook her head. "I don't *know* what we know and what we don't, Cameron. I'm counterintelligence, not counterterrorism."

"You're a spy."

"I'm a field agent," Valerie said with an impatient shrug. "I have a broad assignment to monitor individuals who"—she hesitated—"might have information of interest to our government."

"Which means what?"

"Which means that I have no reason to be briefed on whatever intel Langley might have related to what's happening here. Have we suspected that certain unfriendly governments are intensely involved with developing bioweapons? Absolutely. Was there an indication of an imminent attack within this country? I'm not aware of any such intelligence."

Cam impatiently pushed a hand through her hair. "Can you find out? Or is this information highway only running in one direction?"

Unconsciously, Valerie closed the distance between them and placed her hand on Cam's upper arm. Her face and voice were filled with sympathy. "Cameron, I'll do what I can. But you must know how closed the system is, even to those of us on the inside. There isn't a more guarded organization in the world."

"Try," Cam said quietly. "Just…try."

Valerie nodded, stroking Cam's arm slowly. "I will."

They stared at one another, anger and compassion warring in their eyes.

Felicia spoke into the gathering silence. "What do you think the team from Detrick will do when they get here? That building is a security nightmare now."

At last, Cam turned and looked through the treetops, their leaves a riotous palette of oranges and reds and golds, to where the sun glinted off the windows of Blair's loft. Despite the fact that the apartment was fortified like a prison, within those walls Blair had had a certain degree of freedom. It was the one place where no one watched her; the one safe haven where she could create her art. Now, she was about to lose even that.

"They'll move them. Then they'll quarantine them."

❖

"What did Cam say?" Blair asked.

"Not much, because I don't think there's much to tell yet," Stark answered truthfully. "The team from Fort Detrick will be here soon, though."

"And then what?"

"I'm not sure." Involuntarily, Stark glanced to the far end of the room where the remaining canvases stood, imagining she could still see the white powder drifting on the bright early-morning shafts of sunlight. "I guess it depends on what they think it is."

Blair glanced over to where the male Secret Service agent stood at the window with his back to them, watching the street below. She didn't know him, and although she trusted him on principle, years of habit had made her circumspect; she hesitated to reveal her fears and uncertainties in front of anyone except those she trusted most. "What if they don't *know* what it is?"

Stark thought about the morning briefing and the possibility of anthrax or something far worse. Her stomach rolled, and she quickly suppressed the shudder of fear that followed. Her responsibility was to contain the situation, and although there was nothing she could do if they had been seriously compromised by some biological agent, she could carry the worry herself and spare Blair's peace of mind, at least for the moment. "I'm sure whatever it is, they'll know what to do."

❖

The black van with the revolving red light on top edged slowly through the sea of bodies toward Blair's building, finally coming to a halt with the right front wheel up on the sidewalk. The side door slid open, and two men climbed out. A woman stepped down from the front passenger compartment. All wore Army uniforms. The driver, also in uniform, exited and hurried to the rear. Once there, he pulled open the double doors and reached inside. With efficient movements, he passed full-body coveralls constructed of Tychem F, a material affording the highest level of protection against biological and chemical agents, to the three Army officers.

Cam and Stacy Landers arrived as the team members were suiting up.

"I'm Cameron Roberts, Egret's acting security chief. I want to go up with you," Cam said.

The older of the two men, a well-built redhead with sun-weathered skin and a military haircut, shook his head. "Sorry, Agent…Roberts, was it? It's against protocol."

"Look," Cam said sharply, unable to contain her frustration, "that's the president's dau—"

The only woman on the team, whose name tag read Captain R. Andrews, interrupted quietly. "We know who she is, Agent Roberts. Just as soon as we have determined the nature of the situation, we'll brief you. You'll be far more valuable down here in terms of coordinating the extraction and containing communications than you would be up there."

Cam studied the warm green eyes that looked steadily into hers. Andrews, her collar-length chestnut hair worn in casual layers, appeared to be in her early thirties. She was about Blair's size, but more muscular—a rower or a serious lifter, possibly. Her insignia indicated Army Medical Corps. There was an intensity in her expression that said she understood the source of Cam's concern. Cam nodded. "I want a report on all of them, ASAP."

"You'll have it," Andrews said.

Silently, Cam watched as the three zipped up their suits, pulled on the protective hoods, and adjusted their goggles and gas masks. The NYPD HAZMAT team and Landers's security forces had cordoned off a path to the front door, and the team from Fort Detrick lumbered into the building and disappeared, leaving her to wait.

❖

Blair stood just behind Stark as she pulled open the apartment door. The sight that greeted them was like a scene in a science-fiction movie. Three people in space suits, gender indeterminate, stood in the foyer carrying oversized tackle boxes. *Clearly, whatever they think is in here is something seriously dangerous.*

"Please step back," a male voice said through a microphone. "Move to your left and remain stationary."

"Who are you?" Blair asked, backing up slowly as the three entered in single file.

"I'm Colonel Grau," the first figure informed her, advancing relentlessly, "and these are Captains Andrews and Demetri."

A female voice then said, "Please come with me, Ms. Powell," as the smallest figure stepped away from the triumvirate. "You too, Agent Stark. Follow me to the bathroom, please."

Blair realized, as she and Stark fell in behind the shrouded form, that she shouldn't be surprised that these people knew the layout of her loft. They undoubtedly knew her bra size and every other intimate detail of her life. She glanced over her shoulder and saw the male Secret Service agent being led toward the guest bathroom by the third team member. She stopped walking when she saw Colonel Grau opening his equipment box where her canvases were stored. "I want to see what he's doing."

Captain Andrews caught Blair's wrist in a thickly gloved hand. "I'm sorry, Ms. Powell, but that won't be possible."

Blair's response was immediate and instinctual. She'd been held incommunicado for several hours. She had no idea how grave the threat was, and she was angry and frightened. She couldn't see her lover, her life had once more been invaded, and now her last refuge was destroyed. Swiftly, she broke the restraining grip with a move she had practiced countless times in the dojo and in the training ring.

Captain Andrews did not try to stop her, but only said, "Are those paintings worth your life?"

The only thing Blair saw as she stopped her abrupt charge toward Colonel Grau, who had just cut a postage-stamp-sized piece of canvas from the center of a completed painting and dropped it into a test tube, was Cam's face. The only thing more important to her than her work, her freedom, and even her life, was Cam. If she had the choice, she would never do anything to hurt her. She wouldn't risk her life if it meant Cam would be the one to pay the price. She turned her back on what Grau was doing.

"I want to talk to Agent Roberts," Blair said.

"I know," Captain Andrews said. "Just as soon as possible."

Despite the flat, mechanical sound of her projected voice, Blair thought she detected a note of sympathy. For some reason, she believed her and didn't argue. Silently, she followed her into the bathroom.

The master bath, done in pale gold tiles and granite surrounds, was just off her bedroom. It contained a six-by-four-foot shower stall with two showerheads on facing walls in addition to the other standard features. There was room enough for the three of them to stand comfortably without crowding. Captain Andrews closed the door and knelt to remove a large red plastic biohazard bag from her equipment box. She straightened laboriously in her heavy protective suit and held it out to Stark and Blair. "Would you both please remove all of your clothing and place them in this bag."

While Blair and Stark disrobed, the officer opened the shower door, knelt once again, and proficiently removed the drain cover with a small screwdriver. Then she inserted what appeared to be a water filter in its place.

"What is that?" Blair asked as she crammed her clothing into the red bag. She averted her gaze from Stark, who stood stiffly beside her. Blair knew how embarrassed she must be. It wasn't her own nudity that bothered her so much, but the loss of control that accompanied it. Nevertheless, she was determined not to become a passive player in this drama. "Captain?"

"It's a biofilter."

"What *exactly* do you suspect that we have on us?"

Captain Andrews faced Blair, her eyes unwavering behind the thick polyurethane of her protective goggles. "We don't know, Ms. Powell. But at the moment, we must assume that you have been contaminated with an active biological agent. Until we have determined otherwise, you must be treated as if you are infected."

Infected. Not a chemical agent. Something alive. The thought of something invading her body was strangely more terrifying than the possibility of having been poisoned. Blair drew a slow breath, needing the extra few seconds to force down the surge of panic. "How long before you know?"

"I can't say. Would you please step into the shower now?"

CHAPTER SEVENTEEN

B lair kept her back turned to Stark as the hot water sluiced over her. Although the shower was more spacious than an ordinary stall, if she moved back an inch, her ass would be rubbing up against Stark's. *Government efficiency. Jesus.*

Methodically, she scrubbed her skin with the soft plastic brush and cleansing agent that Captain Andrews had provided, trying not to think about what might already have penetrated the fragile barrier and could even now be coursing through her bloodstream. The last time she'd taken a shower with anyone, it had been Cam. They'd made love while the curtain of water shimmered like a nearly tangible wall between them and all the forces that contrived to keep them apart. She focused on the memory of Cam's face as they joined—so fierce and tender—on the touch of her lover's knowing hands bringing her to orgasm, and on the sweet sound of their passion dancing on the falling water. The acrid scent of something oddly familiar drew her from her reverie.

"What is this stuff?" Blair asked. "Bleach?"

"Sodium hydrochlorite," Captain Andrews replied, opening two large foil packs and extracting synthetic mesh sheets slightly larger than bath towels. "Step down onto the mat and wrap this around you, please."

"Is that a fancy way of saying bleach?" Blair draped herself in the thin covering, discovering strategically placed Velcro tabs that allowed her to close it around her chest just above her breasts and at the waist.

"Yes."

"Well, that's a straight answer, at least."

Although the sheet reached almost to Blair's knees, the shape of her body was clearly outlined beneath it. She glanced once at Stark, similarly covered, noting the curve of her small breasts and strong thighs. *Oh, poor Paula. This must be so hard for her.* Blair indicated the thin white covering. "Tell me you have something else for us to wear."

"Yes, I do." Captain Andrews passed a surgical mask to each woman. "These hook behind your ears with the elastic str—"

"The clothes?" Blair asked pointedly, slipping on the mask.

"Once we exit the building, you'll be provided with temporary coveralls."

"And just where exactly are we going to change?" Stark asked.

"On the sidewalk."

❖

Cam paced the sidewalk in front of Blair's building, alternately checking her watch and scanning the building's façade, as if she might at any moment be able to see through the brick and glass to her lover. She wheeled around when she heard the driver's radio crackle to life and hurried over to him. Stacy Landers reached him at the same time.

"What's the status, Lieutenant?" Landers asked.

"They're on their way down." He carried a stack of silver packs the size of small knapsacks to the zippered front of a white polyurethane enclosure that he had erected between the side doors of the black vehicle and the double glass doors of the building's lobby. The entire structure, resembling a long narrow tunnel, extended like an accordion from inside the vehicle and was supported by thin semicircular hoops at four-foot intervals. When he unzipped the flaps and folded them outward, he created a chute that led directly from the front door of the building to the car. Then he placed a stack of foil-wrapped packages on the plastic floor just inside the front opening.

From a few feet away, Cam observed everything warily. She could feel the dozens of eyes on her back as the first responders clustered behind the barriers that had been hastily erected to keep even the emergency personnel back from the immediate scene. "Environmental protection suits?"

"Yes, ma'am."

"I want you to suit me up so I can go in the vehicle with them."

He shook his head, his eyes fixed on the front door, his posture erect and alert. "I'm sorry, ma'am, but I can't do that. Authorized personnel only."

She took one quick step forward before Landers caught her arm. Cam whipped her head around, a sharp retort on her lips.

"Just hold it together a little longer, Cam," Landers said in a low but forceful tone. "Let them secure the assets, and then we'll worry about access."

Assets. Packages. Targets.

Cam swore, but held her ground. Suddenly, the glass doors opened, and the three officers in protective suits exited in a cluster, each guiding a figure shrouded in white. Cam sought Blair's gaze above the surgical mask, and for one brief instant, they connected. Her lover's blue eyes, so clear and strong, called to her.

"Blair," Cam whispered.

And then she was gone.

Cam stood on the sidewalk, feeling more alone than she ever had in her life, while all around her, activity escalated. Landers ordered the HAZMAT team back into the building to complete decontamination procedures, while firemen were dispatched to secure the main water and electrical supplies. The perimeter that had been hastily erected around the square had traffic snarled for blocks in every direction. The wail of police sirens was a constant backdrop to her own clamoring thoughts. For the first time in her life, she couldn't formulate a plan. Someone had taken Blair, and that single devastating fact left her reeling. It didn't matter that those in charge were presumably friendly. She trusted no one and struggled to subdue the panic that ate at the edges of her reason.

"Cameron."

Cam glanced down at the manicured hand loosely holding her wrist. She recognized the slender fingers, the perfect oval nails, the practiced touch. She raised her eyes to Valerie's and saw that the CIA agent had a cell phone cradled against her ear. Valerie smiled faintly and nodded at her, and Cam's head cleared.

Where? Cam mouthed.

Valerie nodded again but said nothing, obviously still listening to whoever was on the other end of the line. Standing nearby, Felicia watched just as acutely, and the instant Valerie closed the phone, snapped, "Well? Do you have a location for us?"

"Walter Reed," Valerie announced.

"Let's go," Felicia said, starting toward the street.

"Wait a minute," Cam instructed. Both women looked at her in surprise as she removed her radio and clicked to a secure frequency. After a few seconds, she said, "This is Roberts. Are you in the loft? Okay, describe for me the location of the paintings…In what?…Which crate?…Okay, thanks."

She disconnected and turned to her team members. "The HAZMAT officer says the paintings came out of one of the crates labeled 9/6. That's the date of Blair's last show."

"Do you think the toxin was planted at the gallery opening?" Felicia asked, her face creased with concern.

"It's possible. Foster was there," Cam said grimly. "And the crates with the paintings that were sold that night are still there now, waiting to be inventoried and shipped."

"Oh my God," Valerie murmured. "Diane."

Felicia looked at her watch. "It's almost eleven. They'll be opening right about now."

Galvanized, Cam pointed to Blair's building. "Valerie, find Landers and have her dispatch another team to Diane's gallery. Felicia and I will head over there—"

"No," Valerie said sharply. "I'm coming with you."

"Fine," Cam said, knowing there was no time to waste and that she would not be able to dissuade Valerie in any case. "Felicia, brief Landers."

"Got it, Commander."

❖

The five-minute walk to where Cam had left her vehicle seemed to take an hour as they pushed and squeezed their way through the dense crowd. Once they were on their way, traffic forced Cam to drive at five miles an hour even when they were several blocks beyond the cordoned-off area.

"God," Valerie groaned, "I could walk there faster than this."

"It's unlikely that anyone will disturb those paintings," Cam observed, threading her car between two yellow cabs and earning irate oaths from both cabbies.

"Those *bastards*."

Cam glanced at Valerie, fairly certain that she hadn't meant the cab drivers. She could never remember hearing Valerie raise her voice before, let alone curse. She wondered if it was something more personal than the attacks earlier in the week that provoked her response. "Was Diane part of the plan?"

"God, no," Valerie answered quietly.

"But it wasn't an accident you were at the gallery opening." Cam glanced at her watch. It had only been eighteen minutes since they'd left Blair's building, but it felt like eighteen hours. And nothing she could do would get them to Diane's any faster. She doubted that even Landers's team could get there quickly, considering the state of traffic. "Did they tell you to establish a relationship with Blair's best friend?"

"Our orders are never as direct as that, and we often only get a clear picture of the greater plan after the operation has begun. Sometimes, not even then." Valerie stared ahead into the clogged Manhattan streets, her thoughts turned inward. "No. I was just as surprised as you were when I got the call to show up there."

"You hid it well."

"That's my job, don't forget," Valerie said in a slightly mocking tone.

"Are you really an art dealer?"

"As a matter of fact, I am."

Much to Cam's surprise, she realized that her initial resentment at discovering she had been the victim of an elaborate deception had turned now to a curious form of respect. Valerie was, very much like Cam, bound by duty. Both answered the call without question, often at significant cost to themselves and those who loved them. It was difficult for Cam to remain angry when she herself carried much of the same guilt.

"When did they recruit you?"

Valerie smiled softly at Cam. "Even sooner than you. I was a senior in high school."

"Jesus."

"I was bright and idealistic, and I came from a long line of patriots. Both my parents were career Navy."

"Do they know?"

She shook her head sadly. "No. And my father died thinking that I had tossed over the guiding principles they had taught me in favor of an extravagant lifestyle."

"I'm sorry," Cam said, meaning it.

"Well, I could have taken a more traditional route, but," she shrugged and laughed, "there was something about the secrecy that appealed to me."

"No regrets?"

A beat of silence passed, then Valerie answered quietly, "Only one."

"If it makes a difference," Cam said, "I understand."

"That means more than you'll ever know."

Cam finally turned onto the street where Diane's gallery was located, swerved into an illegal parking place in front of a fire hydrant, and cut the engine. As they hurried up the street, she said, "I want you to get Diane and the rest of the employees out of the gallery. If they haven't moved the paintings, there is no reason at this point to believe any of them have been contaminated. You take Diane home while I wait for Landers's team to show up and secure the space."

"She might be more cooperative if you—"

"Someone needs to stay in Manhattan. We need the intelligence on what happened at Blair's. *And* we need to know if there's anything at the gallery. I'm leaving as soon as I can for Walter Reed."

"Then Felicia or Savard—"

Cam shook her head as she reached the front door to Diane's gallery. "No. I need *them* working on the attack on the Aerie. You're going to take the lead on the bioweapons end of things, at least until we find out where it's going."

Valerie had no further chance to argue, because as they stepped into the spacious gallery, which was divided at irregular intervals by half walls covered with paintings, Diane rose from behind a pedestal desk, a pen in one hand and a shocked expression on her face.

"Valerie?"

Cam hurried toward the back of the building where Diane stored artwork in a climate-controlled annex, while Valerie approached Diane.

"Are you here alone?" Valerie asked.

"What?" Diane shook her head, confused. "Why are you here? I don't understand what you're doing."

"I'll explain as soon as I can. I promise." Valerie took Diane's hand and held it gently. "Has anyone been here this morning? Employees or clients?"

"No. I...I don't officially open until noon today. I was just doing the books."

"What about earlier in the week?"

Again Diane indicated no. "I've been closed since the show."

"No one's been in since then?" Valerie leaned over the desk, her palms flat on the surface. "You're sure?"

"Yes, I'm certain. What's going on?"

Cam walked back into the room. "Looks to be all clear. The crates are there, and they all appear to be intact. If there's anything inside, it hasn't been disturbed."

"Good," Valerie said.

Cam's phone rang and she pulled it from her belt. "Roberts...All right, go ahead." As she listened, her jaw tightened. "I'm on my way there now. No, I need you with Felicia..." She stopped and took a long breath. "All right. I'll see you there." She closed the connection and looked at Valerie. "You and Felicia will stay here and work the computers and any sources you can. There was a similar incident yesterday in New Jersey."

"Was that Savard?" Valerie asked.

"Yes. She's heading to DC too."

"Of course she is."

Diane, still holding Valerie's hand, pulled on her arm sharply. "Will one of you *please* tell me what is going on here? Has something happened to Blair?"

Valerie squeezed her hand and then let go. "There's been an incident at Blair's." At Diane's quick gasp, she hastened to add, "She's not hurt. I'll explain after I take you home."

"And if I don't want to go home?" Diane looked from Cam to Valerie. "Do I have a choice in the matter?"

"I'm sorry, no," Valerie answered.

"I didn't think so." Diane turned stiffly away and gathered her purse and jacket. She crossed the gallery and walked outside without looking at either of the agents.

"Well," Valerie said quietly. "I'll see that she gets home."

"Stay there until I call you."

"Yes. Please let me know how Blair is doing."

Cam heard sirens approaching and felt some of the tightness in her chest ease. At that moment, she wasn't interested in national security or bioterrorism. All she wanted was to see Blair. And this time, no one was going to stop her.

CHAPTER EIGHTEEN

The hallways were brightly lit, eerily quiet, and totally empty. Captain Andrews led the way with Demetri following closely behind Blair and Stark, who walked side by side in silence. The rooms lining either side of the passageway were closed, their windowless doors un-numbered. The air carried a faint antiseptic smell. After a twenty-five minute ride to a small airstrip in Queens and another two hours in a helicopter, they'd landed on the rooftop of a building in the sprawling complex that housed Walter Reed Army Hospital. Blair didn't recognize their location and suspected it was a research wing, given the nature of their situation. She'd considered asking, and then realized that in all likelihood she wouldn't get an answer. The whine of the helicopter rotors had precluded any real conversation, even with the White House, other than a terse update and ETA in DC relayed via Grau to, Blair presumed, Lucinda. Now, however, she was besieged by a deep sense of unease. She had a terrible feeling that if she stepped behind one of those closed doors, she might never emerge. She made the one request she didn't think they'd be able to refuse.

"I want to talk to my father."

Beside her, Stark muttered *amen* under her breath.

Captain Andrews continued her brisk stride forward. "The president is fully aware of your location, Ms. Powell. As soon as we complete our tests, you'll be free to call him. We'll bring a phone to your room."

"My *room?*" Blair stopped abruptly, aware of Captain Demetri's breath on the back of her neck. "My room, as in I'm staying here?"

"Temporarily, yes." Captain Andrews turned to face them, her expression serious, but also sympathetic. "Until we have the results of our cultures and other analyses, it's best to keep you under observation."

"Observation." Blair glanced at Stark, who looked grim. "Do I look like I've suddenly lost my ability to reason, Agent Stark?"

Stark's eyes brightened, and her mask moved as if she were silently laughing. "No, ma'am. You look fine to me."

"I actually *feel* fine too," Blair observed musingly. She pointed at Captain Andrews. "For some reason, you seem to think that I'm incapable of appreciating what's going on here. I understand that for security reasons you didn't want me talking to my father earlier, but you and I will get along a lot better if you start giving *me* the facts right now. I don't even require complete sentences."

"My apologies, Ms. Powell," Captain Andrews said smoothly, giving no hint of annoyance. "It's just that I have other priorities right now. I'll be happy to explain as soon as we have you in an isolation room and have completed our tests."

Blair ignored the rush of apprehension at the term *isolation room.* She wanted information and couldn't allow herself to be sidetracked by fear. "Now that's more like it. What kind of tests?"

"I'll explain while we walk." The Army medical doctor turned and started off, and when Blair and Stark followed, she said over her shoulder, "Skin, blood, sputum, and urine cultures. Blood chemistries and cell counts. Baseline chest x-ray. Electrocardiogram. A complete physical examination."

"You think we're going to get sick, don't you?"

"I don't know," Captain Andrews said. "It's possible that the substance in your apartment was completely harmless. But until we know, we're going to treat you aggressively."

They filed into a large room, and Blair noted several windows set into an interior wall behind partially closed curtains. She pointed. "That looks an awfully lot like an observation window."

"It is," Captain Andrews replied. "The nurses' station is just on the other side. The glass allows them to check on you without actually entering the room."

Blair shivered, although the room was warm. Two hospital beds stood side by side with matching institutional bedside dressers between them. A television was mounted on a metal bracket in the upper corner of the room opposite the beds. A bathroom was visible through an open door in one corner. There were no outside windows. The walls were completely bare. Royal blue surgical scrubs in plastic bags were laid out on each bed. "How do we communicate?"

"There's a two-way intercom just above your bed and one by the windows."

"Do those windows open?"

"No."

"Wonderful," Blair muttered. The lightweight EP suit she'd been provided outside her building zipped up the front and covered her from toe to neck. It was unexpectedly durable, but she still felt as if she were practically naked. She pointed to the clothes. "Can we change?"

"Yes. Once you have, I'll examine you both, draw your blood, instruct you in how to provide the other specimens, and then we'll see about your phone calls." Captain Andrews indicated the beds. "For now, why don't you just make yourselves comfortable there, and I'll be back as soon as I collect the necessary specimen containers."

As soon as the doctor left the room, Blair turned to Stark. "Do we have a choice here?"

Stark shook her head. "No."

"What do they think it is?"

"I don't know, I—"

"Bullshit," Blair said mildly. "I know you know, because *Cam* would know. And now, you're Cam."

Stark turned her back to open the plastic bags of clothing, knowing that if Blair continued to study her face, she'd discern the truth. "I haven't heard anything about something like this—"

"Paula," Blair said knowingly, "lying won't work. You're way too obvious. Now tell me what you know."

"I'm not sure—"

"Just tell me what you heard. God damn it, don't leave me in the dark."

With a sigh, Stark dropped onto the side of one bed and unzipped her white coveralls, surprising Blair with her apparent unconcern for her nudity. Blair looked away, sensing that Stark was far more upset than she let on and would be embarrassed later. "What is it, Paula?" Blair questioned gently. "You can tell me. I'll be fine."

Stark pulled the scrub shirt over her head and sighed. "Every morning we get a copy of the Central Intelligence Report—that's the joint release from the CIA and FBI. Yesterday an envelope filled with white powder was delivered to a federal building in New Jersey. They suspect it might be anthrax."

Blair sat slowly on the bed, watching Stark's face carefully. "Anthrax. Jesus. Do you think that's what that stuff was in my apartment?"

Stark squeezed her hands between her knees and shook her head. "I don't know. I think that's what these people think, though."

"What do the reports say about it? Just how dangerous is it?"

"It didn't go into detail. It's treatable, they said." *Seventy percent mortality rate, they said.* Stark indicated the clothing on the bed. "You should change before they come back. It feels better to have real clothes on."

"Yeah. Okay." Swiftly rising, Blair unzipped in the same motion and stepped free of the synthetic coveralls to stand nude by her bed. She ripped open the plastic bags and stepped into the surgical scrub bottoms and then pulled on the top. Barefoot, she stretched out on the bed to wait. If it was what they suspected, things were going to be bad. Very bad. "Paula?"

"Yeah?"

"It's not your fault."

Stark said nothing, unable to take solace in the kindness of what she knew to be a lie.

❖

"Is Blair really all right?" Diane asked. She sat next to Valerie on the sofa in her living room where they had sat together barely a day before, but she felt now as if she were sitting beside a stranger. And of course, she was.

"Yes." Valerie swirled the white wine that Diane had poured for her when they'd both agreed upon arriving back at Diane's that a drink would be welcome. Their cab ride had been silent and awkward, just like the lie that hung in the air between them now. She sipped the wine and broke a cardinal rule. "There was a foreign substance in her apartment. We don't know what it is, and she's most likely been placed in isolation until it can be determined."

Diane's fingers tightened on her glass, and she had to consciously force herself to relax her grip. "Like a poison?"

"That's unlikely, since she and the two agents with her appeared to be fine several hours after they were exposed. It's more apt to be an infectious agent of some kind, if it's anything."

"A...biological weapon?"

Valerie angled her body to look directly into Diane's face. "Possibly."

"Are you supposed to be telling me this?"

Valerie smiled wryly. "No."

"Right. Well." Diane held Valerie's gaze. "Who are you, Valerie?"

"I work for the government."

"Like Cam?"

"Something like that, yes."

"Is your name really Valerie?"

Valerie nodded.

"Did you come here to seduce me?"

"No. I came here to gather information. That's what I do." She leaned toward Diane, but did not touch her. "I didn't want to seduce you until after I'd been in the gallery for almost five minutes."

A smile played across Diane's mouth. "Oh, that was very smooth."

"And very true," Valerie said quietly. She put her glass down on the coffee table and took Diane's hand, ridiculously grateful when Diane did not pull away. "It wasn't my intention to lie to you. I didn't come here to use you."

"But you would have, if it would've gotten you what you needed, right?" Diane asked with an edge in her voice.

Valerie hesitated, then sighed. "Yes. If I'd had to, I would have."

"Do you also have sex with women to get what you want?" Diane stared at Valerie, demanding an answer, and saw the truth in her eyes. "My God. You do. Jesus."

Abruptly, Diane pulled her hand away and stood. She walked rapidly to the far side of the room and stood looking out through the glass doors, her arms wrapped tightly around her midsection. With her back to Valerie, she said, "How can they ask that of you?"

It wasn't the response that Valerie had expected. She stood, but was afraid to approach. She wanted to touch her, just enough so that she wouldn't feel the ache of loneliness that she'd carried with her since she'd left the apartment the morning before. "It's not so much different than expecting soldiers to put their lives on the line in battle. Everyone risks something."

Diane swirled around. "Would you have slept with me?"

"I wanted to," Valerie said immediately.

"But you didn't."

"Because I *couldn't,* not until you knew, and I couldn't tell you." Valerie lifted a hand and let it fall, at a loss to explain how desperately she had not wanted Diane to be Cam all over again. "I didn't want to be having this conversation after we'd made love, because I knew...I knew you'd never trust me again."

"What makes you think I'll ever trust me now?"

Valerie closed her eyes for a second, absorbing the blow, then shook her head sadly. "I don't. I just hope that you will."

The silence that followed was worse than any recrimination Diane could have flung at her. Helplessly, Valerie watched Diane hurriedly leave the room, knowing there was nothing she could say to undo the hurt that had been done. She sank back down onto the couch, picked up her wine, and slowly sipped, tasting nothing.

❖

"What do you think they've done with Fazio?" Blair asked. "Grau took him in the opposite direction when we got off the helicopter."

"He must be in another unit somewhere," Stark said, picking at the Band-Aid they had placed in the crux of her right elbow after drawing half a dozen vials of blood. "You know, he got the full brunt of whatever that stuff was."

Blair remembered him coughing and swearing and brushing the powder off his shirtfront. Her heart raced furiously, and for a second she felt dizzy. "It'll probably turn out to be nothing."

Stark forced a smile. "Yeah."

"Andrews has been gone half an hour." Blair paced. "How far you think they had to go for the cell phones?"

"Langley?"

Blair stopped, stared at Stark, and then started laughing. Langley—CIA Headquarters. "Probably. Like *we're* going to give away secrets from inside here." She stopped laughing as abruptly as she had begun and sank back down on the bed. "God, I wish I could talk to Cam."

A shrill noise filled the room followed by a familiar voice. "Hey."

"Cam?" Blair jumped up and rushed to the glass window as a light came on and illuminated the room on the other side. Cam placed her hand against the glass, and Blair pressed hers to the outline of her lover's palm.

"How are you doing, baby?" Cam asked.

Frantically, Blair looked for the intercom while Stark rose and moved to the far side of the room, giving them a modicum of privacy.

"There's a switch just to the left of the window," Cam instructed.

Blair found it, flipped it, and said, "What took you so long?"

"Heavy traffic."

Smiling, Blair rubbed her fingertips back and forth over the glass as if she were touching Cam's skin, and the illusion of contact made her feel better than she had in hours. "What are they telling you about when we'll get out of here?"

"They're not telling me anything yet, but as soon as I know, you will too. You feeling okay?" Cam tried to keep her tone light, but her stomach clenched as she studied her lover. Blair looked like she usually did when she was steaming. Her eyes were bright, her skin slightly flushed, and her movements quick and tight. Cam realized in that moment just how sexy Blair was when she was angry and understood, too, that it was that very fire that had instantly attracted her to the president's daughter. "Christ, you're beautiful."

Blair grinned. "Be careful, Commander. Stark is here, and you don't want to embarrass her." Blair leaned close to the glass to look into Cam's eyes. When she spoke, she lowered her voice. "Don't worry, sweetheart. I feel fine. We both do."

Cam pressed her hand so hard against the glass her palm was white. She wanted to touch her so badly she hurt inside.

"Cam?" Blair asked quietly, "What's wrong with your finger?"

"What?"

Blair nodded toward the glass. "Your little finger. It's three times its normal size. What happened?"

"Nothing."

"Turn your hand over."

"Blair—"

"Let me *see* it, Cameron."

Reluctantly, Cam complied, repeating hastily when she heard Blair gasp, "It's nothing. It's fine."

"What happened? Sweetheart?" Blair saw Cam's face take on that careful look of consideration she always got when she was about to soften the truth with diplomacy. "And *don't* try to snow me. That finger is broken, isn't it? What did you do?"

"Ah, hell. I lost my temper and jammed my hand up a little."

Blair's heart gave a lurch. Fear for her safety was the only thing in the world that could make Cam lose control. Instantly, Blair forgot her anger at being shuffled about the country with little explanation, forgot her loathing at her confinement, forgot even the dread that something serious might be wrong with her. All she could think of was Cam, worried and in pain. "Oh, sweetheart. It's going to be okay."

"I know." Cam worked up a smile. "I know that."

"You need to have that x-rayed."

"I will."

Blair tapped the glass sharply. "Now."

Cam grinned. "I love when you get tough."

"You'll love me when I get out of here and kick your ass if you don't get that taken care of too."

"Yeah, I will." When Cam spoke her voice was gravelly, and she had to look away to blink her vision clear. "So. Savard is here."

"Good. Paula could use a visit to lift her spirits." Blair narrowed her eyes. "What?"

"She's had it rough. You might want to prepare Stark for that."

"Okay." When Cam took her hand from the glass, Blair said quickly, "Wait."

Cam frowned. "What's wrong, baby?"

"When will you be back?"

"I'm not going anywhere," Cam said, her expression slightly incredulous. "I'll be right here in this room until you're ready to leave."

"Like you don't have anything else to do?" Blair laughed shakily and summoned a smile. "You go get x-rayed and then go back to work.

I'll be out of here in another day."

"Nice try, Blair." Cam ran her index finger down the glass as if she were stroking Blair's cheek. "I love you."

"Oh," Blair whispered, "I love you too."

CHAPTER NINETEEN

Stark pulled one of the straight-backed armless chairs over to the window and sat hunched forward, her hands curled over her knees, her eyes on the glass. Renée stared back at her from the other side. Stark struggled not to let her shock show in her face. It had only been a day since they'd seen one another, but Renée looked as if she hadn't slept or eaten in weeks. Her slender face looked gaunt, her normally brilliant turquoise-blue eyes were a dull gray, and her strong, lithe body appeared frail. Hoping her hand didn't tremble and betray her worry, Stark reached out to flick the switch on the intercom.

"Hi, honey."

Savard straightened her shoulders and smiled more brightly. "Hi, sweetie. You doing okay in there?"

"It's pretty boring, and nobody's telling us much of anything." Stark shrugged. "The usual bureaucratic story. I feel fine. So does Blair. What do you hear?"

Savard shook her head. "Nothing yet. The commander is talking with the medical team right now. I think she was on the phone to the chief of staff too, just a few minutes ago. She won't let them stonewall us. And she won't let them keep you and Blair in the dark."

"Thank God she's here." Stark dropped her gaze, unwilling to inflict her misery on her lover. But she couldn't help thinking that she had fucked up her first assignment pretty badly, and now the commander had to bail her out.

"Hey! Stop blaming yourself. There's absolutely no way you could've known."

Stark's head snapped up. "Less than a week ago there was an attempt on her life. I should've checked her apartment a lot more closely before I let her go in there."

"Paula, sweetie, the commander and I were in that building just a few nights ago. *We* didn't see anything either."

"I know. You're right," Stark said unconvincingly. "So how are you doing? You look tired."

"Nah, I'm fine. Too much time at the computer." Savard looked over her shoulder, ensuring that she was still alone. "Felicia and I have been dogging the computers 24/7 trying to ID the members of the assault team. So far, nothing. Dental records, fingerprints, photo databases. Zip."

"That doesn't make sense. Those guys were trained."

"We *know*," Savard said, sounding frustrated. "But we still can't put names to them. So now we're doing deep background on Foster. It's slow going, because his records were thoroughly buried when he entered the Academy."

"That's routine with the Secret Service so no one can access our personal data and compromise us with it."

"Yeah, the same for us. But it makes our job a lot tougher now." Savard leaned back and pushed both hands through her hair. "But Felicia will sort it all out, if anyone can."

"Any word on what the stuff was in the Aerie?"

"Not yet." Savard's eyes filled with tears, and she scrubbed a hand angrily across her face. "Sorry. I'm just...I just love you. You can't get sick, okay?"

"Don't worry, honey. Nothing's going to happen to me." Stark clenched her hands out of sight, wishing desperately that there were something she could do to ease her lover's pain. It tore at her to see Renée so close to the edge and to be so powerless to help her. "Will you do something for me?"

"Anything." Savard sat forward, her eyes intent. "Anything."

"Will you try to get some sleep?"

Savard considered lying, but she could tell by the worry in Stark's eyes that it was too late for that. "I'll try. It's been...hard."

"You have to take care of yourself. I need you."

"Oh, that's blackmail."

Stark nodded solemnly. "Maybe. But it's true."

Savard indicated the far corner of the room. "There are a couple of beds in here, I guess for the staff when they're monitoring someone around the clock. I'm going to go lie down right now, okay?"

"Promise?"

"I promise."

"I'll be here when you wake up." Stark smiled and tried to sound optimistic.

"Promise?" Savard asked shakily.

"Always."

❖

"How long?" Cam asked as Captain Andrews buddy-taped her small finger to her ring finger, creating a functional splint. She sat on an examining table in a small anteroom adjacent to the monitoring area that looked into Blair's room while the doctor tended to her injured finger. She'd gotten the x-ray only because she knew Blair would ask her, and she couldn't bear to upset her now.

"Fortunately, it's a hairline fracture with no displacement. Ten days of immobilization will probably do it, if you're careful—"

"No, not me. Blair. How long until you're certain she's out of danger?"

Captain Andrews straightened with a sigh and met Cam's probing gaze. "I'm working under Delta level restrictions here, Agent Roberts."

"Understood."

"Define your relationship with Ms. Powell."

Cam's gaze narrowed as she studied the other woman. Not surprisingly, she could read little in her expression. Uncertain exactly where the doctor might be headed, Cam decided that a frontal assault was best. "I'm her lover."

"*And* her acting security chief?"

"That's right." Technically, Hara was next in line with Stark temporarily out of commission, but word had come from the White House via Lucinda that Cam was to "oversee" operations. Not quite a reinstatement, but the closest thing to it.

"Well," Captain Andrews said, crossing her arms over her chest. "The second might not qualify you as being in a need-to-know position, but the first certainly does."

Cam waited, a knot of apprehension tightening in the center of her chest. She gripped the table on either side of her body and squeezed, oblivious to the pain, preparing herself for the blow she feared was coming.

"Be careful with that hand, Agent Roberts, or you'll displace the fracture enough that I'll have to put you in a cast."

"Just tell me."

"The growth of microbial cultures can't be hurried, I'm afraid. It will be a minimum of twelve hours, and more likely twenty-four, before we identify the organism with absolute certainty."

Cam stopped breathing. "You know for certain there was an organism?"

The doctor nodded. "Yes, the gram stains demonstrated that. Basically, that's a quick and dirty way to examine a specimen for living organisms. It doesn't tell us what the bacteria is, only the general class." She hesitated as if trying to judge Cam's reaction. "What we found is a gram-positive, spore-forming bacillus consistent with anthrax. Or smallpox."

"Jesus," Cam whispered, leaning back against the examination table as her legs suddenly went weak. "*Smallpox*? I thought that had been eradicated decades ago."

Captain Andrews dragged over a tall stool and edged a hip up onto it. "That's true, as far as it goes. Frozen specimens, however, were stockpiled in two places—the CDC in Atlanta and the Maximum Containment Laboratory in Siberia."

"Christ, I bet *that* place was secure."

"Unfortunately, no. After the fall of the Soviet Union in 1991, a considerable portion of their stores disappeared. We suspect that they made their way to the Middle East and Asia."

"And you can't tell if this is anthrax or smallpox?"

Andrews lifted a shoulder and sighed. "We're running diagnostic immunoassays right now, which will hopefully give us a presumptive diagnosis while we await the definitive culture results."

"What are we talking about here, in terms of casualties?" Cam's voice was steady, but inside, every cell trembled.

"Look, Agent Roberts—"

"It's Cam."

The doctor nodded. "Ronnie. Look, Cam. We're starting treatment right now. In fact, they've all probably gotten their first dose of antibiotics. Fortunately, with treatment, the cure rate is excellent, *assuming* they're infected."

"Numbers, Ronnie."

"Once symptoms appear, even *with* treatment, the mortality rate is high. Seventy to ninety percent if it's anthrax. With smallpox?" She shook her head. "Closer to a hundred percent."

Cam paled and pushed herself off the table. "I want to see her *now*."

"Wait a minute, Cam. We don't *know* what they were exposed to yet."

Cam turned back. "But you'll know in a few hours, right?"

"We'll have the immunoassay results in just about four hours, yes, but they'll just be prelim—"

"Then I'll see her at 2100 hours," Cam said as she set her watch.

❖

"Hi, Dad," Blair said, holding the cell phone in her right hand as she sat propped up in bed in her surgical scrubs with an intravenous line taped to her left arm. Stark sat in a similar position across from her on the opposite bed.

"Hi, honey. I'm sorry that I haven't talked to you before this. Colonel Grau has been in constant contact, but he seemed to feel it was necessary to complete their preliminary evaluation before—"

"Dad, Dad. Relax. I'm okay." Blair grimaced. *As okay as I can be considering that I'm locked up tighter than Alcatraz and people are poking and prodding me nonstop.*

"I've been assured that you are, or I'd be there right now."

"Don't do that," Blair said instantly. "I don't think there's anything wrong with me, but you certainly can't come here and risk catching something. Besides, you're—"

"I'm your *father*, and if there's the slightest possibility that you're ill, I'll be there."

Blair could hear protesting voices in the background, one of which she was certain belonged to Lucinda. She would not want to be her father's chief of staff at this moment. "Look, Dad, I know the situation.

And so do you. Even if there weren't any risk, the last thing we need is the media around here. So send me a card, but no visits. Come to think of it, no flowers either."

Her father laughed weakly. "You're sure you're okay?"

"I want out of here. Then I'll be fine."

"Where's Cam?"

"She's here. I can't get her to leave."

"Good."

"Dad," Blair said gently, "they're taking good care of me. And Cam won't let anything happen to me."

"I certainly got lucky when you found her."

Blair smiled. "Yeah, me too."

After she said her goodbyes and hung up, she turned on her side and regarded Stark mournfully. "This sucks."

"Yeah. It does."

"You doing okay?"

Stark shrugged. "I don't feel sick." She regarded Blair anxiously. "But Renée looks terrible. Something's really wrong."

"I imagine it's been pretty horrible for her, Paula," Blair said quietly. "But I'm sure that you being in her life is helping her get through it."

Stark closed her hands into tight fists and closed her eyes. "I'm not doing anything for anyone. You ended up in here, and Renée's out there, alone, worrying about me. And I'm no good to anybody."

Blair pushed back the sheets and swung her legs over the side of the bed until she was sitting upright, leaning forward toward Stark. "What the hell is the matter with you? You don't usually sit around feeling sorry for yourself."

"I'm scared." Stark turned eyes dark with misery to Blair. "I'm scared for her, and I don't know what to do."

"Oh, honey, just love her."

"You really think that's enough?"

Blair smiled. "I know it is."

Both women turned at the sound of the door opening, and then Blair shot to her feet. "You can't be in here. Turn around right now and get your ass out of here."

"Hi, baby," Cam said as she hooked an arm around the back of a chair and swung it off the floor. She dropped it next to the bed and sat down a foot from Blair. In a very reasonable voice, she said, "You'll notice, Ms. Powell, that I'm wearing a mask and a cover gown."

"I don't care if you're wearing Kevlar. I don't want you in here." Blair pushed as far away from Cam as she could get. In a voice thin with fear, she said, "Please. Please leave."

"Blair," Cam said gently, making no move to touch her, although she ached to pull her into her arms. It had been only hours that they'd been apart, but the fear had unbalanced her. If she could only hold her—just feeling the heat of her body and the play of those supple muscles beneath smooth skin would set her world right again. She forced a lightness into her voice. "It's okay that I'm here. The doctors cleared it."

"The doctors don't know everything. Hell, they don't *anything*. If we have something, I don't want you getting sick."

Stark spoke up. "She's right, Commander. I'd advise you to leave."

Cam looked from one to the other and stretched her legs out in front of her, crossing her feet at the ankles. "Would you two like to be briefed, or would you rather try to throw me out?"

"You can stay," Blair said after a minute, "but no touching."

"Oh, jeez," Stark muttered.

"So brief us, Commander," Blair said, sitting cross-legged on the bed.

"Captain Andrews will be here in a few minutes to give you all the correct medical terminology. She's on the line with the president right now," Cam said as she looked into Blair's eyes.

"But you know something, don't you?" Blair asked.

Cam never hesitated, because lying was not something she was ever going to do with Blair. "Yes. It seems that the preliminary tests are highly suggestive of anthrax."

Blair's lips tightened.

Beside them, Stark took in an audible breath and then asked, "Does Renée know?"

"Not yet. She's asleep, and I thought it would be better not to wake her. If you want me to get her—"

"No!" Stark said immediately. "But if you'd tell her…" Her voice cracked and she looked down at her hands, struggling to push back her fears.

"Wait, you two." Cam continued in a steady voice, "There's plenty of good news. All three of you have begun treatment before any sign of symptoms, which means that you're very likely not going to get sick." She nodded toward the gauze taped to Blair's upper arm. "They vaccinated you too, didn't they?"

"Yes." Blair leaned forward, allowing her fingertips to brush Cam's sleeve. It was so good to have her close again, and she wanted so badly to touch her. She forced herself to stop before their skin made contact. She had to be sure that Cam was not in danger. "What's the *bad* news?"

"Unfortunately," Cam said with the first hint of frustration, "the incubation period is extremely long, especially for the inhalational form of the disease."

"*How* long?" Blair and Stark said in unison.

Before Blair could protest, Cam slid her hand on top of Blair's. Instantly, their fingers intertwined. "Sixty days after exposure."

Blair stiffened. "They're not going to keep us here—"

"No," Cam assured her quickly. "In fact, Captain Andrews said if you're not showing any signs of illness—which you *won't* be—by the time the cultures come back, you'll all be released on medication."

"What about other people?" Stark asked, thinking of how ill Renée seemed already. "Are we—you know—contagious?"

Cam shook her head. "Not at all. Person-to-person spread of the disease does not occur."

"So what's the bottom line here, Commander?" Blair asked, pulling Cam's hand into her lap and cradling it against her body. That was all the contact she was going to allow herself until she knew for certain that Cam was safe, but the firm grip of Cam's fingers around hers stilled the tremulousness in the pit of her stomach that had been there since the instant she'd seen the white substance burst into the air.

"You need to stay here for a few more days to be certain that the antibiotics and other drugs are working."

Blair regarded Stark with a vehement shake of her head. "I'm not playing pinochle with *her* as my partner."

Cam laughed. The last time Blair had been sequestered, they'd passed the hours playing pinochle. Blair had declared Stark the worst player she'd ever seen. "You don't have to worry about that. The only partner you're ever going to have, Ms. Powell, is me."

CHAPTER TWENTY

Sunday, September 16

Dim light filtered through the window in the door from the hallway into the room where Cam and Savard lay side by side on narrow cots. It had been quiet since the last time a technician had checked on Blair and Stark an hour and a half ago. Cam stared at the ceiling, listening to Savard shift restlessly in her sleep. Every so often she heard a quiet moan. When the moans grew louder and culminated in a sharp cry, she rolled onto her side and reached across the space between them. With a hand on Savard's shoulder, she said gently, "Hey, Renée."

Savard jerked upright, trembling as she fought to orient herself in the near dark.

"Sorry," Cam said, keeping her hand on the unsteady woman's arm. "You sounded like you were having a bad dream."

"Yeah," Savard said shakily. She had promised Paula she'd try to sleep, although she hadn't expected to. She'd stripped down to her camisole and panties after returning from her all-too-brief visit with Stark earlier, and looking down, she realized that she'd kicked the covers off in her sleep. With a small laugh, she reached for the sheet and pulled it up to her waist. "I didn't mean to wake you."

"You didn't." Cam dropped her hand and rolled onto her back again. "Couldn't sleep."

"I'm surprised I did."

"Having a tough time with that?"

Savard hesitated, but there in the dark, with a woman she trusted with her life, she had to believe she was safe. "Can't get it out of my head."

"Understandable."

"Working helps, but only for so long." Savard lay back down, gripping the sheet tightly in both fists. "And now, with Paula in here…" She heard her voice waver and break, but it seemed as if she were listening to someone else. The words kept coming, even though she hadn't intended them to escape. "I keep seeing things. Hearing things."

"When you're awake?"

Savard nodded, her throat constricting around the scream that had threatened to erupt since the first moment she'd realized what the plume of smoke high up in the sky meant.

"Renée?"

"Yes," Savard whispered. "And when I close my eyes."

"How much downtime have you had this week?"

"As much as anyone else," Savard said harshly.

"No one's been getting enough." Cam flashed on how she'd felt that morning when she hadn't known if Blair was hurt, or worse. The terrible fear. The aching helplessness. The soul-sapping powerlessness. She tried to imagine magnifying that a thousandfold or more and couldn't. "Both you and Stark need some downtime after she's released."

"No!" Savard sat up, the sheet falling away unnoticed. "There's work—"

"You're right. There is. A lot of it. Weeks of it, probably. And I need you both." Cam sat up and swung her legs over the bed. She'd removed her shirt and trousers and wore a thin sleeveless silk T-shirt and briefs. "You won't do me any good until you get your feet back under you. Where is your family?"

"Florida."

"Take Paula there."

"She won't go. Not now."

Cam laughed. "She'll go. *And* you need to see someone—a professional—to talk all of this over with."

"You know what will happen if wind of that gets into my jacket," Savard said bitterly. "My security clearance will disappear, and I'll end up holding down a desk in the middle of Kansas."

"Nothing is going into your file because no one's going to know about this except you and me. But I want it done, Renée. And you can consider that an order."

"A week. But I'll see someone."

Cam laughed again, impressed with Savard's toughness. "We'll start there."

❖

"Have you eaten anything tonight?" Diane asked from the archway that separated the living room from the hall and her bedroom at the far end. Valerie stood at the open door to the balcony with her back to the room, a half-empty wineglass in her hand. It was after midnight, as Diane had discovered much to her surprise when she awoke from an unintended slumber. She'd showered hastily and gone in search of Valerie, wondering if she would even still be there and overtaken by a wave of sadness at the thought that she might not be.

A single lamp burned in the far corner of the room, and a nearly empty bottle of wine stood on the coffee table next to her own glass from earlier that day. "Valerie?"

Valerie turned with a weary smile. "No."

"What have you been doing?"

"Thinking, mostly." She finished her wine and crossed to the coffee table where she carefully deposited the empty glass. Diane, she noticed, had changed into a loose, scoop-necked blouse and wide-leg casual slacks. She was barefoot. And she was so beautiful Valerie's throat ached to look at her. She'd thought of her for hours—how she'd looked the first moment she'd seen her in the gallery, what they'd shared that week as they had mourned with the rest of the country, how Diane's strength and compassion had touched the place inside that she usually kept guarded against everyone. "Did you sleep?"

"I did. I can't imagine how."

"Sooner or later the stress catches up to you."

"Does it work that way with you? Does anything ever catch up to you?"

"Sometimes," Valerie said softly.

"What things?"

Valerie shook her head. "Things I chose twenty years ago when I said *yes* to a man who told me I had something special to offer my country."

Diane walked slowly forward, her eyes on Valerie's. "What things, Valerie?"

Valerie was unable to look away from Diane's face. Her mouth was so tender, her eyes so bruised. *God. I've hurt her.* "I'm so sorry."

Diane made an impatient gesture. "What things can't you get away from?"

"Loneliness," Valerie said softly.

"What do you do then?"

Valerie lifted both hands and let them fall, her chest constricting around the sadness and desire that warred within her. She stepped back, knowing that she would keep on hurting her, as she had hurt every woman in her life. She couldn't bear to have this woman's pain on her conscience. "I wait for it to pass. Go back to bed, Diane."

"Did making love with Cam make it better?"

"Don't. Please." Valerie took another step, and her legs bumped into the coffee table. Diane was so close to her now, within arm's distance, and she struggled not to run. She smelled something sweet and tangy, a lotion that Diane had put on after her shower. She imagined how smooth her skin would feel, how soft her kisses. She closed her eyes. "*Please.*"

"Answer me. You owe me that much."

"It wasn't like that," Valerie said desperately.

"Oh, I know you were working," Diane said with just a trace of anger, "but being with her or…others…couldn't have left much room for feeling alone."

Valerie was tired. She was tired of holding herself back, tired of burying her needs so deeply that no one would ever have a hold on her. She'd let her guard down with Cam, and as hard as it had been, she was glad. Glad that she could still feel something for someone. And now, Diane was hammering once again at her defenses, and she was so tired of struggling to keep everyone out. She spoke without thinking. "There's nothing quite as lonely as making love to women who never touch you."

Diane gave a small start. "Are you saying…never?"

"It doesn't matter." Valerie shrugged impatiently. "That's the way I wanted it—the way it has to be."

"It does matter." Diane reached out, her breasts brushing Valerie's, and lightly cupped Valerie's face between her palms. She smoothed both thumbs over Valerie's mouth. "You're trembling. I can feel you hurting."

"No, you're wrong." Valerie tried to pull her head away, but Diane held her firm. "I shouldn't have come here. I'm sorry."

"Why did you?" Diane leaned closer and followed with her lips the path her thumbs had traversed. Valerie moaned quietly as Diane slid her hands to the back of Valerie's neck, deepening the kiss with a gentle exploration of lips and tongue. Then she eased away and murmured against Valerie's mouth. "Why?"

"Because," Valerie said, her voice choked, "when I'm with you, I don't feel alone." She closed her eyes and lowered her forehead to Diane's shoulder as she wrapped both arms around her waist, giving in to the need to hold and be held. Just one minute. Just one minute to touch and be touched. She breathed in Diane's scent and rubbed her cheek lightly against the side of Diane's neck, finding her skin even softer than she had imagined. She tightened her hold and felt the supple strength contained within the lithe form. Marveling at the firm fullness of Diane's breasts, she moaned quietly as her own nipples tightened from the press of flesh on flesh. A tremor started in her legs and climbed into the core of her, and she knew she was falling. Falling from darkness into light, and she pushed away, afraid. "Diane. Go to bed."

Diane laughed shakily and cleaved more tightly to her. "One kiss. One simple kiss. One kiss, and I know I'll starve if I don't have you." She pressed a trembling hand to her heart. "In here, where I hunger."

"Oh God," Valerie whispered, taking Diane's mouth in one fierce motion. She was aware of Diane pulling her blouse from her slacks and felt hot fingers scale her spine. She circled her tongue inside Diane's mouth and groaned as Diane swept her palms around her body to lightly brush over her breasts and then whisper away. "Be sure. Please, be sure."

"I'm sure," Diane muttered, her lips moving along Valerie's throat, "that I'm not going to make love to you standing up out here." With effort, she stepped back and caught Valerie's hands in hers. "Come with me."

"Diane, I…"

"Shh." Diane tugged her toward the hallway. "Later. Later you can tell me everything. Now there's something I want to tell you."

Valerie followed, refusing to think beyond the moment, wanting these few minutes of forgiveness and forgetting. When they arrived by the side of Diane's bed and Valerie reached for the hem of Diane's blouse, Diane murmured *no* and brushed Valerie's hands away.

"I have this need," Diane whispered, her mouth close to Valerie's ear as she deftly unbuttoned the waistband of her slacks, "to touch you. Indulge me."

"Oh yes." Valerie swayed as a languorous heaviness settled in her stomach, and her limbs softened with the slow burn of desire. Lightly, she held Diane's hips, needing the contact as much as to steady herself. Diane's lips shivered over the rim of her ear, and sharp pinpoints of pleasure pricked her consciousness as teeth tugged at her earlobe. She shivered and her nipples ached as they rubbed against the inside of the silk cups that still contained them.

"Lift your arms, my beautiful one," Diane said, her voice husky and deep. Delicately, she slid Valerie's blouse and bra off in one motion, leaving her bare from the waist up. She pressed her thighs and lower body against Valerie's, her loins full and pulsing with arousal. She was determined to go slowly, but her body cried out for contact. She rolled her pelvis into the vee between Valerie's legs, tormenting them both. "Oh God, you feel so good."

With trembling hands, Diane caught the bottom of her own blouse and stripped it from her skin, dropping it mindlessly somewhere behind her. As her teeth closed on Valerie's lower lip, she tightened her arms around the slender body and rubbed her breasts over Valerie's. Their tight nipples chafed, and the beating between her thighs quickened, her clitoris tensing until she moaned.

Valerie edged a hand between them and spread her fingers over Diane's breast, squeezing gently. "I want you so much…so much."

Diane arched into the pleasure even as she pushed away. "Don't. I'm already far too excited."

"Then let me." Valerie covered Diane's other breast and worked her thumbs over her nipples, flicking as she massaged the tense engorged tissue. "Let me give you what you need. I want to."

"No. No." Diane pressed her hands over Valerie's, crushing her breasts beneath their joined fingers, stilling the torturous touch. She drew a breath and then another until her head began to clear. Then she pulled Valerie's hands from her body and jerked her toward the bed, turning them in motion so that Valerie ended up on her back with Diane above her, straddling her body. Her lips curved in a victorious smile, and she stretched full-length upon her, pressing one thigh firmly between Valerie's as she delved into her mouth. Between moans and kisses she worked her fingers between their bodies and finished unzipping Valerie's slacks and then her own. She rolled away only enough to push her clothing down and then to help Valerie shed the rest of hers. As they shifted and struggled and clung to one another, their mouths still joined, desperate not to lose contact, their bruising kisses grew more frantic and their hands more demanding.

"Please," Valerie begged, pressing her hips up to meet each of Diane's ever-more-rapid downward thrusts, "let me touch you. Let me make you come."

"No. You first." Diane's lids were nearly closed, her pupils wide and dark, her breath a rasping groan. She felt Valerie's passion slick her skin, but it was her own control that threatened to break. She braced her body on trembling arms and rocked herself to the brink of orgasm against Valerie's thigh, and still Valerie held back. She could feel her body shuddering beneath her, sense her hands trembling over her back like the frantic wings of a wounded bird, and *still* she held back. "Let go, darling. Let go."

"I can't," Valerie gasped. "Oh God, I can't."

"Oh yes," Diane said fiercely, "you can." And then she pushed herself down on the bed until she was between Valerie's thighs, and in the same motion took her into her mouth with one long slide of lips and tongue and gently grazing teeth. Valerie stiffened, her body rising off the bed as she choked back a scream.

Instantly, Diane gentled her caresses into swift butterfly kisses and short light strokes with the tip of her tongue until Valerie caught her breath and relaxed into the pleasure. Diane stretched both arms upward, finding Valerie's nipples and squeezing to the rhythm of her mouth, drawing the tense clitoris ever closer to the brink.

Valerie covered Diane's hands with hers, joining Diane's fingers on her nipples, guiding her in the twisting, tugging motion that would ignite the orgasm that lingered still in the shadows of her mind. "I'm so closesoclose…suck me harder."

With tender precision, Diane bit down on the base of Valerie's clitoris, and Valerie came instantly. Her shoulders wrenched off the bed as she cried out at the shock, then fell back shivering and twisting as the pleasure ripped through her. She was still coming when Diane pulled herself up and crushed her lips to Valerie's neck, moaning and shuddering, her body on fire.

"Oh, I'm going to come," Diane moaned, her fingers gripping, convulsing on Valerie's shoulders.

"Come in my mouth," Valerie gasped, reaching blindly for Diane's hips, urging her upward.

"Next…time, ohGod I'm coming." Diane buried her face in Valerie's neck and soared.

Valerie tightened her arms around the trembling woman, incapable of recalling a single instance when she had ever felt so satisfied. When Diane quieted and lay breathing softly, her muscles loose and her skin misted with a fine sheen of perspiration, Valerie stroked her hair, the angle of her jaw, her neck, her back, unable to fill her hands with enough of her and desperate to know all of her.

"Mmm, you're wonderful," Diane murmured contentedly.

Valerie laughed shakily. "Oh, my dear, I think that should be my line."

Diane raised her head, her eyes still heavy with desire, and kissed Valerie softly. "I've never wanted to make a woman come quite as much as I did with you just now. I'm feeling positively pleased with myself."

"As well you should be." Valerie stroked Diane's face. "I don't usually…I'm not usually like that with anyone."

Diane was silent for a long time. Then she turned her head and kissed Valerie's palm. "Good."

"Diane, what I do…It's not something I can change easily."

"Do you want to?"

"I want…I want this again, with you. And more. Other things. With you."

"Good. So do I. That's where we'll start." Diane rested her head on Valerie's shoulder and closed her eyes. "We'll work on figuring out the rest of it later."

Diane must have dozed, because she opened her eyes to find herself on her back and the most exquisite sensation she could ever recall building between her thighs. Murmuring her pleasure, she raised her head and smiled down at Valerie. "Whatever you're doing, it's wonderful."

"Remember what I said earlier?" Valerie asked.

Come in my mouth.

"Mmm." Diane shifted restlessly, full and aching. She looked into Valerie's eyes, her want answering Valerie's desire. *Oh please yes.*

"It's next time now."

"Oh yes," Diane sighed as she leaned back and closed her eyes. "It is."

CHAPTER TWENTY-ONE

Diane knocked on the bathroom door, opened it, and handed Valerie a burnished gold silk blouse, white silk panties, and a new pair of stockings. "I think these should fit you."

"Thanks." Valerie, fresh from the shower, stood in front of the vanity wrapped in a towel. Her shoulder-length blond hair was damp, her ivory skin flushed and moist with steam.

There was a great deal more of her uncovered than not, and Diane was struck with an instant rush of arousal. And there was no time. Even knowing that, it took every ounce of willpower she possessed not to tug the towel to the floor and fill her hands with Valerie's breasts. She was already addicted to the way Valerie sounded when she was excited and hungered feverishly to hear her climax again. To touch her that deeply, to claim her so completely. She'd *never* wanted to possess a woman the way she wanted her. "I'm afraid my bra won't fit you," she said in as light a tone as she could manage through a throat tight with desire.

"I'll manage for a few hours." Valerie smiled gently as she set the borrowed clothing on the vanity. The suit she had worn the day before hung from a nearby towel bar. She rested her hip against the counter and sipped the coffee Diane had left for her while she was in the shower. "I appreciate you getting my things from the hotel. I've barely got time to grab a cab to the airport and make the flight."

"Do they do this all the time? Call you and tell you to be somewhere yesterday?"

"I don't usually move around this much. The last few months have been hectic, and then after what happened this week..." Valerie shrugged ruefully. Her identity had very nearly been exposed when the escort service she'd employed as a cover in DC had been the object of a clandestine investigation. She'd expected to remain on the West Coast until a new identity could be established, but she'd been ordered to Manhattan almost immediately for the gallery opening. "Most of the time, we aren't given explanations. I'm given a job to do, and that's what I do."

"I know you can't tell me those things, and I'm not going to ask." Diane grasped the free edge of the towel and pulled slowly until it fell away, watching Valerie's pupils flicker and dance. Surprise and desire. Warning and welcome.

"Diane," Valerie murmured, setting the coffee cup down blindly.

Diane pressed into her quickly, jerking open the tie on her own robe so that their bodies collided, skin to skin. "Just tell me that you're coming back." She worked her fingers into the tangled curls at Valerie's neck and bruised her lips over Valerie's mouth. "Tell me it wasn't just one night."

"One night? Oh no." Valerie angled her hips and spun Diane to the counter, caressing her breasts as she rocked against her. "No. So much more than that."

"God, I want you." Diane arched into Valerie's hands as she circled her tongue over Valerie's lips, tasting her heat. "I want to believe you."

"Believe me." Valerie lowered her head to pull a swollen nipple into her mouth. She licked and bit, then pressed her cheek over Diane's thundering heart. "Oh God, I have to go. I can't do this. I'm so sorry."

Gasping, Diane dragged Valerie's mouth away from her flesh. "I want you to go." At the devastation that flashed across Valerie's face, she shook her head vehemently. "No, darling. Just for now." She laughed weakly. "I can't imagine what they might do to you if you don't show up wherever it is you're going."

Valerie traced the curve of Diane's lower lip with her fingertips. "It's not quite as bad as you think. But I *do* have to go."

"All right." Diane kissed her softly and pushed her carefully away. "I'll be expecting you."

❖

Wednesday, September 19

Stark shifted her shoulders and eased Savard's head onto her chest.

"Sorry," Savard mumbled. "Fell asleep."

When Savard started to move away, Stark tightened her arm around her. "No. Go back to sleep." Even though it seemed that her lover's sleep was far from restful, if the small twitches and moans that accompanied it were any indication, Stark figured if the commander had ordered them *both* to take time off, it was because she thought it was necessary. And she had to agree that the haunted expression in Renée's eyes and the dark circles beneath them warranted attention.

"Where are we?" Savard asked, closing her eyes and tucking her head beneath Stark's chin. She curled an arm around her waist as well, wanting her as close as possible. The nightmare separation in the hospital had nearly snapped the last strands of her control.

"About an hour from the Jacksonville airport." Stark tilted her cheek against the top of Savard's head.

"You have all your medicine, right?"

"Yep. All three vials," Stark assured her yet again. Savard had fretted about her ever since she'd left the hospital early that morning. Even though Stark was beyond the mandatory observation period, Savard remained agitated and hypervigilant, as if she was afraid Stark would suddenly fall ill—or worse—if she let her guard down for a moment. "I'm not going to get sick, honey."

"I know that," Savard said quickly. "I know."

"You really think it's okay to spring me on your family?"

Eyes closed, comforted by Stark's steady heartbeat, Savard smiled and nodded drowsily. "They're going to love you, because they're going to be able to tell that I do."

"Is it okay if they can tell that I love you too?" Stark kissed the top of Savard's head. "Cause I sorta can't look at you without it showing."

Savard squeezed her eyes shut around sudden tears. *Don't leave me. Please, I need you so much.*

"Honey?" Stark rubbed her hand up and down Savard's back. When she got no response, she whispered, "It's okay. You just sleep."

Savard feigned sleep as she immersed herself in the scent and sense of her lover's body. Deep inside, a small corner of the void that had threatened to consume her from the inside out slowly filled with the certainty of love. Long moments later, as the pain and terror of her waking dreams relinquished a fraction of its paralyzing hold on her, she finally slept.

❖

"Tanner's here already," Blair said excitedly, leaning across Cam to look out the side window of the Suburban.

Cam rubbed her hand along the center of Blair's spine, not yet believing that they were actually able to touch. They'd left the hospital and flown directly into Boston, where Felicia and Valerie awaited them with a Suburban borrowed from the local FBI field office. Hara was behind the wheel now with Wozinski riding shotgun. Felicia and Valerie sat across from them. Cam ducked her head to follow Blair's line of sight and brushed her lips over the rim of Blair's ear in passing.

"Careful," Blair murmured, squeezing Cam's leg just above her knee. "We have company."

"Missed you," Cam whispered, but she dutifully postponed the next kiss until they were alone. Even as part of her mind was absorbed with the feel of Blair against her body and the hint of honey that lingered from her shampoo, she scanned the large homes set well back from the narrow road on expansive, wooded lots, assessing the security of their new base of operations. "She chose well."

"Last house on a cul-de-sac," Blair noted. "Situated on the high ground with the ocean behind. Limits the approach points and gives us a three hundred and sixty degree view."

"Very good. You'd make an excellent agent, Ms. Powell." When Blair snorted, Cam laughed and took her hand. "And according to the layout Tanner faxed us, the guesthouse where Felicia and Valerie will be staying is between the main house and the beach. We can secure the perimeter with our ordinary complement of agents."

"I'm so glad you approve, Commander." Blair quickly kissed Cam's cheek and jumped from the car almost before the Suburban had come to a halt.

Cam swore at the security breach and vaulted after her with Felicia and Valerie close behind. By the time they caught up to their charge and stationed themselves in a triangle with her in the middle, Blair had her arms wrapped around a black-haired, tightly muscled woman in a white T-shirt and khakis and was spinning her in a mad circle. Cam met Tanner Whitley's laughing dark eyes when Blair finally set her down. "Place looks good, Tanner."

Tanner, the heir to a corporate dynasty and the owner of Whitley Point, slung an arm around Blair's shoulder and grinned. "I had a feeling this would be the kind of place you needed. All the other houses on this lane are vacation homes, and this time of year they're unoccupied. You should have this corner of the island to yourselves."

"I appreciate it," Cam replied. Were it not for the gold wedding band on Tanner's left hand, her sensuous good looks and confident manner would have suggested she was still the playgirl she had long been reputed to be. Cam, however, had met her partner, Navy Captain Adrienne Pierce, and knew otherwise. While they talked, the other agents parked the vehicle beneath the carport on the side of the two-story cedar beach house and moved off into the scrub to survey the surrounding dunes.

"I can have my team set up with yours, if you'd like," Tanner said, referring to the private security force she employed. The men and women on her personal detail had been with her company for many years, and each had passed a rigorous background check.

"I might take you up on that. For now, though, why don't you have them swing through the general area four or five times a day and report anything that appears unusual to me."

"Will do."

Blair squeezed Tanner's waist affectionately. "Thanks for doing this. I didn't expect to be gate-crashing again so soon." Barely a week before, she had fled the chaos in Manhattan to Whitley Point and the safety of her old school friend's private island. They had stayed less than twenty-four hours before a contingent of Marines had arrived by helicopter to transport her directly to the White House.

"It's no problem," Tanner said seriously. "I'm always glad to see you. And Adrienne will be happy to have a chance to talk to you this time too." Her angular features settled into a frown. "*If* things ease up at the base any time soon. They're still on high alert status. She hasn't been home much."

"This time we'll be staying for a while," Blair said with a sad smile. She was back, and—this time—homeless. Tanner had always been the kind of friend who never asked questions. She and Diane had been Blair's closest confidantes in prep school and had offered her their unconditional support ever since. When she had called Tanner and told her what she needed in terms of a place to stay, Tanner had simply said she'd take care of it. And she had. "You don't know how much this means to me."

"Hey. I'll take any excuse to get you out here." Tanner gave Blair's cheek a light kiss. "Come on. Let me show you around inside."

❖

Cam watched the two women climb the stairs, arm in arm, and disappear inside after Tanner unlocked the door. Valerie joined her at the foot of the flagstone path that led to the house while Felicia left to unload gear from the Suburban.

"It looks like a good location," Valerie noted.

"I agree."

"Blair looks well. A little thin, perhaps."

"So far all the tests have been normal." Cam sighed. "Fazio has cutaneous lesions, though."

"Yes, I know." Valerie had read the update just that morning in the Central Intelligence Report—a summary of all pertinent intelligence data gathered by the CIA, FBI, NSA, and other agencies in the previous twenty-four hours. Of course, she had no way to determine just what data each organization volunteered—or held back—but any intel was better than nothing. "He had the most exposure, correct?"

"Yeah, and razor burns on his face, which was probably the route of infection. Captain Andrews says he'll probably make a full recovery. We got lucky."

"But you're still worried about Blair."

Cam said nothing.

"She's a very capable woman, Cameron. From what I hear, before you came along, she made eluding her security forces an art form. And nothing has ever happened to her."

"Someone almost gunned her down last week," Cam said, her eyes fixed on the door through which Blair had disappeared.

"But they didn't, and every other attempt has failed as well. You have a very good team here, and we're not going to let anything happen to her."

Cam looked away from the house and into Valerie's eyes. "Is that why you're here? To help protect Blair?"

Valerie smiled ruefully. "No, but since I *am* here, I intend to."

"Did you come straight up from Virginia?"

"Yes, why?" Valerie asked warily.

"I was wondering if you stopped in Manhattan."

"I'm afraid my schedule didn't leave room for side trips. And if it had, that would be personal." Valerie's voice held a distinct warning.

"Sorry, that was out of line." Cam puffed out a breath. "Everyone's just a little bit off balance, including me. Diane is Blair's best friend, and—"

"Cameron, I don't want to discuss Diane Bleeker."

Cam regarded Valerie thoughtfully, surprised at the faint tremor she'd heard in her voice, even though her beautiful face remained remote. "Okay. Like I said, I was out of line. Sorry."

"Apology accepted."

"As soon as I get Blair settled in, you, Felicia, and I need to debrief. I'll meet you in your quarters as soon as I can."

"We've got a lot of equipment to set up. I'm sure we'll have plenty to do." Valerie started along the narrow path that wound around the side of the house in the direction Felicia had taken to the guesthouse.

"Valerie."

Valerie looked over her shoulder, a question in her eyes.

"Thanks for the assist with Blair's security."

"Don't mention it." With a soft smile, Valerie turned and walked away.

Cam watched until she disappeared, then climbed the wide wooden stairs to the house and went inside. "Blair?" She walked through the house to the kitchen. Hara stood on the rear deck. "All clear?"

"Tight and tidy," Hara replied. "It's a good site. Easy to cover."

"Good. Put Wozinski out front, and the second team can relieve you at eight."

"Already done, Commander."

"I know I'm not official at this point, but…"

Hara shook her head. "We know who you are, Commander. Everyone in the Service does. We're happy to follow your orders."

Cam knew that Hara was referring to the fact that she'd taken a bullet meant for Blair, the ultimate act for a Secret Service agent. Others considered her a hero. She just considered herself damn lucky that Blair had not been hurt. "Thank you. I'll be with Ms. Powell."

"Yes, ma'am."

On her way upstairs, Cam passed Tanner coming down. "Thanks again."

Tanner grinned. "Don't mention it. Oh, and Blair told me to tell you to get your ass upstairs."

"Aha. Message received, then," Cam replied, taking the rest of the stairs two at a time. As she searched out her missing lover, she heard the front door close downstairs. She opened the only closed door on the ocean side of the house and stepped through into a spacious bedroom. Out of habit, she quickly swept the room, fixing the location of the windows and doors in her mind. The room was appointed with a king-sized bed, matching Mission oak dressers and bedside tables, and a reading chair and lamp. A wide cedar deck was visible through double sliding glass doors on the opposite side of the room. She redirected her survey to the bed. Blair reclined against the pillows, a crisp, snow-white sheet angled diagonally across her waist. She appeared to be naked. "I understand you were looking for me."

"I understand that you're a Secret Service agent."

Cam reached behind her and flipped the lock with one hand. Her eyes on Blair's, she shrugged out of her jacket as she crossed with slow, deliberate strides to the side of the bed. "That's right."

"And exactly what does *service* imply?"

"Well now," Cam whispered, setting her weapon harness on the bedside table and kicking off her shoes, "that would be a secret, wouldn't it?"

"I'll never tell." Blair flicked the sheet aside and slid to the edge of the bed, where she extended a hand and grasped Cam's belt. "Stand still."

Cam looked down, watching through heavy lids as Blair deftly unbuckled her belt and pulled it through her belt loops in one swift motion. She sucked in air as Blair's fingers curved inside her waistband and released the button, then pulled down her fly. When Blair tugged her shirt free and leaned forward to put her mouth against Cam's stomach, Cam tilted her head back and groaned. Eyes closed, she spread her fingers in Blair's hair. "Baby. I've missed you."

"Take off your shirt," Blair murmured against Cam's skin, licking her way upward. "And get rid of these pants."

With trembling hands, Cam hurried to comply, stumbling on quickly weakening legs when Blair circled her navel. She put her hand to the back of Blair's head, stopping her dangerous explorations. "Jesus. Give me a minute here, will you?"

"Oh, I don't think so. It's been *days*." The instant Cam was naked, Blair wrapped both arms around Cam's hips and jerked her down into her arms. She nipped at Cam's neck with her teeth while insinuating one calf tightly around the back of Cam's thighs. "I'm ready to come right now."

Groaning, Cam kissed her throat, her jaw, her mouth. Tasting her after so many days of fear and worry was like finding a crystal pool in the heart of the desert. She drank, feasting, her hands roaming Blair's body, brushing over the peaks of her breasts, smoothing down her abdomen to dance along the inside of her thighs. She lingered inside her mouth, breathing her in, filling the dark places inside with her light. She pushed up until she could look into Blair's eyes. "I love you."

"These last few days—I thought I would scream if you didn't touch me soon." Blair's eyes were already hazy beneath trembling lids. "Don't let me come yet."

"Let me up then, baby," Cam murmured, pulling away.

"Nooo," Blair protested, both hands on Cam's hips, pressing her sex hard against Cam's rigid thigh. The pressure against her hot, hard center tore a cry from her.

"You're going to come if you keep doing that," Cam warned halfheartedly. She wanted her to come. She slid two fingers around one tight nipple and squeezed.

Blair shuddered and groped blindly for Cam's hand, dragging it down her body and pushing it between her thighs. "Fuck me. God, Cam, fuck me now."

Cam curled an arm behind Blair's shoulders and pulled her tight against her body as she pushed inside her, knowing what would follow. Blair jolted in the circle of her arms, her head snapping back as she crashed into orgasm.

"Oh God oh God oh God," Blair keened.

"That's it, baby. That's it." Cam gloried in her responsiveness, loving the sheer, pure beauty of her passion. She drove deep, pulled out, and drove again, wanting to feel her—alive and vital, screaming out her pleasure in the safety of Cam's arms. She pushed her to another orgasm and started again.

Blair groped for Cam's wrist. "I can't…come…one more time."

Instantly, Cam stilled, keeping her hand inside as she pressed her face to the top of Blair's head. She tried to hide the tears that streaked her cheeks, but Blair knew. She always knew.

"Don't cry, darling. Don't cry." Blair pulled Cam's head to her breast and rocked her.

"I just need a minute to get myself together," Cam gasped, burying her face against Blair's neck. "Christ, Christ. I was so damned scared."

Blair's heart twisted, and she held her even more tightly. "You can have all the time you need. I'm not ever letting go. Not ever."

Chapter Twenty-two

When Cam opened her eyes, the room was dark. She lay on her back, Blair's head on her shoulder and their limbs entwined. Blair's breath was warm against her breast, and her heartbeat steady and strong. It took her another few seconds to realize that the hard knot of anxiety in the pit of her stomach that had been her constant companion for five days was gone. She ran her fingertips along the plane of Blair's shoulder blade, then over the curve of her shoulder and down her muscled arm. When she reached her hand, she traced each strong finger, seeing them as they held a brush—applying paint to canvas with swift sure strokes—feeling them on her body, bringing her to orgasm with equal grace.

"I love you," she whispered.

Blair tightened her hold and pressed a kiss to the hollow beneath Cam's collarbone. "You okay?"

"Yeah, I am." Cam cupped the back of Blair's neck lightly and spread her fingers into her hair, teasing the strands over the back of her hand. "I can't believe I fell asleep."

"I think I can take credit for that," Blair said, laughing softly.

"Oh," Cam mused. "I remember now. That was you, was it?"

Blair bit Cam's shoulder hard enough to make her wince. "I'd better be the only one making you come hard enough to fall asleep in the middle of the afternoon."

Cam kissed Blair's forehead. "You're the only one anytime, anyplace."

"That too." Blair circled her tongue over the red mark she'd left on Cam's skin. "You know, we've never talked about that."

"Monogamy?" Cam felt the slightest stirring of unease, but pushed it aside. *Listen first, then react.* In her ordinary dealings that wasn't difficult, but where Blair was concerned her heart tended to rule her head more often than not. "Should we?"

"What?"

"Talk about it."

"Okay." Blair lifted up on an elbow and peered intently into Cam's face. "If I find out that you've slept with anyone else, I'll kick your ass from here to China."

"That's it?" Cam asked as Blair settled back into the curve of her body.

"Yep."

"Okay. As long as it goes both ways."

"Okay."

Cam went back to stroking Blair's hair. "Does that mean we're engaged?"

"Well, two people usually only get engaged if they're planning on getting married."

"I know that." Cam felt Blair grow very still against her. "We're going to be here a few weeks, at least, until we get a clear fix on what happened at the Aerie. There's always the possibility that the FBI or one of the other agencies will break it, but I'm working under the assumption that their resources are spread pretty thin and ours are totally focused."

"Meaning you've got the better shot at getting some answers."

"Yes."

"I don't mind staying here, since I don't exactly have a home to go to at the moment."

"When it's time to leave," Cam said quietly, "I'd like us to find a place where we can live together."

"Is Manhattan okay?" Blair unconsciously cupped Cam's breast, needing the physical intimacy while they strayed into emotional waters that were unknown to her. "I like being near Diane, and it's good for my work."

"Sure. Anyplace works for me."

"So are you proposing, Commander?"

"Yes." Cam lifted Blair's hand and kissed her palm. "Are you accepting?"

Blair shifted on top of her, resting on her forearms so she could look into Cam's eyes. "The media will have a field day."

"That's nothing new."

"Lucinda will probably have a heart attack."

Cam grinned. "Nothing new there, either."

"I want a really, really big wedding with lots of Washington pundits and dignitaries."

"Uh, okay."

Even in the moonlight, Blair could see Cam pale. She couldn't hold back her laughter. "I'm sorry. Just a few friends, my father and Lucinda, and Marcea and whomever you want, of course."

"Rings?"

Blair drew in a sharp breath. "Whoever would have guessed I would have fallen for such a traditionalist."

"You weren't looking when I snuck up on you."

"Oh, I was looking." Blair kissed her, hard and long and deep, then drew away, murmuring her pleasure. "Why now?"

"This week...was hard," Cam said quietly. "I never questioned loving you—I think that started the first time I saw you. But now I know what it would feel like without you—really know. I don't ever want that." She touched Blair's face with her fingertips, and her hand was shaking. "This just feels right."

"Oh," Blair murmured before she brought her mouth to Cam's again. She poured her passion into Cam's body, with her mouth, with her tongue, with her hands streaking over her and, ultimately, into her. She didn't stop until Cam bowed underneath her and shook beneath the force of her devotions. Blair kept her head up, her eyes open, watching through lust-clouded eyes as Cam surrendered every defense, marveling at the trust she was gifted. As Cam came, Blair whispered, "I love you. Always."

Cam fought for breath as her arms and legs lay limp against the mattress, her head still reeling. She swallowed and found her voice. "Did you just say yes?"

"Mmm," Blair answered as she shifted upward, straddling Cam's shoulders and easing down toward her mouth. "I did."

❖

"What are you going to tell your father?" Cam asked as she rummaged in her suitcase for a clean shirt.

Blair ran a comb through her damp hair and leaned against the bedpost, enjoying the sight of Cam, still nude after their shower. "That I'm crazy in love with you and I want to spend the rest of my life with you."

Cam straightened, a pale blue shirt, still in its plastic wrap from the dry cleaners, in her right hand. "Just like that?"

"Yep. What are you going to tell Marcea?"

"That you're the only woman for me and I want everyone to know it."

Blair put out an arm as Cam started toward her. "Don't come near me right now."

Cam raised a quizzical eyebrow.

"Well, you can if it's your intention to go right back to bed. Otherwise, keep your distance, because I seem to be in that *gotta have you every second* state of mind."

"I think that's probably a result of you being locked up for five days."

Blair's expression grew serious. "Jesus, I hated that. Thank God Stark was with me, and you could visit the last few days."

"Yeah, I think you even started to enjoy the pinochle." Cam shrugged into her shirt and crossed to Blair as she buttoned it. She kissed her cheek. "I'm sorry I have to leave tonight."

"You're not going anywhere, are you?" Blair asked quickly, catching Cam's hand.

"No." Cam searched Blair's face with worried eyes. "Hey. I'm just going down to brief with Felicia and Valerie. You okay?"

Blair laughed shakily. "I hate feeling dependent almost as much as I hate being locked up. I just…I just need you around right now."

Cam cupped Blair's face between her palms and kissed her softly on the mouth. "I'm not going anywhere." She kissed her again. "And just in case you were wondering, I need you around right now too."

"If I could just feel like my life is at least *heading* back toward normal."

"I'm going to be spending a lot of time coordinating this search, working out of the command center we've set up in the guesthouse." Cam stepped into her trousers. "It will probably get intense."

"I know. I expected that. Hopefully, I'll be able to paint."

"And Tanner will be around, for company."

Blair nodded. "I love Tanner. And Adrienne. But I was wondering…"

"What?" Cam asked, pulling on her holster.

"There is one thing you can do for me before you leave tonight." Blair reached down and retrieved Cam's belt from the floor, then handed it to her.

"Thanks. What is it?"

Blair told her, and Cam nodded. It was going to cause complications. "Sure. If that's what you need, I'll take care of it."

❖

"How's Mac doing?" Valerie asked as Felicia closed her cell phone.

The two women sat across from one another at a glass-and-chrome table in a makeshift office they had hastily assembled in the dining room of the spacious two-bedroom guesthouse. Through the patio doors the shoreline was visible one hundred yards away. A twisting path led from the wooden rear deck through low dunes to the sandy beach. Under other circumstances, it would be idyllic.

"They're feeding him, so that makes him happy." Felicia smiled softly. "He's been out of bed, but that's about it. It's going to take him a while to regain his strength, but he's young and in great shape."

"Your team took a battering."

Felicia pushed back from the table, stood, and walked to the far side of the room. She opened the patio doors and a brisk night breeze blew in. It was just after ten p.m. "Do you mind?"

"No." Valerie remained seated, unable to read much from her expression but suspecting she knew several of the questions on Felicia's mind. "I know it's not easy working with someone new, especially in light of all that's happened." She didn't think it was necessary to bring up the betrayal of one of the team's own. "But I want to help bring these people down."

Felicia looked over her shoulder, appraising the cool, composed, and almost painfully beautiful woman who, not more than a month before, had been the subject of one of her own investigations. "The only thing I know about you is that you *say* you're CIA."

"You have doubts?"

"It's hard to believe even the CIA would put an agent in *that* position," Felicia said, turning back to the night.

"The Agency makes its own rules." Valerie smiled thinly, realizing that Cameron's team knew the nature of her previous cover.

Felicia snorted. "Oh, we all know that. I just can't believe none of us tipped to it."

"Covert operations are our business. It wouldn't have been easy."

"But you broke your cover for *this* operation."

Valerie smiled fleetingly. "I follow orders too."

"And I don't suppose you're going to tell me why you're here?"

So that anything you find out, my superiors will know about immediately. Because someone thinks that you and your colleagues can do more than an interagency team made up of people who will be too busy trying to take credit to find out anything of value could. Valerie held Felicia's gaze. "I'm here to lend assistance. My understanding is that Camer—Agent Roberts's team is to be given unrestricted access to intelligence from every department. I'm here as a liaison from the Agency to see that happens."

"Just a glorified go-between, huh?"

"That's me."

Felicia shook her head, knowing they were playing a game that they were both too good at to lose. Valerie would not tell her what her true orders were, no matter how hard she probed. And they had work to do. "The commander trusts you."

It was a statement, not requiring an answer.

"So I do too." Felicia walked back to the table and sat down. "Let's go over what we have."

From the doorway, Cam said, "Let me grab a cup of coffee, and you can brief us both."

Valerie rose and said to Felicia. "I'll make it this time. You can get the next pot."

"Sure," Felicia said, watching Valerie follow the commander into the kitchen. She wondered what remained between them, and, despite the fact that Valerie's motives remained suspect, she felt sorry for her. She leaned forward, her elbows on the table, and rested her face in her hands. It had been good to hear Mac's voice. Better than good. He had almost died, and the reality of what losing him would mean had struck her hard. It was time to rethink whether the barriers she had erected around her heart kept her safe or merely kept her alone.

❖

"Okay," Cam said, pushing her empty coffee cup aside. She looked from Felicia to Valerie and then focused on Felicia. "What you're telling me is that we have the bodies of four men, each of which has been autopsied at Quantico."

"Yes, ma'am." Felicia passed the four folders across the table to Cam, who set them in a neat pile to her left.

"And the FBI's finest couldn't find a single thing to identify any of them."

"Nothing from the usual forensic evidence, no," Felicia said in a neutral tone. She was frustrated, they all were, and she needed a clear head to solve the problem. "We've run their fingerprints, obviously, and turned up nothing. We've got DNA—ditto. No matches. Dental impressions were made by the pathologist, but without a geographic area to focus on, it's impossible to even find adequate records to compare these to."

"So, if we ever find out where these guys came from, we might be able to run down the x-rays from area orthodontists, dentists, oral surgeons, and the like, right?"

Felicia nodded. "It will be corroborating evidence after the fact, but it's not going to take us anywhere now."

"What about retinal scans?"

Valerie shook her head. "The only retinal scans we *might* be able to access are from internal sources—the Pentagon, DOD, NSA, and similar agencies."

"FBI, CIA," Felicia added.

"Right," Valerie agreed. "Getting them is going to be tough, and retinal imaging from cadavers is very uncertain. The vitreous begins to coagulate soon after death, and because of the situation in Manhattan the day of the assaults, these bodies weren't retrieved for nearly eighteen hours."

"So no usable images?" Cam persisted.

"Not that we know of," Felicia clarified.

"Find out."

Valerie and Felicia made notes simultaneously.

"Anything else from the bodies? Old wounds, surgical scars—something we could track in hospital records."

"Nothing except they all had similar tattoos on their right upper arm," Felicia stated. She passed a computer image across the table. It showed a pale patch of skin with a tattoo of two crossed assault rifles above a small American flag.

Cam studied and frowned. "An Armed Forces division?"

"Apparently Savard checked that right away," Valerie said, referring to a sheaf of papers in front of her. "It's not an insignia from any division in the Army or the Marines."

"Well," Cam said, "I guess the American flag rules out any other nationality." She placed a fingertip on the lower corner of the paper and slid it back and forth in front of her, staring at the blurry shapes. "Some kind of patriot group?"

"It's possible," Valerie said. "Savard also started a search through the FBI and CIA files on known paramilitary groups here and abroad. Unfortunately, there's no central database tabulating this kind of thing, and thus far we have nothing. It's going to take a lot of digging to assemble the available intelligence."

"These guys had *some* kind of military training, and if they don't show up in the Armed Forces databases, then it had to be well-organized, *unofficial* training." Cam regarded Valerie. "Your people must have some record of mercenary groups that employ a high percentage of Americans. There have been any number of actions in South and Central America as well as Africa where these guys might have been involved."

"It's on the list to check."

"Okay. Top of the list—mercenary and paramilitary groups." Cam pinched the bridge of her nose, trying to ignore the headache that was beginning to throb between her eyes. "And we need to look for a connection between these same groups and Al Qaeda." She swept her gaze from Felicia to Valerie, recalling the conversation she'd had with the president's security advisor that morning. "Because it looks more and more like Osama's claim to being behind the attack on the World Trade Center is true."

"God," Felicia exclaimed. "How did we all miss that?"

"That's probably what everyone in DC is trying to figure out right now," Cam said as she stood. "And that's why *we* have to be the ones to spearhead this portion of the investigation. Let's switch our emphasis from identifying the dead men to collecting everything we can about the organizations we mentioned and finding out all there is to know about Foster. He's our only solid link at this point."

"So far," Felicia said, rising to her feet as well, "he's squeaky clean. An all-American boy. Prep schools, Ivy League colleges, and straight into government service. He came to Treasury by way of graduate school in economics at UVA."

"Find out where he's traveled, especially abroad—and with whom."

"Working it."

"Good. There has to be something there, we just have to find it. Let's compile a list of his family members, girlfriends, boyfriends, roommates, every person he's ever known. These guys"—she pointed to the autopsy photos—"or the guys who trained them, are going to be in there somewhere."

"We're on it, Commander," Felicia said. "But that kind of record search takes time."

"I was told we'd have free access to anything we needed. If you run into a roadblock, tell me about it. I'll make a phone call."

"Thanks."

"Davis, I need you to make some transportation arrangements for the morning."

Felicia joined Cam on her way to the door. "Going somewhere, Commander?"

"No, it's for a new arrival."

Chapter Twenty-three

Thursday, September 20

At just after five a.m., Valerie awakened from a restless sleep. After Cam had left the previous evening, she and Felicia had continued working for several more hours, setting up graphic charts and data grids to organize the plethora of information they had already accumulated, with more to come. They'd finally both admitted their efficiency had zeroed out and it was time to quit for the night. She'd gone to bed, but sleep wouldn't come. She tossed and turned, her mind and body seeking something she couldn't define, until she exhausted herself and drifted into uneasy slumber.

She lay for a moment, staring at her cell phone on the bedside table. She reached out and held it in front of her face, her thumb hovering over the keypad. It would take so very little to banish the loneliness. Thirty seconds of hearing that low, sultry voice welcoming her. It would be so easy to give in, just once. She pressed the first three numbers, then pushed *off* and dropped the phone back onto the table.

Even though she'd had barely three hours' sleep, she got up and showered, then pulled on a soft red cotton V-neck sweater and jeans. She slipped her feet into deck shoes and made her way through the quiet house to the dining room. Working only by the light from the monitors, she continued with the data entry, stopping intermittently to open a Web browser to cross-check facts with additional databases. She registered the sound of the shower running, followed by the rattle of utensils coming from the kitchen, but she kept on.

"How long have you been at that?" Felicia asked as she set a mug of coffee next to Valerie's right arm.

"Thanks," Valerie said with a sigh of appreciation. She checked her watch. "A few hours. Couldn't sleep. Too many things running around in my head."

"I know what you mean." Felicia dropped a hand onto Valerie's shoulder and squeezed. "You should take a break. Too many hours in a row and you'll start missing things."

"I will. Soon."

"Finding anything?"

"It's what I'm *not* finding that's the problem."

"How so?" Felicia sipped her coffee and watched the marsh grass blow outside the window. The sky was an even pewter gray, broken only by darker thunderclouds that threatened rain.

"There's no national registry for identifying marks—scars, tattoos, that kind of thing. Even trying to go state by state is hit or miss. If the various criminal divisions don't input the data, it just never shows up. And even when they do..." She brushed her hair away from her face with an impatient gesture. "It's damn hard to find it."

"We can't even share intelligence between security divisions at the federal level," Felicia noted, settling into a chair at the other computer. "It's too much to hope that the states would be able to."

"I'm willing to bet that situation changes now."

"I think a lot of things in this country are going to change." Felicia regarded Valerie contemplatively. "Do you really think nobody knew what was coming?"

Valerie hesitated for a second, then shook her head. "No, I'm willing to bet a lot of people knew *something*. The problem is not enough people knew *everything*—or even enough. We've been watching Osama—even before the attack on the Cole. But we've never gotten more than bits and pieces of the puzzle."

"Well, let's hope we can find a few of the pieces ourselves."

Two hours later, Valerie pushed back from the computer. "I need some air."

"You should get some sleep."

"Thanks," Valerie said quietly. "I'm okay. A walk will clear the cobwebs out."

"Take a jacket," Felicia said absently, her attention refocused on her monitor. "Supposed to rain."

Valerie pulled on a black nylon windbreaker on her way out through the rear door of the guesthouse. She crossed the deck and started down the narrow sand path to the beach. The wind had picked up and whipped her shoulder-length hair around her face. She hunched her shoulders and put her hands in the jacket pockets, trying to stay warm in the unexpected chill. Within minutes she was at the ocean's edge, surveying the steady march of white-tipped waves that broke and roiled over the small stones and shells that littered the beach inches from her toes. She narrowed her eyes and searched the horizon, but she couldn't make out the presence of any life. They must be out there, the merchant ships and fishing trawlers, fighting the elements, dwarfed by the immensity of nature's power. She looked up into the sky, which had darkened now almost to black, wondering if there would ever come a time again when the heavens would hold only beauty and not the threat of death. With a sigh, she turned away from the house and walked along the ocean's edge, unmindful of the first drops of rain. She had always known her purpose, always understood her place, but in the last few years the world had shifted on its axis and she had lost her balance. What had once been so clear, so simply delineated in black and white, had turned, like the sky, to ever more murky shades of gray. The rain fell harder, and now and then she absently brushed the water from her eyes.

She knew she imagined it when the wind carried the sound of her name, and she kept on. When it came the second time, unmistakable, she turned and held the hair back from her face with one hand. Down the beach, hurrying toward her from the direction of the guesthouse, was a woman in a navy windbreaker much like her own, her hair tucked up beneath a cap. There was no mistaking her gender, however, or, as she drew closer, her identity. Valerie held her breath, afraid to blink and break the spell.

"Valerie!" Diane called.

It was the first time in her life she could ever recall a wish coming true. She stood very still, trying to absorb every detail of Diane's face. The slight frown—worry or anger? Uncertain, Valerie waited for judgment.

Diane stopped inches from Valerie. "You're soaked."

"I got caught out in the rain."

"You should've come back."

"I would have. Soon."

Diane put both hands behind Valerie's head, tangling her fingers in the wet blond strands, and pulled Valerie's mouth to hers. Valerie's lips were cold, but her mouth was molten. Diane moaned softly as she delved inside, swirling her tongue over satin-smooth surfaces until the unexpected sensation of teeth tugging at her lip sent a stab of pleasure straight to her center. Her legs trembled, and she pressed hard into Valerie to steady herself, not surprised when strong arms closed around her waist and held her securely. She tilted her head back and kissed the tip of Valerie's chin. "I missed you."

"Oh God," Valerie gasped, burying her face against Diane's neck. "I missed you too. I'm sorry. I couldn't call. The security…"

"I know." Diane curved one arm around her shoulders while she stroked her face with her free hand. "I thought it was something like that."

Valerie lifted her face. "You did? You didn't think I'd just…walked away?"

A small, sad smile flickered across Diane's face. "Only very late at night, when I was very tired and I ached for you."

"I'm sorry." Valerie cradled Diane's face in one hand, a thumb brushing at the rain that streaked her cheeks. The water was warm. "You're crying."

"I didn't know what to expect when I saw you again." Diane found Valerie's hand and clasped it. "I'm not used to wanting a woman the way I want you. I'm a little…a lot…out of my element."

"Me too." Valerie laughed and tilted her face to the sky. "Oh God, you can say that again." She tugged Diane's hand. "Come on, we need to get in out of the rain. This is crazy."

"I know," Diane said breathlessly as they began to run, still hand in hand. "I'm freezing."

"So am I," Valerie called above the wind. "Did you see Felicia?"

"Yes, she was on her way up to the main house."

"Blair arranged for you to come?"

Diane hurried up the path toward the deck, her feet sinking into wet sand. "Sent a car. Not the usual big ugly thing, and the spookies were cuter." She jumped up the stairs and stamped her feet to rid them of bits of detritus. "I don't think they were the normal Secret Service crew."

"They're probably Whitley's private security." Valerie leaned a shoulder against the wall under the eaves, trying to avoid the rain. She touched Diane's hand, then stroked up her forearm. "Is everything all right?"

"Yes. Blair and I have been best friends forever. She...*we*...needed for us to be together right now. She called. I came." Diane searched Valerie's face. "So I'm a house guest."

"For how long?"

"I don't know. Is it all right I'm here?" Diane caught Valerie's other hand and held them both, squeezing gently. "Because if you don't want me to st—"

Valerie pulled her into her arms and stopped her words with a hungry kiss. When she finally pulled away, she said, "I want you. Don't ever doubt it."

"Tell me that again," Diane murmured, sliding down the zipper on Valerie's windbreaker. She slipped both hands inside and underneath the light sweater, finding warm skin. Her pupils instantly dilated with a rush of arousal. "You're so beautiful."

"Let's shower."

"Felicia—"

"If she comes back, she won't bother us." Valerie opened the door and pulled Diane inside. "I'm still on my lunch break."

❖

"How's it going?" Cam asked, lightly resting both hands on Blair's shoulders from behind. Blair sat on a high backless stool in front of a wooden easel that was angled to allow her an unobstructed view through the wide windows out over the dunes.

Blair looked at Cam over her shoulder, her expression abstracted. "It's an amazing storm."

"The weather report says we're looking at a nor'easter. There's going to be a lot of water coming our way." Cam studied the canvas. It was an astonishing riot of turbulent purples, indigo, and grays verging on black, cut through with slashes of white. She could almost feel the water beat against her skin. "God, that's fabulous."

"You think?" Blair's voice was both pensive and pleased.

"It's…awesome." When Blair rested her head back against Cam's chest, she slid both arms around her, resting her chin against the top of Blair's head. "I've never seen you do anything quite like this. It's…raw. That's not just about the weather, is it?"

Blair gave a small start and then laughed quietly. She closed her hands over Cam's and pulled Cam's arms tightly around her. "How could I forget that your mother is one of the world's finest artists. Of course, you would notice these things."

Cam kissed the top of Blair's head. "I notice you."

"I know you do." Blair was silent for a moment, staring out the window and watching the two women run through the dunes in the rain. Diane's hair had come loose from her cap and tumbled down almost to her shoulders, darkened by the water to a rich burnished gold. Valerie, soaked to the skin, was laughing. Blair thought she'd never seen either of them look quite so happy. "They're a beautiful couple, aren't they."

"They are."

"Did you know?"

Cam shook her head. "I suspected. Did you?"

"Not that things had gone this far. I don't believe I've ever seen Diane in love."

"Is that what they are?" Cam bent down and kissed the side of Blair's neck.

"Oh, I think so." Blair tilted her head back and looked up into Cam's face. "Does it bother you?"

Cam's gray eyes darkened, a reflection of the wild storm pummeling the island. "Are you asking me if there's something between Valerie and me?"

"Darling," Blair murmured, reaching up to stroke Cam's cheek. "I *know* there's something between you. She used to be in love with you. And I know that you cared for her."

"*Cared for.* That's different than—"

"Cameron."

"What?"

"You're being a bit of a jerk."

Cam's mouth twitched. "Am I?"

"I know you're not in love with her. It was just a simple question… more or less." Blair grinned. "Okay, there are moments when I'm jealous. But that's just because she's a beautiful woman and there was a time when she tou—"

"Don't." Cam leaned down further and found Blair's mouth. She kissed her until she felt the tension ebb from Blair's body, to be replaced by a different kind of urgency. Then she drew her head back and said, "I love you. No, it doesn't bother me. Sometimes...sometimes I find myself hoping she'll finally be happy."

Blair stood, turning until she could press against Cam, wrapping her arms around her shoulders. She nuzzled her neck, kissed the edge of her jaw, and finally her mouth. "You see? That's why I love you."

Before Cam could reply, Blair silenced her with another kiss.

❖

"Are you sure about this?" Diane asked, dropping the towel over a wicker chair as she crossed the room. "I don't want to compromise you with your colleagues."

Valerie was already reclining in the center of the queen-sized bed, the sheets thrown back, her skin flushed from their recent shower. She was nude and she was breathtaking. *Like I can walk away,* Diane thought, feeling the heaviness of desire suffuse her. She was used to taking her pleasure from pleasuring women, but as much as she wanted Valerie to come screaming from her touch, she ached for the soft pull of Valerie's mouth on her nipples and her clitoris.

Valerie turned on her side and propped her head on one hand. Her smile was slow as her gaze drifted over Diane's body. "If you're really worried, we can get dressed and watch the storm."

Diane settled one knee on the mattress next to Valerie and leaned over her, her breasts mere millimeters from Valerie's face. "We could do that. I love how wild it is out there."

"Or..." Valerie grasped Diane's hips and, rolling onto her back, brought Diane down on top of her. She slid one leg over the back of Diane's, bringing their centers together. "You could stay here with me, and..." She ran her lips back and forth over Diane's nipple. "We can rage together."

"Keep doing that..." Diane arched her back and groaned. "And I won't care if the entire Secret Service team comes through the door."

Valerie lifted her hips and rolled them both over in one easy motion, sliding down on the bed as they settled. She kissed the tanned, tight skin below Diane's navel. "I can't stop thinking about this. About how you smell. About how you taste. About how much I need to touch you." She turned her head and kissed the butter-soft skin at the very top of Diane's thigh. "Please, please let me love you."

"Darling," Diane murmured, her fingers drifting through Valerie's hair, guiding her lower, "you don't ever have to ask."

CHAPTER TWENTY-FOUR

Monday, September 24

I don't want to go back." Diane refilled her wineglass from the bottle of cabernet that sat in the center of the glass-topped coffee table. She sat on the sofa in khaki shorts and a navy sleeveless blouse with her feet propped on a rattan footstool.

Blair slouched next to her with her legs extended and her bare feet resting on the edge of the low table. Her grey Champion sweats were threadbare and hung off her hips; her red T-shirt with the sleeves and lower half torn off proclaimed "Arnie's Gym." She nudged Diane's knee with hers. "So don't. There's plenty of room here, and I don't get the sense that you're bored."

Diane smiled, thinking of the late-night assignations in Valerie's room and the early-morning walks on the beach, rain or no rain. "Bored. No, not that." She sipped the wine, then watched the bloodred liquid swirl in the glass. "It's been a long time since you and I have had this much time together. It's been good. And I can't say that I mind catching up on my reading."

"And then there are the other benefits," Blair remarked dryly. "Eating pizza every other night, strolling in the freezing rain, or if you're *really* lucky like me, finding strangers in the kitchen when you're in your underwear—"

"God, I thought that guy was going to kill himself trying to get out the door when we walked in that morning. He probably thought Cam would be right behind you and that she'd shoot him on the spot."

Blair laughed. "It wouldn't be the first time one of my security people has seen me undressed."

"Yes, but I'd bet Tanner's crew aren't used to it."

"True, and they've adjusted to our routine very well. She's got good people. I wasn't so sure when Cam decided to have them rotate with the Secret Service agents inside the house, but it's been fine." Blair angled sideways and rested her cheek against her arm, which she extended along the sofa back. Gazing at Diane, she grinned. "And don't forget how much fun it is to report your every movement to the crew chief. How could you possibly think of leaving?"

"Unfortunately," Diane said pensively, "I have a business to see to."

"Diane," Blair said quietly, "there *is* no business as usual in Manhattan right now. It's not going to hurt if you take another week off." She leaned closer and rubbed Diane's shoulders. "Here, turn sideways. Your back is in knots."

When Blair pulled her legs up onto the sofa, Diane shifted into the vee of her parted thighs. She sighed as Blair worked her thumbs up and down along her spine. "God, I've forgotten how good you are at that."

"Oh yeah? Well, it *has* been a long time."

They both laughed.

"I can't remember who seduced whom that first time," Diane said musingly. "Of course, we were fourteen."

"Well," Blair said, circling the flats of her fingers in the hollow at the base of Diane's spine, "you asked me to rub your back when you just *happened* to be naked, but I copped the first feel. So, I guess it was probably mutual."

"We were so innocent." Diane turned her head and looked back at Blair. "I was so crazy about you."

"You never said."

"I know. You were such a little heartbreaker already, and I guess I just didn't want to take the chance of getting hurt."

"I wonder what it would have been like," Blair said, sliding her hands back up to curve over the tops of Diane's shoulders. "If we'd been lovers then—I mean, if we'd admitted it was more than just the sex."

"We wouldn't have this. This friendship." Diane lightly stroked the tops of Blair's thighs where they cradled her body. "And as much as

I've wanted you all these years, this is what I've always needed."

"You're okay with things now, right?" Blair spoke gently, her hands still.

Diane laughed. "I'll admit to having a twinge now and then, when you're looking particularly devastating." She patted Blair's legs. "But I'm not pining, and I can enjoy a back rub without getting wet."

"Well, fuck, I'm slipping," Blair muttered playfully, resuming her ministrations. After a few minutes of silence, she said, "You know what you said about taking a chance?"

"Mmm-hmm." Diane rested her head back against Blair's shoulder and closed her eyes. "God, that feels so good."

"You have to take chances when you're in love."

Diane shifted slightly so she could see Blair's face. "And who might you be? I could have sworn you were my old friend Blair Powell, who used to say that being in love was just a state of insanity."

Blair shrugged. "Maybe it is. But it feels really good, so why not choose a state of insanity that makes you happy instead of sad?"

"I think I know what you mean. After everything that's happened, if there's something—or someone—in life that's precious, we shouldn't lose sight of it."

"So are you?"

"What?"

"Taking a chance. With Valerie?"

"Oh, I have no idea what I'm doing with her." Diane shook her head, her expression rueful. "She's...she's turned everything upside down on me."

"She's very beautiful."

"God yes."

"And terribly sexy."

"Mmm."

"And she might not be who she says she is," Blair said gently, draping her arms loosely around Diane's waist. "You know that, right?"

Diane stiffened, but did not pull away. "Talking about Valerie could get us into trouble."

"Maybe, but we need to." Blair kissed Diane's cheek. "Because I love you and I need you in my life. So, are you in love with her?"

"Yes. Totally."

"Thought so. She looks like she's in love with you too."

Diane sighed. "She hasn't said so. But the way she is with me, the way she touches me…God, she's so tender."

Blair smiled. "Well, it's a done deal, I can see that." She gave Diane a quick hug. "You know, being involved with one of these secret agent types is a real pain in the ass."

"I'm starting to understand that. There are a lot of things she doesn't say. Or can't say."

"They teach them not to trust, you know." Blair's voice was flat, restraining her anger.

"I know. But then, look at us. We're not that much different."

"True," Blair said sharply, "but we're not likely to disappear in the middle of the night on some mission to save the goddamned world. We're not likely to have someone put a bullet in us while we go about our daily business."

"Hey," Diane said, taking Blair's hand. She wasn't going to point out that Blair was as much a target as their lovers. "You can't think about that all the time. It will just make you crazy, and you can't change it. You can't change her. Besides, would you *want* to?"

"Yes. Fuck, yes." Blair closed her eyes, then took a deep breath. "No. But God, I think about something happening to her…" She looked away, her throat working around tears.

"Okay, what's happened?"

"Nothing."

"Yes. Something." Diane turned to face Blair, resting her hand once again on Blair's leg. "Tell."

Blair leaned forward and retrieved her wineglass. Then she set it down, lifted the bottle, and topped off both their glasses with what remained. She settled back, the glass cupped in both hands. She studied it for a while, as if some mystery lay revealed within, then met Diane's compassionate gaze. "Cam and I are going to get married."

Diane sat completely still. While Blair watched her expectantly, Diane finally took Blair's glass from her hand and set both their glasses back on the table. Then she scooped Blair into her arms. "I am so, so happy for you!"

"Thanks," Blair said softly, rubbing her cheek gently on Diane's shoulder. She leaned back and grinned. "Will you help? Because I don't have any idea what to do for this kind of thing. And I'm pretty certain Cam doesn't either."

"Ooh," Diane breathed, her eyes sparkling. "Will you give me a blank check and permission to do anything I want?"

"Nothing fancy."

Diane pouted.

"All right, nothing *too* fancy."

"Wait a minute, won't the White House want to plan this?"

"No fucking way," Blair said succinctly. "This is mine and Cam's, and no one is going to take any part of it away from us."

"Then leave it to me." Diane jumped up and started to pace. "Oh, this is going to be such fun. Can I dress you too? Oh, Cam is going to look *so* drop-dead gorgeous in a tux. Versace this time, I think, although I know she always wears Armani—"

"What makes you think *I'm* not going to be wearing the tux?" Blair asked archly.

Diane stopped and looked at her, a small smirk on her face. "Please. You might be butch in bed, bu—"

"Ah," Cam said from the door, "is this a private conversation?"

"We were just discussing Blair's sex life," Diane said without breaking a smile.

"Really." Cam crossed to the sofa, leaned down, and kissed Blair. Then she straightened and settled a hip onto the arm of the sofa, resting her fingers on the back of Blair's neck. "Past, present, or future?"

"All of them, actually. It makes quite an interesting—"

"Okay," Blair said firmly. "That's enough."

Cam grinned. "I think I might be able to contribute something. On two out of three, at any rate." Blair punched Cam's thigh, and Cam winced. "On second thought, maybe not."

"How are things going?" Blair asked.

"Slow." Cam's expression darkened for an instant, then she forced a smile. "But we're just getting started. I didn't expect the answers to be easy to find. If they were, it never would have happened to begin with." She stroked Blair's hair as she studied Diane. "You look even more happy than usual, which is saying a lot. What's going on?"

Diane's brows rose. "You really are a secret agent, aren't you. Very good, Commander." She took one look at Blair, seeking permission, then at the slight nod of affirmation, replied, "Blair has just given me carte blanche to plan your wedding."

Cam sat up straighter. "Really."

"Uh-huh."

"Tell me when and where to be, and I'll be there." She kissed the top of Blair's head and stood abruptly. "I'm going back to work."

"Chicken," both Diane and Blair called toward her retreating back.

❖

Savard rolled over onto her back and tilted her face to the Florida sun. The ocean sounded a gentle roar twenty yards away, and a breeze cooled the sweat from her skin. She and Stark were the only ones on the beach behind her parents' beachside home. Eyes closed, she stretched out a hand and found Stark's arm, then trailed her fingers down until she reached her hand. Clasping Stark's fingers, she said, "This is wonderful."

Stark turned her head and surveyed her lover. Her caramel skin had darkened in just a few days to a dark bronze, and the shadows beneath her eyes were nearly invisible now. The last two nights she'd slept without awakening. Stark knew it would take more than a few days away from the stress and horror to heal, but her heart felt lighter to see Renée's pain ease even a little bit. "It's great."

"It's our first vacation."

"I know. I never knew you golfed."

"I played on the junior circuit as a teenager," Savard said, turning onto her side and smiling at Stark. "It seems like a million years ago now."

"I was pretty terrible at it yesterday."

"Yeah, you were. But you looked really sexy in those shorts and that tight shirt." She stroked Stark's forearm. "You've got such a great body."

"Jeez," Stark mumbled, but she grinned with pleasure.

"Honey, you know I love you, right?"

Stark frowned. "Sure I do."

"I want to go back to work."

"We've only been here five days. The commander said at least a week."

"I know what she said," Savard replied, drawing random patterns in the sand between them. "But they need me up there. I'm the FBI connection, and I was in the counterterrorism division. They need me working on what happened at Blair's."

"You need a little bit of a break," Stark said carefully, "so you'll be able to work the way you should. That's all."

Savard met Stark's eyes. "I know I almost lost it for a while there. And I know you know."

"Sweetheart—"

"No, it's okay. I'm not embarrassed that you know that I'm not always...strong."

"You are. You're the strongest woman I've ever known. And the bravest."

"I love you." Savard smiled softly. "You know I've seen my old therapist—the one I saw when I was a teenager—twice since I've been down here. It's helped."

"Yeah, but sometimes it takes longer—"

"I know that too. But I can talk to him on the phone from wherever we are, whenever I need to. And I will, I promise."

"I just want you to be okay. I don't care about anything as much as I care about that."

Savard braced a hand in the sand and leaned forward, brushing her mouth over Stark's. "I know. And that's one of the reasons I'm going to be fine."

"Can I tell you something?" Stark said quietly.

"Anything."

"I want to go back to work too. It's driving me crazy that the commander's doing my job."

Savard laughed out loud. "I never would've guessed you were that territorial."

"Oh yeah?" Stark reached out and pulled Savard onto her beach towel, and kissed her hard. "Just try looking at some other woman."

"Really?" Savard's voice rose, surprised at the unexpected show of aggression from her normally laid-back lover. "We *did* need this vacation. I'm learning all sorts of wonderful things about you."

"I'm really glad we came. I love being alone with you like this. Your folks are great too, though."

"I told you they'd love you," Savard said. She frowned and ran her hand over Stark's abdomen. "Did you put on your sunscreen? Your stomach's getting pink."

"I did, and that's not a sunburn." Stark grinned. "It was the kiss."

"Don't tell me you're ready again."

"I've been saving it my whole life just for you."

Savard leaned closer, her breasts nestling against Stark's, and kissed her lightly on the mouth. "You *are* adorable. And so goddamned sexy. And as soon as we shower, I'll take care of that burn of yours."

"We can't."

"Why not?" Savard sat up and dusted sand from the back of her legs.

"Your mother's home."

"Paula, honey, she knows we sleep together."

"Yes, but if we disappear into the bedroom in the middle of the afternoon, she's going to know we have sex."

"Oh, I'm sure that never occurred to her before." Savard smiled. "We'll do it in the shower, then."

Stark's breath caught. "Oh man. Now we're going to *have* to."

"What's the matter," Savard asked, pressing even closer, the bare skin of her stomach sliding over Stark's, "did that just make you wet?"

Stark blushed. "It made everything…happen." She glanced down, half expecting to see her sudden excitement apparent through her bathing suit. "Just thinking about you touching me makes me so excited, I want to…you know. Come."

Savard groaned. "That's it. We're going in the house."

"Yeah," Stark muttered, standing and lifting her towel at the same time. "Maybe we can sneak by your mother."

CHAPTER TWENTY-FIVE

Wednesday, September 26

Cam pulled up a chair and regarded the three women seated around the dining-room table that now served as their conference area. Savard, she noted, looked tired, but not haunted. There was a clarity in her blue eyes that had been missing ten days ago. Some of the improvement, Cam surmised, was due to the fact that Stark showed no evidence of anthrax. Neither did Blair, and Cam knew just how much that meant in terms of her own peace of mind and ability to concentrate. She wouldn't feel completely comfortable until the sixty-day incubation period had passed, but Blair was taking the medication prescribed by Captain Andrews, and at this point she was perfectly healthy.

"Good to see you back, Savard. Are you up to speed yet?"

"Getting there, Commander. And thank you. It's good to be back." She and Stark had taken a night flight and then rented a car, arriving just after dawn. Paula had gone immediately to the main house, and she had sought out Felicia, who briefed her quickly over doughnuts and coffee. Just before the seven a.m. briefing, Valerie had come in through the back door. They hadn't had time to do more than nod to one another.

"We've got our full complement of people back now," Cam said. "So let's hear where we are." She looked first at Valerie. "What do we have on the worldwide situation? Anything to tie in to our four UNSUBs?"

"Nothing specific. Everything points to bin Laden as the mastermind of the WTC attack, although it looks like the terrorists responsible were assembled from an assortment of cells—some from Germany, some from the Middle East, and some who had been living here for at least several years. There's nothing that points to a direct American connection."

"On the other hand," Savard interjected, "there *is* plenty of evidence to suggest that terrorist groups throughout Europe, the Middle East, and elsewhere have begun to collaborate with one another, putting aside their philosophical differences in favor of combined strength. It's not much of a stretch to imagine that something like that could've happened here."

"It works in theory, I agree," Cam said flatly, "but we need facts. What have we turned up on the domestic front?"

Felicia passed out file folders.

Cam opened the top one, as did everyone else at the table. A computer image of a clean-shaven, white, middle-aged male with a buzz cut was on top. His face was square-jawed, with broad cheekbones and a short, relatively shapeless nose—an average face that reflected the melting-pot characteristics of many Americans of far-distant European descent. She looked up, waiting.

"This is August Kreis," Felicia said, "the Webmaster of the neo-Nazi Sheriff's Posse Comitatus group based in Ulysses, Pennsylvania. On September 11, while the World Trade Center towers stood burning, he posted a message praising the 'Islamic freedom fighters' and calling the attacks 'the first shots in a racial holy war that will topple the US government.'"

"Crazy bastard," Savard muttered.

Cam nodded. "I know who he is. He and his 'brothers' routinely get a mention in our internal security reports. So far, I gather he's come up clean for anything related to the attacks?"

"He's been on the FBI watch list for years," Savard said. "There's nothing to connect him to the WTC, other than the timing of his statement. As far as that goes, he either made a very good guess as to who was behind the attacks or he actually knew something. Unfortunately, no one can *prove* prior knowledge. But if *his* group knew, other patriot groups did too."

"What we've got," Felicia picked up the thread, "is a loose association of neo-Nazis, skinheads, white separatists, Christian Patriots, neo-Confederates—and the list goes on and on—who have slowly formed a coalition of paramilitary organizations in this country.

They share intelligence and feed each other's fanaticism. And they don't give each other up. Code of silence and all that."

"We're looking into all of these organizations for something that connects to these four men," Savard said. "The problem is, our intelligence on these groups is scattered among all the various agencies. We're literally reduced to combing through internal memos from FBI field offices and interagency communiqués trying to put the picture together."

"Have you put Foster into the mix as well?" Cam asked.

The agents nodded.

"And?" Cam leaned forward, still believing the answer would be found with him.

"Foster is a cipher," Felicia said, reading from another file folder. "Twenty-nine years old—six years of government service. Nothing exemplary or problematic about his career. His passport, which is reviewed routinely by our agency, showed three trips to Europe other than for assignment-related travel. Each time to Paris, all three trips in the last five months."

Cam narrowed her eyes thoughtfully. "Girlfriend over there? Boyfriend?"

"No sign of any serious romantic relationship here or abroad. And he appears to be heterosexual."

"Savard, pull up the postings of Egret's travel schedule for the last twelve months." It was common practice for the White House press department to post the first family's schedule on the White House Web site as well as in briefings to the press corps, sometimes months in advance. It made the Secret Service's job more difficult, because it provided advance information to anyone who might be a threat, but it was part of the open communication policy that was at least paid lip service on Capitol Hill.

"Got it," Savard said after a minute of clicking through files on her laptop.

"How far in advance was her trip to Paris posted?"

Savard scrolled through data, then raised her eyes from the screen, a look of consternation creasing her face. "Just under six months ago— right before Foster's trips started."

"I'll see what our field agents have to say about the temperature in Paris," Valerie said quietly as everyone at the table grew still. "It's not normally a hot area for terrorist cells, but now? Who knows."

"Nothing happened in Paris last month," Felicia pointed out, referring to Blair's recent goodwill visit to the French capital.

"No," Cam said, her tone hard-edged. "Nothing that we know about." She stood abruptly and crossed the room to the windows overlooking the dune path. She balled her fists and shoved them into her pants pockets, because she wanted to break something. Foster could have been coordinating the attack on Blair for months, probably *had* been, right under her nose. She'd worked with the man, trusted Blair's life to him every day, and the entire time he had been plotting to assassinate her. If she had him in front of her now, she would kill him all over again. She turned back to the team, her expression carefully neutral, and sat down again.

"Pull his vouchers from last month. Maybe he got sloppy and included something that wasn't job-related in Paris. A cab ride, phone calls, anything at all. Track it all down."

Felicia nodded and made a note. "We've pretty much exhausted the deep background check on him, Commander. He's the first of two children, both boys. His father, now deceased, was a Navy fighter pilot in Vietnam. Mother a housewife. Raised in North Carolina, educated in the South as well. No criminal record, no reprimands in his file, no red flags anywhere." With a grimace, she closed the slim file. "Like I said, the all-American boy."

"You're missing something," Cam said quietly, with no hint of criticism. "Because he's *not* the all-American boy. All-American boys may be the privileged class, and they may sometimes be racists and homophobes, but they still don't associate with terrorists. And they don't try to assassinate the president's daughter." She leaned back in her chair and closed her eyes. She thought about Foster, the perfect Secret Service agent. Smart, well-bred, a patriot. And somehow twisted and misguided. What was it that turned a man into something like that. "How old was he when his father died?"

"Uh…" Felicia scrambled with the paperwork.

Savard spoke first. "Almost nine."

"Start there."

"Commander?" Felicia asked uncertainly.

Cam opened her eyes and sat forward. "Find out what, or who, made Foster the man he became." She stood. "Keep looking at the patriot groups. Look back through Egret's files—maybe one of these guys, or one of these *groups*, sent her a threatening message in the past. Hell, maybe she turned one of these guys down for a date. Get me *something*."

"Yes, ma'am," Felicia said smartly, echoed by Savard.

When Cam left the room, Savard turned to Valerie. "I'd like you to work on the Paris end of things. Your people have a far deeper reach internationally than we do."

"Certainly."

Savard hesitated, then said, "I'm glad you're working with us, despite the bad blood between your agency and mine. You just need to understand that for us"—she indicated Felicia with a sweep of her hand—"this is personal."

"I understand perfectly, Agent Savard," Valerie replied. "It's very personal for me too."

"Good," Savard said, resuming command with the feeling that her world had settled into place. "Then let's get to work."

❖

Stark shot to her feet when Cam walked into the kitchen. She'd been waiting for her, knowing that Cam had gone to brief the investigative team. Her coffee sat growing cold in front of her. She'd been rehearsing her speech and had forgotten to drink it.

"Commander, when you have time, I'd like to discuss the transition—"

"You've got Hara and Wozinski…and me, of course." Cam walked to the stove and put her palm on the coffeepot. It was warm. As she grabbed a ceramic mug from a stack on the dish drainer and poured herself a cup, she said, "Plus six of Whitley's private forces. All ex–military police, all very good." She turned and rested her back against the counter, sipping her coffee. "Good to have you back, Stark."

"Thank you, Commander. Is there anything in particular I should know?"

"Business as usual. Except *no one* is given this location. Not FBI, not Secret Service, not the White House security chief. They have one number. Mine. And that's the way it's going to stay. Anyone needs transportation on or off the island, come to me. I'll arrange it."

"Yes, ma'am."

"It's not about not trusting you, Stark. It's about limiting *any* access to her."

"I understand that." Stark weighed her words carefully. "The team needs to know that only one person will be giving the orders, Commander."

A moment passed. Cam lifted a shoulder. "And that would be you."

"Thank you."

"Just know that if she's ever in danger, it will be me standing in front of her."

Stark shook her head. "Only if I'm down. You owe it to her *not* to be the one. Respectfully, ma'am."

Again Cam was silent, her gaze distant. Then she refocused on Stark. "All right, Chief. From now on, I'd like you to sit in on the investigative briefings."

"I'll be there."

"Diane is here, in case you haven't seen her yet. She and Blair have stayed pretty close to the house, and so far it's not been a problem. The beach is secure, but they need to be accompanied. Blair doesn't like it, but—"

From the kitchen doorway, Blair finished, "She doesn't have anything to say about it. Per usual." In a baggy faded blue FBI T-shirt and red-checked boxers that came to mid-thigh, she padded barefoot across the kitchen, paused to squeeze Stark's arm in way of greeting, and made for the coffeepot. She put her palm in the center of Cam's chest and leaned into her for a quick kiss. "Good morning, darling."

Cam grinned. "Hi."

"Please feel free to keep talking about me," Blair said after pouring her coffee. "I'm used to it."

Cam slung an arm around Blair's shoulders. "I think we're probably done with that now."

"Uh-huh." Blair smiled at Stark. "You have a sunburn. Did you have fun?"

"Uh…"

"You are allowed to have fun, Paula," Blair said. "You were on vacation."

"It was good. It was great."

"How's Renée?"

Stark glanced at Cam. "She's good. She's fine."

"I think everyone's getting their legs back under them," Cam said mildly. She kissed Blair's temple. "I've got some calls to make. Can I interest you in a walk after that?"

"Sure. I won't be long." Blair waited until Cam had left the room. "Sorry, I didn't mean to make you uncomfortable asking about Renée in front of Cam."

Stark shook her head. "No, it's okay. I'm just getting used to the commander...well, not exactly being the commander."

Blair laughed. "Paula. Cam will always be Cam, no matter what you call her."

"Yeah, I know."

"Is that a big problem for you?"

"No, not really. It would be silly of me not to take advantage of everything she knows."

"That's a very mature view," Blair said with a grin.

Stark grinned back. "Yeah, I thought so too. But you know, wherever you're going to be, she's going to be. And, well...she's always going to have a say in how we protect you."

"Well," Blair set her mug down on the counter behind her, "I'm glad it's you that took her place."

"Thank you very much. I'm honored."

"I know. I don't understand it, I never have, and I never will. But I believe you." Blair sighed. "Is Renée really doing okay?"

"I think so. She's not having nightmares, at least she hasn't the last few nights."

"How about you?"

Stark looked puzzled. "Me?"

"I was kind of thinking of the anthrax thing," Blair said mildly.

"Oh. That." Stark took a deep breath and let it out slowly. "I don't think about it."

Blair grinned. "Me neither. But I feel okay. You?"

"Fine. Have you heard anything more about Fazio?"

"He's still hospitalized, but responding to therapy. He's going to be okay."

"Man, that's good," Stark said.

"Mac is doing well too. In fact, Cam spoke with him this morning, and he told her they're releasing him in two days."

Starks face lit up. "Yeah? It won't be long before we have the whole team togeth..." She fell silent, thinking about Cynthia. And Foster. She met Blair's gaze. "Nothing will ever be the same again, will it?"

"No," Blair said quietly. "But things never are. We'll all be okay." On her way out of the kitchen, she patted Stark's shoulder. "I'll be going for a walk on the beach with my lover in approximately half an hour, Chief. If you'd like to follow me."

Stark hid her smile. "Yes, ma'am."

CHAPTER TWENTY-SIX

Thursday, September 27

I can't believe you held on to the ace of trump until now," Blair said, tossing down her cards in disgust. "Honestly, Paula, do you think I'm a mind reader?"

"Uh...I thought I was supposed to wait until I could take more points." Stark's face was a study in consternation.

"Not from *me*. Not when I'm your partner." Blair stood abruptly, her chair nearly tipping over as she pushed it back. Everyone at the table flinched. "What exactly do you all do at that training facility of yours when you have spare time? Because God knows, every last one of you is a lousy card player."

"Well," Stark replied with a completely straight face, "we spend a lot of time cleaning our guns."

Blair's eyes narrowed as Diane and Hara tried desperately not to laugh. "You just might become the security chief with the shortest tenure ever."

"Maybe we could work out hand signals or something—"

"Never mind," Blair said through her teeth. "I'm going for a walk."

"Blair, honey," Diane pointed out, "it's midnight. And it's raining."

"I know it's raining. It's been raining for four days. I'm going for a walk." Blair turned on her heel and stalked from the living room.

With a sigh, Diane stood and said to Stark, "I'm going with her."

"Us too," Stark said with equanimity as she and Hara rose.

Diane caught up with Blair on the path to the beach and huddled close to her in the whipping wind and rain. She held the umbrella ineffectually above their heads, where it did little to keep the pelting water from their faces. "God, this is awful."

"Go back, then." Blair shook water from her eyes. "Damned rain."

"*What* has got you so cranky?"

"I'm not cranky."

"Oh yes, you are, and you're taking it out on poor Stark. One of the sweetest spookies you've ever had. And I've seen them all."

"I'm *not*—" She broke off as the umbrella turned itself inside out and nearly set sail. She grabbed it from Diane's hand. "Give me that, before it gets away and kills one of them back there."

"You must be horny."

Blair forced the umbrella closed and shoved it under her arm. "Diane. You're my best friend. But if you don't shut up, I'm going to drown you."

Diane pushed water off her face with both hands. "Then you'd better hurry."

"In case you haven't noticed, Cam has been holed up in the guesthouse for almost three days straight." Blair stomped down to the water's edge, her sneakers filling with ice-cold water. The sky was a solid inky black, storm clouds obscuring the stars. She hugged herself, and when she felt Diane's arms close around her waist from behind, she welcomed her warmth. "When she works like this, she doesn't sleep, and she doesn't eat, and she subsists on coffee. She gets headaches that she thinks I don't know about. She's pissing me off."

"Now I get it. You act the same whether you're worried or horny, and the solution is the same too. You just need Cam in bed."

Blair laughed. "That would be a good place to start." She turned her back to the water and the punishing wind and threaded an arm around Diane's waist. "How about you? Are you suffering from lack of company as well? I don't see you spending much time in your own bed at night."

"Valerie usually calls me when they're wrapping up and I... visit."

"Then you're doing better than me. By the time Cam gets home, she usually falls facedown into bed and gets up again three hours later."

"Well, I haven't had a chance to get used to Valerie yet, so I'm not letting her get a lot of sleep."

"I have a feeling *that* action's probably mutual." Blair steered a path across the darkened beach, noting the shadowy outlines of her two security agents backlit by the lights of the house. She raised her voice to be heard over the sounds of surf and rain. "Go back inside. We're on our way up."

"I'm going to leave you here," Diane said as she reached the point where the path branched to the guesthouse. "I think tonight, I'll surprise her."

"See if you can send mine home before dawn," Blair grumbled as she continued toward the main house.

❖

"I hope you don't mind," Diane said quietly as Valerie slipped into the darkened room. "I let myself in through the back."

Valerie crossed to the bed, her eyes gradually adjusting to the absence of light. She leaned over, tracing the ghostly shape beneath the white sheets with her hand, moving from soft cotton to even softer skin. She combed her fingers through silken strands, her thumb brushing Diane's cheek. She found her mouth effortlessly, as if drawn to her by an invisible force. Soft lips, impossibly warm, enticingly yielding. Her fingers trembled as Diane kissed them. "Oh no. I don't mind at all."

Diane sat up in bed, smoothing her palms over Valerie's shoulders, down her chest, softly outlining her breasts before settling onto the buttons of her blouse. "Let me help you."

Valerie unzipped her slacks and pushed them off as Diane freed her from the rest of her clothing. She slid under the sheets and stretched out facing Diane, supporting her head in her open hand. Lightly, she traced the faint ridge of Diane's collarbone to the hollow at the base of her throat. She placed a soft kiss there. "I'm so glad you're here."

"You've been working terribly hard. All of you."

"There's so much to do, and every day that passes feels like just so much opportunity lost." She sighed as Diane slipped one leg between hers, drawing their bodies closer together. She kissed her, smoothing her palm down the center of Diane's back to cup her buttocks. "Mmm,

I love the way you feel. Your skin is so soft." She parted her lips and gently nipped at Diane's nipple, teasing it with tongue and teeth. "And I love that little mole you have on your breast. So sexy."

Diana arched her back, enjoying the pull of Valerie's mouth on her flesh. She laughed as Valerie traced her tongue around the small birthmark. "I hated that when I was young. I can remember trying to talk Blair and Tanner into getting matching tattoos, so I could cover it up."

"That would have been a shame," Valerie murmured, edging down on the bed. She sucked lightly on the now-turgid thimble of tissue before continuing lower, rubbing her cheek over Diane's stomach.

"I love your mouth. God, what you do to me." Diane gathered Valerie's hair in her hand, tugging gently as Valerie teased at her navel. Dreamily, she recounted, "The two of them were always the daring ones...mmm, that's so nice..." She shifted her legs restlessly as Valerie worked lower. "But they...chickened out."

"I'm glad." Valerie danced her fingers over Diane's thighs and flicked her tongue through the silky curls that lay between them. "I can't quite see you with a heart...or a butterfly...tattooed on your breast."

"Oh, we weren't going to do anything as...mundane as that. We were...thinking of the school mascot...a mountain li—" Diane was brought back from her sensuous haze as Valerie abruptly sat up. "Darling? What is it? What's wrong?"

"What? Oh...nothing." Valerie found Diane's hand and brought it to her lips. She kissed her knuckles. "I'm sorry. Forgive me. I need to get up."

Diane pushed herself up in bed, leaning on her elbows. "Now?"

"Something I have to check." Even as she spoke, Valerie was slipping into her slacks. "I'm sorry. God. I'm sorry."

"Tell me that you're at least suffering a little bit. Because if I'm the only one that's wet and—"

"No. God, no." Valerie sat on the edge of the bed again and curved a hand behind Diane's head, pulling the other woman roughly against her. She covered her mouth with hers, her tongue seeking entrance, and when welcomed, swirling demandingly inside. "Believe me, I'm dying. I've been wanting you all night."

"Good. Then go, and do whatever it is that you need to do. Because when you make love to me, I'm not sharing you with anything." Diane gently pushed her away. "Do you mind if I stay here?"

"I might be a while." Valerie kissed her again. "But I'd like it if you waited. It might be nothing."

"Then I'll be waiting."

"I'll come back as soon as I can." Valerie framed her face and kissed her forehead.

"Careful, I just might hold you to that."

"You do that."

Then Valerie was gone, and Diane curled into the warm space her body had just occupied. She closed her eyes, contenting herself with the scent of her hair on the pillow.

❖

Blair awakened to the insistent ringing of the cell phone. She sat up in bed and leaned across her sleeping lover, fumbling on the bedside table amidst the beeper, the gun, and the radio for the phone.

"God damn it," she cursed, finally finding the small object at the same time as Cam roused.

"I'm awake," Cam muttered groggily, extending her hand.

"No, you're not. And whatever it is," Blair said irritably as she flipped open the phone, "it can wait until morning. They can just call back then." She snapped it closed and dropped it onto the floor on her side of the bed.

"Blair, who was that?" Cam asked quietly, alert now.

Blair circled Cam's shoulders and pulled her down against her body. "No one. Go back to sleep."

"You do realize that was *my* phone."

"Be quiet, Cameron, and go to sleep."

"It might've been Lucinda, or the president."

"I don't care if it was the pope. You need some sleep."

Cam kissed Blair's cheek, then heaved herself up and over her body. She stretched an arm down and felt around on the floor until she found her phone, then rolled back into bed. She opened it and pushed recall.

"You just won't quit, will you," Blair said.

"Roberts," Cam said when the phone was answered. "No, I accidentally disconnected it. What's up?"

"Disconnected it, my ass," Blair muttered. "I'll disconnect it."

Cam instinctively curled her body around the phone, fearing that Blair would snatch it from her grasp and toss it across the room. "I'm sorry. Repeat that?" As she listened, Cam swung her legs over the side of the bed and stood up. She walked to the chair where she'd left her clothes and grabbed her pants in one hand, awkwardly stepping into them as she held the phone between her ear and shoulder. "I'll be right there."

Blair sprang from the bed, naked, and stalked over to Cam. "It's four thirty in the morning. You didn't come in until two. What's so important?"

"Valerie has a lead." Cam kissed her quickly. "Do you think you could find me a clean shirt while I wash up?"

"How's your headache?"

"What?"

"The headache, Cam."

"It's fine."

Blair found a clean shirt in the top dresser drawer, pulled off the protective plastic, and shook it out as she walked into the bathroom. She held it out to Cam with one hand and opened the medicine cabinet with the other. She extracted the aspirin bottle. "Take two of these before you go back over there. And promise me that you'll catch some sleep later on today."

Cam shrugged into her shirt, dry swallowed the aspirins, and kissed Blair again. "Promise. I love you."

"Yeah, yeah." Blair snatched her robe from the bathroom door and walked with her through the house, knowing she wasn't going to be able to sleep. She contemplated waking Diane for company, and then realized that she was at the guesthouse too. Feeling abandoned and out of sorts, she contemplated another walk. It was pitch black and still storming. She contented herself with making coffee, and as she watched the pot brew, heard footsteps behind her. Turning, she saw Stark in the doorway. "Do you have the night shift or can't you sleep either?"

"Night shift."

"Good. Go get the cards. I'm going to teach you how to play pinochle."

❖

Cam walked into the dining room, which was lit by three desk lights and the computer monitors. The overhead chandelier had been turned down to a soft glow. Felicia and Valerie each sat at a keyboard. "What's up?"

Valerie pointed to the printer, where a page was just sliding out. "Grab that, Cameron. See what you think."

"Where's Savard?" Cam asked as she extracted the page.

"Asleep at the main house. I thought we could call her if this turns out to be anything," Felicia said. "I just thought..."

"No, you're right. Somebody might as will get some sleep." Cam frowned at the image from the color laser printer. It looked like a patch from a military uniform, but she didn't recognize the insignia. The resolution was poor and some of the markings indistinct. But what was very clear were the two crossed rifles above the American flag in the upper portion of the shield-shaped design. "What is this?"

"It's a shoulder patch," Valerie said. "We copied it from a web site image and blew it up. That's the tattoo those four guys had on their arms, don't you think?"

"Certainly looks like it." Cam pulled a chair out and sat down, placing the paper carefully on the table next to her. "Where is it from?"

Valerie slid a foot away from the computer monitor and pointed to the screen. "NCMA—North Carolina Military Academy. David Foster was a student there from the age of nine until he graduated at the age of seventeen."

"What's that site?"

Felicia answered, "It's the home page for the school. The commandant is in full uniform, and we pulled the patch off the picture of him."

Cam was quiet for several moments, then she stood and walked closer to the computer, squinting at the images. "We need to know everything there is to know about that place. How long has that guy been the commandant?"

"Checking," Felicia muttered. "Twenty-seven years."

"Then we need to know everything on him too. Starting with his name."

"General Thomas Matheson."

"A real general?" Cam asked. "Because sometimes these guys bestow their own ranks that don't come from any recognized branch of the Armed Forces."

"We don't know that yet," Valerie said. "We're about to start running him through databases now."

"You'd better wake Savard. That's her area," Cam said. "I'll make some coffee. The next thing you need to do is get the student records from the years that Foster was there. Let's see if we can pull some faces that match our dead guys."

"We'll have to…extract…that information from their internal computer systems," Felicia said carefully.

"Fine. Hack into them, Davis. Just don't let them know."

"Yes, ma'am," Felicia said smartly, a small smile of anticipation softening her elegantly remote features.

As Felicia turned to the keyboard, her fingers already flying, Cam signaled for Valerie to accompany her to the kitchen. "Nice job with that. How'd you tip to it?"

Valerie recalled the sensation of Diane's skin beneath her lips, the scent of her, and her heart raced. "Just luck. Someone mentioned getting a tattoo of a school mascot, which made me think of school crests." She opened the cabinet door and passed the coffee canister to Cam. She crossed her arms over her chest, belatedly realizing that she'd forgotten her underwear in her haste to dress earlier.

Cam followed her motion and hastily averted her gaze. "It's the first lead we've had, and it's solid."

"You're thinking that Foster met these men, or at least one of them, at school and then later reconnected with them?"

"Seems like a good possibility."

"God," Valerie murmured. "Why?"

"That's something we may never understand. I'll be happy just to know *how*."

"If this really turns out to be true," Valerie said, "it's going to be a media nightmare. We can't let this get out."

"I imagine that's why you're here, isn't it?" Cam spoke without rancor, watching Valerie's face. "To control the flow of information?"

"Even the CIA can't do that, Cameron. You know that."

"But the CIA is very good at making embarrassing situations disappear, when it's necessary."

Valerie said nothing. She couldn't refute what they both knew to be true.

CHAPTER TWENTY-SEVEN

Friday, September 28

Cam found Blair working on a canvas as the last rays of a cloud-dampened sun faded on the horizon. She'd tied a rolled red bandanna around her forehead to hold her hair out of the way. She wore loose khaki chinos and one of her favorite Grateful Dead T-shirts, paint-stained and holey. A slash of iridescent blue crossed her right forearm where she'd evidently brushed against the corner of her palette when reaching for something. Cam kissed the back of her neck.

"You look terrific."

Blair grinned. "I'm a mess. Don't come too close, I'll ruin your suit."

Obediently, Cam stayed still as Blair moved a few feet away.

"Did you eat anything at all today?" Blair asked distractedly, her focus wandering back to the painting and a problem area she had been trying to correct.

"We had pizza."

"Mmm. That's right. Stark got us some too."

"Can I interrupt you for just a few more minutes?"

There was something in the tone of Cam's voice that immediately captured Blair's attention. She set her sable brush aside and picked up the rag she used to clean her hands. Turning her back to the painting and putting it from her mind, her expression cautious, she said, "What's the matter?"

"Nothing." Cam took her hand, ignoring her vigorous protests about paint stains, and led her toward the bedroom. Once inside, she closed the door. "We've identified the members of the assault team who hit the Aerie."

Blair took a quick breath and backed away. "Who are they? Do I know them?"

Cam took one step forward and, when Blair backed up yet again, she stopped moving and shook her head. "No, as far as we can tell, they have nothing to do with you personally. We cross-referenced their names with every bit of information in your security files. Nothing turned up. You've never met them. They never communicated with you. They've never been known to make a statement about you, your father, or anything remotely political."

"Then *why?*"

"It doesn't matter," Cam said, wishing that she could keep all of this from Blair. Pointing out that the assault had nothing to do with her as an individual, but only with what she represented, was like telling Blair she'd always been right. That *who* she was wasn't important, and all that mattered was what people saw when they looked at her. Just saying the words turned her stomach, but Blair did not want or need her protection. Not from this. "It wasn't about you. They came after you to make a statement."

"But Foster, Foster *knew* me." Blair couldn't hide the horror in her voice. A man she knew—a man who had sat beside her countless times in the car, walked with her on the streets, been there in the shadows as her guardian—had intended to murder her. Face-to-face. It couldn't be more personal. "Where did they come from?"

"We don't have the entire picture yet," Cam said gently. "We identified the men through tattoos that led us to the military academy that they attended as boys. Foster was part of their group." With Valerie, Felicia, and Savard working nonstop all day, they'd been able to access school records, interdepartmental memos, letters to families, interscholastic sports records, and applications to colleges—all manner of personal and academic information that had allowed them to profile the suspects. Eventually, they found the photo archives, and they'd found the faces.

"Tell me their names."

"Blair…"

"Tell me. I want them to be real. Not some ghosts, not some monsters without names or faces."

Cam took a breath and recited the names. She wanted to hold her. God, she ached to shield her. She was afraid to go near her, and that was the hardest part of all. "We think they might have been groomed for the patriot organization while they were at the school."

"You can't be serious. As boys? Recruiting *boys* to become assassins?"

"We don't know that they were trained from adolescence to be assassins," Cam admitted, "but they may have been indoctrinated into a way of thinking that made that next step possible. Don't forget the Hitler Youth and how effective they were in recruiting for the Reich."

Blair shook her head. It should have been inconceivable, but in her heart she knew it was a terrible reality. "Why did you come to that conclusion?"

"It's too much of a coincidence that all four of them have nothing in the public record to identify them. They don't even have driver's licenses." Cam wouldn't have believed the men actually existed if she hadn't seen their autopsy photos. "This, or something *like* this, was planned well before they reached adulthood."

Blair sat on the edge of the bed, her legs shaking. "It's horrible. I...What were they *doing* all this time? Why didn't anyone know this was going on?"

"With the exception of Foster, they've been living normal lives as ordinary citizens, doing nothing that would call attention to themselves. Ordinary jobs, no debt, no criminal records, nothing to make them stand out." Carefully, Cam crossed the room, watching Blair's face. She squatted down in front of her and rested her hands lightly on Blair's thighs. "None of them has ever been fingerprinted or photographed for any reason, even a credit card. They've never held a government or industry job where a security check would have been needed."

"But that could just be coincidence. It doesn't mean anything was planned," Blair insisted.

"If that were the whole picture, I'd agree with you, but it's not. We haven't been able to find applications to military academies for any of the four—not West Point, not the Naval Academy, not the Air Force Academy—even though they surely would have been prime candidates. Well over ninety percent of graduates from NCMA go on to careers in the Armed Forces, and almost one hundred percent apply. Foster went into government service, but these men...It's as if they've been purposefully flying under the radar, just waiting."

"Waiting to be called to do something like this?"

"That's what we think." Cam eased up onto the bed next to Blair and loosely settled an arm around her waist. Blair didn't break her rigid pose, but she accepted Cam's touch. "They probably received all of their assault training at one of the paramilitary camps."

"Like a sleeper cell, only made up of Americans instead of… whoever?" Blair closed her eyes for a second. When she opened them, they were filled with pain. "This can't be. This doesn't happen here."

Cam didn't need to point out that what happened on September 11 didn't happen here either, because she knew they were both thinking it. "I'm sorry."

"What now?" Blair asked.

"We still have work to do. These men are dead, and they can't help us with much more. Hopefully, the commandant of the school they attended will have the rest of the answers. He's proving almost as hard to uncover as these guys were, even though we know his name and what he looks like."

"What happens if he's the one who…planned everything?"

"Then he'll be arrested." Cam wasn't actually so sure what would happen to him, but she knew one thing with absolute certainty. She wanted the opportunity to bring him to justice. And her idea of justice was not delivering him to the FBI or the Justice Department, where he could cut a deal for leniency in exchange for information. In all likelihood, that was what the people in power would want, but their agenda was not hers. Her only interest now was Blair's present and future safety.

❖

"I think I've got something," Savard called from the dining room, her voice tight with anticipation.

Cam levered herself off the couch where she'd been trying to take a nap, rubbed at her eyes, which felt gritty and dry, and shook her head to clear the cobwebs. "What did you find?"

"I've been sifting through Matheson's tax records. He paid a hefty inheritance tax fifteen years ago when his father died."

Cam peered at the screen, frowning at what appeared to be scanned copies of old documents. "You think he's bankrolling terrorists?"

Savard shook her head. "No. I traced back his parents, and then their parents. Matheson's grandfather held a deed for what looks like half a mountain in Tennessee."

"You don't say." Cam smiled. "And Matheson inherited the property. Do you have the precise coordinates for it yet?"

"It's almost midnight on a Friday night, Commander. No one's going to be available at the hall of records in Memphis."

"I'll bet their computer networks are running, because the law enforcement agencies will need access."

"Then we need Felicia for the extraction," Savard said, bowing to Felicia's skill as a computer cracker.

Cam checked her watch and grimaced. "She's only been asleep a couple hours, but I guess we'll need to wa—"

"I might have a contact who can get the location for us a little faster," Valerie said. "I'll make a call."

"All right," Cam said. "And while you're at it, you might request a satellite image for us. You've got something up there with infrared capability, don't you?"

Valerie smiled. "I have no idea what's orbiting the Earth, Cameron. But I'm certain we have some sort of helpful toy up there. I'll see what I can do."

Savard waited until Valerie left the room to make her call. "You think there's a paramilitary compound on his property?"

"Don't you?"

"Yeah. I do. What are we going to do when we find out where it is?"

"I imagine it'll be out of our hands then." Cam kept her face carefully neutral.

"That's not how I want to see it go down." Savard regarded her steadily. "These guys may not have planned what happened at the World Trade Center, but they knew about it. And they sure as hell intended to kill Blair. I want to be there when they go down."

"Yes. So do I."

❖

Blair was still awake when Cam came in shortly after four a.m., lying in bed in the dark with only the light from the vanity in the adjacent bathroom for illumination. "What's happening?"

Cam undressed quickly and slid into bed, reaching for Blair's hand. She threaded her fingers lightly through Blair's. "Valerie, Savard, and I need to go to Washington."

Blair tugged her hand free. "When?"

"Today. Later this morning."

"Why?"

"We're meeting with Lucinda and your father. Probably a few other people as well."

"About what?"

"We've located a compound in the Tennessee mountains. We've got satellite images of a number of buildings and vehicles. We suspect that's where the men who made the attempt on your life came from."

"It's just a briefing, right?"

"I should be back tonight."

"I want to come with you."

"That's not a good idea," Cam said quietly. "We've established excellent security here. We have no way of knowing how deep this may go—who in DC may be a part of it. Foster was on the inside. Maybe there are others. Unless you want to stay in the White House for another few weeks…"

"You know I don't."

"Then this is the safest place for you. The three of us will drive to Boston and get a flight from there."

"And just why do *you* need to go in person?" Blair sat up and snapped on the bedside light. She pulled the sheet to her waist, drew her knees up, and folded her arms around them, drawing in on herself. "What are you going to do in DC? Plan the big operation? Strategize about how you're going to apprehend these guys?" When Cam said nothing, Blair went on, her voice harsh, "You're not a commando, Cameron. That's why we have Special Forces. You're *not* getting involved in this."

"I'm just consulting."

"Oh," Blair said derisively, "don't you dare give me that line. I know you. Consulting, my ass. Tell me you're not going with the strike team. *Tell me* that's not your plan."

"The only thing that's going to happen today is that I'm going to brief the president, Lucinda, and the security chief. That's all." Cam sat up and leaned her shoulder against Blair's.

Despite her anger, Blair found Cam's hand and held it. "What if they don't want to wait? What if they want to go today? Tell me you won't go with them."

Cam was silent.

"Damn you, Cameron."

"I won't be in the first wave. I won't be knocking down any doors."

"I want you to promise me you won't go with them." Blair saw Cam's jaw set. Very gently, she turned Cam's face toward hers. "Make me that promise."

Cam looked into her eyes. "I want to see him in chains. I'd prefer to see him dead, but I won't do it myself. I promise I'll stay far behind the line. I promise you that."

"Why? Why is it so important?"

"Men like him killed my father. And then he almost killed you…" Cam's throat tightened around the words and she turned her face forcefully away, breaking Blair's hold. "I need faces for the monsters too, Blair."

"Oh, Jesus," Blair sighed, wrapping her arm tightly around Cam's shoulders. "I can't stand it when you hurt." She leaned her forehead against the side of Cam's head. "I love you even more than I need you, and that's so much I can't stand it. Please be careful."

Cam turned back, pulling Blair into her arms. She kissed her roughly, urgently, needing to drive the images of flaming cars and automatic gunfire from her mind. She pushed her back onto the bed and followed, covering Blair's body with her own. She let herself drown in her, losing her pain amidst their passion.

❖

Valerie held Diane as she slept. She caressed her hair, her back, the curve of her side, remembering the sound of her pleasure. Fixing it in her mind. She could taste her still, sweetly exotic. She'd made love to her until Diane had begged her to stop, laughing and crying as she'd come the last time.

"Let me make love to you," Diane had murmured drowsily, barely able to move.

"Next time," she had whispered, gathering her close against her body.

Diane, sighing with contentment, had curled trustingly into her arms.

Valerie waited fifteen minutes, thirty, forty—listening to the soft sounds of Diane's breathing, feeling the warm currents of her exhalations drifting over her breasts, counting her heartbeats under her fingertips. When she couldn't wait any longer, she gently kissed Diane's forehead and eased slowly away. She'd had years of practice leaving the arms of women she'd satisfied without waking them. Carefully, she gathered her clothing and the single small valise she'd brought with her.

Two minutes later she stood naked on the rear deck and dressed efficiently in the predawn light. Five minutes later, she was at the ocean's edge and walking briskly away from the house. In fifteen minutes she was three-quarters of a mile away, and the reverberations of the engine on the outboard motor sounded no different than a wave rushing to shore. She climbed into the small craft, and as it pointed away from land and the safe house and the people inside, she did not look back.

CHAPTER TWENTY-EIGHT

Saturday, September 29

Perhaps it was the bed growing cold that woke her, or something in her unconscious that warned her of impending pain. But when Diane rolled onto her side and opened her eyes, she was not surprised to find herself alone. She listened intently for any sound in the quiet house. The baseboard heater hummed quietly. Somewhere far out on the water, a foghorn sounded its mournful call. The house was still—Felicia asleep and Savard in Stark's bed at the main house. Valerie always placed her watch and the gold signet ring she wore on the little finger of her right hand on the bedside table when they made love. There was nothing there now.

Diane strained to hear the shower running in the adjacent bathroom, but she knew that Valerie was gone. The very air had lost its warmth, and loneliness tugged at her heart with new resolve. She lay quietly for a long time, replaying their last moments together. Her body still ached with the memory of desire. She felt Valerie's hands on her, inside her, and remembered the silent promises that had passed between them as they had taken their pleasure in one another. There had been other women who had touched her life, fleetingly, and then had left. She had learned to recognize goodbye in a kiss. That was not what Valerie had said to her as she had claimed her just hours ago.

She had to believe that, or her heart would surely break.

❖

"Damn it, Cam," Blair exploded, slamming her phone down on the kitchen counter. "That was Diane. Valerie's gone."

Cam automatically looked at the clock. 5:10 a.m. Almost an hour until sunup. They had gotten out of bed at five because she, Savard, and Valerie were leaving at five thirty to rendezvous with a helicopter that would pick them up at a small private airport on the mainland and take them to DC. They'd finalized the plan before they'd turned in the night before. She, Savard, and Valerie.

God damn it.

Cam looked out the side window and counted the cars underneath the portico. None were missing. Wozinski had been on night shift, and he would have called her if there'd been any activity on the road in front of the house. Tanner's people were patrolling the entire sector of the island and definitely would have noticed a pickup anywhere in the vicinity, even if Valerie had walked from the house under cover of darkness to the road several miles away. She walked through the adjacent mudroom to the back door, opened it, and said to Hara, "Any activity out here?"

Agent Hara, who had been leaning against the deck post facing the guesthouse and the beach beyond, turned. She wore black slacks and running shoes, a navy windbreaker over a dark polo shirt, and an alert but unconcerned expression. "Good morning, Commander. Nothing out of the ordinary. Agent Lawrence walked down to the beach about"— she glanced at her watch—"thirty-five minutes ago."

"Is that her usual time?"

"Any time between four thirty and six," Hara said. "Almost every day."

Cam realized instantly that the pattern had been carefully, deliberately set, but she followed the questions to their logical end for the sake of procedure. "Does Ms. Bleeker ordinarily accompany her?"

"Not usually this early, Commander."

"How long is she usually gone?"

"Forty-five minutes. An hour at the most. In fact, she should be back any time."

"Was she carrying anything today?"

"Not that I noticed, but it was still dark. I observed her exit the building and checked my watch. By then she was partially obscured by the dunes." Hara looked uncomfortable. "Did I miss something,

Commander?"

"No. I did." Cam stepped back inside and said to Blair, "They must've picked her up on the water."

"Who?" Blair demanded. "Are you telling me she's been kidnapped or something?"

"I doubt that." The muscles in Cam's shoulders tightened as she fought back the anger. "I'd imagine the Agency retrieved her."

"Why?" Blair paced in a tight circle in the center of the kitchen, growing more furious with each passing moment.

"The number of people who know she's here is very limited, and there's no reason to believe she would be a target for a kidnapping." Cam pulled her cell phone from her belt. "It's more likely this was part of the plan from the beginning."

"I can't believe she did this. Do you know what this is going to do to Diane? God damn it. Son of a bitch." Blair stalked from one side of the room to the other. "What plan are you talking about? Whose plan?"

"The CIA's. We've just identified a key player in the assault on the Aerie. We *may* have uncovered a potential connection to the terrorists who hit the World Trade Center. I'm sure that's the information Valerie was sent here to get. Now she has it, her job is done, and they've extracted her." Cam shrugged. "They often relocate their field agents precipitously."

"They sent her to spy on you? My father would never allow that."

Cam caught Blair's shoulders and halted her harried journey. "He probably doesn't even know about it."

"That's ridiculous. He's the president. He knows everything."

"Actually, he doesn't, and there's a good reason for it. There are times when he has to be able to disavow knowledge, especially when something may be…hazy, legally." Cam blew out a frustrated breath. "But I'm willing to bet Lucinda Washburn knows about it. Because she's the one who protects him."

"I'm calling her. Right now." Blair grabbed her phone from the counter and flipped it open.

Gently, Cam reached out and closed it. "She's not going to tell you. She's not going to tell me. *If* she knows, she won't admit it. That's how these things are done."

Blair fixed Cam with an incredulous stare. "Why aren't you angry? Don't you feel betrayed?"

"It's not personal," Cam said quietly. She couldn't view it as personal, because she needed to keep her head clear. The operation depended upon it. And even more importantly, so did the lives of her people.

"Bullshit. Bullshit, bullshit, *bullshit*. That woman…damn it, I *hate* saying this, but that woman is more to you than just another agent."

"No, she isn't." Cam smiled ruefully. "Claire was, once, but Valerie isn't."

"How you can distinguish between the two of them?"

Cam considered whether it was wise to answer. Discussing her past involvement with another woman with Blair was not generally a wise idea. She knew that Blair trusted her. She also knew that Blair knew that she loved her. But Blair was Blair, and she didn't take any intrusion on their relationship lightly. Cam sighed. It went against her every instinct, but her relationship with Blair was something that she couldn't fit into the logic of the rest of her life. The only course that had ever worked with Blair was honesty, no matter how treacherous the path might appear. "What Claire and I had, what we shared, was in the past. We were different people then, and Claire is gone now."

Blair pulled out a kitchen chair and sank into it, then sat drumming her fingers on the wooden surface as she regarded Cam through narrowed eyes. "Do you ever…miss her?"

"Ah, Jesus, Blair," Cam said pleadingly.

"I'm not jealous, I just want to know."

Cam pulled out a second chair and sat facing Blair. She leaned forward and curled her hands around the outside of Blair's knees. She looked directly into Blair's eyes. "Sometimes I'm sad that I'll never see her…Claire…again. But those times are very rare, and they have nothing to do with you and me. It's not about the sex—it wasn't really about that for a long time, even before it ended. It's more like losing a friend."

"And what about Valerie?"

"Valerie…" Cam blew out a breath and shook her head. "Valerie is a woman I don't really know. We're connected, that's true, on a deeper level than just ordinary colleagues, but I don't know what drives her inside. I don't know why she makes the choices she does. I don't *know* her, and I can't be responsible for her. I have Stark and Savard and Mac and all of the others to think of."

"But you like her. I know you do."

"I do. I understand her, on a lot of levels. She's more like me than any of the others."

Blair wanted to protest, but she knew it was true. Cam would sacrifice almost everything for duty—not love, not really—but if you didn't know her very well, it would look like that. "Well, *I'm* really pissed at her. She had no business getting involved with Diane if she knew she was going to be leaving. It's selfish and cruel."

"Maybe she couldn't help it." Cam traced a finger along the tense angle of Blair's jaw. "Baby. Sometimes we fall in love even when we don't want to."

Blair turned her head quickly and kissed Cam's hand. "Don't try to talk me out of being angry."

Cam shook her head again. "I'm not. I know I couldn't. I'm just saying that I've been where she is, and sometimes it's just as hard on the other side. Especially when you can't explain why you're doing what you're doing."

"It drives me crazy the way you all stick together," Blair grumbled.

"If we find out that Valerie isn't working for the Agency, or that the plan all along was to somehow protect the people responsible for what happened at the Aerie, then I will hunt her down to the ends of the earth." Cam's hands tightened on Blair's thighs. "I promise you that."

"What do you mean if she isn't working for the Agency? You mean like a double agent?" Blair dropped her head back with a groan and stared at the ceiling. "This just keeps getting worse. Poor Diane."

Cam said nothing, disgusted with those who professed to share a common goal but whose agenda, ultimately, was only the preservation of their own power. It was a lesson she had learned very early in her life, and one she had temporarily forgotten only because Valerie had been a woman whom she had trusted. It was a mistake she wouldn't make again. She opened her cell phone and punched in Lucinda Washburn's private number.

❖

Blair looked out the kitchen window and saw Diane start down the dune path wearing nothing but a silk blouse, slacks, and low heels. The thermometer mounted outside the window read fifty-three degrees. "Jesus."

She pulled on her jacket, grabbed Cam's from a hook by the back door, and started after her. She crossed the beach beneath a dull gray morning sky, grateful that it had at last stopped raining. The tide was on its way out, and seagulls chattered and picked among the littered shells and abandoned seaweed at the water's edge. She joined her best friend and extended the anorak. "Here, put this on. You're going to get sick."

"Thanks," Diane said quietly, accepting the navy fleece pullover. She shrugged into it without looking away from the ocean. It was too big for her in the shoulders and sleeves, and she wrapped both arms around her waist, automatically pulling her hands inside to warm them. "I'm okay. You don't need to stay."

"Shut up, Diane."

After a minute of silence when it appeared that Diane had taken her advice, Blair snugged an arm around Diane's waist. "This might be the first time in my life I don't know what to say."

"There isn't anything to say." Diane found Blair's hand where it rested on her hip and pulled it inside the sleeve with hers. "Does Cam know why she left?"

"Not really. Do you have any idea?"

"Not a one. I've been going crazy trying to figure out why she did anything she did, including getting involved with me." Diane laughed, a harsh strangled sound. "I'm good, but I doubt it was just the sex."

"Diane…" Blair said.

"I keep thinking I should have sensed something. Seen something in her eyes. God, I should have realized something was wrong when she touched me, shouldn't I?" She turned to Blair, her eyes clouded with pain. "How could I love her so damn much and not know her?"

"I want to kill her," Blair muttered. She'd never seen Diane so defenseless. "I swear to God, I do."

"I love you for that." Diane smiled tiredly and gave Blair's hand a little shake. "But it's not necessary for both of us to be turned inside out by this. She'll have an explanation, and I'll either be able to live with it or I won't."

"You mean you're actually going to give her a chance to explain?" Blair snorted. "Personally, I'd throttle her the second she showed her face."

Diane laughed, and this time there was the smallest hint of pleasure in it. "It seems to me there were a few times that you had the same feelings about Cam. Especially at the beginning, when she did things that made you more than a little crazy."

"*She* never left me in the middle of the night without an explanation."

"No, she didn't," Diane said with a sigh. "But then, Valerie isn't Cam, and I'm not you."

"Oh, please don't be reasonable. Jesus. Aren't you furious with her? You certainly should be," Blair said with indignation.

"I *am* angry. I'm angry that she didn't trust me enough to tell me she had to leave, but"—Diane held up a hand to forestall another outburst from Blair—"she warned me at the beginning that she wasn't always free to do what she wanted." She looked back out to the water, her expression pensive. "There's an explanation."

"Do you really trust her?" Blair's voice was less accusatory now than curious.

"I do," Diane said softly, tracing her thumb in small circles over the top of Blair's hand. "Last night we made love. I can't tell you what it was like, why it was different than anything I've ever experienced. But nothing has ever touched me as deeply as what passed between us. She told me in every way that she could that she loved me. Do you know what I mean?"

Blair sighed. "Yes. I know. I know there are things that I believe because if they weren't true, Cam would never touch me the way she does. And I wouldn't let her."

"Yes. You and I...we know what it's like to make love and never be touched. But it's not like that with them, is it. They get inside." Diane turned back to Blair, not expecting an answer. "If that's not reason enough to trust, then I'm never going to have one."

"If she hurts you," Blair said in total seriousness, "I'm going to hurt her back."

Diane smiled and put both arms around Blair's shoulders. She hugged her, rubbing her cold cheek against Blair's, welcoming the warmth. "I know you would, and I love you for that. But before you make up your mind that she's guilty, let's just wait."

"How long?" Blair stroked her hand over Diane's back, knowing she was in pain and hating the helplessness of not being able to assuage it.

"I don't know. I've never been in this situation before." Diane stepped away, sliding her grip down Blair's arms until she clasped both hands. "I just know that I love her, and I have to believe that she has her reasons."

Blair held back her misgivings, because if she was right not to trust Valerie, time would prove it. If she was wrong, voicing her distrust now would only add to Diane's unhappiness. Instead, she nodded. "Well, you've always had better luck at reading women than me."

"Except for Cam," Diane said with a laugh.

"She would be the exception to all things in my life."

"Thank you."

"For what?" Blair asked.

"For being on my side."

"Oh, sweetie, always." Blair tugged Diane's hand. "Come on. Let's go inside, have some breakfast, and complain about our girlfriends together."

"Wonderful." Diane caught her lip, nearly ambushed by a swell of tears. "That's just exactly what I need."

Blair held fast to Diane's hand as they walked toward the house, her gaze fixed on Cam, who stood on the back deck watching them approach. There were things about her lover she would never truly understand—the fierce drive for justice, the sense of honor that motivated her every decision—and sometimes, like the woman beside her, she just had to trust her heart.

CHAPTER TWENTY-NINE

Stark sat on the side of the bed watching Savard dress, uneasiness coiling in the pit of her stomach like a viper poised to strike. Her fingers cramped as she clenched her hands tightly around the edge of the mattress. The covers were thrown back, exposing the crumpled sheets where they had spent the last few hours curled around one another. How quickly life could move from sated comfort to uncertainty. A litany of entreaties rushed through her mind, but she spoke none aloud.

I don't want you to go. I have a really bad feeling about this. You're not even really recovered from getting shot, and I know you're still a little shaky from what happened on 9/11. You're not yourself. You're not at your best. You're tired, I know you're tired. That's when you get hurt. Jesus, I don't want you to go.

"I'll probably be back tonight," Savard said, tucking a black polo shirt into jeans only a shade lighter. She picked up her holster from the dresser, automatically checked her weapon, and hooked it to her belt on her right hip. She reached for the FBI flak jacket that she'd left over the back of the chair when she'd selected the clothes from the closet. She pulled it on and swept her right hand beneath the garment to reach her gun, assuring herself that nothing impaired her draw. "If I'm delayed, I'll call."

"Okay." *You're not dressing for a meeting.*

Savard turned and looked at Stark from across the room. "Sweetie, don't worry."

"I'm not. Just, you know, be careful."

"I can feel you worrying from over here." Savard crossed the room and gently placed both hands on Stark's shoulders, then bent low to look into her face. "I'll probably spend the entire day debriefing. You know how slowly things happen once the bosses get involved."

Stark nodded. "Well, in case anything…interesting happens, you'll…be fine."

"Paula," Savard said gently, settling into Stark's lap and wrapping both arms around her shoulders. "This is my job. Just like yours is to take care of Blair. I know what that means. I know when you walk out the door with her what that means. If I let myself think about it, it would eat me up."

"You're right," Stark mumbled, burying her face in the angle between Savard's neck and shoulder, embracing her. "I just love you."

"Mmm, and I love you." Savard eased her palm beneath Stark's chin and tilted her face up. She kissed her, taking her time, although she had very little to spare. She knew the commander was waiting for her, but she owed Paula this one moment. Somewhere in the back of her mind she knew that every goodbye could be the last, and she wanted to be certain to say everything that she felt in her heart. She let her mouth slide over Stark's, soft and warm, before she slipped her tongue inside for a final slow caress. "I'll call you later."

"Talk to you soon," Stark said, forcing a smile as she reluctantly let her go.

❖

Blair and Diane reached the back porch just in time for Blair to hear Cam's final words.

"…want in on it. We've earned it. Fine. Yes. Thank you." She closed the phone abruptly just as Blair reached her. "Hey." She kissed her. "I've only got a minute. Sorry."

"Who was that?" Blair asked.

Diane squeezed Blair's hand. "I'm going to go inside and take a shower."

Blair didn't answer, still studying Cam, as she repeated, "Who was that?"

"Stewart Carlisle," Cam said, naming her immediate superior.

"And he's going to do what? Make sure you get your shot at these guys?" Blair grasped the front of Cam's leather flight jacket and gave her a shake. "You *promised* me. You promised me that you'd stay out of this. Cameron, God damn it. You promised."

"I know. I meant it." Cam covered Blair's hands with hers, not resisting. "I *do* mean it. I said I'd stay in the back lines, and I will. I swear."

Blair yanked her forward and kissed her hard. She felt her lips bruise and knew Cam's would be sore too, but she didn't care. If she couldn't keep her from going, couldn't keep her from danger, she would make her feel what there was to lose if she put herself at risk. This love, this life they had made, *that* was what she wanted Cam to remember when she had to make a choice between her desire to see justice done and her own safety.

Cam let herself be taken, helpless before Blair's onslaught. She was breathless from the force of Blair's demanding mouth. She wasn't aware of being pushed until her back smacked up against the deck post and Blair pressed into her. She finally jerked her head away from the kiss, but she couldn't escape the havoc Blair's hands played on her body. "Jesus. I have to be able to think sometime today, baby. Give me a break."

"I *want* you to think," Blair muttered, her mouth on Cam's neck. "You think about *me* today, Cameron. You think about making me love you, about making me need you. And you get your ass back here in one piece."

"I never think of anyone but you," Cam said before she claimed her mouth with as much ferocity as Blair had taken hers. After another hungry moment, she pulled away. "I love you."

"Yeah, yeah." Resting her forehead on Cam's shoulder, Blair tenderly smoothed her hands over the front of Cam's leather jacket, then inside to gently caress her chest. "Like that's the answer to everything."

"Isn't it?" Cam smiled and kissed her forehead. "Be back soon, baby." Then she slipped from Blair's embrace and strode down the stairs and around the building, out of sight.

Blair leaned against the post, watching the sunrise over the ocean. It was so indescribable, so heartbreakingly beautiful. Like love. Before the moment was lost, she hurried inside, dropping her jacket on the floor along the way, and set a fresh canvas on the easel. Her gaze on the sunrise, her heart with Cam, she began to paint.

❖

Savard heard the clump-clump-clump of rotors whirring before the black dot on the horizon became distinguishable as an MH-6 Little Bird—an Army Special Ops light assault helicopter. It was one of the smallest attack aircraft in the Army's arsenal, used primarily for insertion and extraction operations. Ordinarily, it carried six combat troops on its external platforms, but currently the ramps were unoccupied. She glanced at Cam. "Interesting form of transportation to a debriefing, Commander."

"There's been a slight change in plans," Cam said, her eyes on the descending aircraft. "It seems there is some degree of urgency since we have a breakdown in the integrity of our team and our intel may not be secure."

Breakdown in the integrity of our team. Savard played that phrase around in her mind. She deciphered it to mean that someone higher up knew that Valerie was gone, and that she had most likely informed the CIA not only of the location of the paramilitary camp but also of the evidence pointing to Matheson's terrorist link. *Our intel may not be secure.* And someone with a lot of pull was obviously worried that someone *else* would get to the party first. Her vote would be the Department of Defense. They could mobilize this kind of action pretty damn fast.

"It's rather unusual, isn't it," Savard said quietly, "to deploy the military against civilians? I would think it would fall to us in the FBI to take these guys down."

"Ordinarily it would be your people," Cam replied just as quietly. "But these aren't ordinary times. And after the kind of standoff that happened at Waco, with all the publicity that went with it, I expect even the White House is willing to bend the rules to get this done quickly, quietly, and efficiently."

"And…we're going along?" Savard couldn't quite keep the excitement out of her voice.

Cam smiled with grim satisfaction. "We are."

"Uh, if you don't mind me asking, how…?"

"I made some calls."

"Son of a bitch. I mean, thank you, Commander." Savard grinned. *I'll just bet it was a few calls—probably starting with the chief of staff.* Her eyes glinted with anticipation. Her whispered words were lost in the roar of the engine as the attack helicopter settled amidst a cloud of dust and debris. *Here we come, you bastards.*

Heads down, Savard and Cam ran across the tarmac as the door of the helicopter swung open. As soon as they climbed into the body, an Army officer in combat garb with lieutenant's bars on his shoulders crouched down in front of them. The helicopter began to ascend.

"Which one of you is Roberts?" he shouted, handing them headsets to muffle the motor and to allow them to speak to one another in flight.

"I am," Cam yelled back, situating the headgear and flicking the transmitter switch. She grabbed a strap that hung from the ceiling to steady herself and pointed to Savard. "Special Agent Savard, FBI."

The lieutenant nodded to both of them. "We'll refuel in Virginia and rendezvous with the other aircraft, then proceed directly to the target. We've been advised that you are to be considered embedded members of the team. You all will be in the strike zone."

"Understood," Cam replied.

"There're vests under the benches. Do you require assault rifles?"

"We're armed," Cam said. "We'll be fine, Lieutenant."

He studied her face for a moment, then nodded as if satisfied. "Enjoy the ride." Then he settled back on his heels, one hand curled around another hanging strap, closed his eyes, and appeared to go to sleep.

Savard glanced at Cam, raised her eyebrows, and grinned. She mouthed the words, *Let's rock 'n roll.*

Cam grinned and nodded back.

❖

Blair stepped out onto the deck carrying two cups of coffee. She handed one to Stark.

"Thank you," Stark said, taking the mug. The sun was up, but the air was still chilled, and although it usually didn't bother her, this morning she was cold. She shivered inside her regulation-issue nylon jacket.

"Hell of a morning so far," Blair said.

"Yeah. How's Diane?"

"She's okay. She's willing to believe there's a good reason for what Valerie did, at least for now."

"I'm sure there's a reason," Stark grunted. "How *good* it is depends on whose team you play for."

"Well, she never really was part of this team."

"Maybe not officially, but we trusted her. Felicia's pretty steamed. They worked pretty close on this one."

"Do you know what's happening?"

"Not for sure. No."

"Would you tell me if you did?"

Stark met Blair's seeking gaze. "The reason that I think Commander Roberts has been so successful heading this detail is because she never kept you in the dark. Yes, I would tell you."

Blair smiled softly. "You don't think it's because I've fallen in love with her and will do anything she says?"

A second passed while Stark struggled to compose her features, but finally she surrendered and laughed. "Uh, no, that had never crossed my mind."

"Well, just so you don't think that I'm always so easy."

"I think there's nothing easy about the position you're in," Stark said seriously. "And the only thing I want to do is make it as uncomplicated for you as possible."

Blair leaned her hip against the railing, her expression contemplative as she considered Stark's uncomplicated honesty and essential goodness. "You know, I owe you an apology."

Stark looked confused. "I'm sorry?"

"For that night in Colorado."

"No, you don't," Stark said. "Everything that happened that night was mutual."

"You're not blushing. I don't even know how to interpret that."

"Let's just say I'm not embarrassed about something that will always be very special."

To her consternation, Blair found herself blushing. "Well. Thank you."

"Renée doesn't know."

Blair smiled. "And she never will unless you tell her."

"She doesn't seem to care about the past all that much."

"Smart woman."

"Yeah," Stark said with a sigh. She sipped her coffee and studied the empty beach. "I feel bad because sometimes I wish she weren't an FBI agent."

"That makes sense to me. I bet there's times she wishes you weren't a Secret Service agent, either."

Stark nodded. "She said something like that this morning."

"And I don't imagine either one of you is planning on retiring."

"No. Not likely." Stark straightened, shaking off the melancholy. They'd strayed far beyond the boundaries dictated by their professional relationship long ago, and although she welcomed the friendship, she also had a job to do. "So, we should discuss your agenda for the day."

"My agenda?" Blair grimaced. "Anything that will keep my mind off where the hell my lover is and what trouble she's getting herself into."

"I'm sure the commander will be fine," Stark said with absolute certainty. "Anyhow, they're probably spending the whole day meeting with one committee after another."

Blair narrowed her eyes. "You don't really believe that, do you?"

"I wouldn't," she admitted, "except I can't see anyone staging any kind of action so quickly. It takes too much planning, and there's going to be too many people who want to be in charge." Stark shook her head. "I'm sure they'll be meeting with the president's security advisers and maybe the head of the Intelligence committee. That's it."

"Dial the White House on your secure line," Blair said.

Stark blinked. "Excuse me?"

"I want to talk to Lucinda, and I know that no one is supposed to know where we are. So scramble it for me."

"Uh, that's probably not the best idea—"

Blair laughed. "This is where you get to be reminded what a pain in the ass it is being my security chief. Because I can call anyone I want to anytime, anyplace. So if you don't want me to use the phone in the living room—"

"Just one minute, Ms. Powell," Stark said formally, opening her phone. She rapidly punched a series of numbers and held it out to Blair. "There you go."

"Thank you," Blair said sweetly. As Stark started to walk down the steps, apparently to give her privacy, Blair added, "There's no need to go. This involves you too. Hello, Luce? It's Blair."

"Blair. Everything all right?"

"No problem. Well, unless you take into consideration that I'm in hiding because my lover doesn't trust anyone, including you."

"I think for the time being it's reasonable to allow Commander Roberts to make those decisions. The president has every confidence in her."

"Uh-huh. Everyone thinks she's superhuman. That's sort of why I'm calling. All this confidence everyone has in her. Where exactly *is* my lover?" She gripped the railing as she waited for the answer and heard only a faint buzz in the background.

"I'm afraid I don't have an answer on that at the moment. I can assure you, however—"

"Is it that you don't *want* to tell me or you can't tell me?"

"Both, and by now, you should know the reasons why."

Blair thought she heard a sigh, but she couldn't be certain, and it would certainly be out of character. Before she could demand more information, Lucinda spoke again.

"If you call me back in approximately two hours, I may have more to tell you. That's the best I can do, Blair."

Blair looked at her watch. "Don't go anywhere. I'll call back in *exactly* two hours." She hung up and looked at Stark, whose face was a study in barely suppressed anxiety. "I don't think they're in a meeting."

CHAPTER THIRTY

The helicopter set down in a small unpaved landing zone in the middle of a forested area where three other Little Birds, fully equipped with combat troops, waited on the ground. A fuel truck bounced across the rutted field, and when the lieutenant jumped down to supervise the refueling, Cam reached beneath the narrow bench and extracted one of the protective vests. She tossed it to Savard and released another from its restraining clip for herself.

"We let the commandos sweep the front line. I imagine there are more men like the four who hit the Aerie in this camp. You weren't there that morning, but these guys are well trained and very well armed."

"You and your team handled them pretty well, Commander." Savard's eyes glittered with a dangerous combination of adrenaline and anger. "*Without* body armor."

"We were lucky." She didn't think there would ever come a day when she didn't see Foster with his service weapon leveled at Blair's chest. She pushed the image from her mind. She wanted justice. Even more, she wanted retribution. But not at a price that Blair would ultimately have to pay. "We're here to see that these men don't get away with treason and terrorism. We're here to *see* it, not do it."

"I'm going in with my weapon drawn." Savard's gaze lost focus as she remembered the very earth tremble beneath her feet as the Towers came down. "They'll never be able to pay enough for what they did, no matter how small a part they had in it."

"If you've got something to prove, Agent," Cam said quietly, "this isn't the place for it. We bring up the rear, once the area has been cleared. That's an order."

"Yes, ma'am," Savard said smartly.

A clean-shaven redhead of about forty clambered into the helicopter. "I'm Major Simons, in charge of this operation. We'll be airborne in five minutes."

Cam held out her hand. "Cameron Roberts, Secret Service." She indicated Savard. "Renée Savard, FBI."

"Agents," the major nodded. "Flight time is thirty-five minutes. We're working off satellite photographs, but we've got a pretty good picture of the layout. We're going to put down right outside their front gate. I would imagine there'll be sentries posted, if the vehicles we've been able to identify there are any indication of their organization. If I didn't know better, I'd think it was a U.S. Army installation."

"Weekends are when these guys like to play soldiers. There may be a full complement of personnel down there." Cam presumed the strike had been organized so quickly precisely because it was Saturday and Matheson and most of the officers were likely to be present. "Do you have any idea of the numbers?"

Simons shook his head. "A flyby is too risky, because this place is well away from any commercial or tourist routes. Any kind of aircraft would be suspicious. The latest satellite reconnaissance images suggest thirty to forty individuals."

Cam's head count of the troops on the Little Birds put their number at somewhere around twenty-four. Pretty good odds. "If he's there, we need their commanding officer alive."

The major's eyes were flat black disks, devoid of expression. "Then I guess he'd better not put up a fight."

"Do you have any idea where the command center is?"

"Nope. Except for the fact that there's only one main structure right in the center of the compound. That's probably the headquarters, with a lot of little buildings around the perimeter that are most likely sleeping quarters. I would imagine your man's going to be at the big house."

"Most likely." Cam regarded him steadily. She had a feeling that Matheson would not surrender easily, and that if given the opportunity, he would organize his troops for a firefight. If that happened, casualties could be high. She had no doubt that in the end, the special forces would prevail, but she didn't want to see U.S. troops killed, nor did she want to see Matheson die. He had information that was vital to future security. And as much as she might like to extract justice from him personally, she had a greater goal in mind. He had to be taken quickly in the first wave. "What's the chance you can put our bird right down on his front porch?"

Major Simons studied her, then flicked his gaze to Savard. "Why don't I ride with you two and we'll see what we can do about that." He crab-walked to the door and jumped down to the ground, turning to look back inside once he landed. "Let me brief the team leaders, and then I'll be back with the rest of our team."

"Commander," Savard said when Simons was out of earshot, "what happened to our rear-action orders?"

"I figure as long as we're standing behind him and his men, that's the rear." Cam watched the soldiers confer. "And our agenda is slightly different than theirs. I want Matheson alive so we can put him in a room—a very small room—so we can question him. I don't care how long it takes, but he'll stay there until he breaks. I want to know who else we have to worry about in the future. Which of my people," she looked at Savard, "or your people, are like Foster—working beside us every day and just waiting for orders to move against us."

"I want to be in there with you," Savard said fiercely.

Simons walked toward them with three Delta Force commandos.

"Stay by my side when we land," Cam said.

"Yes, ma'am." Of one thing Savard was certain. She wasn't going to let anything happen to Cameron Roberts.

❖

When Diane turned off the shower, she heard her cell phone ringing. She'd left it on the bathroom counter with her cosmetics bag. She stepped out, grasped a bath sheet in one hand, and picked up her phone with the other. She did not recognize the number and thought about letting it go to voicemail. On the final ring, something told her to answer, and she flipped it open. "Diane Bleeker."

"I'm on a pay phone. I only have a minute."

There was static on the line, but the connection was clear enough for her to hear the unmistakable sound of an airplane taking off. She tried to keep her voice steady as her entire body tingled. "Are you all right?"

"Yes. I wanted to say I'm sorry about this morning."

"Where are you?"

There was no immediate response, but Diane had the sense that she shouldn't speak her name. She waited, her stomach tight with anticipation.

"Dulles." There was the sound of a deep breath, then the hurried words, "Everything was set in motion long before I fell in love with you. The only way I could keep your name out of things was to follow the plan."

Diane tried not to be distracted by the phrase *fell in love with you*, but the wild beating of her heart made it difficult for her to think. "Where are you going?"

"I can't tell you."

"What do you mean, 'keep me out of things'?" Diane felt the pressure of the seconds ticking away and desperately wanted to understand.

"Who we're personally involved with—it's a matter of security. They'll watch you, Diane. Your privacy will be gone. I'm sorry. I didn't mean for this to happen."

"Then tell me why you did it."

Her voice came through the line muffled, as if by unshed tears. "I couldn't help it. I needed you. I need you."

Diane closed her eyes. She felt their bodies soar together, their breath mingling, their souls surrendering as one. "Then I'm here."

"Do you understand what that means?"

"I do. I don't care."

"I have to go." A beat. Two. "I love you so very much."

The line went silent, but the words echoed in her heart. *I love you too.*

❖

From the air, the access road through the dense green forest looked like a snake slithering through the grass. If she hadn't known it was there, Cam didn't think she would have recognized it for what it was—a single-track dirt road leading five miles into an unpopulated and undeveloped region of the Appalachians that bordered Virginia and Tennessee. As they descended, she focused the binoculars Major Simons had provided her on a tiny patch of tan that stood out amidst the confluence of green. After a few seconds, she nudged Simons's shoulder and pointed, mouthing the words, *Fire tower*.

He followed her direction and nodded. Then he climbed forward, pointed to the pilot, and spoke into his throat mike. The helicopters veered north to circle around what might be a lookout post. Cam doubted it would make much difference, but minimizing advance notice could only help. She glanced across the aisle to Savard, who looked composed, almost meditative. She almost would have preferred that Savard look a little jumpy. Sun Tzu said that the greatest warriors did not fear death and, therefore, did not hesitate in battle. On this particular day, Cam wanted a little bit of hesitation on Savard's part. If she got hurt, Stark would have a hard time handling it. So would she. She'd just have to see that nothing happened to Savard.

❖

Felicia walked out onto the deck. "Do we know anything yet?"

"Holding pattern," Stark said. She nodded toward Blair. "But it's possible that Ms. Powell may have something for us in an hour or so."

Felicia raised an eyebrow.

"I spoke with Lucinda Washburn not long ago," Blair explained. "She promised to give me an update, but you know how information is handled at that level. It may or may not be the whole story." She shrugged. "Usually, Lucinda tells it to me straight. I could call my father, but…" She considered what Cam had told her earlier about the layers of protection around her father when these kinds of operations were underway. Her lover was willing to risk her life for concepts as hard to define as *honor* and *patriotism*. Blair was not willing to compromise those ideals by asking her father for the details. He might very well tell her, because he loved her, and that was something that she could not ask him to do. He was more than her father. He was the president of the United States. Sometimes, she didn't want to think about that, because it frightened her that there were people who wished him harm. It also overwhelmed her when she considered the magnitude of his importance to the world. He was the man who had held out his arms to catch her when she took her first steps, lest she fall. He was the man who had swung her up to his shoulders to watch the Fourth of July parades when she was too small to see through the crowds. He was the man whose opinion mattered to her more than any person's in the world, except Cam's. But despite all of that, he was also the man whose responsibilities set him apart from everyone else, even her. She shrugged again and tossed the dregs of her coffee over the railing. "Maybe Cam or Savard will call soon and fill us in."

She turned and strode into the house.

Felicia watched her go and as the door swung shut, looked back to Stark. "You okay?"

"Yeah. Everybody's on edge, that's all." She hunched her shoulders against a sudden gust of wind and studied the sky. "I think it's gonna rain again."

"Maybe. The weather's really hinky out here in the middle of the ocean." She squeezed Stark's shoulder. "Why don't you go on in. I'll stand watch out here for a while. I've been cooped up in that damn building for days staring at the monitor—I can handle a little fresh air."

"What do you think is going on with Valerie?"

"Ah, God. I think the CIA wanted to know what we found before anyone else." She buttoned the top button of her navy wool pea jacket as the wind picked up. "She helped break the case open for us. We'd have arrived at the same place eventually, but she helped get us there sooner."

"I was thinking the same thing," Stark admitted reluctantly. "You know, sometimes we don't have a lot of choices."

"I have a feeling no one really knows what's happening minute to minute these days in terms of our security network," Felicia said, her expression uneasy. "I'm glad we're here and that Egret is out of things for a while. They're keeping the vice president under wraps somewhere too. Probably smart. I'm glad I'm not on the president's detail."

Paula snorted. "Yeah. They probably want to keep him in the underground bunker, and knowing President Powell, he's not going to go for that."

"No. That's why I can't be too angry with Valerie. Every day we get closer to these guys, we cut the risk of something really bad happening again."

"So maybe it all evens out in the end?"

Felicia wrapped her arms around her body, wishing, not for the first time, that Mac were with them. "I hope so."

❖

The four helicopters descended in a ring toward the compound. As the layout of the camp became more distinct, Cam noted that the trees had been clear-cut for a hundred yards around the fenced perimeter and the ground bulldozed flat. There appeared to be guard posts on either side of the main entrance, which was barricaded by a double swinging gate. A ground approach, even if they'd *had* armored jeeps, would have been ill-advised because of the absence of cover. As it was, the helicopters would have to deliver the troops right into the heart of the compound.

Simons's voice came through the powerful loudspeaker in their helicopter. "This is the United States Army. All personnel in the compound, assemble on the parade grounds. This is the United States Army. Surrender your weapons and assemble on the parade grounds. This is the United States…"

As the message repeated, Cam quickly scanned the open area between the main building and several smaller ones that probably served as the training grounds. At least a dozen men in fatigues hurried from the buildings. The helicopter to the right of hers, which she could see through the open door, zigzagged sharply away. Through her earphones she heard Simons shout, "The idiots are *firing* on us. Take us down! Take us down!"

The helicopter dropped precipitously, and Cam was thrown back against the inside wall. Across from her, Savard appeared eerily calm.

"All troops, prepare to jump," Simons commanded. "I want these birds back up in the air as soon as we hit the ground."

Cam drew her weapon and glanced at Savard once more before getting in line behind the two Delta commandos who crouched in the open doorway, waiting to drop the last ten feet into the hot zone.

Chapter Thirty-One

Cam was grateful for the enormous clouds of dust that the helicopters kicked up from the hard-packed earth of the parade grounds. At least the impromptu sandstorm afforded them a few seconds of cover as they prepared to drop into the fire zone. She put her hand on Savard's back and leaned close to her. "Go first. I'll provide covering fire. Take cover anywhere you can, but try to follow the front men."

"No," Savard shouted back. "You won't have anyone at your back."

"Do it," Cam said as she saw the second soldier drop from view. She pushed Savard forward. "Go, go!"

The helicopter bounced from side to side as if buffeted by a high wind, hovering as close to the ground as possible. As soon as Savard's head disappeared from sight, Cam jumped after her, mentally repeating, *drop and roll, drop and roll.* She landed with a bone-rattling, teeth-jarring thud and let her legs go soft, pitching forward into a shoulder roll and coming up in a crouch with her weapon extended. Overhead, the steady pinging of bullets impacting on the ascending helicopters sounded like hail on a tin roof. Her eyes were filled with grit and her vision hazy, but she could see well enough to make out that Savard was down and unmoving eight feet away. The only thought in her mind was to get her to cover as she threw herself flat on the ground and started to crawl, ignoring the small puffs of dirt that signaled bullets striking the ground nearby.

❖

Blair walked into the living room, surprised to see Diane curled up in one corner of the sofa with a glass of wine in her hand. "Isn't it still morning, or did I miss something?"

Smiling wanly, Diane shook her head. "No. You're right. But if I drink another cup of coffee, I'm likely to have a meltdown. And frankly, I've been keeping such odd hours for the last week or so, my internal clock is totally disrupted. It feels like seven at night."

"Actually," Blair said as she threw herself down on the sofa beside Diane, "I might join you if we don't hear something pretty soon."

"You don't have any idea what's going on?"

"No. But I'm willing to bet that once they have the names of these guys, which they do now, they're not going to wait around to go after them. *And* I'm willing to bet there's a reason that Cam took Savard, and not Felicia or Stark, to this so-called briefing. Savard's FBI. She's trained in armed apprehension. So is Cam, because she was originally part of the investigative division of the Secret Service. But Stark and Davis have always done protection, and there's a difference. They're not as used to making arrests."

Diane reached over and took Blair's hand. "She's going to be fine. Even if they're involved in something risky, they're not alone. Your father and Lucy aren't going to let Cam do anything really dangerous. They know what she means to you."

"You *are* speaking about Cameron Roberts, my lover, right?" Blair said. "The one who believes that sacrifice is the greatest form of love?"

"Is she any different than you as far as that goes?" Diane spoke gently, but the look in her eyes said that she knew Blair would give up anything to keep Cam safe too.

"It's not the same." Blair turned away from Diane's appraising stare, blinking back the tears that were as much a result of frustration as fear. She sighed. "But her behavior is not a news flash. I should be used to it by now."

"No, not used to it. You'll never be used to it, I suppose, as long as she does what she does." Diane gave Blair's hand a shake. "But perhaps you'll begin to believe that she's coming back, because she always does."

Blair nodded. "I know. And I know that's the only thing I should really be thinking about."

"Good. So practice."

"I'll try." Blair leaned her head back against the sofa and stared at the ceiling, toying with Diane's fingers. "How are you feeling?"

"I'm all right."

Blair turned her head, hearing a calmness in Diane's voice that hadn't been there when they'd walked on the beach. She searched her friend's face. "My God," she breathed, "she called, didn't she?"

Diane said nothing.

"Are you afraid to tell me because you think I'll do something to endanger her?" Blair sat up straight. "Diane?"

"Some people here are very angry at her."

"Cam defended her this morning," Blair said. "Even though she was angry, she said she understood her. She said that sometimes they don't get to choose what they do."

"They do choose, though, don't they," Diane said quietly. "They choose to follow orders, because they believe that what they're doing is right or important or…necessary."

"You've really gotten a crash course in the trials and tribulations of being in love with a spooky, haven't you?" Blair said gently.

Diane laughed, a tremor in her voice. "Oh, I certainly have. No wonder you resisted Cam as long as you did."

"Yeah," Blair laughed, "for all of about two seconds."

"We're a great pair, aren't we?"

Blair slid her arm around Diane's shoulders. "I would never do anything to hurt you. Is she all right?"

"I don't know. I think so. We only…we only spoke for a moment."

"So you don't know anything?"

Diane shook her head. "Not a thing. I don't think she's in Washington anymore, though. So if there's something going on with Cam and Renée right now, she's not a part of it."

"No, probably not right now. But there was some reason that she left the way she did, and I expect there's going to be hard feelings about that for a while with quite a few people."

"What about us? Is it going to come between us?"

Blair reached for Diane's other hand. "Not if we don't let it. Let's agree right now that sometimes our lovers might not see eye to eye. That will be between them. Not us. Okay?"

"Okay."

"You do know what you're getting into, don't you? Because it's probably going to be a very bumpy ride."

"After this morning, I think I've got a pretty good idea just how rough it's going to be." Diane smiled softly. "But when I thought she was gone, really gone, it was as if something inside of me had broken, and I knew I would never be able to fix it. And then the second I heard her voice, everything felt right again."

"Well. That's your answer, then, isn't it?"

"It seems to be. Does it ever begin to make sense?"

"Once in a while," Blair said, "when you feel her next to you, and you know that that's the only thing in the world that truly matters."

❖

"Savard," Cam shouted. "You hit?"

Savard turned her head in Cam's direction, spitting dirt from her mouth. Her face was pale and contorted with pain. "Twisted my knee when I landed. Tore something, I think."

"Can you move?" Cam took in the crimson stain on Savard's leg and the ragged tear in her pants. Bullet wound. Somewhere nearby, men shouted and the intermittent bursts of automatic weapons fire continued. "We need to get out of here," Cam said urgently. "Just crawl."

"Don't think...I can. You go."

"Forget it, Agent. Get moving." Cam gripped the back of Savard's jacket in her fist and pulled, inching forward on her elbows, keeping her belly and hips on the ground. She jerked Savard with her. "Push with your good leg and use your elbow for leverage. Come on. It's only thirty feet or so to the building."

"Commander, I..."

"*Move.*"

"Yes, ma'am."

Together, they maneuvered across the open ground. At one point, Cam saw a figure in faded green camos race around the side of the building, a rifle in his hands. She sighted on his chest, waiting to pull the trigger if he trained his weapon on them. But before she needed to fire, he pitched forward, his rifle flying from his hands. He writhed on the ground, a red patch spreading rapidly high on his back. He'd taken a round in the shoulder. *The Delta Forces aren't shooting to kill, at least not unless they have to.*

"The stairs are just ahead," Cam yelled. "Get up on one knee and put your arm around me. We're going inside."

Cam wrapped her left arm around Savard's waist, her weapon in her right hand. Savard pushed up with her uninjured left leg, and the two of them clambered up the stairs and through the door. The room was empty except for several chairs turned over on the floor and a desk that sat in front of a doorway centered in the far wall.

"You're bleeding," Cam said, easing Savard down to the floor by the side of the desk. She guided Savard's hand to the wound. "Press on this and keep your eye on the front door. Use the desk for cover if you need to. I'll check the back."

Assured that Savard was as safe as she could be, Cam ran quickly to the rear wall and put her back against it. Then, with her weapon arm cocked up by her head, she inched toward the open doorway. She suspected that Matheson's office was on the other side, since this was the building they had presumed was the command center. She hadn't seen anyone come out the front door, unless he'd been one of the first men to rush onto the parade ground as they'd landed. If he was, hopefully he'd been captured already. He might have escaped through a back door, or he could have gone out a window. She hoped that he was still inside, destroying paperwork or just waiting, foolish enough to make a stand.

She took one quick glance behind her and couldn't see Savard. She had probably moved behind the desk. Good. With a quick intake of breath, Cam swung into the doorway, keeping low, hoping to make as small a target as possible. A quick glance left, then right. There was one man in the room, standing behind the desk and looking straight into her eyes, as if he'd indeed been waiting. Cam held his gaze, but her mind was flooded with images. It was surprising the details that one noticed between one heartbeat and the next.

A maroon desk blotter was perfectly lined up in the precise center of the desk. A gold ring with a blue sapphire stone, a class ring of some kind, adorned his right hand. His clean-shaven, tanned face was expressionless save for a small smile on his thin lips, registering neither anger nor panic. That was odd, considering that a chain of rectangular explosive packs were laid out in front of him.

Cam couldn't tell for certain, but if those were C4 charges, she judged there was enough there to blow up a great deal of the surrounding compound, and everyone in it. From what she could see of the coils leading from the pale pink squares, he had not yet set the timer. When he snatched up what appeared to be the ignition switch and dove to the floor behind the desk, she had no time to think about anything, not even Blair. She catapulted out of her crouch, over the desk, and on top of him, grappling for his hand. He elbowed her in the throat, and she gagged, spots dancing before her eyes as she forced his wrist back, trying to dislocate it. He elbowed her in the neck again, and she felt herself losing consciousness. Just as she slipped away, she heard an explosion.

❖

Everyone in the room abruptly stopped talking when Stark's phone rang twenty minutes before Blair was due to call Lucinda Washburn.

"Stark," she said. Her gaze flicked once to Blair as she listened, and she squared her shoulders. "Yes, ma'am, I understand. Forty minutes. Yes, ma'am, we'll be there. Yes, ma'am, ready to receive." She closed her phone and cleared her throat. "That was the chief of staff. They're sending a military escort to pick us up. I should be getting the coordinates by satellite relay right now. Ms. Powell, if you could get ready to leave immediately."

"Did Lucinda give you Cam's status?" Blair asked, her voice surprisingly steady, because she'd stopped breathing with the first ring. Cam would have called her had she been able to. This could only mean one thing. She was hurt. *God, please let that be all.*

"No, ma'am," Stark said hoarsely. "Just that they're airlifting casualties to McDonald Army Hospital in Virginia."

Blair swayed for just an instant before she took a deep breath and steeled herself. "Then we should go."

CHAPTER THIRTY-TWO

A military jet awaited them at the rendezvous point. Hara and Wozinski fell in behind Stark and Blair as they raced across the tarmac to the aircraft. A Marine lieutenant waited at the bottom of the staircase and followed silently behind them as they climbed rapidly aboard. The jet seated ten and had none of the trappings of their usual transportation. Blair made her way to the rear seats and slid into one, reaching automatically for the seat belt. Stark walked slowly up and down the aisle, inspecting the interior, as the jet taxied down the runway.

"Is there anything you need, Ms. Powell?" Stark asked quietly as she slowed by Blair's side on her first pass through the plane.

"No, thank you." Blair was grateful that Paula moved on. She didn't want to talk. She didn't want to think. She just wanted to be wherever Cam was. She'd tried Lucinda on the scrambled line, but got no answer. The significance of that was uncertain, but she suspected that her father's chief of staff was busy handling the aftermath of whatever had happened to result in casualties. *Casualties.* The very word made her feel ill. She leaned her head back, closed her eyes, and concentrated on clearing her mind of all thought. She focused on her breathing, letting the sensation and sound of the air flowing in and out of her body expand until she was aware of nothing else. Her heart rate slowed and her muscles relaxed as she prepared herself for the challenge that awaited her.

❖

Stark crouched down in the aisle next to where Hara and Wozinski sat. She spoke quietly so the Marine would not hear her. "When we land, assume that no one is a friendly. That means medical and military personnel too. *No one* is alone with her except the commander."

The other agents nodded solemnly, neither voicing the question that was foremost in their minds, both wondering if the commander would be waiting for them at the end of their journey.

"Good." Stark stood and took a seat midway down the fuselage between Blair and the cabin door. She sat straight, staring directly ahead, with a death grip on the armrests. She mentally reviewed the things she would need to do as soon as the plane landed. She considered the positioning of the other agents around Egret and the fact that they would be understaffed for what had to be considered a significant security risk. She steadfastly did not think about Renée. She couldn't, because every time she did, a bubble of panic rose into her chest and threatened to choke her. And there was no room for it, no time for it, no opportunity for her to feel anything about anyone except Blair Powell.

So she didn't.

❖

Mercifully, the jet landed at an Army base adjoining the hospital, and a jeep sat idling by the runway, waiting for them. Within ten minutes of touchdown, they were escorted through a rear entrance to McDonald Army Hospital. A muscular, dark-haired, olive-skinned man in his fifties, dressed in scrubs, met them just inside the doors. Incongruously, he glanced at Stark, who walked by Blair's side, and saluted smartly.

"I'm Captain Olivieri, the chief of surgery. If you'll come this way, please." He turned smartly on his heel and strode off.

"Captain," Blair said as she hurried with him, Stark on her opposite side, "we have several of our people who might be injured. Commander Roberts, Special Agent—"

"Yes, ma'am. I was instructed to bring you directly to the treatment room."

"If you could just…"

He pushed aside a curtain that enclosed the last treatment room at one end of a hallway filled with emergency equipment, suture carts, defibrillators, and other medical paraphernalia. "Ma'am."

Blair glanced inside and for one brief instant, everything receded from her consciousness but Cam. "Oh God."

Cam sat propped up on a treatment table, a pillow behind her back and an ice pack on her neck. An angry bruise on her right cheek extended to her lower lid, which was partially closed. Her eyes, however, were blessedly clear, and as soon as she saw Blair, she smiled. Blair smiled back, her heart lifting.

"Hey," Blair said softly as she started forward.

Cam looked past Blair to where Stark stood in the doorway. She tried to speak, but no sound came out.

Captain Olivieri said curtly, "No talking. That was our arrangement. If you try, I'll slap you in the ICU and put a tube down your throat."

Blair saw the oxygen mask sitting by Cam's right hand and realized that Cam must have taken it off. She looked anxiously at the surgeon. "What is it? What's wrong?"

Against doctor's orders, Cam forced out a barely recognizable word. "Star..." Her face contorted with pain and she leaned her head back, closing her eyes as if the effort had exhausted her.

Instantly, Blair reached for the oxygen mask and put it over Cam's lower face. "I take it she's supposed to be wearing this," she said over her shoulder. Her voice was steady but her hands were shaking.

"It's humidified oxygen," the surgeon explained. "She has significant tracheal edema from the blunt injury, and—" He stopped as Cam suddenly sat forward and pulled the oxygen mask off.

Blair narrowed her eyes and followed Cam's hand as she pointed vehemently at Stark once again. Nodding, Blair said, "Captain, do you have any information on Special Agent Renée Savard?"

"Savard?" Olivieri looked confused. "Yes. She's in surgery."

"How is she?" Blair asked quickly, watching the color drain from Stark's face.

"She should be out anytime now. They're just doing a washout of the wound—"

"How about giving us a quick rundown of her injuries, Captain," Blair interrupted when Cam stiffened and made another abortive attempt at speaking. Blair squeezed her shoulder. "Stop it."

"She has a nonthreatening GSW to the left lower extremity. X-rays reveal no evidence of bony injury, but the orthopedic surgeons wanted to irrigate the wound and make sure the lateral collateral ligament had not been damaged. She should be fine."

"Thank you, Captain." Blair smiled at Stark. "If you want to find out where they'll be taking her, Paula, go ahead."

Stark clasped her hands behind her back and locked her knees, trying to appear steadier than she felt. She swallowed once and then said clearly, "Thank you, Ms. Powell. I'll be right outside in the hall here." With that, she stepped back several feet and closed the curtain, giving Cam and Blair privacy. There was no way she could leave. It wasn't even a consideration, and she knew that Renée would understand. Renée was going to be all right, and knowing that gave her all the strength she needed to be patient. She leaned against the wall where she could see the hall in both directions and took a few gulps of much-needed air.

"Now," Blair said to Captain Olivieri. "Tell me about Agent Roberts."

"She has a badly contused trachea and a fracture of the arytenoid… uh, that's one of the cartilages forming the vocal cords. She shouldn't speak, and by rights, she should be in the ICU on a monitor, because if the swelling increases—" He frowned when Cam made a hand motion, waving him to silence.

Blair turned her back to the surgeon and put her face very close to Cam's. "You listen to me. I want to know. And I don't want to hear anything coming from you. Not a single sound." Then, very gently, she kissed her on the mouth. Keeping her arm tightly around Cam, she looked back at the surgeon. "Go ahead."

"Ah—well, that's it really. Vocal rest, a three-week course of steroids, and a laryngoscopy in ten days to check for healing. I recommended twenty-four hours in-house observation, but—"

"I think if you give me explicit instructions, I can see that Agent Roberts is appropriately observed. Several of my security team are EMTs."

He looked sheepish. "Yes, ma'am." He backed up. "I'll see that those are typed up for you."

"Thank you."

Once they were alone, Blair pressed her palm to Cam's cheek. "Does it hurt, darling?"

Cam shrugged.

"The truth."

Cam grinned weakly and nodded.

"On a scale of one to ten?"

Cam held up both hands, eight digits extended.

"Oh, then, that's not so bad." Blair rested her forehead against Cam's and closed her eyes. "I love you. I can't take too many more of these scares."

Cam wrapped her arms around Blair's waist and pulled her as close as she could, sliding one hand beneath Blair's hair to caress the back of her neck.

"I know. It's a million to one chance that it will ever happen again." Blair snuggled against Cam's chest, wanting nothing except to be in her arms. "Don't ever play poker for money, darling."

❖

Diane was waiting for Blair when she came out of the bedroom after situating Cam for the night. "Well? What the hell happened? Where is Stark?"

"We left her in Virginia for the time being. Renée is going to be in the hospital for a couple of days so they can make sure her leg is okay. Paula wanted to come back with us, but I wouldn't let her."

"Is Renée going to be all right?"

"Yes. The surgeon said nothing vital was injured, and her recovery should be pretty fast."

"Thank God." Diane took Blair's hand and led her into the kitchen. "Sit. I bet you haven't had anything to eat all day, have you?"

Blair sagged into the chair without protest and brushed her hair back with trembling hands. "God, what a nightmare this day has been. I don't think I can eat."

"Well, you're going to. Scrambled eggs with cheese and toast. Comfort food, and it will get some protein into you." As she removed items from the refrigerator, she asked, "Do you know what happened?"

"Cam can't tell me, and none of the medical personnel seem to know. I'll call Lucinda tomorrow," Blair said. "But right now, I really don't care."

Diane put the bowl of eggs aside and went to Blair. She leaned down and hugged her. "Neither do I. At least they're all in one piece."

Blair laughed unsteadily and rested her cheek against Diane's body, welcoming the comfort. "More or less."

"I don't suppose you heard anything about Valerie," Diane said softly.

Blair shook her head. "I don't know anything, sweetie. As soon as I do, I promise I'll let you know."

Diane kissed Blair's forehead. "Thanks."

"I did some thinking on the trip back here," Blair said. "I'm going to talk to Tanner about buying this place. I think it will be good for us to get away somewhere truly safe. Tanner should be able to arrange the sale so that no one can trace us, at least not without a lot of trouble. I'm not even going to tell my father where we are when we come here."

"I think that's a great idea. As long as that guesthouse has my name on it."

Blair smiled. "Definitely."

"Perfect. Now, about those eggs…"

To Blair's surprise, she discovered she was hungry, and after finishing the quick meal, she made her excuses and returned to the bedroom. She'd left the bedside light on, turned down low, and she could see from the doorway that Cam's eyes were closed. As quietly as she could, she started toward the bathroom, but stopped when Cam opened her eyes. She changed direction and settled onto the side of the bed, leaning forward with her arm on the other side of Cam's body. "Hey. You're supposed to be trying to sleep."

Cam patted the bed beside her.

"You want company?"

Cam nodded and grinned, stronger this time. She drew one finger along the strong line of Blair's jaw, then brushed her thumb over Blair's mouth. Blair smiled.

"Commander, don't even think about it." She stood, shed her clothes, and slid beneath the sheets. Gently, she eased an arm behind Cam's back. "Can you lean with your head on my shoulder without hurting your neck?"

Carefully, Cam shifted onto her side and settled against the curve of Blair's body. With a sigh, she closed her eyes. Blair held her, wide awake. She didn't want to sleep, she wanted to—needed to—feel Cam beside her. She thought of her conversation with Diane.

"Does it ever begin to make sense?"

"Once in a while, when you feel her next to you, and you know that that's the only thing in the world that truly matters."

CHAPTER THIRTY-THREE

Monday, October 1

Savard heard the sound of footsteps on the deck and watched the door with a combination of anticipation and uncertainty. She'd awakened alone after arriving at Whitley Point late the night before, having cajoled and badgered the medical staff into allowing her to leave the hospital twenty-four hours early. Paula had slept in a chair by her bed and had risen early to check in with the commander. She wanted Paula's company, her comfort, but at the same time, she wanted to be alone. She needed time to find a place for the anger and terrible disappointment that had plagued her since 9/11, and she didn't want to inflict her doubts and disillusionment on her lover.

"I've got coffee and scones," Stark said as she edged through the doorway with a tray. "Hungry?"

"Yes." Savard smiled. She couldn't help it.

Stark appraised the position of Renée's leg, propped up on several pillows on the sofa. "How are you feeling?"

"It doesn't hurt much at all. Just a big old cut is all it turned out to be. If it hadn't been for the temporary shock to the nerves, I probably would've been able to walk on my own." She grimaced, still embarrassed that she'd put the commander's life in danger.

"You couldn't help getting shot, honey." Stark poured coffee and placed a blueberry scone on a paper napkin. She set them both on the end table within Renée's reach.

"I nearly blew the whole thing. Big time."

Carefully, Stark settled onto the sofa and laid her hand on Renée's thigh.

"But you didn't, did you."

Savard looked down at the strong hand. Paula loved her. Paula also was one of the few people in her life who could really understand what it meant to struggle against an evil so pervasive that the fight felt endless. Paula would understand that sometimes she just wanted to give up, to give in, to say it was all too much and to walk away. To have a normal life, where it was still possible to believe that the world was safe. She sighed and traced the tendons and veins on the top of Paula's hand with her fingertip. "It was close, for a while. I wasn't certain we were going to make it." She looked into Paula's concerned brown eyes. "For a while now, I haven't been sure *I* would make it."

"Do you want to talk about it?" Stark asked gently.

"No." Savard kissed Paula softly, knowing that the love this woman offered her was the one safe place in her world. "But I will."

And as she told her everything, she felt the first stirrings of peace.

❖

Blair watched Stark disappear into the guesthouse and turned to smile at Cam, who sat at the table. "Between Savard on crutches and you barely able to manage a whisper, I feel like we're running a rehab center around here."

Cam grinned.

"Don't talk," Blair warned, joining her at the table. She sat down and reached for Cam's hand. "I'm going to talk, and you're going to nod. Okay?"

"Yes," Cam whispered.

"Cameron, don't push. I've been going easy on you because you were hurt." Blair's eyes flashed. "But I haven't forgotten that you said you'd stay with the rear action, and you ended up practically getting yourself blown up."

"No—"

Blair held up a hand, cutting her off. "I didn't say anything to you yesterday because you needed to rest, but I spoke with Lucinda. I got some of the details."

Cam frowned.

"Oh, I know. You would have preferred to tell me yourself, so that you could downplay the danger. I know how you operate." Blair reached for Cam's hand and held it. "They put up more resistance than anybody figured, didn't they?" When Cam nodded, a frustrated expression on her face, Blair continued, hoping to fill in the blanks so that Cam wouldn't need to speak. She knew that Cam probably needed to talk about it almost as much as she needed to hear it, even though Cam wouldn't want to share all the details. Well, she'd just have to. "And that's how you ended up right in the middle of things. There *was* no rear action." She lifted Cam's hand and rubbed it against her cheek. "You wouldn't have put yourself in danger like that unless you had to, right?"

Cam shook her head carefully while holding Blair's gaze.

"I know, you promised." Blair tried to sound matter-of-fact, but Lucinda's dispassionate recounting of the events still terrified her. She shivered with the chill of what might have been. "I believe you."

"Thanks." Cam's voice was a whisper, but she gave no indication that it pained her to speak. Blair put her fingers against Cam's mouth nevertheless.

"Hush. Wait until I get to something I don't know the answer to, and then you can tell me." She leaned forward and kissed Cam's cheek. "You're being very good. I love you." She took a breath. "Some things Lucinda told me you *don't* know. The assumption is that he was going to blow himself up along with most of the compound and everyone in it to prevent you finding what was in the office—cabinets full of transcripts and tapes of incriminating conversations with all kinds of people, personnel files, maps, schedules—a gold mine of vital information." She brushed her fingers gently over Cam's injured cheek. "From the looks of your neck and face, you kind of made it difficult for him to finish setting the charges."

Cam lifted a shoulder.

"Here's what no one is clear on. Who shot him in the head, Cam?"

Cam was silent for a long minute, staring out the back door into the blazing sun. The rain had finally stopped. The storm clouds had blown out to sea and had been replaced by clear, cold air that signaled the first hint of fall. If she knew how much forensic evidence was available, she could formulate an answer that might protect Renée from any kind of investigation. But she didn't, and a lie could put her at greater risk. She met Blair's questioning gaze. "Renée."

"Well," Blair said quietly, "I owe her a great deal, then, don't I?"

"She…won't…think so."

Blair smiled tenderly. "Oh, I know. And I won't embarrass her about it." She stroked Cam's cheek. "I spoke with Lucinda again this morning, darling. It wasn't Matheson."

"I know." She'd known the instant she'd seen him behind the desk. The man had probably been Matheson's number two, designated to destroy the evidence if Matheson wasn't there to do it himself.

"According to Lucinda, Matheson seems to have disappeared. There's no record of him leaving the country, but he's just…gone."

"CIA."

"Lucinda won't say even if she knows, will she?"

Cam shook her head.

"But you think they took him?"

"Yes." Short words were less painful than moving her neck.

"Valerie?"

"Not…her…personally."

"No," Blair said, "but they probably picked him up as soon as she told them who he was. Is that what put you all in danger? What Valerie did?"

"No."

Blair was relieved. Diane had left that morning to return to Manhattan in the same vehicle that had brought Stark and Renée back to the island.

"I think I want to get away for a while," Diane had said. "Maybe Paris."

Blair had kissed her cheek and wished her luck. "I'm glad, because Diane loves her. I think she's gone after her."

Cam smiled wryly. "Valerie…will…find…her."

Blair rose and came around behind Cam's chair and rested her hands on Cam's shoulders. She gently massaged her. "Luce said that there's so much information in what they confiscated from that camp that it will take months to go through it all, but these people…they're just one link in a much bigger chain that extends around the world, like a global net of terrorism." She closed her eyes, trying to absorb this new horror that was now a part of their daily life. "What you did, what all of you here did, was buy us time to prepare for whatever is coming next."

Cam reached back and clasped Blair's hand. "I love you."

"Thank you for that. It means everything to me." Blair crouched down by Cam's side, put her arms around her lover's waist, and leaned her head against her shoulder. "And thank you for being who you are, Secret Service Agent Roberts."

Cam leaned her cheek against Blair's and held her tightly, knowing that whatever the future held for them, they would face it together. And they would win.

About the Author

Radclyffe has written numerous best-selling lesbian romances (*Safe Harbor* and its sequels *Beyond the Breakwater* and *Distant Shores, Silent Thunder*; *Innocent Hearts*; *Love's Melody Lost*; *Love's Tender Warriors*; *Tomorrow's Promise*; *Passion's Bright Fury*; *Love's Masquerade*; *shadowland*; and *Fated Love*), two romance/intrigue series: the Honor series (*Above All, Honor*; *Honor Bound*; *Love & Honor*; *Honor Guards*; and *Honor Reclaimed*) and the Justice series (*Shield of Justice*; the prequel *A Matter of Trust*; *In Pursuit of Justice*; *Justice in the Shadows*; and *Justice Served*), and the Erotic Interlude series: *Change of Pace* and *Stolen Moments: Erotic Interludes 2* (ed. with Stacia Seaman). She also has selections in the anthologies *Call of the Dark* and *The Perfect Valentine* (Bella Books), *Best Lesbian Erotica 2006* (Cleis), and *First-Timers* (Alyson).

She is the recipient of the 2003 and 2004 Alice B. Readers' Award for her body of work and is a 2005 Golden Crown Literary Society Award winner in both the romance category (*Fated Love*) and the mystery/intrigue/action category (*Justice in the Shadows*). She is also the president of Bold Strokes Books, a lesbian publishing company. In 2005, she retired from the practice of surgery to write and publish full time. A member of the GCLS, Pink Ink, and the Romance Writers of America, she collects lesbian pulps, enjoys photographing scenes for her book covers, and shares her life with her partner, Lee, and assorted canines.

Her upcoming works include *Turn Back Time* (March 2006), *Lessons in Love: Erotic Interludes 3* ed. with Stacia Seaman (May 2006), and *Promising Hearts* (June 2006).

Look for information about these works at www.boldstrokesbooks. com.

Books Available From Bold Strokes Books

Grave Silence by Rose Beecham. Detective Jude Devine's investigation of a series of ritual murders is complicated by her torrid affair with the golden girl of Southwestern forensic pathology, Dr. Mercy Westmoreland. (1-933110-25-2)

Honor Reclaimed by Radclyffe. In the aftermath of 9/11, Secret Service Agent Cameron Roberts and Blair Powell close ranks with a trusted few to find the would-be assassins who nearly claimed Blair's life. (1-933110-18-X)

Honor Bound by Radclyffe. Secret Service Agent Cameron Roberts and Blair Powell face political intrigue, a clandestine threat to Blair's safety, and the seemingly irreconcilable personal differences that force them ever further apart. (1-933110-20-1)

Protector of the Realm: Supreme Constellations Book One by Gun Brooke. A space adventure filled with suspense and a daring intergalactic romance featuring Commodore Rae Jacelon and a stunning, but decidedly lethal Kellen O'Dal. (1-933110-26-0)

Innocent Hearts by Radclyffe. In a wild and unforgiving land, two women learn about love, passion, and the wonders of the heart. (1-933110-21-X)

The Temple at Landfall by Jane Fletcher. An imprinter, one of Celaeno's most revered servants of the Goddess, is also a prisoner to the faith—until a Ranger frees her by claiming her heart. (1-933110-27-9)

Force of Nature by Kim Baldwin. From tornados to forest fires, the forces of nature conspire to bring Gable McCoy and Erin Richards close to danger, and closer to each other. (1-933110-23-6)

In Too Deep by Ronica Black. Undercover homicide cop Erin McKenzie tracks a femme fatale who just might be a real killer...with love and danger hot on her heels. (1-933110-17-1)

Stolen Moments: Erotic Interludes 2 by Stacia Seaman and Radclyffe, eds. Love on the run, in the office, in the shadows...Fast, furious, and almost too hot to handle. (1-933110-16-3)

Course of Action by Gun Brooke. Actress Carolyn Black desperately wants the starring role in an upcoming film produced by Annelie Peterson. Just how far will she go for the dream part of a lifetime? (1-933110-22-8)

Rangers at Roadsend by Jane Fletcher. Sergeant Chip Coppelli has learned to spot trouble coming, and that is exactly what she sees in her new recruit, Katryn Nagata. The Celaeno series. (1-933110-28-7)

Justice Served by Radclyffe. Lieutenant Rebecca Frye and her lover, Dr. Catherine Rawlings, embark on a deadly game of hide-and-seek with an underworld kingpin who traffics in human souls. (1-933110-15-5)

Distant Shores, Silent Thunder by Radclyffe. Dr. Tory King—along with the women who love her—is forced to examine the boundaries of love, friendship, and the ties that transcend time. (1-933110-08-2)

Hunter's Pursuit by Kim Baldwin. A raging blizzard, a mountain hideaway, and a killer-for-hire set a scene for disaster—or desire—when Katarzyna Demetrious rescues a beautiful stranger. (1-933110-09-0)

The Walls of Westernfort by Jane Fletcher. All Temple Guard Natasha Ionadis wants is to serve the Goddess—until she falls in love with one of the rebels she is sworn to destroy. The Celaeno series. (1-933110-24-4)

Change Of Pace: Erotic Interludes by Radclyffe. Twenty-five hot-wired encounters guaranteed to spark more than just your imagination. Erotica as you've always dreamed of it. (1-933110-07-4)

Honor Guards by Radclyffe. In a wild flight for their lives, the president's daughter and those who are sworn to protect her wage a desperate struggle for survival. (1-933110-01-5)

Fated Love by Radclyffe. Amidst the chaos and drama of a busy emergency room, two women must contend not only with the fragile nature of life, but also with the irresistible forces of fate. (1-933110-05-8)

Justice in the Shadows by Radclyffe. In a shadow world of secrets and lies, Detective Sergeant Rebecca Frye and her lover, Dr. Catherine Rawlings, join forces in the elusive search for justice. (1-933110-03-1)

shadowland by Radclyffe. In a world on the far edge of desire, two women are drawn together by power, passion, and dark pleasures. An erotic romance. (1-933110-11-2)

Love's Masquerade by Radclyffe. Plunged into the indistinguishable realms of fiction, fantasy, and hidden desires, Auden Frost is forced to question all she believes about the nature of love. (1-933110-14-7)

Love & Honor by Radclyffe. The president's daughter and her lover are faced with difficult choices as they battle a tangled web of Washington intrigue for...love and honor. (1-933110-10-4)

Beyond the Breakwater by Radclyffe. One Provincetown summer three women learn the true meaning of love, friendship, and family. (1-933110-06-6)

Tomorrow's Promise by Radclyffe. One timeless summer, two very different women discover the power of passion to heal and the promise of hope that only love can bestow. (1-933110-12-0)

Love's Tender Warriors by Radclyffe. Two women who have accepted loneliness as a way of life learn that love is worth fighting for and a battle they cannot afford to lose. (1-933110-02-3)

Love's Melody Lost by Radclyffe. A secretive artist with a haunted past and a young woman escaping a life that has proved to be a lie find their destinies entwined. (1-933110-00-7)

Safe Harbor by Radclyffe. A mysterious newcomer, a reclusive doctor, and a troubled gay teenager learn about love, friendship, and trust during one tumultuous summer in Provincetown. (1-933110-13-9)

Above All, Honor by Radclyffe. Secret Service Agent Cameron Roberts fights her desire for the one woman she can't have—Blair Powell, the daughter of the president of the United States. (1-933110-04-X)

This book is due on the last date stamped below.
Failure to return books on the date due may result
in assessment of overdue fees.